Linda Fairstein is a former prosecutor and one of America's foremost legal experts on crimes of violence against women and children. For three decades, she served in the office of the New York County District Attorney, where she was Chief of the Sex Crimes Prosecution Unit. In 2010 she was presented with the Silver Bullet Award from the International Thriller Writers Association. Her Alexandra Cooper novels have been translated into more than a dozen languages and have debuted on the *Sunday Times* and the *New York Times* bestseller lists, among others. She lives in Manhattan and on Martha's Vineyard.

Visit Linda's website at:
www.lindafairstein.com

SILENT MERCY

When the burnt, headless body of a young woman is found on the steps of a Baptist Church in Harlem, Assistant DA Alexandra Cooper is quickly on the shocking scene. With NYPD cop Mike Chapman, Alex investigates, but soon another woman is slaughtered and found on the steps of a Catholic Church in Little Italy: her throat slashed and her tongue cut out. The killings look like serial hate crimes, but the apparent differences in the victims' beliefs seem to eliminate a religious motive. Convinced that another young woman's life is at risk, Alex uncovers a terrible truth that takes her beyond the scope of her investigation and leads her directly into the path of terrible danger.

Books by Linda Fairstein
Published by The House of Ulverscroft:

THE KILLS
HELL GATE

LINDA FAIRSTEIN

◆

SILENT
MERCY

Complete and Unabridged

CHARNWOOD
Leicester

First published in Great Britain in 2011 by
Little, Brown
An imprint of
Little, Brown Book Group, London

First Charnwood Edition
published 2011
by arrangement with
Little, Brown Book Group
An Hachette UK Company, London

The moral right of the author has been asserted

British Library CIP Data

Fairstein, Linda A.
  Silent mercy.
  1. Cooper, Alexandra (Fictitious character)- -Fiction.
  2. Public prosecutors- -New York (State)- -New
  York- -Fiction. 3. Detective and mystery stories.
  4. Large type books.
  I. Title
  813.6–dc22

  ISBN 978–1–4448–0831–5

Published by
F. A. Thorpe (Publishing)
Anstey, Leicestershire

Set by Words & Graphics Ltd.
Anstey, Leicestershire
Printed and bound in Great Britain by
T. J. International Ltd., Padstow, Cornwall

This book is printed on acid-free paper

For Cyrus R. Vance, Jr., District Attorney,
New York County,
whose wisdom, vision, integrity, courage, loyalty,
and gift for friendship inspire me

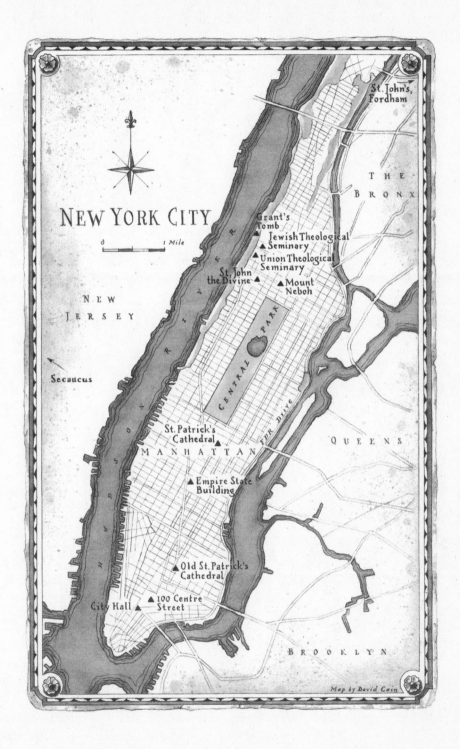

1

'Is that you with the broad, Detective?' the fire captain shouted at Mike Chapman in the darkness of a frigid March night. 'Keep her back there, across the street.'

'Got that, Coop? Stay put.' Mike left me in the middle of the double-wide roadway, wedged between unmarked police cars and bright red fire trucks as he charged in behind the huddle of uniformed cops on the sidewalk on the far side of the street.

I took my own blue-and-gold badge out of my pocket — no one would stop to read that the small print beneath my name said Assistant District Attorney, not NYPD — and flapped it over the breast pocket of my ski jacket, slinking between rowdy onlookers to get within inches of Mike.

'Alexandra Cooper. Special Victims,' I said to one of the firemen. His scowl softened and he nodded to let me pass.

Chaos had enveloped the corner of 114th Street and Seventh Avenue. Flames still danced around something that lay on the portico of a stately old church, teasing the water that spouted from steady-stream nozzles the firemen aimed at it. Emergency Service Unit cops wielded axes to try to break open the locks on the wrought-iron gate that guarded the front steps, and a growing herd of neighborhood rubberneckers crowded

1

the first responders who were trying to get the job done.

I was on the tips of my toes, hoping to catch a glimpse of what was burning. Amidst blackened fragments of some kind of fabric and the occasional glitter of embers atop that, I could make out something white — almost flesh-colored. The shape of a human arm, maybe, but that thought was too awful to imagine.

More firemen rushed past me to aid their brother officers, one of them knocking me back a step. There was no point in slowing anyone down to ask questions.

I raised myself up again. It must have been sensory overload because I thought I could see a hand, but there weren't really any fingers, and a terrible smell made me dizzier than the confusing sight.

'Who on fire?' one tall kid yelled out at no one in particular, then started to pull on the sleeve of my jacket as I passed in front of him.

'Don't know,' I said, breaking loose from his grip and inching forward, but his choice of pronoun focused me.

No question that within the fiery pile was a human being. The putrid odor of burning flesh — coppery and metallic — permeated the air. Holocaust survivors and soldiers who had liberated camps in World War II claimed it was a stench they would never forget.

'Go!' It was one of the ESU cops who had pushed back the gate he'd hacked open, calling out to the firemen who'd been spraying hoses impatiently from the sidewalk.

The pair took the church steps two at a time, rushing toward the smoking mound. While uniformed cops turned their attention to crowd control, Mike dashed in through the gate.

'I'm his partner,' I lied to the startled cop at the foot of the steps, running up behind Mike. I could see feet — small, pale, and bare — protruding from the remains of what might have once been a blanket that had covered them. They didn't move.

The taller fireman dropped to his knees and did what he must have done thousands of times after dousing the flames at a scene, whether or not he believed the victim would be able to respond.

He grabbed the ankles and pulled them toward him, then threw off the charred material that had concealed the corpse. He leaned over to begin an attempt at mouth-to-mouth resuscitation, but his back bucked and broke sideways as he braced himself against one of the massive columns and retched.

I stepped forward to see what ended the fireman's effort so abruptly, and a wave of nausea swept over me too.

The body of the young woman had no head.

2

'Don't you think the guys should move her inside?' I asked. The fire had been out for almost an hour and everyone on duty was growing restless.

Mike Chapman didn't look up at me when he answered. 'She can't feel the cold quite like you do, Coop.'

My gloved hands were deep in the pockets of my ski jacket. 'I'm not talking about the weather. I'm talking about the size of the crowd we're attracting.'

'Breaking into a church is against my religion. Besides, the arson investigators have to check her out before we can take down the scene.'

I glanced at the pathologist who'd been dispatched from the medical examiner's office. He was standing against another of the six columns at the far end of the portico, talking on his cell phone.

'The ME's word isn't enough?'

'Not when the perp was playing with matches. Got to make nice with the fire department,' Mike said, standing to turn and look down the steps at the growing number of passersby pressed against the wrought-iron fence.

'What do you want us to do, Chapman?' asked one of the four uniformed cops guarding the gated sidewalk entrance. It always seemed harder to get things done on the midnight shift.

Mike didn't answer. He scanned the crowd of faces — all African American, mostly young-adult men with a handful of women among them. 'It's two o'clock in the morning. You mooks got nothing better to do with your time? Come back on Sunday for the full service. Be sure to bring something to throw into the plate.'

'I know you — you ą DT,' one tall kid yelled out, using the uptown street name for detectives. 'I seen you lock up dudes in Taft Houses last year, after that pimp got whacked. Who dead?'

Mike waved him off and speed-dialed the veteran lieutenant in charge of the Homicide Squad, Ray Peterson. 'How about that backup you promised, Loo? Northeast corner of 114th Street and Powell Boulevard.'

This stretch of Seventh Avenue that spiked into Harlem, north of Central Park, had been renamed Adam Clayton Powell Jr. Boulevard in honor of the pastor turned politician, the first black congressman from New York.

'What did he say?' I asked Mike as he flipped his phone shut.

'Should be lights and sirens any minute now.'

'Who's the shorty, man?' The kid with the big voice was pushing through the crowd, referring to me — despite my five-foot-ten-inch frame — with another street term used by many teens in Harlem to tag their women. When that question failed to get Mike's attention, a string of curse words followed.

'Yo, keep it sweet. This is sacred ground, don't

5

you know that?' Mike pointed over our heads to the large white wooden sign that appeared to have been added to the limestone façade of the old building more recently. I knew it read MOUNT NEBOH BAPTIST CHURCH, though I wasn't sure how visible the lettering was in the early morning darkness. 'And the shorty is my sister. So keep it sweet.'

I suppressed a smile at Mike's form of crowd control. It was less controversial to claim me as kin than announce to the agitated onlookers that I was the prosecutor in charge of the Sex Crimes Unit in the Manhattan District Attorney's Office.

'Chapman!' the uniformed cop shouted again. 'I asked if you got a plan.'

I could see the revolving red lights as a fleet of squad cars approached from both directions on the boulevard.

'Here comes your mob management, guys,' Mike said. 'They'll help you clear the sidewalk.'

An unmarked car moved through the vehicular snarl with urgent repeats from its screaming whelper. When it braked to a stop across from the church, I could see Mercer Wallace, one of the city's only African American detectives to make first grade, his six-foot-four inches towering over the noisy kids.

Officers began to push back against the curious crowd as one of the sergeants from the local precinct came through the gates and up the steps, followed by Mercer.

'Counselor.' Sergeant Grayson nodded at me as he shook Mike's hand. 'What's going on here,

6

Chapman? Why'd you pull Alexandra out of bed in the middle of the night?'

'She got something better to do I don't know about?'

I walked behind Mike to try to get a closer look at the body, wrapping the end of my scarf around my mouth and nostrils, although it provided little protection from the powerful odor. We had all put on booties and been cautioned to minimize foot traffic close to the dead woman because of the need for the crime-scene team to collect debris that might also yield valuable clues.

'You just can't learn to stay back, can you, Coop?' Mike said as Mercer joined us at the top of the staircase, in front of three pairs of tall wooden doors that fronted the six columns of the old church.

I stared at the parts of the young woman's body that were visible. Her left thigh was bruised, her torso was badly burned, and mutilated fingers protruded from beneath the tattered blanket.

'Who's the ME?' Grayson asked, glancing over at Mike.

'Rookie named Bixby, who's about to die from a cell phone being forcibly impacted in his cochlea if he doesn't hang it up and get back over here,' Mike said, whistling to get the doctor's attention. 'I take it you've met Ms. Cooper.'

'About six rapes and thirty-seven domestic assaults ago,' Grayson said. 'How you doing, Alex?'

7

'Okay, Sarge.'

'Coop's been handling a bias crime from last summer,' Mike said. He walked away from the steps and led us behind another of the columns, farther away from the dead woman. Bixby sauntered toward us. 'Gay guy whose body was mutilated.'

'A barbecue, like this?' Grayson asked.

I shook my head.

'It's pretty obvious the girl wasn't burned alive,' Dr. Bixby said, squinting to read a message on his BlackBerry. 'I want the arson team to have a look before I disturb the body, but I think the fire was set to cover up the manner of death.'

'What kind of cover-up? She's behind a locked fence, on the steps of one of the most prominent churches in Harlem, and she's torched like a bonfire in the middle of a dark, cold night,' Grayson said. 'That's hardly hiding anything. It's like inviting all the locals to stop by for a drink.'

'I got a call at eleven. Pair of cops in the Charlie/David sector of the precinct,' Mike said, running his fingers through a shock of black hair against the direction that the wind was trying to take it. He was wearing his trademark navy blazer and chinos, and as always, no matter how bitter the weather, no overcoat. His explanation for why we were together, so close to the crime scene, was directed at Mercer. 'They found fingertips — four of them — nicely manicured, most likely a woman. Garbage pail on Lenox near 120th Street.'

'Like, six blocks from here,' Grayson said. 'No head, huh?'

Chapman grimaced.

'I had a decapitation once. Guy carried the head all over town in a bowling bag. Left it on the six train going downtown in rush hour. Some jerk thought he scored himself a major steal. Opened the bag and the damn head rolled out. Cleared the whole freaking train in thirty seconds. Don't worry — it'll show up.'

'I'm not worried, Sarge,' Mike said, turning back to Mercer. 'I knew Coop had that other mutilation case, so I thought I'd pick her brain. Never even made it to Lenox Avenue to scope the fingers when this call came in.'

'That victim last summer was a guy, right?' Mercer asked me.

'Yes, but cross-dressing. Perp might have thought he was picking up a woman and gone berserk.'

'Now I've got a naked cadaver dumped in a public place. Headless. I gotta think sexual assault, I gotta think torture, I gotta think mutilation again,' Mike said. 'And I gotta think possible hate crime 'cause the perp picked a religious institution for the drop. Sex crimes, torture, hate — it's got Alex Cooper written all over it.'

I had run the Special Victims Unit in Paul Battaglia's office for more than a decade and partnered often with Mercer, who worked in the counterpart NYPD bureau almost as long. Mike was assigned to the elite Manhattan North Homicide Squad — responsible for all of the

9

murders above Fifty-Ninth Street — and knew that so many of the sadistic serial rapists Mercer and I investigated often escalated to killing their prey.

Mercer walked over to the body and kneeled to pull back the sheet Dr. Bixby had placed over it so he could eyeball the woman. 'And she's white. Dead center of Harlem and you've got a white girl snuffed out on a big stage.'

'We've been gentrified, Mercer,' Grayson said. 'Don't go playing the race card here.'

'I'm betting you she's not from the 'hood.'

'When's the last time you stopped into Sylvia's for some ribs?' the sergeant asked, referring to the legendary soul food restaurant. 'Looks like the limos full of ladies who lunch got lost on their way to tea at the Plaza.'

Mercer's jurisdiction was countywide, like mine. He knew about the cross-dressing victim who had been bludgeoned to death in the Ramble by a guy he'd picked up on the street. The gay man who got his signals mixed was black. His fingertips had been mutilated, probably in an attempt by his killer to slow down the identification process. His penis had also been cut. The NYPD had classified the unsolved murder as a hate crime, though it was safe to say that most assaults that occurred within the thirty-six-acre enclave of Central Park's densely foliated Ramble were assumed to have an element of bias.

'We're on this, Sarge,' Mike said. 'Thanks for your help.'

'She staying?' he asked, pointing at me.

10

'I am.'

'Coop's useful sometimes, Sarge. You ever give that a try?'

It wasn't unusual for a Manhattan prosecutor to come to a crime scene. Smart detectives called us into cases early on, to work as a team so that the most important evidence could be preserved and presented in the courtroom if the investigation was solved and the case went to trial. Matching seemingly unrelated crimes, overseeing forensic testing, and giving legal guidance for search warrants, lineups, and confessions had proved invaluable teamwork in seeking justice for those victimized.

'I'll hang around, too, then,' Grayson said.

Mercer rose to survey the rest of the scene. 'That gate was locked when you arrived?' he asked Mike.

'Yeah.'

'So, you're saying the murderer got over the gate carrying a dead body, Doc? You're not thinking he killed her on this portico?'

'Most likely the former,' Bixby said. 'She's rather petite, easy to move around. Lighter without, you know — '

We all knew. Lighter without her head.

'Or he had a key,' the sergeant said, trying to make himself relevant. 'Or maybe he came out of the church with her. It's possible he killed her inside there.'

'A regular Quasimodo,' Mike said. 'Hunchback of Mount Neboh. Why don't you go check the bell tower, Sarge?'

I had noticed two towers on the church as I

approached it earlier. Its neo-Gothic design looked squarely out of a London landscape. The cops would obviously have to sweep the entire building before any determination could be made about whether this distinguished house of worship had harbored a killer.

'Where's the preacher man?' Grayson asked. 'He's a good guy. He'll help.'

'Lieutenant Peterson reached him on his cell. He's in Atlanta, at a church retreat. The custodian is supposed to be coming over to let us in.'

A red-and-white station wagon was guided around the parked vehicles by one of the cops. Two men got out and were admitted through the gates, quickly mounting the steps to introduce themselves as fire marshals, Dan Daniels and Frank Russo. Both of them knew Mike.

'Who's the deceased?' Russo asked.

'Don't know,' Mike said.

'Any kind of ID?'

Bixby tore his eyes away from his BlackBerry and introduced himself. 'I didn't do a full exam. Didn't want to turn her over until you gentlemen arrived. Have you got a camera?'

Daniels put his heavy case on the ground and opened it to get his equipment out. A camera and large flash attachment were on top. As he set up, I checked the progress of the uniformed cops, who were hanging yellow crime-scene tape to establish a wider perimeter on the sidewalk in front of the church, pushing back the ever-growing group of gawkers.

'Looks like they used straight-stream to put

out the fire,' Russo said.

Mike had talked to the men on the truck that had first responded to the 911 calls of a blaze at Mount Neboh. 'Said they had no choice. They didn't know when they got here if whoever was under that blanket was dead or alive.'

The straight-stream nozzle was effective in dousing the flames quickly, but more destructive in dispersing the evidence.

'She must have been decapitated first, don't you think?' I asked Bixby while Daniels finished dressing himself to move in and work on the body.

'I assume so.'

Something more interesting than my questions caught Bixby's attention as his BlackBerry vibrated in his hand. His lack of focus was annoying.

Mike caught it too. 'Hey, Doc, you with us, or do you plan to tweet your way through the autopsy?'

'Sorry. Trying to advise one of my colleagues.'

'She appears to be badly burned,' I said. 'Can you tell how long the fire was going?'

'The body itself is part of the fuel load, Ms. Cooper. The clothing — or blanket, in this case — provides fuel; so does the body fat, and even the skin and muscle.'

A lanky black man, dressed in a pea jacket and jeans, was escorted through the gate and up to where the group of us was standing. 'One of you, Detective Chapman?'

'You got me.'

13

'Amos Audley. This here's my church. I'm the caretaker.'

He opened the jacket to reveal a large brass ring with more than a dozen keys on it. He sniffed at the strong odor while he sorted his stock to produce the two that would unlock the building.

'Go ahead, please,' Mike said. 'I'll follow you in.'

Audley turned the large dead bolt and unlocked the knob below it. 'Not like the days you could leave a church open for the poor souls what needs it in the dead of night.'

'You're not old enough to know those days.'

'I've been knowing this place since I was a boy, Detective. Be sixty-seven years come November. Used to be, whether the Lord's lions or lambs came calling, doors was wide open and all was welcome twenty-four hours of the day.'

'This was a lamb, all right. To the slaughter, Amos. We're going to have to bring her in now, if you don't mind,' Mike said. 'C'mon, Coop. Step inside.'

I paused at the entrance as Audley marched in the dark to the panel of light switches that illuminated the vestibule and this part of the church. When he came back to us to explain that he'd be going to the far end to turn on the rest of the lights, I extended my hand to introduce myself.

'I'm Alexandra Cooper. I'm an assistant district attorney. Sorry to bring you here for such an unpleasant mission.'

'Pleased to make your acquaintance,' he said,

14

head down as he walked up the nave. 'You need to set yourself down and have a little prayer, young lady. That's what you all be needing.'

'If you don't mind, Mr. Audley,' Mike said, 'I'll have to ask you to stay close. We've got to look around the church before you touch anything, just in case the killer was in here.'

Audley narrowed his eyes and stared at Mike as though he was crazy. 'Not likely, Detective. I won't cause you any grief, but not likely. Not a fit place for a killer.'

From this point in the entryway, I could see enormous stained-glass windows in the ceiling of the sanctuary. It was streaks of moonlight from above that made me conscious of them, although it was still too dark for me to make out any of the images.

'You heard Mr. Audley,' Mike said. 'Take a seat.'

'Well, since everybody's here now, and both Bixby and Russo have done a visual and taken photos, why don't you just take her straight to the ME's office?' I asked.

'No can do.'

'Why not?'

'Her body's going to be pretty brittle because of the fire.'

A blast of cold air blew in the doors that Audley had opened. I looked over my shoulder at Russo and some of the cops who were spreading another clean white sheet on the ground beside the victim.

'Brittle?' I said, shivering against the chill of the night and my thoughts of the deceased.

'Just the ambulance ride downtown could jostle things. Change the way she presents at autopsy. That sheet will capture any trace evidence that falls off the body. Keep her as intact as possible.'

Mike watched, too, and inched a few steps closer to the doors as the team took direction from Russo and moved in to lift the woman. I stood beside him. When he walked back out onto the portico to oversee the change in positioning to the sheet, I went along.

'Jeez, Coop. In or out,' he said, stooping as Bixby raised the woman's left arm several inches away from her body. 'Something there, Doc.'

I leaned over his shoulder as Mike used a pair of tweezers to lift what looked like a piece of blue silk fabric from the fold beneath the woman's right arm. I gagged at the sight of her body and neck — closer up this time than I was before — and from the smell that intensified with the cold wind.

'Man up, Coop,' Mike said. 'This is as ugly as it gets.'

He stood and offered the material around for the others to see.

Mercer motioned to me but I wasn't moving. 'I'm okay.'

'May be as close as we come to figuring what she was wearing before she was set on fire,' Mike said.

Dr. Bixby talked to me as he explained. 'Even on the most badly charred bodies, fragments are protected in the flexures of the armpits or groins. Might help you later on.'

16

Russo asked everyone to step away from the sheet as he ran his flashlight across the section of the portico where the body had been. There was a glint of something sparkling on the ground.

'Mike,' I said, 'see that?'

The men who were tending to the deceased looked around, too, as Russo's beam fixed on the tiny object that caught the light.

'Coop could find a freaking nugget in a pile of manure, as long as it's gold,' Mike said to Russo. 'Take a picture of that, will you?'

'What is it?' I asked.

The flash went off several times before Mike lifted the paper-thin object with the tips of his tweezers.

'It's a star. A six-pointed gold star. One of yours, Coop,' he said. 'A Jewish star.'

Bixby ordered the cops to hold up before folding the sheet over the deceased. He rolled her body gently to one side, examining the skin on her back.

'You can see the form of it here, Detective. And even the suggestion of a chain extending up from the star. The heat almost embedded it in her back. It may prove to be a chain she was wearing when — uh, before she was killed.'

When she had a neck, is what he started to say.

Russo photographed the faint outline of the tiny symbol that was etched in the skin of our victim. Then she was finally ready to be wrapped in the sheet and lifted into the church vestibule so the rest of the scene could be examined for evidence.

'Go ahead, Coop,' Mike said. 'Wrong church, wrong pew. Got to be something in this. More than your average murder-and-dump job.'

Sergeant Grayson didn't agree. 'Some local kills a girl. Maybe it's a rape, maybe not. What else is he gonna do but toss the body? Maybe he's a parishioner here. Could be he's looking for salvation.'

'Aren't we all?' Mike said. 'The star might have belonged to the killer.'

'Too feminine a piece,' I said. 'It's tiny. And wafer-thin.'

'You still can't assume it was hers. She could have ripped it off the guy's neck during a struggle.'

I walked ahead of him, past Amos Audley, who was standing watch over the entrance to his beloved sanctuary. 'I realize how unusual a decapitation is. What else did you mean about this not being an average murder, Mike?'

'Somebody went to a lot of trouble to make a statement. Kill a woman, decapitate her, get up and over that tall fence or come from within this place. Could have dumped his prey somewhere a lot more remote and make a much easier escape than climb to the front steps of Mount Neboh, get away clean. If the murder happened inside the church — and I guess we'll know that shortly — he could have just left the body here. And if she's Jewish, then what's the point of bringing her to a Baptist church?'

Amos Audley mumbled something, but I couldn't hear him.

'I'm sorry. What did you say?'

18

'The dead girl, she a Jew?' he asked.

'It's possible. We don't know who she is yet.'

'Well, maybe the Lord just brought her on home,' Audley said.

'Home?' I didn't get where he was going.

'Take a look, Ms. Cooper.' Audley favored his left leg as he limped out of the vestibule.

I continued on after him, and saw that there must have been more than a thousand seats in the barrel-vaulted sanctuary of the church. A great organ with towering pipes filled most of the wall at the opposite end.

'Overhead,' he said.

I stretched my neck for a better view of the trio of splendid stained-glass windows that arched above me, forming a triptych of gigantic skylights.

'You see that?' Audley asked. 'Those letters in the glass?'

'It — it looks like the writing is in Hebrew. Is that possible?'

'Indeed it is.'

I couldn't read the ancient language, but the lettering was clear, as were the various symbols of the Jewish faith etched into the amber, emerald, and cobalt-blue glass. In the middle frame were the two tablets displaying the Ten Commandments, topped by a six-sided Star of David.

'Mercer — Mike,' I called out to them, 'you've got to see this.'

'A hundred years ago, Ms. Cooper,' Audley said, proudly showing off the church he'd been associated with since his birth, 'this here was built to be a synagogue.'

Mike rested his hands on my shoulders as he leaned back to look up.

'What kind of detective you be, Mr. Chapman?' Audley asked. 'In that pediment up over the columns, above the front door, didn't you see those tablets with the Ten Commandments?'

Mike didn't have a ready answer.

'Didn't you even notice those numbers carved in the cornerstone as you walked past? Big as you are? Says 5668. That's the Hebrew calendar, year she was built. Sherlock Holmes wouldn't miss no clue like that. Means 1908, when Harlem's population was mostly Jewish. Rich and powerful ones, merchants and such. This girl just come home.'

'That's one view of it,' Mike said. 'I'd like you to show us all these things in daylight. I'll bring Dr. Watson along. Make sure we don't miss anything.'

'Just you come back with Ms. Cooper. I think she gets it.'

Maybe it was a hate crime after all. If the Star of David was in fact the victim's, maybe it was no coincidence that her body was deposited on the steps of this particular church.

'The Lord moves in mysterious ways, Mr. Audley,' Mike said. 'Strange and mysterious ways.'

'Amen, Mr. Chapman. The Lord be making these mysteries, He can help you solve them too. Just you figure it out before anybody else get dead.'

3

'My name is Wilbur Gaskin, Detective. I'm a member of this congregation. Our pastor is out of town and I'm hoping to be of some assistance to you in his place.'

It was shortly after three a.m. The body had been bagged and removed from the church, and the remaining uniformed cops had ushered in this gentleman when he appeared at the gates in response to a call from Amos Audley.

'Mr. Audley said you could help us with whatever we need.' Mike made the introductions, and Gaskin gave each of us his business card. I guessed him to be in his midfifties, and the title on the card identified him as an executive in private banking at Chase.

'Do you know the name of the deceased?' Gaskin asked. He was about Mike's height, and lighter-skinned than Mercer, dressed in gray slacks and a crewneck sweater that he must have thrown on when Audley awakened him.

'Not a clue.'

'Do you think she worshipped here?'

Audley bowed his head. I thought he wanted to speak, but he deferred to Wilbur Gaskin.

'She's Caucasian, Mr. Gaskin,' Mike said. 'You tell me.'

The banker bristled. 'You may not be familiar with our church, Mr. Chapman. In addition to a long, fine reputation in the religious community, we've got one of the best gospel choirs in the world. You'd be surprised what a service looks like here. Perhaps you'll come. You won't be the only white man. And you certainly won't be the only cop.'

'I'll do that,' Mike said. 'And I apologize for my rudeness. Is there someplace we can go to talk?'

Gaskin glanced around at the four detectives who were making their way through the sanctuary of the church, fanned out between the rows of seats as they looked for any evidence of an intrusion or violent crime. 'Is all this necessary, Detective?'

'It is, Mr. Gaskin. One way or another, a dead body wound up on your front steps.'

'She could have come from anywhere,' he said, gesturing with both hands as if in protest to Mike's suggestion.

'I'd say her mobility was limited, sir. Just like her access. But we can rule out the inside of your church pretty quickly, if you'd let us.'

'There's a small office through that door to the left, behind the altar. Come with me, please.'

Amos Audley limped ahead of us, keeping a keen eye on the detectives as they scoured the sanctuary. Mike suggested to Sergeant Grayson that he wait at the entrance to the building to direct the comings and goings of investigators, and to keep out the press.

Mercer and I followed as Mike walked behind Wilbur Gaskin. The small room he led us to — bare except for a table and six wooden chairs — was cold and drafty. I seated myself away

22

from the old lead-glass windows that rattled whenever the March wind kicked up.

'Isn't this about the point when I'm supposed to tell you to get a search warrant?' Gaskin scratched his head and phonied up a smile, though I didn't think he was as unsophisticated as he tried to appear.

'This church is a crime scene. Up to me, I think we're entitled to scope it out. But my specialties are dead folk and the detritus of their late, lamented lives, Mr. Gaskin. Ms. Cooper's your law jock. Ask her what you'd like and the decision's up to you.' Mike started toward Audley, who moved out of the way of the door, as I leaned forward to express my opinion.

'That's all right, Detective. I don't want to hold things up. Suit yourselves.'

'How many people have keys to the church?' Mercer asked.

Gaskin pointed a finger at Amos Audley, who answered, 'Ain't but a few that can unlock the front — '

'How many, exactly?'

'I said a few,' Audley snapped at Mercer Wallace. 'I can't give you a number. But there's more than a dozen to the entrance on 114th Street, right by the pastor's office.'

'A dozen people with keys?' Mercer repeated the number.

'Last I knew. The pastor hisself, his assistant, his secretary. Then there's the choir director and his number two. A couple of parishioners who help with the finance business. Not sure who all else got them.'

'There must be a list?' Mike asked.

'Surely,' Gaskin said, 'when the office opens in a few hours. We'll get you that.'

'Have you had any problems recently? Any feuds that were brought into the church?' Mercer asked.

'Any psychos showing up to pray?' Mike added.

Wilbur Gaskin shook his head. 'Nothing I'm aware of. Amos?'

'Not my business, Mr. Gaskin. Not none of my business who comes for the Lord's word.'

Every now and then I could hear the footsteps of the detectives, climbing stairs to the choir loft or opening doors that led from the chapel. Audley's head turned at the same sounds. The mass of keys on his belt clanged against one another whenever he moved. 'You mind if I step out, Mr. Gaskin?'

'I'd prefer you stay close, Amos. You've got more answers than I do.'

'I understand that this church was built to be a synagogue,' Mike said. 'You know anything about that?'

'You spend enough time here, it's hard not to notice. It's the story of most cities, Mr. Chapman, and of many houses of worship,' Gaskin said. 'The population changes and the demographics shift. One ethnic group replaces another, one religious community takes over the temples the others left behind. It's not so strange.'

'What was the synagogue called then?' I asked.

'In English, it was People of Mercy. I can't

properly pronounce the Hebrew,' Gaskin said, jotting the words 'Ansche Chesed' on a piece of paper he withdrew from his pants pocket. 'I don't suppose any of you can read this or tell me if I'm right?'

'Give it a whirl, kid,' Mike said to me, explaining in the next breath. 'She was 'Cooperized' at Ellis Island. Some really complicated name was totally neutered.'

'My father's parents were Russian Jews,' I said. My mother's Finnish roots revealed themselves in my blond hair and pale green eyes. She had converted to Judaism when she married my father, and although I was raised as a reformed Jew, I was embarrassed at how little of the Hebrew language — or religious tradition — I knew. 'But I can't help with this one.'

'That's all right. I came by Gaskin the hard way too. My great-granddaddy's owner made sure all his slaves took his name.' He winked at me, and I noticed that his eyes were nearly as light in color as mine. 'But our church isn't unique around here. Mount Olivet Baptist, that was a synagogue too. So was Cross Church of Christ, on 118th. Look around here a little more carefully.'

'I never imagined.'

'A hundred years ago, when this place was built,' Gaskin said, 'Harlem was the third largest Jewish settlement in the world — in the world — after the Lower East Side and Warsaw. It was a thriving community dominated by Jewish culture and heritage. There are remains of it in buildings all over the neighborhood.'

The part of Manhattan known as Harlem ran east to west from river to river, and from 110th Street north to 155th.

'In 1910, we were only ten percent of the population here, Ms. Cooper. Twenty years later, the great migration started from the South. By the fifties, Harlem was ninety-eight percent black.'

'And the Jews?' Mike asked.

Wilbur Gaskin shrugged. 'The diaspora continued. They moved once more. This time because they wanted to, not because they had to. To Riverside Drive, to Park Avenue, to the Grand Concourse, and up to Westchester. These churches — these magnificent synagogues — are the silent vestiges of their years in Harlem.'

Footsteps again, like a couple of cops were running inside the church. Audley was in the doorway, checking out the activity.

'Neboh,' Mike said. 'What's that?'

'One of the four holy mounts, Mr. Chapman. The Bible says it's the place from which Moses first saw the Promised Land.'

'This girl wasn't quite so lucky.'

'One more thing about our church, Detective, to confuse you further. Before we Baptists took it over, it had a short incarnation as a Roman Catholic sanctuary. I think that trifecta is true of only two institutions in Manhattan.' Gaskin went on in Spanish, 'Iglesia de Nuestra Señora de la Medalla Milagrosa.'

'Our Lady of the Miraculous Medal,' Mike said.

Now there were loud noises, like men arguing in the sanctuary.

'Your Spanish isn't bad,' Gaskin said, patting Mike on the shoulder.

'Can't do homicide in this city without a smattering of español.'

I was ten years beyond cringing at Mike Chapman's political incorrectness. But I wondered if the interim Catholic incarnation of the building did anything to influence Mike's theory of why the body landed here.

A sharp voice shouted a command as a heavy door slammed shut.

'What's the ruckus?' Mercer asked, following Amos Audley through the door.

Now I could hear many more footsteps. It sounded like cops were running through the building, along the south wall. I recognized Scotty Jaffer's voice calling out that he wanted help in the basement.

Mercer broke past Audley, who was moving as fast as he seemed to be able to, and Mike sprinted after Mercer. I stood in the doorway with Wilbur Gaskin at my shoulder.

'Let it be,' Amos Audley called out, obviously distressed by the massing of officers, two with their guns drawn. 'No harm there.'

'Bringing out four,' Jaffer called.

I could see a large oak door, and from the echoing sound of the detective's voice, I assumed he was still downstairs.

Wilbur Gaskin panicked. He opened his cell phone and speed-dialed someone, starting to explain the situation in which he found himself at three twenty in the morning.

'Nice and easy,' Mercer said, holding both arms in front of him and backing away from the basement door toward the main sanctuary. 'Come forward one at a time. Slow. Hands over your heads.'

The first to emerge was a young man in his early twenties. He was about my height, with a shaved and waxed head, dressed in a filthy sweatshirt, torn jeans, and unlaced high-tops.

Mercer's calm seemed to be controlling the unexpected encounter. 'Sit right there,' he said, pointing to a seat in the front row of pews.

'You know him?' I asked.

He covered the mouthpiece of the phone. 'I've never seen him.'

'Put your guns down,' Mercer said quietly to the cops who flanked him. 'Let's get this done right.'

'Send out the next one, Scotty,' Mike said. He was always edgier than Mercer, a bit frenetic and pacing now, to distance himself from Amos Audley, who was muttering something at Mike's back.

The second guy was heavier-set than the first, but just as unkempt and unhappy to be disturbed in the middle of the night. Mercer seated him a good distance away from his friend and directed two of the four cops to stand behind him.

It sounded as though there was some scuffling — and some physical urging by Scotty Jaffer — before the next trespasser came up the steps,

28

lifting his head as he entered the large barrel-vaulted space.

'Dammit!' Gaskin said into the phone before he shut it. 'It's Luther again.'

'What do you mean?' I asked as he strode forward.

Wilbur Gaskin waved me off with his free hand.

'You,' Mercer said, turning his head to look at us when he heard Gaskin's outburst. 'Back row.'

'Let me speak to this,' Amos Audley said, grabbing Mike's arm.

'What?' Mike shook him off. He wanted his hands free.

'He's mine.'

'Last man standing,' Jaffer said. 'On the way out to you.'

The fourth kid didn't come easily. He was cursing at the detective and banging on the walls with his fists as he climbed up.

'I thought Luther was still upstate, in prison,' Gaskin said. 'Looks like he's been living here, doesn't it?'

'Step back, Amos,' Mike said. 'Out of the way.'

'You don't understand, Mr. Mike.'

'You'll explain later. Stay out of the way.'

The fourth player showed himself. Dreads hanging out from under a do-rag, a long-sleeve T-shirt with a skull on the front, and tattered black pants made him look like he was wearing an unofficial gang uniform. The long scar across his nose and cheek was thick and dangerously close to his eye.

'They've done nothing, Mr. Mike. These

freezin' cold nights, boys need a place to stay warm.'

Then I could have sworn I heard Audley say the word 'blood.'

'I'm telling you to take it easy, Mr. Audley,' Mike said, swiveling to get the anxious custodian out of the path he intended to send the last kid.

Audley took two steps to the side and the young man saw his opening. He bolted past Mike, clearly familiar with the interior of the old building, and around to the rear of the chancel. He was thin and wiry, and his head start made it impossible for any of the cops to catch him. I was simply grateful that none of them drew a gun.

'What's back there?' I asked.

'A couple of doors, Ms. Cooper.' Before Audley could finish his sentence, I heard one slam shut.

Mercer called out to Grayson, who sent men running through the church and, I'm sure, out on the street as well.

Mike was furious. 'These kids don't move. Cuff 'em and let 'em sit till we sort this out.'

Amos Audley hadn't figured out how to keep out of Mike Chapman's way. He pointed at Luther, his finger trembling with fear. 'It's the Lord's house, Detective. No harm in them being in the Lord's house. He's my grandson, Mr. Mike. That boy's my blood.'

4

'No harm in them being in the station house, either,' Mike said.

'How old are you, Luther?'

The young man neither looked up nor answered.

'How old?'

'He twenty-two,' Amos Audley said.

'Luther. Look at me.' Mercer Wallace's booming voice got the young man's attention. 'Don't go dissing your grandfather, 'cause you do that and you're taking on me and Chapman and a whole bunch of guys you don't really want to butt heads with. Let's go inside and talk.'

Luther appeared to be more sullen for being singled out from his friends by a detective. He didn't budge.

'Get up on your feet,' Mercer said.

He rose slowly, and his two companions hissed their disapproval.

'Mr. Audley,' Mike said to Amos, trying to distract him from his grandson's predicament, 'I think the sergeant could really use your help. Don't get yourself in knots over these kids.'

Mercer frisked Luther from top to bottom and then led him back to the small room in which our conversation with Wilbur Gaskin had started. Luther's jeans hung so low on his body that Mercer grabbed the waistband and hoisted them, startling the vacant-looking young man

31

and probably pinching one of his testicles, from the sound of his squeal.

'Wassup with that?' Luther asked, trying to wrest himself away from Mercer.

'R-e-s-p-e-c-t. If the lady really wanted to see your ass, Luther, she'd probably invite you to drop your pants all the way.'

Mike was giving Grayson orders to search and cuff the two others and separate them for some initial questioning before taking them off to the 28th Precinct station house.

'What does your gut say, Detective?' Gaskin asked.

I had almost caught up to Mercer, but I paused to listen to Mike's answer.

'Unlikely they're involved. I haven't been this lucky — or fast — catching a perp since my first domestic when the guy stabbed his wife to death with a carving knife in their bed then fell asleep next to her, waiting for a response to his 911 call so he could tell me she must have forgotten it was there and fell on it. They'll be more valuable for anything they saw or heard. You know them?'

'Just Luther. The kid's done everything possible to break his grandfather's heart.'

Amos Audley's limp was more pronounced as he struggled to follow Grayson while keeping an eye on Mercer's charge.

'Banger?'

'Sorry?'

'Is he in a gang? A gangbanger?'

'Yeah. Something to do with that dead rap gangster they all idolize,' Gaskin said.

'Tupac Shakur,' Mike said, shaking his head.

32

'Rapist and rapper. One of Coop's best teammates prosecuted him for molesting a teenage fan, which only helped confer sainthood on him.'

''Course they idolize him. He was a total thug.'

'PacMen's Luther's gang, then. A most unsuccessful group of losers.'

Mike's stage whisper was intended to irk the two young men now handcuffed to the armrests at the end of the row in the handsome church.

'We've got a program here,' Gaskin said. 'An initiative working with kids at risk, kids who've been in the system. Called something like Fair Chance.'

'Should have called it Fat Chance,' Mike said. 'Fat chance anything but the max and a little attitude adjustment works on these bastards.'

Mike left Gaskin in the sanctuary and by the time we opened the door to the small office, Mercer was sitting on the edge of the long table, forcing his attention on Luther Audley.

'Twice, juvenile. Three more since I turned sixteen.' Mercer's first question had obviously been about the number of Luther's arrests.

'How much time have you done?'

'Two years. Got out in December.'

'You like it upstate?'

Luther Audley tilted his head and screwed up his mouth, looking at Mercer like he was crazy.

'You like it enough to go back?'

'I ain't never going back.'

'Then who are your friends? These other three guys?'

'I don't know.'

'You stupid, Luther, or you just look like you're stupid?' Mike asked, pulling up a chair to sit opposite Mercer.

Mercer held out his arm to tell Mike to back away. 'The two guys inside, who are they?'

'I only know their faces. Not their names.'

'How about the dude that ran off?'

Luther just stared at the tabletop. 'Don't know him.'

'Shit. So when you want to hang out with him,' Mike said, 'you just ask around for the ugly mother with the big scar across his cheek? That how you find him?'

'What's he running from?' Mercer asked.

'Just running, I guess.'

Mike slammed the table and Luther sat up. 'Olympic trials, don't you think, Detective Wallace? Fastest ex-con with his butt crack showing, sprinting away from a murder rap.'

'What you mean, murder?' Luther swallowed hard and looked to Mike, who stood up and turned his back.

'Scotty?' Mike called out into the sanctuary. 'Any blood downstairs? Body parts?'

'Not so far. A crack pipe and a dusting of white powder. Smoke and coke.'

'Your buddies are giving you up, Luther. They're sitting inside the church, telling the other cops why they're here,' Mercer said. 'And they're here because of you. Because your grandfather was kind enough to let you crash inside this church. Risk his job and everything he cares about. So who are they?'

'They just guys. We hang out sometimes.'

'PacMen,' Mike said. 'Gangsta-wannabe assh-oles. What'd you do time for?'

Luther licked his lips.

'Let me guess. At least once for drugs. Then, two years? Armed robbery, I'm figuring. Botched job at best. Nobody got hurt, you weren't the one carrying heat. You were too dumb to get away clean. Copped to the attempt and got a deuce up the river. Am I warm?'

'My lawyer made me take that plea.' Luther Audley rolled his head around and looked up at the ceiling.

'Always the damn suits that make you do things you don't wanna do, isn't it?' Mike asked. 'Ms. Cooper here, she's a mouthpiece too. She finds out you know something about this murder and she'll have your parole revoked, then ship you right back up to the yard. She actually enjoys doing that.'

Luther's head dropped and he fixed his vacant gaze on me. 'What you keep talking about murder?'

'There was a body found on the steps of the church tonight,' I said, trying to edge Mike farther away from the young man. 'A woman was killed and — '

'We didn't kill nobody.'

'I'm going to start easy, back it up a few hours, and find out what brought you here,' I said, pulling my chair closer to the slow-to-anger interloper.

'Whoa, Ms. Cooper.' Wilbur Gaskin had

appeared in the doorway. 'How about Miranda? How about the right to — '

Mike interrupted him and rose to back him away from the room. 'Nobody's in custody, Mr. Gaskin. Let's not put a plug in the works yet.'

'Not in custody? You've got the kid closeted in back here, while his God-fearing grandfather is going to pieces right outside,' Gaskin said. 'You hear that, Luther? Get your tail out of this place.'

The young man's mouth was open but he didn't move fast.

'I'd sooner lock up Grandpa for aiding and abetting,' Mike said. 'I'd get my answers damn fast, and they wouldn't be full of lies and laced with crack.'

Luther lit up like he'd had a snake bite. He stood and shouted at Mike, his finger jabbing at the air. 'You can't be all gettin' on Amos. You can't be all — '

Mike was walking out the door and directing Gaskin to come with him as he looked back for a last comment. 'You'd be surprised at the things I can do, Luther. Hold tight and tell Ms. Cooper what she wants to know. Who comes and goes is up to me.'

Luther Audley stared at me and laughed.

'Talk to her,' Mercer said.

Mike's bluff had worked. If the kid was agitated about nothing else, he still wanted to protect his grandfather. He snarled at me but took his seat.

'Tell me why you're here tonight,' I said.

'I'm here every night. My mother won't let me

be at her house. She got a boyfriend who don't want me there.'

'And Amos?'

'He don't have space for me. Him and my grandmother live in a studio. Ain't no room.'

'How do you get in here?'

Luther fidgeted with the belt loops on his pants. 'Amos. He the last one to leave every night, first one to come in the morning.'

'Your friends, he lets them crib here too?' Mercer asked.

'Not exactly. He don't like most of them. Used to be you could sleep on the steps of almost any church. Even get food and all. Now every one got bars on them.'

The city's religious institutions had long been havens for the homeless. That situation, neither safe nor sanitary, had ended with the gating of most of them when a homeless man who had lived outside a church on the Upper West Side for three years froze to death just feet from the entrance.

Luther described the habit that had developed because of his grandfather's affection for him. Those nights that were too cold and raw, he called Amos and asked for shelter. His crew knew he would let them in later, when alone, and they'd leave at daybreak, before Amos arrived. In exchange for a warm place to crash, they would bring drugs to feed Luther's habit.

'What time did you get here last night?' I asked.

'I don't remember.'

'Don't mess with her, Luther,' Mercer said. 'She's got more juice than I do.'

Luther closed one eye and studied me with the other.

'What time did your grandfather let you in?'

He didn't like it when we brought Amos into the mix. 'It was, like, midnight. A little earlier than that.'

There was no watch on either of his skinny wrists. 'How do you know?'

''Cause of the bells. I was in here when they rang, when they done twelve times.'

'And the others?'

'I texted them when he left. Maybe fifteen minutes later.'

'Give me your cell phone,' Mercer said, holding out his hand.

Luther frowned.

'Give it up.'

The messages he sent to his friends, and their responses, would be captured in the memory of his phone. He drew the razor-thin machine out of his pocket and placed it in the large palm of Mercer's hand.

'What did you do?' I asked.

'Nuthin'.' He was watching Mercer scroll through the messages.

'What did you do, Luther?' I asked again.

'Me and them, we always hang in the basement. They brung me some food, is all.'

'And crack?'

He blew me off. 'I don't do that shit.'

'Coke?'

'L'il bit.'

38

'So these guys you don't know,' Mercer said, reading the name off the cell history, 'which one is Shaquille?'

Luther bit his tongue.

'Shaquille, the one you texted.' Mercer leaned in closer. 'He one of the dudes inside, or is he the one who skipped out on you?'

The answer was slow and deliberate. 'Inside.'

'Which one deals?'

No answer this time.

'Must be Shaquille or you wouldn't have been so anxious to invite him to join you.'

Luther had nowhere else in the room left to look but at Mercer.

'Go talk to him, Alex. I'll get Luther here up to speed.' Mercer handed me the phone. 'What else did you hear besides church bells last night?'

'She gonna ask Shaquille. I don't know nuthin' else.'

As I turned the corner into the sanctuary, I noticed another kid was gone. The remaining one was still cuffed to the end seat of a pew. His knee was bouncing up and down, nervously, at a furious pace, and when Mike stepped away from him, I could see that tears were streaming down his cheeks.

'What happened?' I asked. 'Where's — '

'Scotty took the tall one back down to the basement for a once-over.'

'What'd you do to make this guy cry?'

'He's fifteen, Coop. Wants his mama, I think.'

'Which one's Shaquille?' I asked.

The knee jerked and the kid shook his head.

I held up Luther's cell and texted a few words.

I could hear the noise of the vibrating phone in his pocket over the insistent tapping of his foot.

'I guess you're Shaquille,' Mike said. 'That solves that piece of the puzzle. Now, why don't you tell Ms. Cooper what you saw last night? And remember, she doesn't believe in ghosts.'

'I was waiting for Luther to call me.' The kid wiped his eyes with the filthy sleeve of his sweatshirt. 'I was around the corner, on 114th.'

'You know what time it was?' Mike asked.

Shaquille shook his head.

I looked at Luther's outgoing messages. 'A little bit before twelve forty-five.'

'All three of you there?'

'Nope. I was alone.'

The bounce in his leg was like a lie detector. It sped up whenever the topic got more sensitive. He didn't seem to care about the time of night, or his companions.

'What'd you see?' Mike asked.

The knee was rocking now. 'I told you, I don't know. It was like a man, but then it didn't move like any man I ever seen.'

'How's that, Shaquille?'

'It was almost like he could fly. Like a cartoon character, you know?'

'I don't know. You tell us,' Mike said. 'What'd he look like?'

'Too dark to tell,' the kid said, sniffling back his tears.

'Black? White? Big? Small?'

'He was a big guy, that's the thing. Big but he moved real quick and light. Couldn't see his skin 'cause he had a hoodie on. Black hoodie and sweatpants. Just figured he black 'cause — I don't know — 'cause it's, 'cause . . . '

''Cause it's the middle of Harlem in the middle of the night?'

'Why some white guy be breaking into Mount Neboh?' Shaquille asked.

'Breaking in?' I said. 'Is that what he tried to do?'

'I didn't stay to see that. I just know if he was any friend of Luther's, he'd be goin' by the back door.'

'Tell her what you saw. Tell her where he came from.'

'Don't know where he came from. He was already near the gate when I got to the corner. He had a sack with him. Big sack, like a duffel. I mean, really big. First thing he did when the street got quiet, he reached up and dropped the bag over the gate.'

'Were you smoking yet, Shaquille?' Mike asked.

'Let him tell his story,' I said. 'Stop interrupting.'

'I just want you to understand he wasn't high. Okay, Coop? What'd he do?'

'He got himself up that fence. Like he hung on to the railing from the side, and then he kind of flew himself over.'

'Threw himself?' I asked.

'Flew, ma'am. He, like, flew.'

'Don't roll your eyes at me, Coop. That gate is tall,' Mike said.

'We've tried lots of times to get over that fence, ma'am. You can't do it. It's really tall.

41

Must be like ten feet, and there's no cross-pieces to climb on.'

'Did you watch him after that?' I asked.

'Yeah. I wanted to see what was in that bag.'

'The man opened the bag?' I asked, wondering how this kid — how anyone — could have watched somebody be set afire on the church steps and walk away from it.

'Yeah. He took it up the steps and unzipped it.'

'Anyone else around besides you?' Mike asked.

'Nope. There were cars on the boulevard, but it was too dark for people driving by to notice much.'

I positioned myself directly in front of Shaquille. 'What did you see when the man opened the sack?'

The kid's knee was going wild.

'I thought it was, like, a person. Like, I thought I saw legs coming out, you know? Then I figured out it couldn't be a real person, like a body or anything. That it must have been some other thing he got flopping around. It was real creepy-like, so I just left, is what I did.'

'Why did you think it wasn't a person? That it wasn't a body?'

''Cause there couldn't be a body, ma'am, without no head.'

5

'What time do you have to be in court?' Mercer asked.

'Not until eleven. The judge has to take care of an abscessed tooth first. Don't worry, I'll get to put my head down for a couple of hours.'

It was four a.m. and we were sitting in an all-night coffee shop on 125th Street. Luther Audley and his pals had been released after Mike's Homicide Squad partners took statements from them. Sergeant Grayson had two teams looking for the fourth kid, who fled — with information from Shaquille, a willing snitch — in the unlikely event that he had any useful tidbits to offer. The Crime Scene Unit had started its painstaking work on the church steps and inside the sanctuary. And Amos Audley was left with the sad task of cleaning up behind them and his wayward grandson.

We left as the tabloid newshounds and photographers had clustered in front of Mount Neboh, grumbling to Grayson that they had missed their most salacious shots.

Murder never got in the way of Mike Chapman's appetite or conscience. While Mercer and I sipped coffee, Mike was working his way through an order of scrambled eggs with onions and a slab of crisp bacon, using cornbread to mop up the grease on his plate.

'I know, I know,' Mike said. 'You're wondering

how I can eat like this after what we saw this morning, and I'm wondering why you're drinking black java when you're already so wired you could tap dance in the well of the courtroom while you're cross-examining your worst enemy and not even come up for a breath of air.'

The three of us had worked together on some of the city's most horrific cases for more than ten years. We knew our respective foibles and strengths, considered ourselves family, could shoot barbs directly to the heart of either of the others without a second thought, but covered the others' backs from any outside attacks. We came to this alliance from backgrounds so different that sometimes it was inconceivable to me that we understood one another as well as we did.

'How soon till we find out who she is? That's what I'm thinking about.'

'Somebody'll miss her, Coop.'

'And who did she cross to come to such a hideous end?'

The counterman walked over to the booth to refill our mugs.

'It's the setting that gets me,' Mike said. 'Does Neboh speak to you, Mercer?'

Mercer had been born in Harlem and worked in Manhattan North Homicide with Mike before transferring to Special Victims. He knew the streets and the people, even though he had been raised in Queens by his father — a mechanic for Delta at LaGuardia Airport — after his mother's death in childbirth. He was forty-two, five years older than I, and married to another detective, Vickee Eaton, with whom he had a young son.

'I'm not sure. Like Gaskin said, Mount Olivet Baptist, that was built as a synagogue too. It was Temple Israel in 1906. Abandoned with white flight. Baptist since 1926. They took the ark the Torah used to sit in and turned it into a baptismal pool.'

'So?' Mike asked, crunching the bacon while he talked.

'You said that you and Alex were headed to 120th and Lenox because of the fingertips in a garbage pail on the street.'

'Yeah.'

'That's only one block from Mount Olivet. Gives something to your theory that the dead woman's religion may be tied up in this. I mean, the best-known Baptist church in Harlem is Abyssinian. Built Baptist, stayed Baptist. Your murderer wants to send a message about Baptists, that's where he goes. Not to both of these recycled synagogues.'

'Maybe he didn't know Neboh's history,' I said. 'I certainly didn't.'

'Too much of a coincidence, then, that he chose both Neboh and Olivet. I think Mike's onto something.'

Mike's investigative instincts were probably in his DNA. His father, Brian, had been one of the most decorated cops in the NYPD, proud that his son had excelled in academics and had chosen Fordham University, majoring in history, as a way out of the dangerous street life in which his own career had been forged.

Two days after retiring from the force, while Mike was in his junior year at Fordham, Brian

45

Chapman died of a massive coronary. Mike honored his promise to get his degree but immediately enrolled in the Police Academy to follow his passion, to shadow the steps of the man he most revered. Six months older than I — thirty-eight — Mike's bachelor existence had only once been threatened by a serious romance, which ended in the accidental death of the young architect to whom he'd been engaged.

'You got a dish of ice cream? Chocolate, two scoops?' Mike called out to the waiter. Then to Mercer, 'So how did Abyssinians get involved with New York City Baptists?'

'Goes back two hundred years, right down near the courthouse. Way before we were known as black or African American, seems the Negroes didn't like being segregated — forced to sit apart — while they were worshipping in God's house. It was a bunch of rich Ethiopian merchants who broke away from the First Baptist Church, way down on Worth Street, to start this one.'

'Where do you begin to look for a woman's head?' I asked.

'She's fixated on that, Mercer.' Mike was starting to soften his frozen dessert by swirling the spoon around and around the dish. 'Coop's not going to be happy until we have all the body parts.'

'Don't play with your food,' I said.

'They teach you that at Wellesley, Miss Manners?'

I was the most incongruous part of our trio. My parents' middle-class existence changed radically during my childhood when my father, a

46

cardiologist, and his research partner invented a half-inch piece of plastic tubing that was used in almost every open-heart surgical procedure worldwide for nearly two decades thereafter. We moved to Harrison, an upscale suburb in Westchester County, and my parents were able to provide my brothers and me with the best educational opportunities available — for me, at Wellesley, where I majored in English literature before getting my JD degree at the University of Virginia School of Law.

They fostered my interest in public service and were pleased that I found such fulfillment in my work as an advocate for women and children who'd been victims of intimate violence. The Manhattan District Attorney's Office was the premier prosecutorial model in the country, and I had thrived there under the leadership of Paul Battaglia and his hand-chosen staff of dedicated lawyers.

If my work seemed depressing to some, they had no understanding of how uplifting it was to help this long-underserved population triumph in the courtroom. In just the past thirty years and through the diligence of those who came before me, archaic laws that treated women as chattel were abolished, investigative techniques had been developed to match forensic advances, and the application of DNA technology to law enforcement methods had revolutionized the criminal justice system.

'You know what I learned at Wellesley, Mike?' I smiled at his ability to bring humor to the most dire situations. 'If you've been out all night with

47

a guy, and he's about to ask you to pay for his meal, you ought to find someone else to take you home. Ready to go, Mercer?'

'Even when the sucker who's had you out with him doesn't even bother to try to jump your bones?' Mike asked. 'That's a sorry situation, kid. What's today, anyway?'

'Wednesday. Soon as the sun comes up, it'll be Wednesday.'

'Put it on my tab, Coop. I'll catch up to you on payday.'

'By my count, you're about three years of payday overdue, Mike. You'll be at the autopsy?' Mercer asked.

'Yeah. Late this afternoon.'

'Could you tell anything about the killer from looking at the neck injuries?' I asked.

'Other than that he meant what he was doing, what is it you want to know?' Mike asked.

'The obvious questions. Do you think it was done by a surgeon, or by a butcher? You know, someone skilled anatomically?'

'Don't go all Jack the Ripper on me, Coop. Somebody whacked off the poor broad's head. The only thing I'd say about him for sure is that he was powerful. Not artful and no surgical precision. Really strong. Must have used something like an ax or a hatchet. A machete, maybe.'

I leaned back against the cracked vinyl padding on the seat of the booth. 'Where do you even begin on this one?'

'It's got 'personal' stamped all over it,' Mike said. 'Nothing random about this victim.

Nobody goes to all this trouble hacking up a stranger. Get a make on her, it'll tell us half the story.'

'You know, Alex,' Mercer said, 'morning news shows will blast this story everywhere. All the nuts respond to gruesome. Your office, the local precincts, the squad phones — they'll be ringing off the hook. Every woman who didn't come home last night will have someone looking for her. Prepare yourself for the onslaught.'

'I'll be in court. Thoroughly preoccupied.'

'And we'll be pawing through every Dumpster and incinerator north of the DMZ,' Mike said, referring to 110th Street, where Harlem unofficially began. 'Hoping this madman didn't toss her head or the murder weapon in the river. And the zoo. I'll send Grayson to the Bronx Zoo. Keep him out of my way. Egg on my face, Coop?'

'Not the usual kind,' I said, reaching over with my napkin to wipe the ice cream from the side of his chin. 'I'll bite. Why the zoo?'

'Could be an orangutan, no?'

'You lost me.'

'Everything you ever taught me about Edgar Allan Poe. 'Rue Morgue.' The monstrously fierce killer who defied Parisian police 'cause he could scale the sides of buildings and kill women, getting away undetected.'

'Perfect, Mike. The monkey did it. Flew over the gates of Mount Neboh with his headless torso before making his escape. The DA'll be impressed.'

'Great ape, Coop. Orangutans are apes, not

monkeys.' Mike was chewing a toothpick, his dark eyes flashing with the energy his breakfast provided. 'How do I start, you want to know? Just like Poe. Ratiocination. Forget the hysterics that are going to surround this case and think rationally. Make sure no orangutans escaped from the zoo.'

We had worked a murder at the home of the great poet and storyteller years earlier, and Mike had devoured his tales of the bizarre and grotesque.

'You keep your eyes peeled for a head,' he said, pointing the toothpick at me and tugging at a few straggling strands of my hair as he stood up. 'Or somebody carrying a bag that might weigh — oh, I'd say about nine pounds six ounces.'

The counterman handed me the check and I left cash on the table as we stood up.

'How'd you come up with that number?'

'My last decapitation, Coop. The human head accounts for less than ten percent of the body mass, usually in the eight-to-twelve-pound range.'

I wouldn't sleep at all now. Facial features were flooding my imagination. The manner of this woman's death would haunt me. I didn't know the first thing about her, but I was wildly creating a visual image, a life and a family, and of course a brutal death.

'And you arrive at nine-six by? . . . '

'Eyeballing her, kid. Much shorter than you. Maybe five-five. Brunette, from the rest of the hair on her body. And she wasn't from the streets.'

'How so?'

'Pedicured toes. No track marks. No tats. About your age, I'd say. Breasts were firm. Skin was unwrinkled and smooth. My money's on midthirties.'

I had turned away from the broken body of the victim on the church portico, while Mike studied it to learn as much about her as he could in just the few minutes spent with her in the dark and cold.

'I'll drop you at home, Alex,' Mercer said. 'Let's see what the day brings.'

'Expect the usual,' Mike said, gnawing the toothpick from one side of his mouth to the other. 'A handful of domestics, child pervs scouring the playgrounds and cyberspace, identity theft up the wazoo. Let's meet up at the end of the day, guys, okay? See where we stand, what we find out. 'Cause this friggin' beast will be back before you know it.'

'Why do you — ?' I started to ask.

'There's a bloodlust here you don't see very often, Coop. He's not done. That bastard tossed the head so his next vic won't connect the dots. Whoever she is, unless we find her first, she'll never see him coming.'

6

Mercer dropped me at the entrance to my high-rise apartment on the Upper East Side, and one of the doormen escorted me to the elevator. I rode alone to the twentieth floor, unlocked the door and bolted it behind me, comforted by the familiarity of my well-appointed home. It wasn't the way most young prosecutors lived, but at moments like this, the security it offered provided a safety net for which I was enormously grateful.

I didn't disturb the sheets. I pulled back the duvet and slipped in beneath it, knowing that I needed to calm down but aware that I was far too restless to sleep. Daylight would soon flood the large windows, so for an hour, I closed my eyes and tried to transport myself to a more tranquil surround.

Photographs on my night table allowed me a brief escape from the night's dreadful scene and Mike's unpleasant prophecy. My parents smiled at me from the porch of the beach home on the Caribbean island to which they had retired, and my brothers' kids were oblivious to the camera lens as they body-surfed in the Atlantic during a visit to my summer house on Martha's Vineyard. My lover, Luc Rouget, waved from his red convertible in the tiny village of Mougins, near the Côte d'Azur in the south of France, and thankfully didn't seem to be an ocean away when

52

I rested the silver picture frame next to me on the pillow.

I must have dozed despite my apprehension of revisiting visions of the body in my nightmares. My alarm sounded at seven, and I allowed myself another hour after listening to the headlines — still vague and devoid of essential facts — on the local all-news station.

At eight, the time I was usually at my desk in the criminal courthouse in lower Manhattan, I got up and showered. I dressed for the trial, in a gray, chalk-striped suit with a pleated skirt and a man-tailored ivory silk blouse. Lyle Keets, the trial judge, was an old-fashioned gentleman who liked all the niceties of the practice of law as it was done forty years ago — professional attire was almost as important to him as professional conduct. He had once forbidden a colleague of mine to reenter his trial part in slacks after a juror remarked that he had been distracted throughout the proceedings by the tight panty line he could see as she stood behind the lectern.

I had missed rush hour, so I grabbed a yellow cab for the fifteen-minute ride down the FDR to the courthouse.

'Morning, Ms. Cooper,' one of the uniformed cops on security said as I passed through the metal detector at the One Hogan Place entrance to the building. 'Half a day, huh?'

It was easier to smile and nod at him than expect him to have linked my night's activity to the morning news.

My office was on the eighth floor of the massive courthouse structure, just across the

53

hallway from the district attorney's executive wing. I had enormous respect for Battaglia, whose long tenure and innovative policies as Manhattan's chief prosecutor had made him a legend in law enforcement. The pioneering Sex Crimes Unit, created three decades earlier, was one of the jewels in his crown. Battaglia was not a micromanager. He left daily details of running investigations in the hands of me and my staff of dedicated lawyers, but he insisted on being kept up to speed on any high-profile matters that would affect his standing in the community or his political base.

'You're running late.' My secretary of many years, Laura Wilkie, knew when not to waste words. I rounded the corner into my office and she followed with a handful of phone messages.

'Sorry. I thought I told you Keets had a dental emergency to deal with.'

'You did. But I didn't know you'd be out with my boyfriend half the night.'

Laura had an unrequited crush on Mike Chapman. There were days I think she came to work just in order to talk with him on the phone, or be dazzled by his broad grin when he perched on the edge of her desk to flirt.

'He ratted me out already?' I untied my cashmere scarf and hung it with my coat behind the door.

'Nope. But Mercer did,' Laura said, reading from a list on her steno pad. 'Told me to keep Mike's calls away from you so you could get done what you needed to do in front of Keets.'

'Okay.'

'Nice thought, but I've already had to scratch the idea of giving you space. Battaglia skipped his meeting at City Hall to get in early. He wants you to brief him on the murder.'

'He picked up from the news that I was out on that? I didn't think they made me.'

'No again. Some guy named Wilbur Gaskin called him to complain about how you were all browbeating a bunch of kids at his church. Gaskin's on some charity board with the boss.'

'The guy was more upset about our questioning trespassers than finding a headless corpse on his doorstep?' I took the messages from her and flipped through them. 'Have you Googled Gaskin for me?'

Laura handed me a two-page printout. She'd never let me see Battaglia unprepared, if she could help it. 'The profile I found reads a tad self-serving. Doesn't say what the man eats for breakfast, but gives you the rest.'

'Sound legit?' I brushed my hair and reapplied some lipstick in the small mirror above the coat hook.

'Banker. Family man. Do-gooder. Moved here from Atlanta a few years ago. I'll run a broader search.'

'I'm looking for an ax murderer, Laura. See if you can find me one before the end of the day.'

'Got it. And Mercer told me to check with the press office. Tell them to let us know about calls coming in through the switchboard on the news reports.'

'Any yet?'

'Minor flood. Not a tsunami, so far.' Laura

55

read from her notes. 'Some of these missing girls go back months. Who's going to vet the callers?'

'I'll look these over. Can you find Nan Toth?' She was one of the most experienced lawyers in the unit with plenty of homicide experience, as well as one of my closest friends. Nan could be the liaison to the squad for the remainder of the day. 'Maybe she'll have time to take it from here.'

I grabbed a legal pad from my desk to list the things Battaglia would tell me to do. If the pastor of Mount Neboh had pulled out votes for his last election, I'd be reporting to the boss with updates four times a day and ordered not to step on the toes of any more parishioners.

'On the lighter side, Alex,' Laura said, checking off her notes, 'am I confirming that reservation for four at Patroon Saturday evening? You still expecting Luc for the weekend?'

'Yes, ma'am,' I said. The owner of the restuaurant, Ken Aretsky, was a great friend to Luc and me, and Joan Stafford was one of my closest confidantes. She moved between homes in Washington, D.C., and Manhattan, and I was looking forward to spending time with her at dinner. 'Fingers crossed. And will you ask Ken if we can dine in the wine cellar? It's a surprise I'd like to arrange for Joan.'

'I thought I could make you smile. You'll have your appetite back by then. If not, well, you can always just drink, right?'

Luc was a restaurateur whose father had been one of the most prominent men in that business on both sides of the Atlantic. While his main outpost was a destination spot for fine dining in

Mougins, Luc's plan was to reestablish Lutèce, his father's great culinary creation that had once been New York's swankest French restaurant. Until that time, the elegance and quality of Patroon made it his favorite dining experience whenever he reached Manhattan.

'Dead right about that,' I said, thinking about the assistant DA who was my trial partner in the case. 'One more thing. Would you please call Barry Donner?'

'Damn. Back to business. I so prefer the social side of your life.'

'Me too.' I looked at my watch. 'Ask him to meet me here at ten thirty so we have a little time together before we go up to court.'

'Sure. And Rose says the boss is in a perfectly good mood. Somebody just comped him four tickets for opening day at the stadium.'

'That always helps,' I said as I left Laura to pass yet another security officer in order to enter Battaglia's inner sanctum.

Rose Malone, my good friend and the DA's longtime executive assistant, was the most trusted person in the office. She was the personification of a loyal and devoted employee who knew where all the bones were buried, with the side benefits of great looks and style that belied her age. Battaglia and his predecessors had no secrets from Rose, nor did any young assistant who caught the attention — for better or worse — of the front office.

'Good morning, Alexandra. That's a handsome suit,' Rose said. 'How is everything?'

'Too good to be true, till last night.'

The city's murder rate had dropped to an all-time low. The mayor claimed credit for it, Police Commissioner Keith Scully went on air regularly to remind voters that dynamic policing techniques were responsible, and the DA ignored them both with arguments that he had jailed most recidivist criminals and successfully used diversionary programs to rehabilitate the rest. There was no logical explanation for the phenomenon. We all knew that such trends were cyclical and that the numbers would eventually spike again.

'You can go right in. He's alone.'

Rose was my barometer for the measure of Battaglia's temperament. In the few seconds I had before entering his office, the warmth of Rose's greeting let me know how the DA's day was going. The strong odor of cigar smoke that wafted over her desk suggested that he had just walked away from her post to settle back into his own suite.

'Have a seat, Alex.' The cigar — a contraband Cuban, no doubt, that someone had given him to curry good favor — was plugged into the middle of Battaglia's mouth, and would be replaced throughout the day by one after another. If you hadn't worked with him for a period of time, you'd need an interpreter to understand the words that leached out around the thick stub. 'Rough scene last night, I take it?'

'Unimaginable.'

'What does Chapman think?' I could barely see his mouth over the top of the *Wall Street Journal*. He was examining yesterday's market results while he talked to me.

I was tempted to tell him that I had a full plate and he was welcome to call Mike for his thoughts, rather than my own, if that was the reason he'd brought me in here. Battaglia had a much more welcoming attitude about women in the criminal justice workplace than the lead prosecutors who came before him did, but like most of the guys who had been in this business a long time, he still viewed homicide investigators as members of an elite professional men's club.

'That the killer knew his victim, chose her purposefully. That this isn't his first kill, nor will it be his last. That he picked his venue for a reason.'

'Good people at Mount Neboh. Don't let the guys hassle them.'

If Wilbur Gaskin described that little encounter as a hassle, I thought, wait till he sees Mike and Mercer close in on a suspect. 'Of course not. There's no reason to.'

'Who was she?'

'We don't know.'

'I realize no face, no fingerprints, but no paper in her pockets?'

'No clothes, Paul. A dump job. Naked, with a blanket that was torched.'

'Cops hold anything back from the press?'

They always did, in hopes that when a suspect was confronted and interrogated, he would reveal a scintilla of evidence that had never been made public.

'She might be Jewish. Or the killer is. There was a Star of David found beneath her body — a

59

delicate piece of jewelry.'

Battaglia flattened the newspaper on his desk. 'For all his bullshit, Chapman always comes up with the goods.'

No point correcting his conclusion. Mike needed the credit for occasions on which his outspoken manner and his gallows humor offended the district attorney. I nodded and smiled, explaining the history of the old church. 'That's why there may be significance to the victim's religious affiliation.'

'You ever think about running for this job, Alex, remember what I tell you. There are three hundred seventy-one Catholic churches in the Archdiocese of New York. I've worshipped at one of them all my life, so I've got to attend. The rest are part of the must-do stops in every campaign. God knows how many Baptist and Protestant churches — the Separatists, as my mother called them all her life, even though they separated from Rome four hundred years ago.'

He laughed at his own remark. He often did.

'Ten minutes apiece on Sunday morning for every primary race, till the sermons come out your ears,' Battaglia went on. 'Then Friday night or Saturday morning for the seventy-seven synagogues on this island. Shecky Feinberg contributes to your race? You've got to show up at his kid's bar mitzvah — and that's before you do the O'Donnell christening. Cold little piggies in soggy blankets and more rubber chickens than you can count. The one sure place you don't want to find bodies is a house of worship. Got that? This one will cost me a month of Sundays at Mount Neboh.'

'Got it.' The campaign poster that hung in my office had Battaglia's head shot over one of his favorite slogans: You Can't Play Politics with People's Lives.

'More likely you'll come to your senses and settle down with your Frenchman and have a brood of little litigators who can also cook a mean omelet.'

'Now, that doesn't sound very enlightened of you, Paul,' I said, wagging a finger at him.

'Be realistic. I got Sonia Sotomayor a seat on the Supreme Court, didn't I? That kind of lightning won't strike twice for my best staffers.'

He was in his late sixties and had been reelected five times, with no signs of slowing down.

'When you tell me you're ready to step aside, I'll have it figured out.'

I had my own unique piece of the criminal law in our Special Victims Unit, and loved everything about my ability to do advocacy for victims who'd been denied voices for so long. The political aspect of the DA's job — trying to be all things to all voters — left me cold.

'Whatever you need, pull it together for this one. Don't hesitate to ask for anything,' he said, reaching across his desk for the daily court calendar, the multipage roster that reported every trial case and disposition in the Supreme Court parts, where all the felony cases were argued. 'How's that Koslawski matter going? You're doing a good job keeping it under the radar screen.'

'Flip to page five — you'll see it there. We're in front of Lyle Keets. I left an update memo with Rose before I went home last night. I just assumed you'd seen it.'

'Must be in this pile,' he said, twizzling the cigar butt between his lips as he looked for the memo.

'Barry Donner caught the case when it came in. He's a good junior assistant, so I didn't want to take it away from him. But once the defense waived a jury in front of Keets and we figured out there might be a surprise witness, I decided to second-seat Barry in the event he needed a hand.'

A second seat in the courtroom — literally an extra chair at counsel table — was usually occupied by the less-experienced lawyers who were assigned grunt work for the bigger guns. In our office, they wheeled the evidence cart of exhibits to and from the trial, put on witnesses of lesser importance, and made routine notifications to get cops and civilians to court at the proper day and hour, often haggling with police bosses about bringing essential players in on overtime.

This time we turned the tables on the tabloids. The defendant — a private-school teacher charged with molesting a fourteen-year-old student — had no name recognition to attract media attention, and by listing Barry Donner as the lead prosecutor, the crew in the press room failed to attach any high-profile connection to the case.

'I made a lot of promises there'd be no grandstanding on this one, Alex.'

'Promises to? . . . '

Battaglia ignored my question. 'No grandstanding. I made that clear to you.'

I could see the memo I'd dashed off the previous evening about what was going to happen today at the Koslawski trial on top of the in-box file. Of course the district attorney had read it first thing this morning. It was the real reason I'd been summoned, to be given an extra admonition. Of course Battaglia was talking directly to Cardinal McCarron about the trial.

'It's not my fault that Koslawski's lawyer decided to call Bishop Deegan as a character witness, Paul. The bishop testified on direct yesterday afternoon, and it was as plain vanilla and coddling of the defendant as you would think. It was nonsense.' Dishonest is what I wanted to call it, but that would be pushing the district attorney too far. 'Enright's just trying to appeal to the court's old-fashioned sense of religious propriety, but I think her plan is about to backfire.'

Denys Koslawski, now a private-school teacher, was a defrocked priest.

Barry Donner had done a tremendous job securing records from the archdiocese in which Koslawski had served as a much younger man. Now we needed to get the evidence of his prior uncharged crimes — swept under the church carpet at the time — into the record.

'Watch whose feet you step on.'

'I'm not looking to embarrass anyone here.' It

63

wasn't the moment to remind Battaglia of his other favorite campaign slogan — that justice would be done in his office without fear and without favor. 'You can't give this perp another pass.'

'I'm not suggesting anything like that, Alex. But there's no need for you to play Torquemada in this either. Young Mr. Donner can probably do fine on his own.'

'I'll pass along your vote of confidence to him, Boss, and remind you of it when it comes time to evaluate the staff for raises. Is that it?' I asked. ''Cause I'd better get up to the courtroom.'

'Chapman didn't see any connection, did he?'

'Connection to what?' I stopped. 'Rose has Mike's number, Paul. Feel free to call and ask him whatever it is you want to know.'

'Any link between a murder victim deposited on the church steps and the fact that you're on trial at this very moment, going after a priest. The timing of that is tricky, don't you think?'

'A fallen priest, thrown out of his position because he couldn't keep his hands off teenage boys, and a decapitated woman — probably Jewish — '

'Like you. Could be a message in that.'

'A decapitated woman who was tortured and dismembered? Left on the steps of a Baptist church? None of us saw a connection to Denys Koslawski, Boss. Maybe if she'd been dumped on the doorstep at St. Patrick's Cathedral, I'd think differently.'

'Don't be facetious, Alexandra.'

64

'Well, please don't look for trouble where there isn't any.'

'I'd hate to think you brought on a tragedy of this magnitude when a slap on the hand would have sufficed as punishment for Koslawski.'

'You think something that I did brought on this murder? You can't be serious, Paul.' Maybe if Koslawki's hand had been slapped enough times to leave some bruises, I stopped short of saying, it would have kept him from reaching for the zippers of the vulnerable young men who looked to the church for spiritual guidance.

'I think Cardinal McCarron was simply worried on your behalf. I expressed that poorly.'

'Thank the cardinal for his concern, Paul. Hope you can both keep the faith.'

7

'The boss said that to you?' Donner asked. He'd overheard my short conversation with Mercer before the elevator doors closed to take us up to Part 67 of the Supreme Court, Criminal Term, of the state of New York, on the fifteenth floor of the monolithic and dreadfully outdated WPA-designed courthouse.

'Why? Can you see steam coming out of my nose and ears? Blood oath, Barry — you never heard what I said about Battaglia or the cardinal. I just needed to vent to a friend so I can calm down and focus on what we've got to do today.'

'I didn't think I'd be making enemies in this job.'

'Nothing to get paranoid about. You won't. This is a tough issue for Battaglia. He's one of the city's most visible Catholics in public office, and the church has been notoriously ineffective in acknowledging the problem of sexual abuse in its ranks.'

'Have you prosecuted other priests?' Donner asked as the doors opened and we made our way past paroled perps and bedraggled relatives waiting for short visits with imprisoned sons and husbands and brothers whose cases were also on the court calendars.

'I was a rookie when I handled my first complaint, a dozen years ago. A Dominican woman from Inwood had an eleven-year-old kid. The local parish priest took an interest in him when he started struggling in school.'

'That must happen all the time.'

'It does. So Mrs. Caceres was fine with it. In fact, she thought it was the best of all possible worlds. Father Leopold offered to tutor the boy in his apartment the evenings that Mrs. Caceres was working late. She was saying more novenas for Leopold's well-being than anyone on the planet. What better? In a neighborhood where gangs roughed up or recruited all the kids, this boy had a guardian angel keeping him off the streets.'

'Till the kid complained?' Barry asked.

'He couldn't bring himself to tell his mother, which is common with most adolescents. He just became very withdrawn and wanted to stop going to see Father Leopold. His mother insisted otherwise, telling him he'd better cooperate and do everything the priest wanted him to do. Everything. Listen to him, she kept insisting, and obey him. No disrespect.'

'And he did, right?'

'Yes, he did. For several weeks, until he had a breakdown in school, after Leopold had moved from touching the boy to sodomizing him. It was a doctor at Columbia-Presbyterian who notified child welfare and the police. That's how I got the case.'

'Did you have Leopold arrested?'

The court officer unlocked the door and let us into the empty courtroom. We walked down the aisle and I pushed the gate that admitted us to the well, taking our assigned table closest to the jury box.

'It was my rude awakening to how the church operated. At the first whiff of a complaint, the priests were moved to another archdiocese. Another state, thousands of miles away. Beyond the subpoena power of the state of New York. Leopold had come from some town in Wisconsin, where he'd run the youth group. Before the ink on the Caceres complaint was dry, he was relocated to a really poor parish south of Austin, Texas. The church leaders just shuffled their problems around, hoping no one would notice.'

'But you're usually a pit bull about this stuff, Alex. Didn't you go after Leopold? Didn't you bring the boy in?'

'Once. I had one shot at an interview with a painfully shy adolescent who would rather have had a root canal than talk to me about Leopold's sexual advances. I had a whole plan for gaining his trust over time and building the case. But the church lawyers moved faster than I did. They offered Mrs. Caceres a settlement she couldn't refuse.'

'Money? She took money to kill the case?'

'You bet she did. She didn't want to start a scandal, publicly accusing a priest of molesting her son. Wouldn't be good for the boy, and it certainly wouldn't be good for her beloved church.'

'And Leopold, what became of him?'

'Typical of the pattern, Barry. A couple of years in a small parish in a remote part of Texas hill country, then on to Oregon, then up to Bridgeport. And always gravitating toward his target population. Supervising the altar boys, organizing retreats for the youth choir. You've seen stories about civil cases against priests, but you'll search pretty hard to find any criminal cases that have been successfully prosecuted. Not one in this county when I got to this job.'

'Is that why you've been so adamant about no plea for Koslawski?'

'That's part of it,' I said. 'He's had lots of chances, over and over again. He's hurt so many young lives and walked away from them each time, protected by the Mother Church.'

'And if Sheila Enright hadn't been so hell-bent on putting Koslawski's character in evidence through Bishop Deegan, the religious background wouldn't have tiptoed its way into this case.'

We were spreading our files on the table when Enright and her client walked into the courtroom. She was an associate in a white-shoe law firm in which her senior partners billed their clients at $850 an hour. That representation was the first sign that Koslawski had someone with a deeper pocket trying to protect him. When I checked the list of archdiocesan settlements, the McGuinn, Hannon, and Cork name came up repeatedly.

'Good morning, Sheila,' I said.

She mumbled a greeting to me and to Barry, but her client was stone-faced. 'Any sign of Keets yet?'

'His secretary called to tell us to come up. She

69

said he's ready to go.'

Enright put her briefcase beside her chair and began whispering to her client. It was a smart move for a sex offender to have a woman at his side for trial. It often made a defendant seem more benign and unlikely to be threatening to anyone. It might have backfired in this circumstance because of Enright's manner. Her attack on the victim had been strident and nasty in tone and substance. There was nothing to corroborate his version of the events — there rarely was, since sex crimes were not likely to be committed in front of witnesses — but the youth's calm demeanor and forthright responses to her questions reflected the confidence of his candor.

One of the court officers banged twice on the side door that led to the judge's robing room. 'All rise. The Honorable Lyle Keets entering the courtroom.'

The black robe draped over his shoulders and the leather-bound notebook he carried suited the judge's patrician bearing. Keets mounted the three steps to the bench, followed by his law assistant, and ordered us to be seated as he pulled in his chair. The stenographer took her place in the well, between the witness stand and the judge's chair above her.

'Ladies and gentlemen,' he said, lifting a fountain pen while checking the previous day's notes. 'We suspended after the direct examination by Ms. Enright of her witness, Bishop Edward Deegan. Are we ready to resume testimony?'

'Yes, sir,' Barry Donner answered.

'Your witness. You may go ahead.'

'Actually, Your Honor, Ms. Cooper is going to handle this cross.'

I could hear Sheila's chair scrape across the floor as she half rose to her feet before thinking twice — she had no grounds for an objection — and reseating herself.

This was a circumstance of Sheila Enright's own creation. Koslawski had his constitutional right to a trial by jury, but Shelia had chosen to waive that right with advice from two of her senior partners after they scoped the pool of prospective jurors. The tactic was occasionally used by savvy lawyers who suspected that their clients might not get a fair shake if a dozen of their peers found charges like these distasteful, and chose to rely instead on a judicial temperament that might be cooler rather than emotional, arguing the case to the bench.

If jurors had been seated in their usual role as triers of the case facts, then the judge would be responsible only for applying the law to those facts. The prosecution would need a unanimous verdict of twelve in order to convict. The defense team could claim a partial victory by hanging the group with only one not-guilty vote. Here, Lyle Keets would not only be responsible for all questions of law, but he would also be the sole trier of fact, the final arbiter in the defrocked priest's case.

So the McGuinn trio of high-priced legal talent had decided to take their chances by opting to not allow Denys Koslawski to be

71

judged by a jury of his peers. The voir dire of a large panel of citizens would have been certain to elicit his background in the clergy, and word would have spread through the courthouse like wildfire, attracting the tabloid press to cover this now anonymous case. You could never guess what personal views a devout practitioner — or a lapsed Catholic — would bring to the jury box.

'Would you please ask the bishop to retake the stand?' Lyle Keets nodded at the officer to bring in the witness while Sheila Enright smirked her discontent at me.

Once the case was assigned to Judge Keets, the defense team made an educated guess that the elderly jurist, who'd been on the bench since the days when the testimony of a sexual assault victim required corroboration — independent evidence of the elements of the crime, which didn't exist in the present case — might buy into their denials. We had all done enough research to know that Keets was High Episcopal, but none of us could figure which way that would cut when it came to his jurisprudence.

Bishop Deegan, close to eighty years of age — about ten years older than the judge — swept into the courtroom, his head erect and his gold pectoral cross highlighted against his black suit and white clerical collar. He took the stand and sipped from the cup of water offered to him before making himself comfortable.

'May I remind you, Your Grace, that you are still under oath?' Keets said.

The defense had also made a lame effort to close the courtroom, but the law was well established that with rare exceptions the public was entitled to be present at criminal trials. Deegan peered over my shoulder as if to reassure himself that no spectators had entered present. Then he looked expectantly at Barry Donner and seemed surprised when I rose to my feet to begin the questioning.

'We haven't met, sir. I'm Alexandra Cooper and I'm working with Mr. Donner on this case.'

'Very well then. Good day, Ms. Cooper.'

Deegan's credentials had been established by Sheila Enright the previous afternoon. He was presently Bishop of the Diocese of Chicago, with degrees that included a doctorate in canon law — a codification of the law of the Catholic Church.

'You spoke yesterday about the time, fifteen years ago, when you served as an auxiliary bishop in the Diocese of New York, is that right?'

'That is correct.'

'And you met Mr. Koslawski during that period, when he was a priest in a local parish?'

Deegan nodded in the defendant's direction. 'Yes, I was the vicar in charge of education, and Denys was one of our most able teachers back then.'

That was a point he had made over and over again the previous day. Enright had taken the bishop through all of the good deeds of the young priest to hammer home his sterling character.

I asked a series of questions regarding the interactions between the two men and accepted the praise that Deegan heaped on the defendant.

I wanted it clear that I had respect for his exalted position, for his religious leadership and community influence, and for the pride he so richly took in his many years of church leadership.

'During your time in this archdiocese, did you ever hear any allegations against Father Koslawski regarding sexual abuse?'

The bishop's answer was out of his mouth before I could finish the question. 'I had no duties that involved me in issues of sexual abuse.'

'Most respectfully, sir, my question was whether or not you heard any allegations, whether in or apart from your duties?' I changed the course of my inquiries, though Deegan was determined not to give me an inch. The law allowed me to ask a character witness not only about specific acts within his direct knowledge, but also the defendant's reputation for morality within the community.

'No, I did not.'

'Did you ever hear any allegations that Father Koslawski put his hands on the knees and thighs of a young man in a movie theater?'

'Objection.' Sheila Enright didn't rise from her seat. 'Asked and answered.'

'You may respond,' the judge said.

'I don't recall.'

'Let me back up a step, Bishop Deegan. Would you consider such conduct — the unconsented groping of a minor's thigh and knees, by an adult — to be sexual abuse?'

'Objection, Your Honor.'

'I'll allow it.'

I had studied Deegan's answer to this question in a deposition he had given in a civil case involving another priest.

'No, I would not.'

'Is there some other way you would describe that conduct, sir?'

Deegan cleared his throat with a cough. 'I would say that it's improvident, Ms. Cooper. Improvident touching.'

Exactly the language he had used in the civil matter two years earlier, which had led to a furious interchange with the plaintiff's lawyer.

'So, 'not sensible or wise' would be your conclusion about such touching. Improvident, but not a sexual violation.'

'Correct, Ms. Cooper. I don't consider those — those, well — areas to be sexual parts.'

He ought to talk to women who ride the subway in New York, subject to the uninvited stroking of strangers on crowded trains.

Enright was on her feet. 'Your Honor, I think Alex — Ms. Cooper — is already venturing beyond the scope of my direct.'

'I'm just trying to get the semantics right, Judge. I don't want to use a conclusory term like 'sexual abuse' if the bishop doesn't agree with the legal definition.'

'Ask your next question, Ms. Cooper.' Keets stared at me over the rim of his reading glasses.

'You were responsible for hearing complaints against priests, were you not?'

'Most certainly.'

'And what were the nature of those complaints?'

75

The bishop smiled at me now, almost beatifically. 'Some were liturgical, Ms. Cooper. Some were theological.'

'Can you be more specific?'

'I received complaints that a priest's sermons were too long,' Deegan said, 'or that he sang poorly. On the more serious side, there might have been a charge that a priest was promoting a practice in violation of church teachings, that kind of thing.'

'And abuse of alcohol?'

'Yes, certainly. Those came to me.'

'So sexual abuse was the only parish problem that was not under your jurisdiction.'

'Those weren't my words, Ms. Cooper.'

'I guess we can have your testimony read back, Bishop. I believe you said that oversight of such allegations wasn't part of your duties as vicar of the archdiocese.'

A less enthusiastic smile this time. 'I suppose I should say there were no records of any such misconduct, so nothing came to my attention.'

'Well, sir, were there written records of any sexual abuse allegations in this diocese during your tenure?'

'Written, Ms. Cooper? Specifically, written?' He was speaking to me but looking to the judge as though for help.

'Exactly.'

'No need for that. No need for anything in writing.'

'Why not, sir?'

Bishop Deegan tapped the side of his head with his arthritic forefinger. 'Because I kept all

76

that sort of thing up here, Ms. Cooper.'

'In your head?' I said. 'Let the record reflect that the bishop is pointing to his head while speaking.'

'Precisely.'

'And neither you nor anyone else in a position of authority in the Archdiocese of New York thought it necessary to make any formal record of such complaints?'

'Why should it be necessary, Ms. Cooper? They trusted me, of course.'

I glanced at Judge Keets to see whether he was as unimpressed with that answer as Barry and I seemed to be, but his expression was glacial.

'By the way, Bishop Deegan, how many parishioners are there in this archdiocese?'

'Two and a half million, young lady.'

'And you keep it all up here, is that correct? Every complaint and allegation?'

'Objection,' Enright said. 'She's just getting argumentative with the witness.'

'Sustained.'

'Then let's move on from these files,' I said, tapping my own forehead.

The bishop reached for the paper cup of water. I didn't know whether the tremor in his hand was related to his health or was a reflection of his discomfort. 'I'd like to do that. Where to, Ms. Cooper?'

'I'd like to discuss the secret archives of the church.'

'The what?' Judge Keets asked, over the shouted objection of Sheila Enright. 'Is there such a thing, Bishop Deegan?'

The bishop didn't answer the judge.

'There are indeed secret archives, Your Honor,' I said. 'I'd like to inquire about them.'

8

'I've given you some scope, Alexandra, because there's no jury here,' Keets said, pushing his readers to the top of his head as Enright, Donner, and I stood at the bench. 'Would you mind telling me what these secret archives are?'

'I'd also like to know,' Enright said.

'I'm sorry if you didn't do your homework, Sheila, but this goes to the heart of the matter. They're church records, and I believe I'm entitled to inquire about them.'

'Do they have anything to do with this defendant?'

'Certainly.'

'She's just fishing, Your Honor,' Enright said. 'You can't let her do that.'

Keets turned to the bishop and asked him to step down, letting the court officer lead him away as our voices raised beyond a stage whisper.

'You think what this man has said is credible?' I asked, trying to keep some semblance of respectability in the tone of my voice. 'Every diocese in this country has been rocked by these scandals. The settlement numbers are over four billion dollars now, and at least six dioceses have had to file for bankruptcy. They're closing down churches and parochial schools all over the country. Parishioners in the poorest communities are suffering, and it's primarily because of the failure of the Mother Church to confront this issue for more than fifty — *fifty* — years.'

'That's not my client's fault.'

'I'm well aware of that, Sheila. But Deegan has been part of the problem. Philadelphia, Your Honor, and Boston, for example, are places typical for the kinds of reports that are involved. Their diocesan personnel files show that more than seven percent of the priests in their cities had been accused of abusing children in the last half century. At least seven percent. And you know what the numbers are in New York?'

Keets lowered his glasses and made notes as I talked. 'Go on.'

'One point three percent. The lowest in all 195 dioceses in the country.'

'How fortunate for the children of New York,' Enright said with obvious sarcasm.

I couldn't think of the legal term of art for the word 'bullshit.' 'That's absurd and you know it. It's totally artificial.'

'Ladies, ladies. Let's not have a catfight,' Keets said. 'What reason would you offer for that, Alexandra?'

'Two things, Your Honor. First is that our numbers are ridiculously low because we have the most restrictive statute of limitations of any state. There are many, many more reports, but they aren't legally viable because the complaints came in too late.'

'You mean that in most jurisdictions, the reporting can be done for a period of time after the youths have attained majority?'

'Yes, sir. That's so very logical. Most minors don't have the knowledge or wherewithal to take on the church at such a young age. So the statutes have been extended. And secondly, we're the only city in which prosecutors have been denied access to the chancery's records.'

'There are no chancery records here,' Enright said. 'Didn't you listen to the bishop?'

'Isn't it lucky that Deegan hasn't been hit by a bus, Sheila? Or lost his head?' I said, thinking of the body I had seen just hours earlier. 'Fifty years of unholy acts right out the window, 'cause the only place they were tracked in the entire archdiocese is in the bishop's eighty-year-old cranium. That's what the secret archives are about.'

Barry and I had piqued Lyle Keets's interest. 'Step back, ladies. I'll let you run with this a bit, Alexandra.'

Enright was practically frothing at the mouth as she continued to object. 'But — but Ms. Cooper is going way beyond — '

'I've heard enough, Ms. Enright,' Keets said, pointing a finger at her. 'Will you resume your seat, Your Grace?'

I waited until the bishop arranged himself in the wooden chair and looked at me. 'Would you explain to the court, sir, what the secret archives are?'

Deegan frowned and paused for an objection, but none followed.

'Am I correct that this diocese has such archives?'

'Yes, Ms. Cooper. It's a canonical requirement that every diocese has them,' Deegan said, now turning his body toward the judge. 'The

81

'secretive' designation really means only that certain documents are set aside, Your Honor. Historical papers, if you will, that relate to the founding of the diocese and such things. It's not as mystical as it sounds.'

'If one of your colleagues were to receive a complaint about a priest's misbehavior? . . . '

'What kind of misbehavior, madam?'

'Any kind. Liturgical or theological,' I said. 'Even sexual. Anything deleterious to a priest's reputation or career. Would that complaint be written up for the secret archives, in addition to being stored in your memory bank?'

Whatever these archives held, it was obvious that Deegan thought I was prying open Pandora's box. He didn't want to answer any questions.

'Sorry?' he said, leaning forward to better hear me, I thought.

But he was drawn to the opening of the courtroom door behind me, so I turned to look as well. A man entered alone, his dark hair slicked back, disappearing behind his long neck into the scarf he wore. It looked as though he had on a clerical collar beneath his winter coat. He was wearing sunglasses, which made it difficult to discern his features, but his skin was such a ghostly shade of white that it seemed he hadn't been exposed to daylight in ages.

I repeated my question, shifting position so that I could follow the spectator's movement. He seated himself in the next to the last row behind Denys Koslawski — the groom's side of the aisle, as Mike liked to call it. It seemed as though

82

Bishop Deegan nodded at him, almost imperceptibly.

'No, Ms. Cooper. Nothing like that exists in the secret archives of this diocese.' Each word was delivered with emphatic confidence.

'Would it be possible, sir, for me to examine those — '

'Objection, Your Honor. Did I say this was a fishing expedition, or what?'

'Sustained, Ms. Enright.'

What I couldn't get one way I would try to do another. I would be permitted to continue my cross if the candor of the witness himself were at issue, as I believed it to be. 'Are you aware, Bishop Deegan, of how many claims of sexual abuse in this diocese were settled out of court?'

'I'm afraid I cannot say.'

'Because that information is not 'up here'?' I asked, mimicking his motion of tapping the side of his head.

He snapped back a reply. 'Because there are things called confidentiality agreements in such lawsuits, Ms. Cooper.'

'Yes, of course, Bishop Deegan. So then you are aware of the claims?'

'Objection!'

'Sustained. Ms. Cooper,' Lyle Keets said, clearly growing annoyed with my line of questioning.

'For what reason, Bishop, did Denys Koslawski leave the diocese?'

His trembling hand reached for another sip of water. The lone spectator stood up and moved a few rows closer to the front of the room. The dark glasses hid his expression from me and blocked his features, but his skin seemed rough with angry red blisters on one cheek.

'Do you recall?'

The bishop's voice was softer now. 'It was a medical dismissal.'

'Medical?' I asked, trying not to show my surprise. I liked to prep my cases with a nod to the axiom that advised not asking a question to which one didn't know the answer. I wasn't expecting this one.

'Entirely that,' the bishop said, picking up his head with renewed satisfaction and smiling at Koslawski — or the man who had come in to observe.

'And what condition might that be?' I asked as the Mike Chapman voice that often played in my brain despite my best efforts to keep it at arm's length was laughing and repeating the word 'priapism' — the persistent, painful erection of the penis.

'Objection. Mr. Koslawski's health condition is privileged.'

'Hardly, Judge. The bishop was not his physician.'

'I'll allow it. Go ahead and answer, Your Grace.'

'Hepatitis. Denys suffered from hepatitis, which required a lengthy period of hospitalization and recovery.'

'And did you ever hear, Bishop Deegan, that Father Koslawski — before suffering this medical setback — had invited a teenage boy to

84

his room in the rectory and engaged him in oral sex?'

'No, I certainly did not.'

'And would you agree with me, sir, that such conduct would not only be 'improvident,' to borrow a phrase from you, but that it would also be illegal?'

He closed his eyes and answered, 'Yes.'

'Are you aware of where Mr. Koslawski went when he left this diocese?'

'In hospital, as I recall. Out of state.'

'Isn't it a fact that he was transferred first to another diocese in the Midwest?'

Deegan seemed to look for the answer in the light fixture high above his head. 'I don't remember that.'

'Do you recall that one of your colleagues asked him to sign a document requesting laicization?'

'No.'

'But if that were a fact — if such a document existed — it would be in the secret archives of the New York diocese, would it not?'

'Slow down, Ms. Cooper,' Judge Keets interjected, lifting his fountain pen from his notebook to refill it. 'For the record, Your Grace, why don't you tell us what laicization is?'

'Certainly. It is the act of reducing a priest to the lay state, Your Honor. Relieving him of his duties.'

'And that would be within your power to do?' Keets asked.

'Indeed it would. There are certain authorities in the Catholic faith that a priest has — to

85

preach, to minister the sacraments, to say Mass, and so on. I'm able to suspend him from those acts.'

'And are you aware that one of your colleagues performed that suspension in regard to Denys Koslawski?' I asked.

'I . . . was . . . not.' Deegan shifted in his chair as he spoke a firm answer.

'Did you ever correspond with Father Koslawski while he was in New Mexico?'

'I did not.'

'Did you know he stayed for a period of time at the Via Coeli in that state?'

'I don't recall.'

I fingered a piece of paper — a copy of a letter Koslawski had written to the bishop many years ago.

'What is Via Coeli?' Keets asked. 'Do you mind letting me in on this?'

'A church-run facility,' the bishop answered, responding more politely to the judge than to me.

'I see,' Keets went on. 'For medical treatment, for his hepatitis?'

'No, Your Honor,' Deegan had lowered his head. 'It's a monastery.'

'A monastery of sorts, wouldn't you say?' I asked. 'Bishop Deegan, is it more accurate to describe Via Coeli as a facility to which priests accused of sexual abuse — priests whose deeds were recorded in secret archives, or in the deep recesses of your brain — were sent?'

'Yes.' The bishop gave me another quiet yes. 'They were transferred there for a good reason,

86

Ms. Cooper. For rehabilitation.'

'Are you aware, Bishop Deegan, that most professionals in the therapeutic community don't believe that there is any kind of rehabilitation that is effective for sexual predators, most especially for child molesters?'

'Objection,' Sheila Enright said. 'Your Honor, this is a hearing. It's not a bully pulpit for Ms. Cooper's views on sex offenders.'

'Sustained. That objection is sustained. Move on, Ms. Cooper. I've given you plenty of latitude.'

'Yes, sir. Well, if you didn't correspond with Denys, Bishop Deegan, do you recall receiving any mail from him?' I said, raising my copy of the old letter.

The heavy doors creaked open again. I leaned against the railing at the jury box and looked back to see Pat McKinney, the chief of the trial division and my archnemesis in the bureaucratic structure of the office. Although he wasn't one of my regular supporters, he made his way to the front of the room and seated himself behind me, on the bride's side.

'No, I don't.' Deegan's eyes narrowed and he glanced from the first visitor, dragging his line of sight like the cursor on a computer across the aisle to McKinney.

'Your Honor, I've had this exhibit pre-marked as People's eighteen. I have a copy for the defense and for you,' I said, passing them to the court officer to deliver to each party. 'I'd like to offer it in evidence.'

'Any objection, Ms. Enright?'

'I need a minute to read it,' Sheila said, accepting the document and slumping in her chair, tilting her head to talk with her client.

'Psssst.' It was Pat McKinney, trying too hard to get my attention.

'Mr. McKinney,' Keets said. 'Always nice to have you in my courtroom. Do you need Alexandra? She seems to be oblivious to you.'

'Just for a minute, Judge, while Ms. Enright examines the exhibit.'

I walked over to the wooden barrier that separated the well of the courtroom from the benches. My arms were folded against my waist and my lips pursed as I turned my back to the defense table. There could be no good news wrapped into McKinney's appearance.

'I know you didn't drop in for a lesson in the art of cross-examination, Pat,' I said. 'What's up?'

'Just making the rounds for Battaglia. You're not beating up on the bishop, are you?'

'Hardly. But he is stubborn.'

'Ever gone after a rabbi, Alex?'

'Actually, I have. A guy I grew up with who led a congregation in Greenwich Village. He was drugging teenage girls and sleeping with them. That's the thing about these cases, Pat. Equal opportunity crimes. My perps come in all shapes and sizes. You don't think this is some kind of religious persecution, do you? I'm beginning to get the picture that Battaglia does.'

'Try and wind it up this morning, Alex. You may have some media wandering around here in

88

the afternoon. The house press is looking for red meat.'

'Red meat — or me? As of this morning, no one knew I was involved in this case.'

'Guess you didn't have time to fill me in on last night's excitement. Don't forget the chain of command, Alex. You still work for me.'

'Funny. I thought I served at the pleasure of the district attorney. You're just his ass-wiping yes-man.'

McKinney glared.

'Ready, Your Honor,' Enright said. She wasn't going to challenge the authenticity of her client's handwriting or the letter itself. 'No objection.'

'People's eighteen, Ms. Cooper. You may proceed.'

'Channel that gentle, feminine charm that must be lurking somewhere within you, Alex,' McKinney said. 'Deegan's a very popular figure in my circles, you know.'

'I'm almost done with him. Meanwhile, keep your eye on that guy sitting behind my defendant. You think he's a priest?'

We both turned our heads, but the man was gone.

'Like magic, Alex. You made him disappear just like magic,' McKinney said. 'Just like that woman's head.'

The letter captured all the anguish of the young priest. I passed it to Deegan through the court officer and let him read it.

'Have you ever seen this document before?'

'Not that I recall.'

I repeated the date and referred to the

89

postmark of New Mexico on the envelope. I asked Deegan to read aloud from the exhibit.

The paper rattled ever so slightly in the old man's hands. ''Eight months have passed, Your Excellency, since I have been here at Via Coeli. I realize the serious duties to which you must attend, but I plead to you again for some word of encouragement about whether I might return to the diocese.''

The bishop hesitated and lowered the paper.

'Please go on,' I said.

''I do feel so alone here, even though at peace with God. I am hoping to hear from you, as my spirit is heavy and my heart longs to serve the church again, in all the ways that I can be of good use.'' This time Bishop Deegan rested the page on his lap. 'Must I continue?'

'That's not necessary,' Keets said.

'Do you recall reading that letter shortly after the date it was posted?' I asked.

'I don't open my own mail, Ms. Cooper. I never saw this letter. I can't account for every piece of paper sent to me,' Deegan said, coming to a slow boil. 'Father Koslawski was a fine young man. That's what I know.'

'And your opinion wouldn't change, sir, if you believed he had molested seven teenage boys in the rectory?'

'That never — '

'Would your opinion change if such a fact were true?'

'Of course not. I'm a man of my word,' Deegan said, almost shouting now. 'Judge Keets, if I may, the district attorney himself promised

90

me I'd be on and off the stand in fifteen minutes.'

'You have spoken with Paul Battaglia about this matter?' Keets asked, faster than I could form the words myself.

I stared at the large gold cross on Deegan's chest.

'By chance, Your Honor. I ran into him quite by chance.'

'I have no further questions,' I said, sitting and pushing Barry Donner away as he leaned in to talk to me.

'Then we thank you for your testimony,' Keets said, standing to excuse the bishop as he stepped out of the witness box and signaling to Enright at the same time to hold her comments.

The court officer led Deegan out of the room as Sheila Enright got to her feet.

'Judge, I want to know what kind of contact the district attorney had with my witness. What have we got here — tampering?'

'Deegan wasn't even on the witness list you turned over at the start of the case, Ms. Enright,' I said, hoping my shock showed slightly less than hers. 'I wouldn't get too carried away with accusations yet. Ask the bishop which one of them initiated the encounter.'

'I intend to.'

'And you, Ms. Cooper,' Keets said. 'You'll inquire the same of Mr. Battaglia, won't you?'

He banged his gavel on the bench and frowned at all of us. 'Two o'clock. We'll resume at two o'clock sharp.'

9

'Who's with him, Rose?' I asked, skipping the niceties.

'Pat came down from court twenty minutes ago, and he called in Brenda Whitney,' she said, referring to the head of Battaglia's public relations office. 'They're working on a press release for later today.'

'It's urgent. May I go in? You don't need to buzz him.'

I had passed her desk and was opening Battaglia's door, startling the threesome as they huddled over the conference table at the far end of the room.

'You finish with the good bishop?' Battaglia asked, grinning broadly as he sucked on what was likely his third cigar of the day.

'I figured he'd stop by to tell you himself. Maybe take you to lunch.'

My old friend Brenda realized immediately that she was caught in the crossfire. I was trying to keep my tone appropriate but finding it difficult.

'Skipping lunch. Too much to get done.'

'That's not my point, Paul. Sounds like Deegan was calling the shots.'

'You're mistaken, Alexandra. Badly mistaken.'

'I didn't know you had a dog in this fight. Are you on Koslawski's team?'

Brenda picked up her pad and started away

from the table. 'I'll come back later, Boss.'

'Don't leave, Brenda. I've got no secrets from you. We'll need Alexandra for this, too.'

He usually had secrets from everyone. This time, he didn't want to be alone in the room with me. He didn't want to have a private conversation or a chance for me to question him.

'I gather you know Deegan?' I asked.

Pat McKinney walked over to the bookshelf and busied himself in the first volume of the Penal Law. He liked nothing better than an argument that might distance me from the district attorney's favor.

'We've met many times, but fortunately never in the confessional,' he said, laughing at what he must have thought was a joke. 'Cool down and sit down, Alexandra. You here about last night?'

'I'm here because a key defense witness just told the court that he'd been talking to you about the case. Judge Keets asked me to get the details on that.'

That comment erased Battaglia's smile. He removed the cigar from his lips. 'You tell the judge to invite me to court if he wants to ask me questions. I don't need an interpreter, even if it's you, young lady. I've got ten thousand cases pending in the office at any given time. Every Tom, Dick, and Harry in town wants a favor. I can't remember each person I talk to. Goes in one ear and out the other. Where's Chapman?'

'At the morgue, I expect. I haven't been back to my office yet. I came straight here from the courtroom.'

McKinney turned on a dime. 'You haven't

spoken with Mike?'

'In the middle of my cross, Pat? You saw what I've been doing this morning.'

'Then maybe you haven't heard. The victim on the church steps has been ID'd,' he said.

'They've found her head?' I asked, adrenaline kicking in to override annoyance.

'Turns out the fingertips were all they needed.' Battaglia took the reins, glad to be in charge of breaking news. 'Naomi Gersh. Thirty-four years old. Have I got that right, Brenda?'

'Yes, Boss.'

'What am I missing?' I asked. 'DNA? Something in the databank that identified her?'

'Simpler than that, Alexandra. Seems Ms. Gersh had an arrest record.'

'Here?' I asked, and Brenda nodded. 'What for?'

'Two collars,' Pat McKinney said, holding up the first volume of the Penal Law. 'Both times for OGA.'

Obstructing governmental administration — usually an action that interfered with a law enforcement function and made the arrestee unpopular with the cops.

'We're pulling up the court papers for you,' Battaglia said. 'Get to work on this, pronto. Leave the Koslawski business to Mr. Donner. You're off that case.'

'I'm what?'

The district attorney ignored me, and Pat McKinney simply smirked. I bit my lip to stop the venom from spurting out and left the inner sanctum as abruptly as I had entered.

94

'Mike called,' Laura Wilkie said as I stormed into my office. 'I'll get him on the line while you take some deep breaths. You look wild.'

'I'll get over it.'

'The other messages can wait,' she said. I heard her talking to someone before she told me to pick up my second line.

'We got a vic,' Mike said.

'I know. Naomi Gersh. Battaglia had a call from the commissioner. I should have all the court papers shortly. Where are you?'

'The autopsy's over. I'm on my way to notify her younger brother, Daniel. Pick him up at his job — moves scenery at a small theater off-Broadway. He's next of kin.'

'If you want company, I'm available.'

'I assumed you were a full-time trial dog this week.'

'Battaglia thought I was getting too rowdy in the courtroom. He just booted me off the Koslawski case and told me to work with you on the murder.'

'Let me start with Daniel. If I get lonely by dinnertime, I'll give you a shout. Battaglia tell you anything about the obstructing arrests?'

'He didn't know facts. Brenda's digging up the old files.'

'What's your bet?' Mike asked. 'Antiwar? Pro-choice? Fur coats?'

'Be serious.'

'I'm very serious. For one of those causes, she was willing to go to the mats. Pushing the envelope to get something she believed in.'

Laura stood in my doorway, her arm blocking

the eager young woman who wanted to enter. 'Emily is from IT — with court papers for you.'

I waved the girl in, took the blue-backed misdemeanor cases from her hand, and cupped the receiver against my neck.

'Here's your answer,' I said, folding the disposition sheets over so that I could see the date and place of occurrence on each of the complaints. 'Both arrests occurred at the same place. Dag Hammarskjold Plaza. One last December and another in January.'

The small, tranquil city park on the entire south side of the block between First and Second Avenues on East Forty-Seventh Street had been named for the Swedish diplomat and Nobel peace prize winner who had been Secretary-General of the United Nations.

'Right opposite the U.N.'

'Exactly. But it's not about war,' I said. 'Naomi was leading a protest, a day of international solidarity for an Israeli feminist group that has been denied the right to pray, like men do, at the Wailing Wall in Jerusalem.'

'Well, Coop. Maybe we've got a holy war on our hands after all.'

10

Mike extended a hand to help me out of the yellow cab in front of a recently renovated tenement building on Avenue B at four the same afternoon.

'What happened to Daniel?' I asked.

'Strike one. Manhattan South sent a team to his old job, 'cause the commish was afraid he'd hear about Naomi on the news. But he hasn't worked there lately.'

'Someone told him?'

'Yeah. Yeah. One of the guys he used to hang with told him. Good way to piss me off.'

'So he's crushed. Give him a break. And let's get out of the drizzle,' I said, pushing open the vestibule door.

'Not so broken up as you'd think. He hasn't seen much of Naomi in almost six years. His buddies at the theater didn't even know he had a sister.'

'But this is her apartment.' I knew the address from the court papers. 'How did Daniel get in? If he didn't have much of a relationship, you wouldn't think he'd have a key.'

'Nope. The super opened up for him. Now he's stonewalling me.'

Mike pressed the buzzer with the paper marker labeled Gersh next to the mailbox for 2D. It took almost three minutes for a voice to respond through the intercom.

'Yes?'

'I'm still here, Daniel. I'd like to talk to you.'

'What about that warrant, Detective?'

'I got one right here. A living, breathing warrant. Meet Assistant DA Alex Cooper. Open up, Daniel. This is a condolence call, not a strip search.'

There was another short hesitation before the buzzer sounded. Mike entered, climbing the steps in front of me. When we reached 2D, the door was ajar and the chain was bolted across the opening.

'Let me see your papers.'

'I realize this is a difficult day,' I said, 'but we don't need a warrant. You have no legal standing to keep us out of your sister's apartment. We're simply here to talk to you.'

'Me, I'm the battering-ram type, Daniel. Works every time and it gets the neighbors' attention. Coop here favors the more polite approach.' Mike pressed his arm against the door to test its give.

Daniel pushed it closed and removed the chain.

'May we come in?' I asked.

He shrugged and stepped back to let us enter. Mike scoped the room — a large studio apartment lined with brick and board book-shelves, with little more in it than a double bed against the wall, a pair of beanbag chairs, a couple of crates that served as a living area, and a tiny kitchenette. Two doors were opened in the back, revealing a bathroom and a closet. I introduced myself to Daniel, trying to figure whether his reserve was grief or a natural shyness as I expressed my sympathy for his sister's brutal death.

'May I sit down?'

'Yeah, sure.' He motioned to the chairs, but I chose the side of the bed. I knew I would sink into the shape-shifting beans and end up below eye level with him. Daniel wasn't ready to sit, answering me but keeping a watch on Mike.

'I've got a lot of questions about Naomi that I'd like to ask you,' I said. 'Is there anything you want to know before we begin?'

'Nah. The cops told me the stuff about her body,' he said. 'I really don't want to hear any more of that.'

'How old are you?'

'Twenty-seven.'

'What do you do?'

'Right now I'm a prop guy. Move scenery and equipment at a theater. I'm supposed to start acting classes in the summer.'

'Have you worked at the show very long?'

'It's a temp job,' he said, scratching his sandy brown hair, which hung below the collar of his sweatshirt in a long, tangled snarl. 'I only moved to New York in the fall.'

'From? . . . '

'Chicago. I lived near Chicago with my mother.'

'Does she know about Naomi yet?' I asked, hoping to distract Daniel while Mike lifted a suitcase out of the closet.

'She's my mother. Not Naomi's,' Daniel said. 'You mind leaving her luggage alone, Detective?'

'All packed up and ready to go,' Mike said. 'Your sister do that, or you?'

'Just don't touch it, okay?' Daniel Gersh walked toward Mike. He was tall and well built, with a jangly kind of energy that made him appear skittish and nervous.

'Ms. Cooper's talking to you.' Mike backed off the suitcase and walked over to the windowed wall that housed the sink and small oak dining table.

The apartment was neat and clean. I knew it would be gone over by crime-scene detectives and was confident — as Mike was — that Daniel wasn't leaving with the suitcase or any other property of his late sister's, if that was what he had come here to do. Nothing appeared to be out of place. It didn't look like the young woman had been butchered in her home.

'Can I just get you to focus on some questions that would help us try to figure out what happened to Naomi?' I said.

'Then stop asking about me, okay? What do you want to know about her?'

'Why don't you start with the family background?'

Daniel had planted himself in the middle of the room. 'Naomi's a lot older than I am. Seven years. My father — our father, I mean — he met her mother in college. Got her pregnant and her family put a lot of pressure on them to get married. So they did. But it didn't last very long. Like a year after Naomi was born, it was over.'

I could hear the rustling noise as Mike pulled back the shower curtain in the bathroom, and

Daniel hurried over to look at what he was doing.

'The toilet's still running,' Mike said. 'What'd you flush before you let us in?'

Daniel held up his arms as if puzzled. 'Like, what are you talking about? Maybe it's just broken.'

'Drugs? Pills? Why're you so jumpy, Daniel?'

'I'm not jumpy, man. I'm still, like, shocked about this.'

'Then answer Ms. Cooper's questions.'

'I take it your father remarried,' I said. 'Did you and Naomi grow up near each other?'

'At first, yeah.' Daniel settled himself in, leaning against the refrigerator and lighting a cigarette. 'My mom and dad lived in a suburb of Chicago. Naomi's mother taught at the university for a while — they lived in Hyde Park. Then, like my dad said, she was always trying to find herself.'

'Naomi's mother?'

'Yeah. Her name was Rachel. My dad used to joke that he was glad she did eventually find herself — and that it was as far away from him as possible.' Daniel inhaled and smiled, his affect as inappropriate to the situation as his remarks.

'Where did they go?' I asked.

'They made *aliyah*, Ms. Cooper. You know what that is?'

'They immigrated to Israel.' I knew the Hebrew word that was a basic tenet of Zionism and would explain the Israeli Law of Return to Mike later on. It allowed anyone of Jewish descent the right to settle in Israel, to return to the Promised Land.

'Rachel took Naomi away with her? There wasn't a custody battle?'

'Not from what my mom says. By that time my father was already — um, he was diagnosed with Lou Gehrig's disease when I was pretty young. He died when I was twelve, and no, he wasn't really interested in Naomi. Or me, for that matter. He was too sick to do much of anything.'

'Did you stay in touch with your sister?' I asked.

Daniel didn't seem to object to my calling her that, as separate as he tried to paint their lives. He took a deep drag on his cigarette. 'Sometimes. She came back to the States when our dad died. Stayed with my mother and me for a few months, but they didn't have much to say to each other. Naomi went off to college after that, in London.'

'Do you know what she studied?'

'Yeah. Philosophy. Philosophy and religion. I think she wanted to — tried to — have some kind of relationship with me. She used to send me things all the time.'

'What kind of things?'

'Letters. Souvenirs and shit like that whenever she traveled.'

'Tell me about the letters, Daniel.'

'I don't remember much. Naomi was trying to be all grown up and intellectual, and me, I was just a goofy kid. Just read them and threw them out.'

'*Shhhhhhh*,' Mike said, placing his forefinger

102

against his lips. 'Hear it?'

'Hear what?' I asked.

'The quiet.' Mike was getting right up in Daniel's face. 'Think of the money you'll save, Daniel. Plumbers charge almost as much an hour as good defense lawyers.'

'So what?'

'So the toilet stopped running. Not a long-standing problem in the pipes, I wouldn't think. Why won't you tell me what you flushed?'

'Maybe I just had to use the john, Detective. Ever think of that?'

'I did, actually. 'Cause if you've got these tiny pieces of paper coming out your ass, you ought to see a doctor.'

Something had been ripped into shreds and it looked like Mike had picked up a few damp remains and spread them on the countertop, on paper towels, to dry.

'Daniel, you've got to be candid with us. We're at square one on Naomi's case. If there's something about her lifestyle we need to know, if that's evidence you're trying to destroy or conceal — '

'I know what you people are going to do.' He was staring at the torn bits of paper. 'You're going to rip every inch of her private life apart and hang her out in public, like she asked for this.'

'Nobody asks for this. We're in here because we're looking for something that might connect her to the man — to the people — who did this to her,' I said. 'What did you try to hide?'

Daniel turned to the sink and put out the butt

103

of his cigarette under the kitchen faucet. 'She's got nobody, man. You understand that? Even I let her down.'

'How do you mean?'

'She wanted me to help her. When things happened.'

'What things?'

'Trouble. Not big trouble, but — I don't want to go there.'

'Like her arrests?' Mike asked.

Daniel reached into the cupboard over the sink for a glass and filled it with water. 'You already know about that?'

'Yeah. That's how she was identified, and that's the reason we got to you as next of kin. She listed you on the arrest papers.'

'Naomi called me from jail,' he said with a half laugh, not intended to be funny. 'I was the only family she had. She needed me to go to the bank and get some money, and agree to be her contact in the city, even though I'd been here only a few weeks less than she had.'

'But you'd spoken to her not long before that?'

'E-mailed. That's mostly how we stayed in touch.' Daniel twisted his long hair into a knot at his neck, working his spindly fingers around one another while Mike wrote down both their email addresses.

'Is her mother still in Israel?' I asked.

'Rachel?' Daniel put the glass down and looked at me. 'She was blown to bits by a suicide bomber on a bus in East Jerusalem. Two, maybe three years ago.'

I'd never thought of a possible terrorist angle

104

to Naomi's murder. When Daniel said that she had no one close to her, he wasn't exaggerating.

'Did Rachel live in one of the settlements?'

'Yeah. Naomi gets all her activist energy from her mother. Lucky she was in London that time when the bomb went off.'

'What do you know about your sister's religious beliefs, Daniel?' I asked. Now I wondered if there could be any kind of connection between her mother's violent death and her own.

'Very little.'

'Your father — was he Jewish?' I asked.

'Raised as a Jew. But my mother's agnostic and so was he. That's why Naomi and I didn't talk about it much.'

'But the arrests, Daniel, were they because of her religious beliefs?'

He thought for a few seconds and reached into his back pocket for another cigarette. 'Less religion than over her feminist views. That's what all her preaching was about. Always rubbing certain people the wrong way.'

Certain people. 'Like your mother, for one?'

'Yeah. You could say that.'

'So why was she arrested?' I asked. 'Do you know?'

'I had to sit through the arraignment, so I heard most of the facts, and then Naomi told me more of it when they let her out.'

'What's the organization?'

'It's called Women of the Wall,' Daniel said. 'It's a group that Rachel helped start up twenty years ago, in Israel.'

'For what?' Mike asked, moving the tiny bits of paper around like figures on a chessboard, trying to form words from the letters written on them.

'Naomi said that ultra-Orthodox Jews didn't allow women to pray at the Wailing Wall, didn't allow them to dress in traditional prayer shawls. Stuff like that.'

'You know anything about this, Coop?' Mike asked.

Daniel walked across the room to take a matchbook from the pocket of a jacket he had thrown on one of the chairs.

'A bit. Tallith — that's the ritual prayer shawl. I know that some of the extreme factions of Judaism consider it wrong — arrogant, and against biblical commands — for women to wear these garments and pray publicly at places like the wall.'

'Hear that, Daniel? We've come to the right place. Coop's got all her feminist ducks in a row.'

I turned my back as Daniel lit up and whispered to Mike, 'Wrong time to make fun of it, Mike. You've got to look into this,' I said. 'Discrimination against women sheltered under the wings of religion — every religion — is a really serious problem. It's been that way for centuries. It's excluded us from education and social opportunities, from positions of authority. You want me to go on?'

'Later for that,' Mike said, cocking a finger at me like he was pointing a pistol. 'After I calm you down with some Dewar's.'

'What else do you know about the demonstration?' I asked Daniel as he rejoined us.

'That it was supposed to be a day of solidarity with the women in Jerusalem. Naomi said the first protest brought out some real animals. Guys who spit at her and threw things. Then their women actually joined in, too, doing the same.'

That fact didn't surprise me. Sadly, women often were the worst jurors in cases of sexual assault and domestic violence, far too judgmental about the conduct of their peers. The sisterhood wasn't always the friendliest group in town.

'I take it Naomi resisted arrest,' Mike said.

'That was the whole point, Detective. She figured the only way to get press about the issue was to be a little outrageous. She wasn't exactly a novice.'

'Sure, kick a cop. Spit at him like the bad guys did at her,' Mike said.

Daniel held up both hands like he was surrendering to Mike Chapman. 'Hey, I'm not defending what she did. My mother didn't want me to have anything to do with her. Naomi might as well have been a leper, the way she lived.'

'What do you mean — a leper?' I asked.

'She'd been an outcast for so long, it made it easy for her to embrace that over-the-top conduct, whatever the cause of the day. Fling herself down on the ground, refuse to move on when the cops broke things up. Yeah, I'm sure she did some fine kicking and spitting. She's had lots of experience with it.'

'Not just once, here,' I said. 'In December and then again in January. She must have believed deeply in this cause.'

'Or maybe she just liked the attitude,' Mike said, playing with his paper chips.

'A pariah, Ms. Cooper. That's what my mother liked to call Naomi. She was the perfect pariah.'

11

'You want to make sense of this alphabet soup for me?' Mike asked Daniel. 'These are the bits that were clinging to the inside rim of the toilet bowl. Didn't go down with the rest. You mind telling me what you were trying to get rid of?'

I walked to the countertop and looked at the scraps of paper. Daniel's expression was glum, but he didn't respond.

'Is this Naomi's handwriting?' I asked, nudging a few pieces toward him.

'Yeah.'

'Can't you understand how important it is that we learn everything there is to know about her?'

Mike's displeasure was palpable. 'So far there's not a whit of evidence to connect a killer to Naomi's body. I just came from the autopsy and there's nothing. No seminal fluid, so no DNA inside her — '

'I said I don't want to hear about it,' Daniel said, closing his eyes and waving Mike away with one hand.

'Listen up, buddy. Hearing about it might be the only way to reach you. Whoever did this to Naomi had the time and place to slaughter her like an animal. It didn't happen here, obviously. And it likely didn't happen on the street, or someone would have found a whole mess of blood by now.'

Daniel clapped his hands to his ears and Mike pulled them away just as fast.

'Could be she was abducted by a stranger, but my money's on somebody who knew her well enough to hate what she stood for. Hate everything about her. You don't get this personal with your violence — you don't sever the head of a woman — unless you're so full of vitriol that swinging the ax is what gets you off.'

Daniel tried to keep his eyes squeezed shut so the tears that had formed wouldn't be visible to us.

'Who did she know, Daniel?' I asked, softening the tone to get him to talk to me. 'Who were her friends?'

'I told you, she didn't have friends,' he said, turning to face me.

'We'll get the names of the people who demonstrated with her. At least the ones who were also arrested. Did she talk about them?'

'Maybe so. But I didn't listen. There were antiwar groups and pro-choice marches. Save the whales. Protect the rain forests.' He was mocking her now, ticking off a list of issues, just like Mike had done, only this list was for real. 'Anti-smoking, pro-mammograms, anti-handgun, pro-opening the borders, free Tibet.'

'And most recently a full-on involvement with a religious organization,' I said.

'Not up my alley, Ms. Cooper. I was the get-out-of-jail-free card. I was there when she needed me. That's all.'

'How much time did you spend with her after she was released the first time?'

110

'Hardly any. We had lunch together once when I was between jobs. And she came to a Christmas party with me, when the first show I worked on was breaking up.'

'A party?'

'Yeah. Naomi said she wanted to meet new people. She was living in an ivory tower.'

'I don't get it,' Mike said. 'She was on the barricades, Daniel. She was on the street for all these causes. It doesn't get more common ground than that.'

'No, I meant her intellectual life. She was taking courses and everyone was so serious. She said she wanted to hang with me 'cause I made friends easily and I didn't have the emotional baggage that she did.'

'Where was she taking courses? The ivory tower?' I asked.

Daniel looked sullen again. 'I don't know, Ms. Cooper. Some religious school, I guess.'

'Did she actually meet any of your friends?' Mike asked.

Daniel squirmed and looked away. 'Like, I knew they weren't her type anyway. She came 'cause she thought there'd be actors and people she could talk to. By the time Naomi got to the party, it was mostly a bunch of inebriated stagehands and prop guys.'

'Did she stay? Did she hook up with anyone?'

Daniel gave Mike his best what-are-you-crazy expression. 'I think she stayed long enough to insult a couple of the crew. I mean, just talking her usual way to them — stuff nobody really cared about.'

'Did she leave with you?'

'Nah. Naomi left before I did. I wasn't in the mood to get stuck taking her home, getting a lecture about how we should be family and all that. It was her new kick, and quite frankly it didn't interest me a bit.'

'So what have we got here?' Mike asked, pointing to the scraps of paper.

'Junk. I was just trying to clean up. Gonna have to start packing and sorting out Naomi's things.'

'Clean up? If this place was any neater,' Mike said, 'I wouldn't think anyone lived here. Who put you in charge?'

'Like I said, I'm the next of kin.'

'Let me guess. Your sister inherited some money when Rachel was killed.'

'I — I, uh, don't really know. I don't know much about that.'

'You went to her bank to withdraw money when she was arrested, didn't you?' I asked. 'Any idea how much was in her account?'

'Oh, no. This isn't about money,' Daniel said, shaking his head.

'Did Naomi have a will? You know who her lawyer is?' Mike had a laundry list of questions ready to pop.

'Sure she had a will. Ever since her mother — since Rachel was killed so suddenly — Naomi was always spooked about being . . . well, like, ready to die.'

'Who's the lawyer?' Mike asked, opening dresser and night-table drawers with his vinyl-gloved hand.

'How the hell would I know?' If I'd thought Daniel Gersh was jumpy ten minutes earlier, he was bouncing off the walls by now.

Mike turned back to the small rolling bag he had removed from the closet earlier and hoisted it onto the couch.

'You've got no business touching that,' Daniel shouted, circling the kitchen counter and moving to the middle of the room.

'I think I've got a better claim to it than you have at the moment,' Mike said, bending over to unzip it. 'The luggage tag says it belonged to Naomi. Did she keep it loaded or was that you, planning how to take some of her things away while I waited at the front door?'

Mike threw back the lid. The suitcase was practically full. I could see a checkbook on top of a stack of other papers. He picked it up and lifted the cover. 'Well, well. It's Naomi's. Three thousand, seven hundred, ninety-six dollars and change in her checking account, packed and ready to go.'

Daniel's hands were flailing. 'It's not what you think, Detective. I didn't want anybody stealing anything from here.'

Mike laid the checks on the arm of the sofa and started to dig through the rest of the things. I didn't see any items of clothing, but there were spiral notebooks, manila file folders, and, crammed among them, what looked like the kind of ritual prayer shawl that had started the brouhaha at the Wailing Wall.

Mike opened one of the pads and began to read aloud. It was a diary that Naomi had

113

written in the period after her mother's death. The language was full of despair, appropriate to the dreadful circumstances of the bombing.

He set it aside and picked up several volumes, flipping through two or three of them before coming to a more recent period that documented her stay in New York. He held up the pages to reveal that strips had been torn out of the journal — paper that matched the scraps on the kitchen countertop.

'What's with this, Daniel? What have you got to hide?' Mike asked, circling back to the sink with the notebook.

Daniel had no intention of answering. Before Mike or I could get anywhere near to stop him, Naomi's brother turned and bolted out the door of the apartment.

12

'Hey, Loo,' Mike said, wasting no time calling to let the lieutenant know that Gersh had skipped out on us. 'I guess Daniel thought I was getting ready to throw him into the lion's den. Make sure somebody runs background on him and gets to his crib before he makes it home.'

'Have you got extra gloves?' I asked.

Mike pulled a pair out of his rear pants pocket and handed them to me so I could begin to do an informal inventory of the items in the suitcase, looking for leads to move the investigation forward.

The notebooks were in no particular order, but each one had Naomi's name and a date — month and year — printed on the first page. They seemed to cover the last five or six years of her life and were a mixture of scribbled recollections of a day's events, paragraphs filled with serious reflections, and collages of news stories or photographs pasted into the pages.

'What do you think, blondie? Can you tell if Naomi was packing up, or do you think Daniel was sniffing around for something?'

I was holding three of the notebooks but put them down to look around the apartment, starting in the bathroom. The toothbrush was still in the small plastic stand on the sink, and all the daily hygiene products were in place. In the medicine chest behind the mirror, a cosmetics

115

bag — lipstick, blush, eyeliner, and mascara — was nestled between a box of condoms and a vial of pills: a mild tranquilizer packaged by a pharmacy in London. A nightshirt and robe still hung on the hook behind the door.

'The don't-leave-home-without-them things of a young woman's life seem to be accounted for,' I said. 'I found this piece on the bathroom floor, at the base of the toilet bowl.'

'I feel like we've signed up for a high-stakes game of Scrabble.' Mike took the paper from me — it had portions of letters torn in half, written in the same boldface as the notes in Naomi's books — and set it next to the others he had dried out. 'What the hell was Daniel doing?'

'Let me take a stab.'

He moved aside and I tried to align the snippets to make any kind of sense, but it seemed too much of the paper was missing to tell a story. 'What have you got?' he asked.

'An *L* ripped off alone, and another one with a *T* and an *R* on it. Here's an *S*. This one is clipped at the edge, but it's a *U*.'

'Trial. Maybe she was worried about her case.'

'Trial, trail, traffic, truck, train, tryst, triangle.'

'Lust,' Mike said.

'Rust. Struck. This is a task for another time. Max can do this in her sleep.' My brilliant paralegal, Maxine Fetter, could probably have cracked the World War II Enigma encryptions over a slow lunch period.

Mike started to put the dried scraps in envelopes while I went back to the suitcase. I carefully removed the prayer shawl and checked for stains like blood, knowing that the lab would do a proper search when it was delivered to them. I saw nothing unusual.

Beneath the notebooks were tracts on feminist theory in a range of theologies. I took a folder out of my tote and listed the volumes and authors, looking inside for any margin notes or dog-eared pages Naomi might have made.

Under the religious tracts were scads of photographs — old ones of Naomi as a child, posed between young adults I guessed were her parents. There were more recent shots of her with Daniel. The background was distinctly suburban, the yard of a home and an SUV with Illinois plates in the driveway.

Interior scenes showed both of them smiling at the camera across the table with a Thanksgiving turkey in the foreground. Daniel's mother probably took the photograph — there was no other sign of her — and the handsome man leaning in behind Naomi and her brother, flashing a big smile, must have been the stepfather. Then in Daniel's room, with Naomi standing at his shoulder while he was hunched over his computer, someone had snapped another remembrance.

The last trio of photographs was printed out on glossy four-by-six paper and worn from travel or repeated handling. I sucked in a gasp as I looked at it.

'This may be why Daniel's mother called Naomi a pariah,' I said, studying the shots before I passed them to Mike.

The first two were pictures of Naomi, wearing

117

only black bikini panties edged in lace, smiling from a bed in what looked like a guest room. The same suitcase we'd found in the apartment was sitting on the floor next to a chair.

'Mother of God,' Mike said, looking at the image. 'You think that squirrely kid who just blew us off was actually in bed with his sister?'

'I doubt it. I'm guessing the reason Daniel's mother wanted nothing more to do with Naomi is because of her newfound appreciation for the seventh commandment. Thou shalt not commit — '

'Adultery.' Mike finished the sentence for me and stared at the photos as I handed off the third one in the pile.

The naked man on the bed, smiling at the camera, was the same guy who appeared in the Thanksgiving dinner photo — arms around the half-siblings. Even without his horn-rimmed glasses and his clothes, Daniel's stepfather looked handsome and happy.

13

'Do the notebooks go back as far as Naomi's visit to Illinois?' Mike asked. We were both riffling through them to see what months and years were covered.

'Not any that I've found yet. How about the one you had with the torn-out pages?'

'That's pretty recent. All about this winter and what she was up to.'

'Let's make copies before you voucher it. What did Daniel rip from it?'

'The pages after Naomi was arrested in January. The half that's left reads like a description of what she was doing with the other protestors. Has some names. Then a sweet bit about how she was grateful to Daniel. How she went to meet with him a couple of times.'

'Names?' I asked. 'Her fellow protestors? Friends of Daniel's?'

'Looks like he was ripping out most of what came after he got involved with her, whether to protect someone else or himself. You hoping to find an avenging angel here?'

'Anything that will help. We'd better do a run on Daniel's father — who he is, whether he's in the Midwest or traveling. Few things more personally virulent than an intimate partner gone bad. Is that your phone or mine?'

I dug into my bag, but Mike had answered his phone on the second ring. 'Louder, Loo. I can

119

barely hear you,' he said, sticking his forefinger in his other ear.

As he listened to Ray Peterson talk, he turned his back and walked away from me. 'What do you mean 'just now'? Where? Exactly where?'

There must have been a break in the case.

'We're in Alphabet City. The vic's apartment. I can be there in twenty if you can get uniform from the precinct here to secure the apartment. Hold tight, Loo, okay? I'll check.'

Mike leaned over the sink and looked out the window, up and down the street. 'Coop, you want to go out and give a yell to the cops in the patrol car?'

'Sure.'

'She'll sit with the guys till Crime Scene gets here. It's not a big job. I just want them to photograph the place and do a routine check.'

'Don't even think about parking me here. Wherever you're going, I'm with you,' I said, opening the door to summon the officers while Mike gathered the papers and books he wanted to bring along. 'It's Naomi, isn't it?'

'Suit yourself,' he said as he nodded to me.

When I returned to take a last look around the small apartment, Mike was on the phone again, his back to the sink. I passed by him and he took a firm grasp of my forearm, stopping me in place until he finished his conversation.

We were face-to-face as he flipped his cell closed with his free hand. 'You don't have to prove anything to me by coming along, Coop.'

'What would ever make you think that was my purpose?' I said, raising my right hand to shield my eyes from the glare of the late-afternoon sun that streamed in over Mike's shoulder, while trying to wriggle free from his grip. 'It's ridiculous. What's eating at you today?'

I didn't mean to sound as arch and strident as I did with just those few words.

'Easy, girl. I know you've got balls as big as any guy in the squad, and I know you can outthink me from here to the moon, but you don't belong on the streets with all the garbage we're used to chasing after and corralling. You should be in the courtroom, Coop — '

'Battaglia threw me out of the trial I was handling,' I said, confused by the tender tone of Mike's voice. The sentiment was familiar, but he was softer and calm, not baiting me as he always did in front of the cops. 'I told you that.'

'Then sit behind your desk and write a brief, for Chrissakes. Analyze the latest Court of Appeals decisions. Break some defense attorney's chops.'

'What is it you don't want me to see today?'

'It's gonna get to you, kid. It gets to every one of us sooner or later. The street has a way of settling in your gut like a malignancy, small at first, then spreading till it infiltrates every pore in your body. It's not just about today. Not just this case.'

He let go and I thought for a second that he was going to touch my face, cup my chin between his fingers. 'I understand that, Mike. I've seen my friends, our friends — '

'But you think you're different, is that it?'

'Not for a minute. There's nobody here but us,

121

you know?. You don't have to make me the butt of your jokes. Take out your frustration on something else.'

'Trust me, Coop. I'm not frustrated. You'd be the last to know about that.' He turned away from me and opened the faucet, splashing some cold water on his face. The moment had passed and now the edge was back in his voice. 'You've got some kryptonite coating that protects all this shit from creeping into your soul and your brain and that underutilized thing you call your heart? You think you're immune from it?'

'Not in the least. You asked for my help last night. I started out with you because you thought I had something to give you.'

'My mistake,' he said, wiping his face with a piece of paper towel. 'I didn't guess I'd be dragging you into what came next.'

I wanted to reach up and straighten the lock of hair that had lodged itself below his shirt collar at the nape of his neck, but when he stood, it fell into place. The line between my annoyance at his sniping and the affection that had grown for years was pencil-thin. 'I might surprise you, Mike. Maybe I can help with the bigger picture.'

'Then saddle up, Coop. Let's see if you can cross-examine a severed head.'

14

Mike's estimate of how long it would take us to get uptown was off by half an hour. The circuitous route from the narrow one-way streets of lower Manhattan, up the FDR Drive, and across the width of the island to West 112th Street and Amsterdam Avenue seemed to take an eternity in traffic that was snarled and tangled despite the lone siren of our unimpressive Crown Vic.

The area around the Church of St. John the Divine — the largest cathedral in the world, set on thirteen acres of land — was already cordoned off with police tape and a phalanx of uniformed cops who had established a perimeter. This time, reporters and photographers had beaten us to the scene and were angling for a gruesome money shot, the sort they had missed at Mount Neboh less than sixteen hours earlier.

Mike double-parked the car on Amsterdam, and in an uncharacteristic display of patience, waited for me to catch up with him before approaching the barricade of wooden horses and yellow police tape. It wasn't chivalry — he usually threw himself headlong into the mix with no concern for my whereabouts — but rather the fact that I'd explained my connection to the cathedral as we crawled through the late-afternoon traffic.

'Which way?'

I pointed to the right, and he shoved the stanchion aside to make room for both of us to pass through. 'The sculpture garden,' I said. 'The Fountain of Peace.'

My mother, Maude, raised on a dairy farm in Massachusetts by her Scandinavian parents, was confirmed in the Episcopal Church, and had been bused with her teenage classmates to this grand hybrid of Romanesque and French Gothic design for that ceremony. She had never forgotten the elegance of its architecture, so we came often in my youth to admire the 601-foot nave, the Great Rose Window made of ten thousand pieces of colored glass, and the stunning procession of thirty-two limestone matriarchs and patriarchs — Abraham and Sarah, Isaiah and Jeremiah, Ishmael and Hagar — who now appeared to be frowning down at Mike and me as we jogged beneath the Portal of Paradise to circle the massive building.

The cloistered park, usually swarming with children and their mothers and nannies, was a sea of NYPD blue. It looked as though all the civilians had been chased from the area.

A sharp voice yelled 'Chapman,' and off to the side I could see Ray Peterson, standing on a bench to oversee the operation and waving us to approach.

'Sorry it took so long, Loo,' Mike said. 'What'd I miss?'

Mike extended a hand and Peterson stepped down, crushing the end of the burning butt that he tossed from his mouth as he did. Then he picked it up and pocketed it so his team didn't

124

mistake it for something the killer left behind. 'There's gonna be a couple of toddlers with nightmares for months to come.'

'Who found the head? You're saying kids?'

The lieutenant extracted another cigarette from his pocket and lit it. 'Put something in a bright yellow backpack with cartoon characters and smiley faces all over it and what child wouldn't glom onto it?'

'Who's got it now?'

'ESU. Katie Cion wedged through the fencing to retrieve the bag. She's hangin' here for dear life to see you, Chapman. Won't give it up to Crime Scene or the medical examiner. You got some motley harem is all I can say.' Peterson inhaled and started marching us toward the center of the circle of cops. He was pushing sixty-two, grizzled and slightly stooped, with the smell of tobacco well saturated into every piece of clothing he owned, especially the polyester suits that were standard for cops of his generation. 'Like to know your secret.'

'If I told you I'd have to kill you, Loo. Katie Cion's a sucker for my sensitivity. That a fact, Coop?'

The Emergency Services Unit was as exclusive a group of cops as you could find anywhere in the world. They pulled despondent jumpers off the cables of the city's tallest bridges, rescued infants from abandoned elevator shafts, dragged crazies from precarious window ledges, managed the most dangerous hostage situations, and in Katie's case, once safely maneuvered a corpse from the bottom of an antique city well while

125

dangling upside down, supported by the partners she trusted daily with her life. She was courageous, cool, and clever, all packed in a pint-size police uniform.

'Sounds right to me. She's only human.' I let Peterson lead because he was known to everyone at the scene. The men and women who were working the small park in a grid formation, scouring the ground and bushes and paved pathways for any traces of evidence, briskly stepped aside for the lieutenant. He was universally respected for his decades of experience and vast knowledge of the workings of the most complex homicide investigations in the city.

'Mike says you know this place fairly well.'

'Social visits and a few funerals.' The cornerstone was laid in 1892, but even to this day the construction of the great building was barely two-thirds completed. Its design was the customary cathedral shape of a cross, crowned at the crossing by a towering spire, with a main altar surrounded by seven Chapels of the Tongues to represent the growing immigrant masses in nineteenth-century New York. Despite early financing by wealthy trustees like J. P. Morgan, the ambitious project ran out of funding somewhere along the way. 'Saint John the Unfinished is what my mother calls it.'

'I'd laugh, Alex, but the scaffolding around the base of the church serves too well to conceal anybody who wants to lurk around here at night. It's dark and massive, and it's sheltering in ways that I don't think the Good Lord had in mind.'

I spotted Katie Cion thirty feet ahead, holding

court with one of the ME's death investigators and a few of her ESU colleagues.

'Scrape up that gum,' Peterson shouted to a detective who was using the toe of his highly polished leather shoe to poke around a patch of damp sod. 'Get on your knees and bag that chewing gum, Gonsalves. You got a good dry cleaner, the grass stains will come out.'

'It's a friggin' playground, Loo. You want DNA from the gum? We got a vat full already. We got a whole kindergarten class ready to upload in the databank. The saliva of a future generation of moguls, memorialized in the city lab. You think we need more?' The dapper Benny Gonsalves bent down and probed at something with his pen.

'If I don't see dirt on your pants by the end of the day, don't even think about putting in for overtime.'

Mike had passed the lieutenant and walked directly over to Katie Cion, who was explaining what had happened as we caught up to him.

'A pack of five-year-olds, you know what I mean? A couple of the moms were off to the side, yakking about Botox or something serious like that.' Katie paused to greet me but kept right on talking. 'One of the kids got frisky and started to climb into the bowl of the fountain while nobody had an eye on her.'

It was still too cold and windy for the four strong heads of the fountain to be opened for the spring season. Then, they would shoot steady streams of water into the air to cascade over the pedestal, merging and foaming into a maelstrom meant to evoke the primordial chaos of the earth.

Rainwater, dirt, and small bits of garbage had pooled in the base of the giant sculpture. 'The kid didn't mind stepping in this muck,' Katie said. 'She had her eye on that backpack.'

'Was it just sitting there on the edge?' I asked.

'Nope. It was out of reach, beyond the wooden gate that was erected around the inner circumference, probably for the purpose of keeping people away. She got her skinny little arm right through the slats and pulled it close. Got enough of a glimpse to scream bloody murder.'

We were losing the late-afternoon sunlight to the west, behind the tall buildings. The enormous wings of the sculpted figure above our heads cast a bizarre shadow.

'Who's the flying dude?' Mike asked as Katie's gloved hands reached to unwrap the backpack, which was covered with a tarp, under the watchful eyes of the death investigator and the ESU team.

'The Archangel Michael,' I said.

'Ah, leading the heavenly host against the forces of evil. The Bible told me so. Guess he was asleep at the wheel last night. Show me what you got, Katie.'

I was nervous, averting my eyes from the tarp and studying the figures on the sculpture that rose above the fountain, remembering from my youthful visits that its many images celebrated the triumph of good over evil.

'It's not a coincidence our killer picked this

church, either,' I said.

Mike had gloved up, too, and was crouched next to Katie, ready to look at what she had. 'What do you mean?'

'That's the Archangel's sword,' I said, pointing at the weapon extending from his hand, and following the tip of it with my finger. 'He's vanquished his enemy.'

'Keep it coming, Coop,' Mike said, parting the zippered pouch of the backpack to look in.

'Satan. He's just decapitated Satan. There's the devil's head, dangling beneath the crab's claw.'

Our killer hadn't discarded his trophy. He had placed it in this spot to make a statement.

It was a full minute before Mike spoke to me. He stood up, one hand brushing his dark hair back as he often did when he was agitated, the other planted on his hip.

'Here's the rest of your vic, kid. You wanted the whole experience, didn't you?'

He stepped back and Katie Cion offered me up the backpack like it held something inside that I might actually want to see. I steadied myself and met the sightless stare of the pale, waxen, bloodied face of Naomi Gersh.

15

'You couldn't have two more different institutions,' Peterson said. 'Mount Neboh and Saint John the Divine. But they're really just a stone's throw away from each other. We're two blocks south — '

'A few broad avenues west and in between them lies one of the most dangerous strips in the city,' Mike said, referring to Morningside Park. 'Not the most direct route I'd expect someone to take, escaping with a body part.'

'Hey, it's all Harlem.'

The ME's office workers had taken over the process of removing the backpack and the possible evidence that had been found around it. Most of the detectives paused and stood silently as Naomi's remains were carried out of their circle and packed into the van.

'Don't let any of the folks who send their kids to Columbia hear you call this neighborhood Harlem,' Mike said, wagging a finger at Peterson. 'They plunk down the big bucks for a college education they think is in a genteel part of town called Morningside Heights.'

The Columbia University campus continued to expand and swallow up most of the surrounding area, between its academic buildings and real estate bought up for student housing. It suffered the crime problems of most urban schools — the town-gown dichotomy

— but the overwhelming number of criminal cases that came to my attention from the Columbia campus were actually date and acquaintance rapes between kids who knew one another, usually fueled by drugs and alcohol.

'Call it what you want, Chapman, this here's still Harlem. You're just lucky her head didn't wind up at the bottom of the Hudson. Zip. Nada. Nothing to work with then.'

Having seen the gruesome discovery, I wasn't sure what clues this find would yield. 'Don't you think the choice of crime scenes is a more important focus right now, while the lab works up some forensics? Why these churches? Like Mike said, there's nothing random about this.'

'What she's really thinking, Loo, is what's a nice Jewish girl doing in a place like this? Maybe a not-so-nice girl. Think of that angle.'

'I figured for certain the tabloids would start blaming the victim before you did.'

'Motive?' Peterson asked, using the embers of his cigarette to light the next one. 'You're already writing your closing argument, Alexandra. We'll never get there till we find this bastard.'

We had lost the sunlight altogether now, as shadows lowered themselves down the sides of the cathedral and over the somber faces of the disapproving martyrs and prophets. Beyond the yellow lines of police tape, the gawkers were dispersing as some of the medical personnel and uniformed cops left the scene.

I shielded my eyes with my hand, spotting a familiar face as a man emerged from a yellow

131

cab on Amsterdam. He headed directly toward the entrance of the cathedral, through the gold-plated doors of the main portal. 'Mike, isn't that Wilbur Gaskin? The guy from Mount Neboh, last night?'

'Good eye, blondie,' Mike said, taking off after him. 'Hold that thought, Loo.'

I was a few paces behind as Mike called Gaskin's name, but the determined banker never looked back as the heavy door started to close slowly behind him.

Mike broke into a jog and managed to wedge himself in the entrance, getting Gaskin's attention this time as he yelled loud enough to fill the huge nave of the church.

'What brings you here, Mr. Gaskin?'

I was inside the cool, damp building, my five-foot-ten-inch frame dwarfed by the immensity of the interior space.

Gaskin was obviously surprised to see Mike, fidgeting as he tried to make me out in the background. 'I heard the news, Detective. I heard the terrible news on the radio and thought I should talk to the bishop.'

'About the case? About something you know that I don't?'

'About our churches, Mr. Chapman. By the time this is on the nightly news, we'll both have the same — uh — issues on our hands.'

'Publicity? You got yourself all worried about the PR aspect of things, while me and my buddies just have to think about who killed the girl.'

'We have security problems to consider, and I

think it would be tasteful to offer a prayer service in her memory.'

'The bishop know you're coming?'

'Well, no. I didn't call.'

'Just hoping to get the bishop in his seat, huh?'

'There'll be somebody here to help me, Chapman. It's a church,' Gaskin said, snarling at Mike as he kept glancing over his shoulder as though expecting someone to appear.

'Why don't we take this walk together? You must know the way to the office.'

I could see Gaskin hesitate before turning to start down the long nave. 'I think I do.'

I was twenty steps or so behind the two men as they passed through the center of the church, having walked at least the length of an entire football field in silence.

Out of the corner of my eye, as I glanced over my shoulder, I could see a flash of movement in the ornate choir loft that ran half the distance of the nave, built out as though suspended above the end of the pews to my far left.

I cocked my head and turned to see whether we had company. Mike said something to Gaskin and I swiveled back to try to hear their conversation at the same time.

I couldn't shake the sense someone was moving in that space overhead, and though I continued forward to keep up with Mike, my eyes swept the choir loft again.

Now I could see the figure — a tall, thin young man with a clerical collar visible beneath his overcoat, weaving a path to the rear of the loft, closer to the massive church door behind me.

His head was bowed and he seemed to be talking to himself. His skin was a ghostly white, blurring into the bleached collar beneath it.

I tried to get Mike's attention, but the man had slipped behind one of the colossal columns that extended from the floor of the church up to the great ceiling. Not a sound accompanied his fluid movement.

I slowed down for another look just as Mike turned to wave me forward to him.

The man looked familiar to me, just as Wilbur Gaskin had. But this time I wasn't so sure. Maybe I was spooked and looking for quick solutions when there wouldn't be any.

'Put a move on, Coop,' Mike said.

'Excuse me, sir,' I called after the silhouette, shimmying my way across one of the long pews to get closer to the area below the choir loft, looking down so as not to trip over any of the prie-dieu kneelers along the way.

There was no response.

I picked my head up again and leaned back, but the loft above was empty.

Only seconds had passed, but off to my left the church door opened, and though the man was farther away from me now, the feature that was most prominent in my memory showed clearly as I viewed his back. The long hair, bunched together like a ponytail, was tucked into the rear of his coat — just as it had been in the courtroom that morning.

I broke into a trot to get to the door before it closed behind him, struggling to remember from earlier visits to the cathedral whether there actually was a staircase in that corner of the loft. Even if there was one, how had this man descended it so quickly and silently? I'd have to figure that out later. Now all I wanted was to find out who he was and why he had twice crossed my path.

I dashed out and gasped as the wind whipped at my face while I continued the hunt for this fast-moving apparition. The CSU detectives were still working off to my left, so I ran down the steps and around to the right — the north side of the great cathedral.

Against the blue-black sky and the dark gray stone of the old building I could barely see more than a few feet in front of me. I came to an abrupt halt as the walkway ended fifty yards from the corner I had turned. I found myself pressed against the waist-high railing that formed a balcony over the steep incline toward Morningside Drive.

No one there. I thought for a second that I heard a sound coming from below the ledge on which I stood, but that didn't seem possible. I was sure it was just me, panting to catch my breath before turning back to go inside.

16

Gaskin was fuming about being intercepted in the cathedral, and even more annoyed when Mike left him to follow me out onto the church steps. Darkness had overtaken the streets, and we looked in vain for any sign of the elusive cleric.

'Is there a staircase that leads down from the choir loft?' I asked.

'Not on that end, Coop.'

'Then he must have moved even faster than I thought he was going.'

'Or he sprouted wings,' Mike said, exasperated with me. 'Let me get this right. You didn't recognize his face.'

'I didn't really see his face in court this morning.'

'But it was well-lit there.'

'Yes, but he had on a big pair of sunglasses. I didn't see any of his features, except that his face was long and angular, and his skin was unusually white with irregular red scabs or something.'

'So, you're giving me a make on a tall, thin guy with a ponytail?'

'I told you he was wearing a collar. And I said a gray overcoat.'

'Detail on that?'

'Generic.'

'One of retail shopping's best consumers and you can't detail the coat? Would you buy this scrip from a witness, Coop? 'Oh, yeah, Ms. DA. Ask the man to turn around so I can see the back of his head. Bingo! That's the guy who did it.' Come in out of the cold, Madame Prosecutor. I think you're having a brain freeze.'

'I'm not exaggerating, Mike. See if that's who Gaskin was here to meet. Maybe there are connections between this murder and the trial of the defrocked priest, but I'm just too thick to make them. It's almost like Battaglia wished this on me.'

Mike pushed open the door and practically rammed it into Gaskin's chest. 'I asked you the nicest way I know to stay right where you were, didn't I?'

'I thought you'd gone off and left me, Detective. You're correct about my calling the bishop first. I should have done that. I'll go back to my own church and make a plan.'

'You happen to see the young man who just left the cathedral?' I asked.

'I'm sorry? I didn't notice anyone,' Gaskin said.

'He must have been waiting in the choir loft when you entered.'

'Waiting for what? Are you implying? . . . '

'He only started to move when Mike and you got halfway down the nave, closer to him.' I was creating a scenario that had the two men planning an assignation in the cathedral.

'You were off base last night when I came to my own church to try to help, and your techniques of information-gathering are even more preposterous today. What young man are

137

you talking about?' Gaskin said. 'Who is he?'

'Ms. Cooper was hoping you could tell us that. Might be a man of the cloth, Mr. Gaskin. Caucasian. Tall and thin, hair in a kind of ponytail, hasn't outgrown his acne.'

'I'll sleep on it, Chapman.' Wilbur Gaskin pulled on the door handle and let himself out as the cool evening air rushed in, the chill attaching itself to me like a second skin.

Mike's fingers were riffling through his hair, and when his eyes wouldn't meet mine, I knew he was trying to curb his annoyance with me.

'What's wrong?'

'Nice job, Coop.'

'Hey, I told you I saw Gaskin — '

'And then you freaked him out so he wouldn't even wait to talk to us.'

Two young men, both in the garb of Episcopal priests, appeared through a large oak door behind the altar, looked up when they heard our voices, and started toward us down the long nave.

'I'm telling you I think that guy with the collar was the one who showed up at the Koslawski hearing.'

'Heads up, Coop. Everybody in this joint has a collar. It's a church. Your guys wear beanies, our team likes the white choker around the neck. Makes sense that whoever came to court to watch Bishop Deegan testify was one of his troops.'

'Then what's he doing in an Episcopal cathedral, at the precise moment when a crucial piece of evidence is found?'

'Tall guy, long hair, gray overcoat, and acne. Won't exactly make for a riveting AMBER Alert. Let's hit the road.'

'May we help you?' one of the young priests said as he approached.

'NYPD Homicide. We're just about to leave, thanks. Is the bishop in, by any chance?'

'No. He's not. I'm his secretary. May I give him a message?'

'Sorry this happened here is all. Some of the Homicide Squad detectives will be questioning your staff — what they saw, what they know.'

'We understand that, Detective. We'll do everything to help. They've already told us they'll be searching the cathedral.'

'So long as you understand. You know a man called Wilbur Gaskin?'

'I don't recognize that name.'

Mike gave me a self-satisfied grin. 'I knew he was full of it.'

'There was a gentleman who left the church about five minutes ago,' I said.

'I just asked about him, Coop. They don't know Gaskin.'

'Possibly a priest,' I said. 'Tall, thin with very long hair and — '

'I believe we're the only two in the church this afternoon,' the bishop's secretary said. 'The police officers took the names of people who were here when the young lady's — uh — when her head was found. Then they asked everyone to leave. Perhaps it was a tourist. They're in and out all the time.'

Mike pulled his phone from his pocket and

139

answered the call. 'Hold on, Mercer. Let me get out of church and back on the street.'

He turned and thanked the two men and we were on the broad cathedral steps, walking down to Amsterdam Avenue.

'It's Mercer, for you. Wants some legal advice.'

'Good evening, Mr. Wallace,' I said as I took the phone. 'It's been a long day. What have you got?'

'Cops at Port Authority are holding Daniel Gersh. He was about to board a bus to Chicago.'

'Holding him? What's the charge?' Giving me the slip earlier in the day wasn't exactly a criminal offense.

'That's what they want to know.'

'Where's his stepfather?'

'All signs are that he hasn't left home — you know, the house and his office — in more than a week. He bought Daniel the ticket and made all the arrangements.'

'Mike can whip me down to the terminal. There's no way to keep him with what we've got now. But I have so many more questions to ask him.'

'Too late for that, Alex. His old man has him lawyered up. He's tighter than a tomb.'

17

'Of course she's drinking, Adolfo,' Mike said to the maitre d' at Primola, an Upper East Side Italian restaurant that was my hangout several times a week. 'I told you she's tired, but I didn't say she'd lost her mind. Dewar's on the rocks. Tell Fenton not to be stingy with the scotch.'

'And for you, Detectivo?' Adolfo smiled at me as I held up my thumb and forefinger to show him I wanted only a short cocktail while he took Mike's order.

'A vodka martini with the works. Olives, onions, capers. Back it up when you see me running low.'

Mercer arrived ahead of us and was already sipping a glass of red wine. I excused myself to go downstairs to the restroom. When I emerged five minutes later, refreshed after scrubbing my face and reapplying some makeup, Mike was waiting for me with my drink in hand.

'Giuliano said we could use the television in his office. It's all tuned up.'

For more than a decade, Mike had engaged us in his habit of betting on the Final *Jeopardy!* question every weeknight. He did it at the morgue and in station houses, at crime scenes in mansions and tenements, in front of startled witnesses and crusty old NYPD bosses. He had no time or use for the entire show, but was fascinated with the trivia of the last brain teaser often worth many thousands to the contestants, and happy to wager twenty dollars of his own.

'So much for my privacy.' I took the glass and clinked it against Mike's.

The owner of Primola — Giuliano — had been charmed by Mike's humor and intelligence for years and was always pleased to let us into his tiny business office for the three minutes that closed the evening game show.

'You look a hell of a lot better than you did an hour ago. D'you put that blush on for us? I thought you said you wanted an early night, but here you go trying to be your most fetching for Mercer and me. Wish you could do something about those dark circles under your eyes. I've seen raccoons more attractive than you.'

Mercer was sitting on the edge of the desk. 'If we're talking attractive through your eyes, Detective Chapman, then we've got to build in a whole new set of standards. Rumor has it you were spotted at closing time at Elaine's last week with a real — '

'Don't go telling secrets on me. It was the forty-eight-hour rule.'

'What rule?' I asked.

'Still within forty-eight hours after the St. Patty's Day parade — like a temporary blindness sometimes sets in, on account of the green beer. Errors in judgment don't count.' Mike passed behind me, giving a quick squeeze to the back of my neck, and took the cushy leather chair, resting his feet on the desktop. I plopped down on the small stool in the corner of the room, barely able to see the wall-mounted television.

'Who was she, Mercer?' I said, smiling for what seemed like the first time in hours. 'What did you hear? Spare nothing.'

'Code of silence, m'man,' Mike said, pointing his finger at Mercer.

'Can't go there, Alex. Sorry.'

'So back to business, then,' I said, drumming my fingers on Mike's knee. 'What happened with Daniel Gersh?'

'Port Authority police managed to delay the departure for about fifteen minutes, to give us a shot at the kid. But he wasn't the least bit cooperative. I think his old man really put the fear of God in him.'

'With good reason. I'd like to talk to the stepfather as badly as to Daniel,' Mike said. 'Shh. Here's the category — it's ASTRONOMY. Let's see your money.'

'I'm good for it. I left my bag upstairs.' It was safer there than just about anyplace in the city.

'Ready to double down?'

'Not a chance. Unless you tell me more about the girl you were ogling at Elaine's.' The famous watering hole was a last-call stop for many reporters and detectives on their way off duty in the early morning hours.

'She reminds me of you.' Mike was inhaling his drink and already seemed more playful.

'Brace yourself, Alex. This won't be pretty.' Mercer laughed.

'Too skinny for my taste, for starters. Actually, that's where the resemblance ends.'

'See, Mercer? Painless for me.'

'Almost forgot. Good-natured. Quick to laugh.'

'Who's faster than I am when it's not over a dead body?'

'Very solicitous of my needs. Patient with me and all that.'

'She's got me there. Not happening. Ever.'

'And instead of the ice water that courses through your veins, she's all heart. Somehow, I have the feeling that girl gets under the sheets and gives in to it, you know? Isn't all Miranda warnings and Fifth Amendment, reciting sections of the Penal Law and worrying if what you're doing is okay with Paul Battaglia.'

'That's your idea of me in bed, Mikey? Love-locked because of the law and too much Battaglia on the brain? Sweet.'

Alex Trebek read the Final *Jeopardy!* answer aloud: ''Friday the thirteenth, April 2029, this object will come uncomfortably close to Earth.' Too close to Earth, folks. That's your final answer.'

The three contestants earnestly peered at the game board before starting to write.

'You good for forty, Mercer?' Mike asked.

Each one of us had our favorite subjects. For me, with a heavy concentration of literature studies at college, I usually cleaned up on book and author questions. Mike knew more about military history than most scholars I'd ever encountered, and his knowledge of war and warriors took him deep into myths of ancient cultures. Mercer's lifelong fascination with geography made him a whiz in that category, and most of the time we hedged our bets on the strength of our friends' wisdom.

The *Jeopardy!* time clock ticked on as Mercer nodded to Mike.

'Don't be a bad sport, Coop. Give me your best guess.'

'What's an asteroid? It's got to be an asteroid. You really think I've got ice water?'

'Of course it's an asteroid. Any fool could answer that. What's its name? You got tons of compassion for every victim or fool who sits in front of your desk. But your love life? Totally lacking in substance.'

'I have no idea of the asteroid's name. Mercer, you got this?' I said. 'What about Luc? Doesn't he count for anything?'

'Case in point. The guy lives for foie gras. How do they make it? Tap-tap-tap — first you nail the damn goose in place, then you force-feed it to fatten it up. After that you kill it, just to make a little pâté for some rich customer and his babe. You and Luc are a perfect match in that department. Cool as ice. He's got his head back on the pillow, fantasizing about his next meal, and you're dreaming about how many convictions you can get in this quarter.'

'She's all heart, Mike. Ask my kid,' Mercer said. 'What is Apophis?'

Trebek was consoling the two contestants who gave wrong answers.

'Looks like we split the pot, pal. What is Apophis?' Mike asked.

'That's the stuff. The damn thing might get

close enough to dip beneath our communications satellite. Set off a tsunami that would clean up Venice Beach and all the whackjobs on it. Named for the Egyptian god of death.'

Mike knew everything there was to know about death. He clicked off the TV with the remote. 'Let's feed her and send her home.'

None of us needed a menu. We could probably recite the choices from memory as well as the waiters. Adolfo told us the specials and we ordered. A veal chop with three hearty side dishes for Mike, grilled Dover sole and a salad for Mercer, and a linguine con vongole for me.

'What's the plan for tomorrow?' I asked.

Mercer opened his notepad. 'The squad had a few calls in after Naomi's name was released this afternoon. She'd been taking a course at the Jewish Theological Seminary. I thought I'd take a run up and do some interviews.'

'I'd like to be with you.'

'You want to go to your office first?'

'I do.'

'Pick you up there. Figure late morning.'

We were nibbling on breadsticks and antipasti as Adolfo opened a bottle of wine for us.

'There ought to be more information after the story breaks wide,' Mike said. 'The guys will still be canvassing the neighborhoods around the churches, talking to Naomi's neighbors, finding out more about Daniel and whoever he socialized with at work.'

'The autopsy set?'

'In the morning. I'll be there while you two go to the seminary.'

As always when the three of us segued from the intensity of investigative work to a casual meal together, the conversation would have confused anyone listening in. One of us would think of something that had to do with the murder — in this case, Mike describing the condition of Naomi's head to Mercer — then would go on discussing Mike's mother's health or Mercer's son's allergies or the last time I'd been to my ballet class.

I had the sense to pass up espresso, counting on a good night's sleep before the frenzy of the next day. I dipped my biscotti in Mike's cup, yawning despite the early hour.

'C'mon, Alex,' Mercer said. 'I'll drop you at your door.'

Mike lived in a tiny studio apartment east of the restaurant. He called it 'the coffin,' for its small size and light-starved interior. We left him nursing his coffee and sipping the dregs of the fine bottle of wine that Giuliano had sent over to us. He was more likely to work out the day's demons at the bar than in his bed.

Mercer drove me the short distance to my building. My father's trust fund afforded me the luxury of a beautiful co-op apartment twenty floors above the racket of the city streets, secured by two doormen on duty twenty-four hours a day. I was grateful for the comfort and peace of mind my home provided me, as well as its convenience to the office.

'Say hi to Vickee. We're overdue for a dinner. And tell Logan that I'll be taking him to the zoo on the first nice spring day.' I leaned over and kissed Mercer on his forehead.

'Will do. Rest up and I'll see you tomorrow.' He waited and watched through the glass windows that fronted the driveway, making sure that Vinny and Oscar greeted me, gave me my mail and dry cleaning, and held the elevator open for me.

I locked the door of my apartment, tossed my jacket onto a chair, went into the bedroom, and hit the playback button on my machine while I put away the day's clothes. Most of my friends called and texted to my cell, but Luc enjoyed leaving intimate messages to be played alone when I came home after a grueling day. The six-hour time difference often meant that we couldn't speak frequently while I was working, but it was comforting to me to hear his voice and know that he was sound asleep in Mougins, after a busy night in the restaurant, just as I would be settling in.

'*Bonsoir, ma princesse.*' His deep, calm voice and the elegant French accent were instantly soothing to me. I had left Luc a voice mail explaining that a new case had interrupted the day and I would be hard to reach. He understood the demands of my schedule now in a way he had not when we first met, and respected the fact that my work took me away from friends and family, inconveniently and unpredictably.

Although he made fun of my schoolgirl French, my comprehension had only improved in our time together, so the messages were all in his language. I hung up my suit while he told me about friends who had visited the restaurant that evening, and about his motorcycle trip to Cannes in the afternoon to buy some of my favorite things — perfumes, a scarf, and a few surprises — for his trip to New York on Saturday. I slipped off my underwear and threw it in the hamper, wrapping a bath towel around me while I listened to his promises to make me forget all the trouble I'd seen this week while we were together.

The second message was from Joan Stafford, one of my closest girlfriends. Although she never hesitated to call my cell — and actually preferred it when she caught me at a crime scene or police precinct — she was excited that she and her husband, Jim, would be coming to the city for dinner with us this weekend. Joan, a novelist and playwright, and Nina Baum, my Wellesley roommate who lived in Los Angeles and was an entertainment lawyer with one of the big studios, were the two closest friends outside my orbit of prosecutors and cops who covered my back daily. I spoke to them each almost every day, my lifelines to a trusting world that wasn't punctuated by violence and victimization.

'Alex? Pick up. Why aren't you home yet? Call me,' Joan said. 'You've got to tell me everything about this case. It's so gruesome.'

Luc again. He was sleepless and restless, and I could hear the rustle of his sheets in the background as he changed position to get more comfortable while he rambled on. It amused and excited me, and his visit gave me something to look forward to while immersed in such turmoil.

'Don't you dare call Joan before you call me. I'll bet she's looking for you.' It was Nina Baum, at her most protective. 'I'm worried about you. Heard the news on the radio and assume this could be your case. Take care of yourself, sweetie. Have a nightcap and try to separate your work from your dreams. G'night.'

I ran a steaming hot bath, poured in my scented oils, and agreed with Nina that a nightcap was in order. Ten minutes of letting some of the stress soak out of me worked wonders. I toweled off, put the drink on my bedside table, and stretched out under the covers. I usually read for half an hour before turning out the lights, but I didn't think George Eliot was up to keeping me awake.

I slept soundly. When the landline rang at 4:47 in the morning, I reached for the receiver, almost knocking over the cocktail that I had thankfully left unfinished before dozing off.

Mike's cell number was displayed on the caller ID. 'I know there's a perfectly good reason you're calling me at this hour.'

'What is it exactly you told me that you said to Battaglia, about where the body was found and whether it could be connected to the priest you've got on trial?'

'What's this — a 'refresh your recollection' wake-up call?'

'Not really. What'd you say?'

'That it would be a different story — or something like that — if the victim had been dumped on the doorstep at St. Patrick's Cathedral instead of a Baptist church.'

'Now you're beginning to scare me.'

'Why? Are you drunk?'

'No. But there's a second body.'

I sat bolt upright and switched on the light with my free hand. 'A woman? You think it's our guy? Was she decapitated?'

'Yeah, a woman. Her throat was slit. Looks like she just bled out on the site. Really fresh kill. You either got a crystal ball or the DA has a point. She was dumped at the doorstep of St. Pat's.'

Adrenaline moved faster than the speed of light. The questions tumbled out of my mouth before I could complete them. 'Was she sexually assaulted?' I asked, though it hardly seemed to matter. 'Mutilated. Was she mutilated too?'

'The perp cut out her tongue, Coop. He slit her throat and he took her tongue.'

18

'There's got to be witnesses,' I said. 'You can't kill someone on the steps of the most famous cathedral in America, no matter what time of night, when Fifth Avenue is as well-lit and heavily trafficked as a shopping mall.'

Mike was waiting for me in the driveway, throwing the clutter from the front seat of his department car into the rear. 'You get any sleep?'

'Yes, thanks. Six hours. And you?'

'A few. Here's the tabs.'

I unfolded the *New York Post*, never tasteful in its insatiable appetite for crime stories. The headline ran: UNHOLY AX — and beneath it, in bold print, A DIVINE PLAN? I skimmed the first few paragraphs and found the expected buzzwords — 'headless torso,' 'flaming flesh,' 'baptism by fire,' and 'St. John's divine resting place.'

I tossed the paper over my shoulder, into the back with Mike's junk. 'Now the newsroom boys have got a full twenty-four to work on something irreverent for the new girl. They live for this.'

He handed me a hot cup of black coffee. 'There's probably a stale bagel in one of those bags at your feet.'

'Which bag is yesterday's and which is last week's? I'm afraid I'd break my teeth on it. What do you know about her? Any ID?'

'Starkers. No clothing, not even a blanket this time.'

'You didn't answer me. What about witnesses?'

The first major American cathedral built in Gothic Revival style was once a city landmark visible for miles. Now its twin spires were surrounded by the modern office complexes — including Rockefeller Center — that pressed upon it from every direction.

'Old St. Pat's, Coop. The original one.'

'I don't know what you're talking about.'

The cathedral that had been the centerpiece for the city's Catholic population since 1879, and the scene of great ceremonial splendor for visitors of every faith — or no faith — from all over the world, was just twenty blocks from my home. But Mike was speeding east to go downtown on FDR Drive.

'Two hundred years old. 1809. New York's first cathedral church.'

'Where?'

'So close to your office they can probably hear you sounding off when someone lies to you and you go ballistic. The corner of Mott and Prince Streets. NoLita.'

North Little Italy — NoLita, bordering on SoHo — was less than ten blocks from the courthouse.

'You know it?' I asked.

''Course I do.'

Mike had been raised in a devout family, attended Fordham University after parochial school, and though not a regular churchgoer, had an abiding trust in his religion that carried

153

him through the incomprehensible depravity of our work. His widowed mother and her siblings had steeped him in the knowledge of all things Catholic, about which he loved to lecture me.

'How did I miss it all these years?' The drive was empty and Mike was cruising down the center lane.

'It must have been grand when it was built two hundred years ago, but once the neighborhood deteriorated, brick and mortar walls were put up to protect it from vandalism. You've probably seen it, but didn't know what was behind the walls.'

'And it's still active?'

We had passed the United Nations building, and the earliest glimmer of light reflected from all the glass of the Secretariat onto the East River. The city was beginning to wake up and shed the eerie quiet of the still night, although only a few tugboats were moving on the choppy waterway.

'The Irish and Italian congregants have long given way to the Dominicans and Chinese, but it's still active.'

'You know anything else about this girl you're not telling me?'

'Quit it, Coop. We'll be there in five. You know all I got.'

The lights on the Manhattan and Brooklyn Bridges danced above the crossing cars and trains as we sped toward them.

'You think Battaglia will really try to connect this to me?'

'We'll know the minute he demands to put a

154

bodyguard on your ass.'

'That could be you. We're working together anyway.'

'Been there. Never doing that again.'

'What's the part you didn't like?'

Mike took his eyes off the road and grinned at me. 'Think of a better question.'

'All right. What's the difference between a church and a cathedral? I thought St. Peter's in Rome was the largest church in the world, but St. John the Divine claims to be the largest cathedral.'

'St. Peter's isn't a cathedral. It's a papal basilica. Holds sixty thousand. Aunt Eunice took me over every square foot of it. Said more novenas than the pope. A cathedral holds the seat of a bishop.'

'So this little church in NoLita is a cathedral?'

'Not so little in its day. And yes, it was built to be the seat of the bishops of the newly formed Diocese of New York. Held that honor until part of it was destroyed in a fire. Enough wealthy Catholics had moved uptown so that the bishop, too, headed to Fifth Avenue. The new cathedral is St. Patrick's to most of the world. But this beauty is the original.'

We were off the FDR, threading the narrow one-way roads of the Lower East Side to get to the corner of Mott Street. Mike was on the phone to the sergeant in charge of the Night Watch Unit. 'Where are you exactly? We're just a few blocks away.'

He got an answer as they talked back and forth about how many men were on hand and what reinforcements were needed.

The streets we drove through held a mix of the modern and remains of the scores of tenement buildings that had warehoused the immigrants who poured into this city in the 1880s and thereafter. Families crowded together — usually several generations plus in-laws and boarders — sharing toilets in the hallways and bathtubs in their kitchens. Before World War I, this densely populated area of the Lower East Side was home to five hundred synagogues and religious schools. I wondered if that fact would figure into the case of the woman who'd been found at the old cathedral.

'You check the crypt, Manny?' Mike asked the sergeant on the phone.

I drained the coffee cup and stashed it in an old paper bag. 'This place has an underground crypt? I've sworn off those. I'll wait in the car.'

'See you in three, Sarge. At the back entrance, on Mulberry Street.'

The pizza parlors and bodegas on Prince had been replaced by fancier latte shops and designer boutiques, as SoHo style crept into the old neighborhood.

'That's the front door, on Mott, Alex. See it?'

The high wall shielded most of the church from view, until Mike parked the car and walked me to the wrought-iron gates that fronted the old building. There was a restrained simplicity in the design of the cathedral, easy to see how I had failed to notice though I had passed by it many times. From this side, there was no sign of police activity.

We cornered the street again and continued onto Mulberry. The investigation was still small, because of the remote location and the time of morning. The morgue van was already parked in the middle of the street, and several RMPs — radio motor patrol cars — blocked off both ends.

Manny Chirico was the sergeant in charge of Night Watch, the detail that caught all the major crimes on the midnight shift, sometimes getting to a murder scene before homicide detectives were available. He was one of the smartest men on the job. Both cops and prosecutors liked working with him, which wasn't always the case.

'Hey, Mike. Alexandra,' Manny said. 'I didn't bother to call the South. Had a briefing on your case before we turned out and there didn't seem to be any doubt they're related.'

'Thanks for sparing me that,' Mike said. This half of the island was the jurisdiction of Manhattan South Homicide, but there was no point bringing another layer of supervision into this case. 'Where is she?'

Manny pointed first to the sidewalk adjacent to a small stone archway that was attached to the church. 'Blood, don't you think?'

Mike squatted and looked at the strip of dark red stains that dotted the cement. 'Probably so.'

Then he stepped through the threshold and we followed, emerging from the darkened entryway to a short hall lined with windows. Outside was a tiny eighteenth-century cemetery, fenced in by the wall, with several dozen primitive granite headstones — weathered and eroded by age. Most of them were leaning as though about to topple over with a gusty March wind.

'There she is,' Manny said.

CSU had beaten us here this time, and Hal Sherman was already at work taking photos of the body.

'How do you get into the cemetery?' I asked. Many of the centuries-old churches of lower Manhattan still had adjacent graveyards. Trinity Church and St. Paul's were even tourist attractions, and my route to the DA's Office took me past the last man-made remnant of Manhattan's seventeenth century — the cemetery of Sephardic Jews from Brazil who immigrated here in the 1600s, neglected but still standing on St. James Place.

'This entrance is the only way, Alex, but it was gated and locked.' Manny led us down the corridor and onto the damp soil of the burial ground. 'Maybe it was a couple of men — one helping the other scale the wall and carry the girl over. I've got Crime Scene checking out this old oak inside the walls, as well as the tree branches that overhang from Prince Street, for any trace evidence.'

'Still liking my orangutan theory, Coop. The guy must have been swinging from a tree.'

The exposed body of the young woman lit up in the flash of the camera. I stood about three feet from her, taking the measure of her young life. She might have been a few years older than I. She was certainly shorter — probably only five feet five or so — and rounder in the stomach and

158

hips. Her cropped brown hair looked wet from the dew, and the gaping wound in her throat appeared to be large enough to spill out all her innards.

'Who found her?' I asked.

'The caretaker,' Manny said. 'He doesn't usually show up until six a.m., but he's got a guy coming in to fix the organ this morning, so he just woke up early and strolled over at four o'clock. No better reason than that. I'd say he missed our perp — or perps — by less than an hour.'

Mike and Manny were crouched around the body like a pair of bookends. They had gloved up, and Manny was showing Mike the back of the victim's head.

'I think he must have bludgeoned her with something to subdue her, in order to bring her in here and finish her off. See that crack in the rear of her head?'

Mike nodded. 'The ME say anything?'

'They just sent a cleanup crew. No docs. Shorthanded. Hal got all the photos, so we'll just ship her off to them.'

'What do you make of the tongue, Manny?' I asked. 'It's still Little Italy. You think the Mob?'

Mike stood up and I could see that he was taking a measure of the entire setting. There were five tall stained-glass windows that decorated the south side of the old cathedral. The body had been deposited directly below the one in the center.

'The Mob cuts off balls, Coop. Not tongues.' Now Mike was back to examining the dirt around the body. There were so many imprints of footsteps, it would be impossible to know what the disturbance had looked like before the cops arrived.

'If she was a snitch, I'd say of course it could have been an organized-crime operation. They might go for the tongue. But after last night's case? There's something else going on. This isn't an OC dump. Doesn't have the look or feel of that. And no way wiseguys would desecrate an old Catholic church in the 'hood. There's a different message here, even though I don't know what it is.' Manny Chirico got to his feet. 'I leave that to you and Mr. Chapman.'

'I'm working on it, Manny.' Again, Mike turned his attention to the windows. 'Our first vic winds up on the steps of a church that used to be a synagogue.'

'What does that tell you?'

'I'm trying to brain it out. At least it's what I got Coop here for,' Mike said, pointing to the dark images worked into the old glass windows above our heads. 'You think maybe this placement wasn't accidental? I mean, the cemetery for sure. But maybe she's dumped under this particular image for a reason.'

'I was thinking where she is has something to do with the tombstones, not the stained glass. Maybe these names are meant to connect, once we get a make on her.' Manny Chirico shrugged, then began to pace around the grave markers, reading the names aloud. ' 'Right Reverend John Dubois, Third Bishop of New York. Francis Nealis. Brendan Callahan.' '

'Possible, but not a lot of broads buried here,' Mike said. 'Can you have one of your men do a list of all the dearly departed? Who they are and where, relative to her body?'

'On it.'

'Can we get inside? I'd like to see what the stained-glass windows depict. Is the caretaker here?'

'Yup. He's in the church.'

We let the crew with the body bag get to work and retraced our way to the narrow corridor through which we had entered.

Manny took us into the main chapel, which was dark and cool, much grander than it appeared to be from the street. It indeed had the feel of a large, old cathedral interior.

I couldn't see anyone at first, but I was surprised by the beauty of the huge white marble altar that spanned the entire western wall, and by the stunning collection of carved gold-leaf reredos, the ornate religious statuary that surrounded it.

Only when I glanced around did I see the caretaker, on his knees in the very first pew, bent over the railing as he wept.

We stayed in place, giving him a few minutes alone. When he got to his feet, Manny asked him to turn on the lights, and Mike started along the wall to look at the windows, which displayed themselves far more vividly from within the church.

I planted myself below a striking image of Madonna and child, straining my neck to look up at it, wondering whether that feminine portrait had anything to do with the position of the corpse in the graveyard.

'Can't you count, Coop? Wrong one.' Mike was twenty feet away from me. He stepped up onto the seat of one of the pews for a closer examination of the center window, and I walked directly in front of him.

Below the figure of a solemn, gray-bearded man, pen in hand, apparently writing his gospel, was a name, the lettering made of deep-brown stained glass, barely visible with such low lighting.

'Matthew the apostle,' Mike said. 'Matthew the Evangelist.'

'What does that say to you about your killer?'

He leaned a hand on my shoulder and got down. 'I'm not sure yet. But if Mount Neboh wasn't a random dropping-off point, then neither is this place. I got things to do, kid. You get the tombstone map and start reading your Gospels, and we'll talk later.'

Again I followed Mike, this time from the chapel through the corridor and out onto the street. As we emerged from the church, I could see Mercer approaching from behind the parked RMPs.

'Bad way to start the day. Slow down, Mr. Wallace,' Mike said. 'You haven't missed much.'

'I got waylaid. Something else to stir the pot.'

'What's that?' I asked.

'Port Authority cops cut short my sleep. Daniel Gersh was quick to board that bus to Chicago last night. Get himself out of our hair. Problem is, the first stop was Philadelphia.'

162

'Don't tell me — '

'He got off there and crossed town to the Thirtieth Street Station. Used his credit card to buy a ticket on the last train back to New York.'

'So he was here? . . . ' I wasn't able to finish the sentence. *In time to do this*, was what I was thinking.

'By midnight. It's no wonder he didn't fly. Daniel Gersh had no mind of leaving town, no matter what his stepfather told him to do.'

19

We found a dive a few blocks away for coffee and eggs. Our plans for the day hadn't changed. The forensics work on the new case would be under way, and the investigative piece would pick up steam as detectives tried to make an identification.

Mike left for the morgue at seven thirty, while Mercer and I made the short trip to my office.

'I've just got a few things to clear on my desk. I'd really like to get out of here before Battaglia shows up. Just leave a message with Rose that we're on top of this.'

'I got calls to make. Do what you got to do.' Mercer made himself comfortable in Laura's cubicle and I turned on the lights in my office.

There was a note on top of the center pile of manila case folders. Barry Donner was going to sum up today in the case of Denys Koslawski. The judge was giving signs that he was going to reserve decision, so there might not be a verdict in the case for a couple of weeks. I'd expected better of Lyle Keets, but I guess he didn't want to embarrass Bishop Deegan and rule so quickly on the heels of his testimony.

I dialed Luc's number at Le Relais, his restaurant at Mougins, and held until the hostess got him on the phone. As I waited, I took the Xerox I'd made of the letters Mike had found in

Daniel Gersh's apartment and placed the pieces in front of me, trying to move them around to form parts of words. When Luc said his faint '*Oui?*' I swiveled my chair around, my back to the door.

'*Ça va*, darling? Is everything all right?'

It was unusual for me to try to find him in the middle of a working day.

'I'm okay. It's — well, another young woman was killed a few hours ago. Her throat was slit, and we're sure it's the same perp.'

'That's so awful — I don't really know what to say. Are you taking care of yourself? Do you want me to come immediately?'

'No, no. I'm fine. I just wanted you to hear it from me and not some Internet news report. I know I haven't been easy to find, but I adore coming home to your messages.'

Luc laughed. 'Less of a nuisance than coming home to me, with all this going on.'

'Probably so. Mercer's here at the office with me now.'

'So, you can't talk?'

'You mean tell you I love you? Of course I can.'

'I hope that's why you called.'

'I needed to hear what you have to say. To get me through the day.'

'*Je t'aime*, Alexandra. I'll say it as many times as you'd like and loud enough so everyone in Mougins can hear.'

Mercer whistled to get my attention, and I spun the chair around. 'I hate to break this up, Alex, but you've got your first customer.'

'How fast can you talk, Luc? I've got a new case. Have to run.'

'Three days, darling. Hold tight. Tell Mercer and Mike to keep you safe.'

'That's not their job, Luc. I take care of that myself. Talk to you later.'

'That's Ms. Cooper,' Mercer was saying to the young uniformed cop.

'Good morning. I'm Terence Seckler. Nineteenth Precinct.'

'What have you got?' I reached for his arrest report and paperwork.

'Unlawful surveillance. Second degree. They told me to bring it up to your unit — Special Victims.'

'Thanks. I'll look it over and we'll assign it to someone as soon as my secretary gets in. Looks like it's got a twist.'

'Yes, ma'am. Different angle. Technology is amazing.'

'Inside Bloomingdale's?'

'Riding the escalators up and down all day.'

For ages, up-skirting had been a sport of many perverts. Sitting on the sidewalk or on the steps of institutions like our great museums or on crowded subway cars, these men found ways to position themselves to be able to see — and sometimes photograph — the more intimate zones of a woman's body. The actions had never been criminal until, with the proliferation of pocket-size cameras, the conduct got so out of control that the legislators went back to work on it. Now it was a crime — section 250.45 of the Penal Law.

166

'He strapped a camera to his shoe?'

'Yes, ma'am.'

'And you recovered that too?' The jury might have to see the contraption to believe it.

'It's vouchered. The captain told me to bring the camera on down to you, so you could view the images. It's got crotch shots — excuse me, I don't know what else to call them — of about three hundred girls — teenagers, mostly.'

'You find any of the victims?'

'Three. The last one sort of figured it out and attacked him. She nailed him pretty well, right on the beak.'

'Good for her. How was the camera attached?'

'I took a photo here, with my cell,' Seckler said, showing me a close-up of the image. A small device had been set into the panel of laces of one of the perp's sneakers, held in place when the shoe was tied tightly.

'Nice job. Have a seat in the hallway. My secretary will find you an eager prosecutor as soon as she gets in.'

'Why don't you just let me steer all this away?' Mercer asked as Seckler left the room.

''Cause it's what keeps me sane. Not everything that crosses my desk is a murder or a rape. It keeps things in perspective for me to handle all the daily fallout of street life in the big city. Sometimes it even amuses me. Like what could possibly be so thrilling about taking pictures up a girl's skirt?'

'And on the downside, what does that perversion lead to? Used to be peeping Toms were the first step in a rapist's training regimen.

167

From peeping to break-ins to sexual assaults. How many of these fools go on to forcible touching? That's what you've got to worry about.'

'I do. That and how fast our killer seems to be moving.'

'Sorry to interrupt. Ms. Cooper?'

'Yes,' I said. Mercer stepped aside and I nodded to the woman standing behind him.

'I'm Alison Borracelli. You have an appointment with my daughter this morning. At eight thirty, I believe.' She was softspoken, with a hint of an Italian accent.

Gina Borracelli. I had completely forgotten the Thursday-morning lineup. I flipped open my diary and saw the notation.

'Yes, of course I do. I'll be with you in just a few minutes.'

It was only in movies that the detectives and DA caught the big case, and everything else on the table stayed quiet. In real time, rapists continued to attack, pedophiles preyed on kids, victims needed legal guidance and hand-holding, and death never took that longed-for holiday.

'But Gina — she wouldn't come. She insisted on going to school today instead. She said you didn't believe what she told you. That you were very tough with her. I came to talk to you about that, Ms. Cooper.'

I wasn't completely surprised that the sixteen-year-old was a no-show. This would have been my third go-round with the arrogant teenager.

'Give me a few minutes with Detective

Wallace, please, and then I'll be happy to discuss the case with you.'

'I've got to get to work myself. Can we do this quickly?'

'Just step out for a moment and let me pull the paperwork,' I said, moving in front of my desk to close the door between us.

'You need me to back you up on this?' Mercer asked.

I stood up and went to the last in a wall-length row of filing cabinets and pulled out the case folder. 'Alan Vandomir's case,' I said to Mercer. 'I caught this kid — Gina — in so many lies, that's why Alan hasn't made an arrest. She asked me for the chance to go home and tell her mother the real story herself. But she obviously hasn't done that yet.'

'You get to be the bad guy.'

'Again. It's wearing thin.'

It was smart to have a witness present when the possibility of confrontation so clearly loomed, and I couldn't ask for a better one than Mercer.

Gina was a sophomore at an expensive prep school on the Upper West Side, the daughter of two professionals. The accused, Javier Valdiz, was a scholarship student at the same school. On the night she claimed a crime occurred, Gina's parents had invited Javier to spend the night at their apartment, in her older brother's empty bedroom, after a party that both kids attended.

Unbeknownst to the Borracellis, on the way to the party, Gina had filled an empty sixteen-ounce seltzer bottle with her father's vodka. She

169

and a girlfriend had finished drinking the entire thing by the time Gina and Javier returned home.

I went over the facts with Mercer and invited Mrs. Borracelli to sit down opposite me. She knew the claim — that two days later, Gina told her boyfriend that Javier had forcibly raped her in her bedroom that night, while her parents slept in the next room.

I began by asking Mrs. Borracelli to repeat the story to me, as Gina had related it. I listened, but my eyes were still playing with the letters of the alphabet that Naomi Gersh had scribbled on a piece of paper, trying to make sense of them.

'Did you know Gina had been drinking that night?'

Mrs. Borracelli pulled herself up, looking at me indignantly. 'No, not at my house. She's too young, but for the occasional glass of wine with dinner.'

'Would it surprise you to know where she got her vodka, and how much she had?'

'From Javy, I'm sure. From the boy.'

'That's not what she told me. I suggest you ask her that directly, and check your own liquor cabinet.'

'I would be totally shocked. I'll ask, but that would shock me.'

'Does Gina have a drinking problem, do you think?'

'All the girls at her school drink, Ms. Cooper. What's your point? I can't police her all the time. You think that means she can't be raped?'

'Not in the slightest. A great percentage of our

170

cases occur when the victim has been drinking. The alcohol intake often makes them more vulnerable. I'd just expect my witnesses to be honest about it. I can't help girls who won't be candid with me. A judge and jury won't help them either.'

'And my Gina — she didn't tell you?'

'No, she didn't. It was the other girls at the party — and Javier's lawyer — who told me. She denied it completely until I confronted her with what her best friend had said.'

Many of these investigations took more time than a straightforward stranger rape. In those instances, victims had no reason to dissemble. They didn't know their assailants and hadn't spent time together, as acquaintance- and date-rape survivors did before the assault. The latter sometimes tried to make themselves appear more 'proper' — to family and to law enforcement — by minimizing their alcohol and drug intake, or the amount of consensual foreplay. In the end, there was often a rape charge, but it was muddied by facts the witnesses foolishly tried to conceal.

'What else, Ms. Cooper?' Mrs. Borracelli was arch now. 'Gina said to ask you about other things she told you. She said it was easier for me to hear them from you.'

'Why don't you stay calm, ma'am? Ms. Cooper isn't trying to give you a hard time,' Mercer said.

'Whose side are you on, anyway?' she asked. 'You're Gina's lawyer, aren't you?'

'No, I represent the state, Mrs. Borracelli. My

job is to get at the truth, before I take Javier or any individual to court.'

'I want someone to represent Gina.'

'Ms. Cooper will be the best ally your daughter ever had,' Mercer said, 'if she's forthcoming. You think this boy isn't telling his lawyer everything that happened that night? You think both sides of this story won't come out at a trial, if there are two sides?'

The expression on Mrs. Borracelli's drawn face wavered between confusion and anger.

'Did Gina tell you that Javier was wearing a condom?' I asked.

'So, what difference does that make? I've read about rapists. How they carry condoms with them sometimes so that they don't leave their DNA behind.'

'He didn't bring any along that night. They weren't his.'

Javier's lawyer had told me how his client claimed the encounter became sexual. Not that I didn't often get total fabrications from the defendants. But frequently I got a nugget of truth that broke down some of the elements of the victim's story.

'Do you know about the little box that Gina keeps in her bathroom?' I inquired.

Mrs. Borracelli was not so quick to talk. 'What box?'

It was Javier's lawyer who told me to ask the girl about it. Her 'box of bad things' is how she'd laughingly described it to her schoolmate.

'It's a small enameled case she keeps under the sink.'

'I don't ever look at her things. The maid cleans that room.' I had the feeling that any minute now this entire episode would be blamed on the family maid. I'd be right behind her.

I didn't need to tell Gina's mother right then about the marijuana and the rolling papers she hid in the box. 'It's where she keeps a supply of condoms.'

Mrs. Borracelli slumped back in the chair. 'You're saying she gave Javier the condom? Is that what she told you?'

'On her third visit here, that's what she told me.' Getting a statement from the teenager had been like pulling teeth. I had chipped away at her story with bits of information that came from the alleged rapist and her closest friends.

Gina had admitted that after she and Javier were 'fooling around' on her bed, she left the room to undress — he never pulled her clothes off, as her original statement read — and to bring a condom for him from her stash in the 'box of bad things.'

This back and forth of deconstructing the evidence went on for another ten minutes. Mrs. Borracelli dabbed at tears with her embroidered handkerchief. Her voice softened as she looked to Mercer as an ally in this.

'But why would she do this, Mr. Wallace? Why would she exaggerate so much?'

'It's not the first time, ma'am. I can't answer that.'

'Gina may have given the reason in the texts she wrote, just minutes after Javier left her room.'

173

Mike referred to that kind of message, which cyber cops had pulled up and printed out for me, as TWI: texting while intoxicated. Rare that the contents of them didn't come back to haunt the sender.

'But he spent the night in our home. How could he do that if he raped her?'

'You can put all the facts together, Mrs. Borracelli. I don't think you'll find that there was a rape. I suppose like most kids, Gina thought there'd be no record of her texts,' I said, removing a sheaf of papers from my file. 'But they're all saved in the memory of the cell phone. I've given Gina a copy. I had hoped when she left here last week she would show them to you herself.'

'What do they say, Ms. Cooper?'

Gina had texted Javier after he tiptoed out of her room and went down the hall to sleep. She was giddy with the mix of intoxication and what she described as lovemaking. Her only concern was that he not tell any of the kids at school that they had hooked up, for fear that one of the girls might call her boyfriend — her 'real' boyfriend — who was away at boarding school.

'I'm going to let Gina tell you that. I want you to hear it from her. Ask her to show you the photos she sent along with the message.'

Sexting — using the cell device to send photos, in this case, nude shots of herself, usually wound up circulating among school friends and out to the world on Facebook or some other social network.

After Javier left the Borracelli apartment, Gina

174

slept till noon, then kept a doctor's appointment to get shots for a trip to Africa for which the family was preparing. She mentioned nothing to the doctor, missing an opportunity to be examined for injuries or possible DNA. It was only two days later, when girlfriends began asking her if it was true that she had slept with Javier, that Gina was compelled to come up with a story: that he had forced himself upon her.

Mrs. Borracelli looked defeated. I had been in this unhappy position countless times before, but it saddened me on so many levels whenever it occurred. 'I don't know if she will tell me anything at this point.'

'Why?'

'She said this morning that she didn't want to see Javier prosecuted.'

I was glad she had reached that conclusion. I couldn't find any evidence of a crime.

'Gina just wants him to be thrown out of school,' Mrs. Borracelli continued. 'She doesn't wish to see him anymore.'

Doesn't wish to see him? So she calls their tryst a rape? I had a new training case for the office rookies who came fresh from law school, anxious to grow the skills to reach the pinnacle of prosecutorial ranking: homicide assistants. They would have to work their way through drug deals and petty thefts, learning how to dissect cases and discern truths from every witness who walked through the courthouse doors.

'Gina's probably embarrassed at this point,' Mercer said. He knew me well enough to recognize that despite the early hour, my temper

175

was ready to snap. 'That's a pretty harsh sanction for what the two of them embarked on together, don't you think, ma'am?'

The woman didn't respond.

'Javier's on a college track, just like your daughter,' I said. 'There was no force here, Mrs. Borracelli. There isn't a crime I can charge. I don't see any reason to eject him from school, just to make things right between Gina and her boyfriend. And one more thing, may I?'

'I'll never be able to explain this to my husband. She's still his baby.' Mrs. Borracelli was wringing the handkerchief now. 'Yes? What else is it?'

'Ask Gina to tell you what she did with the condom.'

'You mean, you fault her because she didn't save it as evidence?' The anger rose in her again.

In more than a dozen years on the job, I had rarely known a witness to be as cavalier as Gina, or do something as revolting. I understood throwing condoms in the toilet or garbage — ugly reminders of the forced sexual act — at a time when the police lab wasn't foremost in one's mind.

'No, I don't fault her for anything she did. Except lying.' I wanted that point to be clear. 'Gina tossed the condom out the window of your apartment, Mrs. Borracelli.'

'I don't believe you.' Her words were sharp and meant to be stinging.

'The police recovered it from a flowerpot on the terrace of a neighbor, three floors below you. You don't have to believe me. The detective has

176

photographs. And Mr. Delson, in 6B, was rather disgusted. He's not likely to forget it.'

'What happens now?' Mrs. Borracelli asked.

My phone rang and Mercer walked over to Laura's desk to answer it.

'I'd like Gina to make a statement — she can do it in writing, or she can sit down with Detective Vandomir. I think she gets along with him.' She liked anyone better than she liked me. I had played the eight-hundred-pound gorilla often enough to feel as though I had gained the weight necessary to look the part. 'I want her to tell the story — the truth — from beginning to end. If it doesn't spell out a crime, the entire matter will be dropped.'

'And my Gina? What will happen to her?'

Mercer stood in the doorway, one hand cupped over the receiver of the phone. With the other, he pointed his thumb over his shoulder, signaling me to get rid of Mrs. Borracelli.

'She'll have learned a very hard lesson in the worst way.'

'But for lying, you won't arrest Gina, will you?'

I stood up to escort the woman out of my office. I had mounted many prosecutions for filing false police reports. The fabrications wasted time and energy for dedicated cops, but mostly made it more difficult for the next rape victim to be credited by people to whom Gina had disclosed the bogus crime.

'No. Fortunately, we caught this before Gina testified under oath. I think she needs counseling, Mrs. Borracelli.' I put my arm behind her

177

back, trying to move her along more quickly. 'I think she needs attention to her drinking and drug issues.'

'Ms. Cooper,' she said, stopping in her tracks when I most needed to get clear of her, 'will you help me tell my husband these facts? He's a very difficult man. I doubt Gina will be able to talk to him about this.'

'I'm working on a murder investigation, Mrs. Borracelli. Two murders, in fact. Detective Vandomir will do everything possible to help. Would you mind stepping out while I take a call?'

The witnesses who lined up in the complaint room of our office every morning, seven days a week, needed triage as badly as patients in an emergency room. This woman was about to go to the back of the pack.

I returned to my desk and picked up the phone. Mercer stayed on the line and told me it was Manny Chirico on hold.

'Hello again. Past your bedtime, isn't it, Manny?'

'Just playing around on my computer before I knock off. Mercer said you haven't had a minute yet to get back on the case.'

'Real life intervened. You got an ID on her?'

'No such luck. Listen, I'm playing around on CrimeDex.'

'That'll make Commissioner Scully happy. So much for pounding the pavement.'

The social networking fad that gave birth to Facebook and Twitter led a private company to create a site that eroded many of the

178

bureaucratic boundaries between law enforcement agencies around the country.

'You got us a perp?' Mercer asked.

CrimeDex had effectively linked everything from police reports to surveillance tapes from departments all over the country, challenging privacy protections in cases that had not yet led to arrest or convictions.

'Not yet. But this guy didn't wake up two days ago in Gotham and start offing church ladies for no reason at all.'

'What'd you find?'

'Wayland, Kentucky. Four months ago, in early December, a pastor — lady pastor — was killed right inside her church. She was found lying behind the altar with her arms outstretched. Naked.'

'This info is all online?' I said.

'The autopsy report is right there — no arrest, no suspect, no leads.'

'What's the cause of death?'

'Multiple incised wounds. Gaping hole across her neck that the doc believes was an attempt to decapitate her. Oh yeah, her hair was singed too. The bastard tried to set her on fire.'

20

'Where's Wayland?' Mercer asked.

He was driving us up to the Jewish Theological Seminary, where Naomi had been studying, and I was looking through a road atlas I had taken from Rose Malone's bookshelf when I stopped by to give her a message for Battaglia about the second murder.

'Eastern corner of Kentucky, not all that far from the Virginia — West Virginia border. Looks like the Appalachians. Did you find anything out while I was talking to Rose?'

'I called the local sheriff's office. The church was the Sanctified Redeemer.'

'Baptist, by any chance?'

'No. Pentecostal.'

'Any more details about the killing?' I asked. I was tracing imaginary routes with my fingers. First from Chicago suburbs where Daniel Gersh's family lived, through Pikeville and on up to New York, and then, for no good reason, from the Atlanta hometown of Wilbur Gaskin back to Manhattan.

'Just that the killer staged the body behind the altar. Took all the woman's clothing with him.'

'Did he take any money? Any religious items of value?'

'Not a thing.'

'How did he get into the church?'

'The pastor always left the doors open. Still a

small-town lifestyle. Sheriff says all the other religious leaders in town have been jumpy ever since.'

'What goes on in Wayland?' I asked.

'Coal. Population holding at about three hundred, so the good ol' boys are pretty sure it's not one of their own. He's going to pull together all their files and fax a set up to me. No leads, no forensics of value. No money for all the bells and whistles our labs have.'

'So now?'

'Manny Chirico's on a tear. He's trying to find connections to this kind of kill anywhere he can. Thinks we got a transient maniac on our hands.'

There was nothing unusual about that idea. Sooner or later, most madmen with felonious intent found their way to one of the big cities. New York, Los Angeles, Detroit, D.C., Miami, Houston, Oakland — even the small-town perps wanted to make it to a bigger stage.

Mercer and I bounced ideas off each other all the way uptown, but nothing worthwhile came of the conversation.

'You have an address for the seminary?' I asked as we passed the main Columbia University campus on 116th Street.

'Northeast corner of 122nd and Broadway.'

We parked on a side street and approached the entrance of the redbrick building that sat catty-corner on Broadway, exactly at the point where the subway emerged from belowground and the tracks ran through the center concourse.

There was tight security at the entrance, and the guard who had Mercer's name on his list called for someone to escort us to the administrative offices.

There were glass doors leading to an interior courtyard. The setting was tranquil and elegant — beautiful plantings and a small fountain, arranged in a quadrangle.

'Welcome to JTS. I'm Rabbi Levy. Zev Levy.' The handsome, bespectacled man who greeted us didn't look any older than I am. He was dressed in a sports jacket and dark slacks, and was wearing a yarmulke.

Mercer and I introduced ourselves.

'Why don't we go over to my office? I can see you're admiring the view, so we should take the scenic route. Our first donor was insistent that we look 'American' rather than Eastern European. That's why we copied a typical New England campus. Come, I'd rather be somewhere private. I know you have questions about Naomi Gersh.'

'That's a good idea,' I said. 'I didn't realize this beautiful oasis was tucked away here.'

'We're one of the city's best-kept secrets. Do you know anything about us?'

Several students made their way through the quad, most doing a double take at Mercer and me, probably because we didn't fit the traditional profile of rabbinical students. 'Very little,' I said, while Mercer echoed me by answering, 'Nothing.'

'We like to think we're the central institution — the flagship, if you will — of the Conservative movement in American Judaism. We're here to produce modern American rabbis. Do you

182

understand the difference between Orthodox and Conservative theology?'

'I think I do, Rabbi,' I said. 'I grew up in a Reform household. My mother converted to Judaism after marrying my father. His ancestors had been Orthodox when in Russia, but not once they immigrated to this country.'

'Please call me Zev,' he said. We walked through the quiet gardens, the day slightly milder and sunnier than yesterday. 'The Orthodox are the most traditional Jews, of course. They believe in the strict interpretation and application of the laws and ethics that are canonized in the Torah. They believe that the Torah and its laws are divine in origin, transmitted by God to Moses. That those laws are eternal and unalterable.'

He stopped to greet a student who passed us on the walkway.

'The rumblings of Reform Judaism started in Germany, in the nineteenth century. There were still the beliefs in monotheism and morality, but Reform leaders thought most of the rituals were connected to the ancient past, no longer for Jews of the modern era to follow. In this country, the Reform movement took hold in Charleston.'

'South Carolina?' Mercer asked.

Zev Levy smiled. 'Not your first idea for a hotbed of Jewish intellectual thought.'

'I never considered it.'

'It was the largest Jewish community in America in the 1820s. Charleston was one of the four biggest ports in the country and took in many Spanish and Portuguese Jews who left

183

England to come here. The members of a synagogue there first petitioned for reforms.'

'Like what?' I asked.

'They wanted English-language sermons. They wanted Hebrew prayers to be repeated in English. German immigrants joined them later in the century, setting up magnificent houses of worship like Temple Emanu-El here on Fifth Avenue.' Levy held back the door to let us through. 'The boiling point came to a head over kosher dietary laws.'

'With all the other principles at stake, that's hard for me to imagine.'

'It represented so many of the cultural changes in the new world. There was a banquet organized for the first graduating class from Hebrew Union College in 1883. The more radical element planned a provocative menu that included shrimp. Trefa, if you know what I mean. It just highlighted the conflict over whether kosher law — and therefore rabbinical law — would be binding in Reform Judaism.'

We reached his office and Levy's secretary rose to usher us into his room. While she took orders for coffee, he went on.

'Our Conservative movement arose as a reaction to the more liberal positions taken by Reform Jews. It has nothing to do with political conservatism, you understand. The name signifies that we believe Jews should attempt to conserve Jewish tradition, rather than jettison it as the Reformers did.'

I wondered where Naomi Gersh would fit into all of this.

'So who wrote the Torah?' Mercer asked, smiling at the good-natured rabbi.

'Most Conservatives believe it was written by humans, but divinely inspired. Here at the seminary, I'd say our feet are firmly planted in two places — tradition and modernity. We maintain the tradition of prayer, but we've been known to reinterpret it.'

The secretary closed the door.

'So on to Naomi Gersh. That's what you want to talk about.'

'Thanks, Zev. Yes, yes it is,' I said. 'Was she enrolled here?'

'No, she wasn't. Although we are rather small,' Levy said, 'we offer a diverse number of programs. We have three professional schools for students with college degrees. One is for rabbinical training, another is for cantors, and the third is a more generally Jewish education. We offer an undergraduate degree as well. Naomi hadn't made up her mind to apply to that, to devote herself to a course of study. But she sought us out to explore the idea of coming to school here. She liked our mission, I think.'

'And what is that?' Mercer asked.

'A learned and passionate study of Judaism. I'd say our vision joins faith with inquiry. We strive to service Jewish communities and strengthen traditions.'

'What about Israel?' I asked. 'Did Naomi talk about her time there?'

Levy bowed his head. 'Most definitely. Our movement has intense involvement with the society and state of Israel. That's probably why

Naomi came here to begin with.'

'How long ago was that?' I tried to keep eye contact with Levy while Mercer took notes.

'Maybe four months ago. Sometime in December, I believe. The first course she signed up for started in January, in the new semester. That's how I got to know her. I taught the class. Jewish Philosophical Thought.'

'Tell us about Naomi, please. Anything you can remember, no matter how insignificant it may seem to you.'

Zev Levy stroked his chin with his hand. 'My first impression of her was about how much a loner she seemed to be. The graduate students here are an exceptional group. Brilliant, many of them, and scholars all. Some are more vigorously and intellectually engaged with the others, while some are more intense and reflective. Naomi wasn't in either league. While she remained remote, it wasn't because of an inward spirituality.'

'What, then? Did you attribute it to anything?'

'There was a sadness she carried with her,' the rabbi said. 'A sadness she wore like a weight around her neck.'

'Was she close to any of the other students?'

Levy shook his head. 'Not that I'm aware. They've set me up to talk with you because I probably spent more time with Naomi — and that's not a lot — than anyone else.'

'Did she confide in you, Zev?' I didn't want him to invoke the clergy-penitent privilege. I wasn't looking for Naomi's admissions of wrongdoing, if there were any, and I didn't believe they would survive her death. I wanted to know if she trusted him with any personal information that would be of use to us.

'You mean as a rabbi?' He knew exactly where I was going. There was no privilege if she had merely leaned on him as a friend. 'Not that way. Sometimes she would come to me with questions about things I'd said in class. Then she'd linger to get to what was really on her mind.'

'What kind of things?'

'She was still haunted, of course, by what had happened to her mother. That tested all the depths of her religion and beliefs, into politics, back to threatening her faith completely, over to obsessing about the Israeli-Palestinian peace process. You know about her protests?'

'Maybe not as much as you do,' Mercer said.

'No, don't assume I got any substance out of her on that. Naomi was just proud of her activism. Much of it was sincere, although I think some of it was a way of calling attention to herself.'

'What's the role of women here at JTS, Zev?' I asked. 'How are they accepted in the Conservative movement?'

'That's a good question, Alex. You might not get the same answer from any two people. It's not like you Reformers, who have been much more welcoming to women and to gays. It's one of the topics that drew fire from Naomi.'

I was beginning to flesh out a better picture of her. She had been thrust into the outcast role early on by her life circumstances. But she also

187

seemed to have grown comfortable in that skin.

'Have you ordained women as rabbis?'

'We have. But only for the last twenty-five years. I don't think Naomi had the intellectual rigor to go there, but she was fascinated by the feminist role in religion. Women as clergy have emerged from a grassroots push, after a very long debate. Now about thirty percent of our rabbinical students are female.'

'Does that still cause division in the ranks?' I asked.

'Not here, I don't think. But you will find many Jews — just as you will in every Christian denomination — who don't believe that women belong in this role. Didn't you face that in your work?'

'Not openly, Zev. Not my generation of litigators.' But I knew that the women who had come before me in the law, as in many careers, had faced insurmountable obstacles simply getting through the door of the courtroom. Even legendary prosecutors like Frank Hogan thought that trial work was too tawdry for lady lawyers. 'Did Naomi come up against any of that here?'

'Not that I know. I hope you'll look in at our synagogue on your way out. You'll see the balconies that existed so that women were seated separately from the men in the old days. They couldn't have dreamed at that time of leading services.'

'And now?'

'There are always a couple of students who arrive believing they won't have to participate with women. It's no longer possible here.'

'Did Naomi clash with any of them?'

'I can ask about that. She liked to argue. Maybe she thought she was debating, but I'd say the better word is argument, in her case. I don't think she made enemies here. No particular friends, although the dean is asking around about that. But no real enemies.'

'Do you know anything about Naomi's social life? Did she date anyone here?'

Zev blushed as he answered. 'That's outside my calling. I simply wouldn't know.'

'Nothing you observed in her actions with other students? Nothing she said?'

'I had the impression there was a man in her life. Not here at JTS. I had the sense that he was somewhat older than she. That there was something inappropriate about the relationship, or she might have been more open in discussing it with me.'

I saw Mercer jotting down notes. He must have wondered, as I did, how serious Naomi's involvement with Daniel's stepfather was, and whether it had been ongoing in the recent past.

'Did she ever talk with you about her brother?'

'This is the first I'm hearing she had any siblings. Naomi never mentioned him.'

'When was the last time you saw her?'

'One week ago, to this very day. My course is given on Wednesday, and she had missed it. I saw her in the library and asked if she was okay. She didn't usually cut classes.'

'Did she tell you why she had?'

Zev Levy blushed again. 'I'm sorry that our last conversation was a bit confrontational. She

189

didn't like answering to me. She thought I was prying. Perhaps she thought I was — how would you say? . . . ' He looked at Mercer and raised his shoulders.

'Coming on to her?'

'Maybe so. I can assure you that I was not. But she snapped when I asked how come she had cut class if everything was okay.'

'She got short with you?' I said.

'I misspoke. Out of character for me, by hindsight. Completely out of line.'

The earnest young rabbi seemed shaken by the recollection.

'Naomi told me she had a friend who was ill — a guy. She said something about the fact that he was being treated at Bellevue. I should have just left it at that.'

Bellevue was a city hospital, the oldest public medical facility in the country. It had a grim history and was not a place in which you wanted a loved one to wind up. Bellevue was best known as a psychiatric facility for the indigent.

'What did she say about her friend?' I asked.

'She wouldn't talk to me about him after I opened my mouth. 'What is he crazy, this guy?' I should have held my tongue before speaking. I just couldn't think of anyone being treated at Bellevue except a psych case. 'What do you need with a madman?' That's the last thing I said to her.'

21

Zev Levy had walked us back to the building entrance. Before we said good-bye, he had something else to tell us, a bit sheepishly. 'I want you to know that I called Naomi a few times over last weekend. I left messages at her home.'

Mike had checked the answering machine at the apartment. There was nothing on it, whether because she had picked up the calls herself or because Daniel had listened and erased them.

'The tech guys in the PD will be able to retrieve those,' Mercer said, half bluff and half wishful thinking. 'Remember what you said?'

Levy shifted uncomfortably. 'I — uh — I think I just apologized for being so rude. That's right, I offered to meet her for coffee too. I did try to make a — uh — an appointment.'

'At school?'

He reddened again. 'No, down near her apartment. But she never returned my calls. And then, of course — well, the murder. I never saw her again. Maybe I wasn't so far off when I called her friend a madman.'

'Thanks for your time,' Mercer said. 'The Homicide Squad will probably send a few detectives over to talk with some of the students. We'll try not to intrude too much.'

'Whatever is necessary. We're very willing to cooperate.'

We made our way back toward Mercer's car.

'You think the rabbi was trying to make an appointment,' Mercer asked, 'or a date? Bad choice of words today, that he should have held his 'tongue.''

'I get that he's nervous, and that any involvement in a murder case is an extreme situation for Rabbi Levy and for the seminary,' I said. 'But it certainly sounds like he had more than a professional attraction to Naomi. Can you push the lieutenant to get some guys up here for a more thorough interview?'

'That and scoring his phone records for starters.'

'I hate how this job makes me distrust everybody. I mean, maybe he was just picking up on her despondency.'

'And maybe he was just picking up on her, Alex. Gotta check it out.'

'I know we do, but sometimes it's the worst part of my work. Makes me wish I'd been a prima ballerina,' I said, giving a tug to the sleeve of Mercer's black leather jacket.

Both of us reached for our cell phones to check for messages. It was almost one in the afternoon. I held mine at arm's length while Pat McKinney railed at me at the top of his lungs for not sticking around to give him details about the morning's murder. Rose Malone, calling on Battaglia's behalf, made the same complaint with more dignity.

'Hot water?' Mercer asked.

'Tepid. It will come to a boil by the end of the day, I'm sure. McKinney will be in the front office stirring the pot to try to nail me. Nothing from Mike about the autopsy?'

'Should be done by now,' Mercer said, checking his watch. 'One from Special Victims. The serial rapist in the transit system hit again. Brooklyn, this time. And Vickee, warning me that headquarters is getting hell from the mayor's office about these cases. He doesn't want any more bodies in churchyards, can you imagine?'

'I need to be careful what I wish for,' I said as the phone vibrated in my hand and Mike's number came up on the screen. 'And the mayor better pray a little harder. Hello?'

'Who's buried in Grant's Tomb?'

'What?' I hadn't heard that question since reruns of Groucho Marx went off the air.

'You heard me. Grant's Tomb. Who's buried there? And why don't you smile when you see me?'

My head jerked and I looked up the steep hill we were climbing as we crossed Broadway going west. I couldn't help but break into a grin and wave when I saw Mike at the top.

'Ulysses S. Grant, Detective Chapman.'

'Half right.'

'And Julia Boggs Dent-Grant. First Lady. Beloved wife.'

'Cross-eyed, she was. D'you know that surgeons wanted to correct her crossed eyes when she moved to the White House? But General Grant said he liked her just that way.'

'You ought to learn some tolerance from Ulysses's attitude, Mikey. Why are you here?'

'Came to pay my respects to the general.'

Mercer and I continued due west, up the steep

193

incline and across Riverside Drive, where the wide expanse of the Hudson River opened up below the stately granite and marble monument — the second largest mausoleum in the Western Hemisphere — built by a mourning nation as a tribute to Grant's leadership to save the Union.

We sat on the great steps, catching the sunlight that brightened the dull March landscape, flooding the area between the two huge sculpted eagles that guarded the tomb.

'Any surprises at Naomi's autopsy?'

Mike was halfway into a ham-and-cheese sandwich. He'd brought a second one for Mercer and a yogurt for me. 'Nope.'

'Signs of sexual assault?'

'Inconclusive. No seminal fluid. Minor bruising on the thighs, but that could have come during a struggle anyway.'

'Mercy, mercy.'

'How can you say that, Mr. Wallace?' Mike asked. 'You see any mercy in this matter? You think it was such a blessing to be beheaded by a dull hatchet?'

'The ME says that's what the weapon was?' I asked.

'Let's leave it at the fact that it wasn't such a clean slice. He's not sure what kind of blade, but it might have done with a good sharpening. Probably same one as for this new victim. Naomi's killer didn't get the job done with just one strike.'

'Any thoughts about drugs? That maybe Naomi was unconscious before she was mutilated?'

194

'I hope it's the case for both women, but tox won't be ready for at least a week.'

The complicated tests for toxicological finds in the blood and tissue were impossible to be rushed. It often took weeks, depending on the substance tested for, to get an answer to whether drugs were present and in what amounts.

'Did Chirico have anything to add?' I asked. Not that there were any good thoughts to have about this case.

'Not yet. Wound himself up in this one tighter than a tick on a dog's ear. He doesn't like anybody screwing with the Mother Church. The guy won't budge from his desk. What'd you get?'

Mercer repeated what Rabbi Levy had told us about Naomi Gersh. All of it fit with her brother's description of her as a pariah, and of her profound loneliness as she struggled to find a way to live her life. He also noted the rabbi's apparent interest in helping Naomi relieve some of that gloom by suggesting a date.

'Then there's this Bellevue piece,' Mercer said. 'If you ask me, Naomi's quirks were growing on the rabbi. She might have pushed back because she thought he was coming on to her. She told him she had a friend she had to see who'd been sick. Said he'd been at Bellevue.'

'A veritable whackjob? Now we're talking,' Mike said.

'I thought I'd ride down there and rattle some cages. We have a pretty specific window. Naomi told the rabbi about this guy last week, and if he's a Bellevue psych patient, I can start to look at discharges in the days before the murder — '

'And escapes. Eyeball the escapes too.'

'You're going to need a subpoena. I'll cut you a few when I get down to the office.'

'Ask one of your posse to do it for him right now,' Mike said. The stunning team of lawyers who worked Special Victims — Nan Toth, Catherine Dashfer, Marisa Bourges — would drop most of what they were doing to back up Mike and Mercer on any case. 'I'm going to take you for a ride, Coop.'

'Where?'

'The Bronx. I got a hunch.'

'About Naomi?'

'No. About a church.'

'I wouldn't dream of crossing you on that subject. Mercer, when you get to Bellevue, you should think about the emergency room too.'

New York had some of the finest private medical centers in the world, including the New York University facility adjacent to Bellevue. But cops knew the best trauma treatment was in the ERs at hospitals one would never choose for open-heart surgery: Harlem, Metropolitan, and Bellevue.

'Already doing that. Maybe Naomi didn't like the rabbi calling her friend crazy 'cause she didn't think he was crazy. Could have been at Bellevue for an injury. Treated and released.'

'Maybe he was giving his machete a practice run,' Mike said. 'Hurt himself in the process. Or drugs.'

There were scores of people a day in and out of the Bellevue ER. Hundreds more who were in outpatient programs or coming in to receive meds. If you wanted to do one-stop shopping for the mentally ill in Manhattan, this hospital was the place to start.

'I'll go straight to administration. Will you call Laura and ask her to fax up the subpoenas?'

'Right now.'

'Coop's office at six tonight?' Mercer asked.

'Deal.'

Once again we went in separate directions, Mercer downtown and Mike and I heading due east to take the Triborough Bridge to the Bronx.

'You're not telling me where?'

'No secret. It's a long shot, not a secret. I'm taking you to my alma mater. The old church there — St. John's — may have a clue or two.'

'Another St. John's?' I asked. 'Obviously not the Divine this time?'

'Nope. Just a little parish church built in the Bronx way before that one got under way.'

Mike had majored in history at Fordham University, one of the premier Jesuit institutions in the country. While the school had expanded its campuses into Manhattan, the original Rose Hill site was where Mike had studied.

'Time for confession?' I said, dialing Nan's number to implore her help.

'Just like there's a reason for Naomi to be dumped at Mount Neboh, this woman's at St. Pat's to make a point. If the perp has done that much homework, maybe I'll get lucky.'

Mike was weaving between cars and trucks while I brought Nan up to speed on the events. She would put a team of our most trusted colleagues together and run interference with

197

McKinney until I could return to the office.

The Gothic Revival church, St. John's, was built in the 1840s as the house of worship for the parish of surrounding farms in what was then the bucolic village called Fordham. Today, with an overbuilt urban population on every side of the campus, the buttresses, gargoyles, and great bell tower of the church seemed a pleasant anachronism.

Mike and I had worked a case that took us to this neighborhood often just a few years earlier. As he turned onto the Fordham grounds from Southern Boulevard, I looked across at the serene Botanical Gardens that held such deadly memories for me.

'Tintinnabulation,' Mike said. 'Your man Poe.'

'What?'

We were driving toward the chapel as he pointed to the tower. 'Most scholars think these old bells were Poe's inspiration for that poem.'

The cottage to which Poe moved with his young, terminally ill bride was a short distance away, and he walked this area almost every day that he lived nearby. 'Hope you've got more to show for the ride than that.'

'Boy, does this bring back memories,' Mike said, getting out of the car and heading toward the plain wooden doors of the chapel.

I followed Mike inside. As we walked down the nave of the simple Gothic church, natural light streamed onto the white marble altar through the blue, yellow, and green stained-glass windows that lined the walls. Below them were a series of panels depicting the Stations of the

Cross, scenes from the trial of Jesus by Pontius Pilate to his burial in the tomb.

Mike's right hand was busy combing through his hair. He looked around, as though taking everything in anew, but didn't speak.

'What is it, Mike?'

'Who was the last king of the French? That's a subject dear to your heart,' he said, beginning to pace, staring up at the windows as he walked through the crossing.

'Look, it's a little early for *Jeopardy!* Why did you bring me here?'

'Last king of the French.'

'Louis-Philippe. The July Monarchy, as it was called.'

Mike was motioning with his cupped fingers to give him more. 'When?'

'Eighteen thirty to eighteen forty-eight.'

'I'll take you the rest of the way, Coop. See these six windows? Three on each side? The most brilliant-colored ones?'

I looked back and forth. Of the sixteen windows that lined the nave, six were larger and far more exquisite than the others.

'So, Louis-Philippe had the idea to make a grand gift to the Catholics in America. He had these six stained-glass windows, said to be the most beautiful in the world, designed for St. Patrick's Cathedral — the old one — '

'The one where the body was found today.'

'Exactly. They were created in Sèvres, France, and shipped to New York as the king's — what do you call it?'

'Beau geste.'

'Yeah. But these windows didn't fit at Old St. Pat's. Imagine that? A king's ransom worth of stained glass, but the wrong dimensions for the fancy new cathedral in Manhattan,' Mike said. 'So the bishop shipped them up here to the little farming village of Fordham, so they could be the centerpiece of this new seminary that was still under construction and could be modified to hold them.'

I studied these glorious works with a deep appreciation of their magnificence — the depiction of handsome biblical figures, which were indeed so much richer in color and style than the other windows in the chapel, and than their replacements at Old St. Pat's.

'Sorry for my ignorance, Mike. Who are they?'

'That's Saints Paul and Peter, holding the Keys to the Kingdom. Then you've got the four apostles — John, Luke, Mark, and Matthew.'

The artistry of the glasswork was extraordinary.

'Now, here's what got me thinking, Coop. You remember where the body was this morning?'

'Between two old headstones, and beneath the window that depicted Matthew.'

'Exactly. Manny Chirico was fixated on the names on grave markers for clues, but I kept thinking about the portraits in the stained glass, 'cause there was something unusual about that image.'

'In what way?'

'I mean, most of the time — in Christian art — the apostles are portrayed like this.' Mike was at his most animated, taking me by the hand to stand before these masterpieces of religious glasswork. 'See? Each of them is painted with one of the living creatures described in the book of Revelation.'

The larger-than-life-size evangelists were posed on golden pedestals, and at their bases were bright blue enamel medallions — the same color as their halos — bearing their names.

'So that's John, with an eagle at his feet,' I said. 'Mark with a lion, Luke beside a bull, and then — '

'That's what was different at St. Pat's,' Mike said, breaking into my sentence as we stood beneath the stunning portrait of the fourth apostle. 'There were no beasts, no creatures in those windows. But look, Coop, look at this.'

The French medallion below the figure in the fourth soaring window bore the name Matthieu.

He was robed in magenta, composing his gospel, pen in hand, as he gazed toward heaven. Holding the emerald-green writing tablet for him and glancing back at us was a young man — a young man with wings on his back, feathered and tipped with gold.

'A winged man,' I said in a whisper.

'He's gaming us, this killer. Somehow he got himself over the gates at Mount Neboh — '

'Like Luther Audley said, the guy flew.'

'Well, he did it again this morning, into the graveyard. At least, that's what he wants us to believe.'

'Like the symbolism at the fountain at St. John the Divine, when you asked me about the flying guy in the statue,' I said, visualizing the

Archangel Michael, hovering over a decapitated Satan.

'Yeah.'

'You're thinking that the killer left the body at St. Pat's this morning, and cut out her tongue. You're thinking he brought it here. That he knew about the connection between the two churches because of the windows, because of the classic portraits of the apostles.'

Mike nodded at me.

'But he couldn't possibly have known there'd be a homicide cop at the scene who'd worshipped in this very chapel,' I said, brushing off the idea that had seized both of us so completely. 'No one could expect this to be put together so quickly.'

'Of course not, Coop. But this bastard is showing off how well he knows his Bible, his religious readings, the haunts of the faithful — like this little jewel of a sleepy village church, with its legendary royal windows,' Mike said. 'Forget about me piecing this together — '

'But you did.'

'Yeah. And by the time Commissioner Scully sits down with the cardinal tonight to talk about the desecration at Old St. Pat's, you can bet the cardinal himself will make the very same connection. This is well-documented church history, kid, even if it's news to you. Keith Scully went to Fordham Law School. He'd have this figured out even if I was walking a beat in Coney Island,' Mike said. 'See that altar right there?'

I'd forgotten the police commissioner had a Fordham Law degree. I nodded as Mike pointed to the rear of the church where a decorative piece, elaborately carved with a relief of the Last Supper, stood next to the entrance.

'Yes. It looks like it came out of a museum.'

'Well, it's the original altar from Old St. Pat's, and it was installed here by Cardinal Spellman in the 1940s, a gift from the archdiocese. I may have encroached on a bit of the killer's lead time, but the church hierarchy would have come to the same conclusion and connected that cathedral to this little chapel before the sun sets tonight.'

'So you're right, Mike. The perp's gaming us and he's gaming the whole religious establishment as well. What are you doing now?'

Mike was running his hand along the wall, back and forth below Matthew's window. 'One more thought. I was looking for a crevice, a hiding place — but the stained glass is mounted flush into the wall.'

Although the window's elevation stretched almost to the ceiling, its bottom was not much higher than our heads.

'You still think? . . . '

'One more place. There's a reliquary here, at the end of the east transept. A shrine to Saint Jean de Brébeuf. There's a Frenchman for you.'

I jogged to try to catch up with Mike.

'He was a Jesuit priest who was captured by the Iroquois and tortured to death,' Mike said. 'Mutilated.'

That sort of eliminated any questions I had about why this would be a fitting place for a connection to our victim.

'He was so brave he never even whimpered

during the torture,' Mike said, before he turned away from me again. 'So the Iroquois cut out his heart and ate it, to try to internalize his courage.'

The reliquary was in the darkest recess of the church, marked by a small plaque that listed the other martyred Jesuit priests it honored. It was mounted high on the wall. On a shelf beneath it, far above us, was a silver chalice, like the kind used at communion.

Mike stood as tall as he could but wasn't able to reach the shelf.

'What are you doing?' I asked as he ran past me and up the steps of the main altar.

'Stay put.'

He disappeared through one of the doorways to the right, and less than a minute later emerged carrying a wooden ladder I guessed to be six feet tall.

'What? . . . '

'Watch it, Coop. Every altar boy needs a boost now and then to get up to the candelabra to put out the flames. There's always a ladder backstage.'

I steadied the legs as Mike climbed the steps. Directly over his head there was a crossbeam, closer to the ledge of the reliquary than he could get with his outstretched arm. I closed my eyes for a second and imagined a winged man suspended from it. The exhaustion was playing tricks with my imagination.

'Get me closer,' he said.

I pushed the ladder slowly so as not to dislodge him.

Mike reached out again and grasped the stem

of the chalice. He glanced into it, then pulled it to his chest to secure it, holding it there with his right hand while he guided himself down the rungs with his left.

When he had both feet on the floor, he extended the silver cup toward me. There within it was the discolored, putrefied tongue of the woman who'd been murdered at Old St. Patrick's Cathedral earlier that day.

22

It was almost five o'clock when Mike dropped me off at the Hogan Place entrance to the District Attorney's Office. Lawyers were pushing shopping carts full of case folders and evidence back from courtrooms in the overflow civil courthouse across Centre Street, ending wearying days on trial. I crowded into an elevator with two of the junior assistants and rode up to the eighth-floor office suites.

'Hey, Laura. Start with the good news.'

'Can't think of any. You're going to need a shovel to get through all the stuff that's been piling up since you left.'

'Battaglia?'

'Better send out for a cocktail before you go in there. Something to steady your nerves. He's been like a raging bull today.'

'Now?'

'Go rescue Nan. She and McKinney have been in with him for an hour.'

'Take off. See you tomorrow.'

'Not a prayer. You need an air-traffic controller for these messages. I'll wait till you're out.'

'Thanks.' I picked up a legal pad and headed through security to the executive wing. Rose looked as grim as an executioner.

Pat McKinney practically exploded with delight when Battaglia, who was talking on the phone, scowled at my entrance. 'What was it?

206

Chapman's class reunion that took you back to the Bronx?'

'And to think Mike didn't invite you to come along, Patrick. You could have been homecoming queen.'

News of our important find hadn't reached the DA yet, or McKinney wouldn't have been quite so snide about my absence.

I sat next to Nan at the conference table and leaned over to whisper to her. 'I am so sorry to have dragged you into this mess.'

'I'll get you back,' she said, patting my hand. 'You'll owe me for months.'

'Alexandra will be a little late for that meeting, Keith,' Battaglia said, crushing the cigar with his teeth as he raised his voice. 'We've got some business here first.'

Battaglia had been talking to Commissioner Scully. I didn't know whether that would be worse for Mike or for me, since we had both disappeared for the afternoon.

'So what else does your crystal ball tell you?' McKinney asked. 'You sure nailed that St. Pat's location for the second body.'

I didn't answer. I was most anxious to ask Battaglia to find out from Bishop Deegan who the man in the courtroom during his testimony was. I was certain I had seen him at St. John the Divine the day before, but for the first time in my years under Battaglia's watch, I worried about giving up information like that when there was clearly a backstory between the district attorney and the bishop to which I was not privy.

'They had a solution for that kind of

207

prognosticating in Salem,' McKinney said. He was, as usual, the only one to laugh at what he thought passed for humor.

'Nan was just telling us that there might be a Bellevue connection,' Battaglia said, eyeing me, waiting for me to speak.

'Mercer come up with anything solid yet?' I asked her.

'Risk management's doing their usual dance,' she said, referring to the legal arm of the hospital, always vigilant against the potential for lawsuits. 'Patient privacy, medical privilege — we'll be lucky to have our first shot at records by Monday.'

'Surely Chapman's got a hot nurse or two he can lean on there to break the rules,' McKinney said.

'I won't forget to ask him.'

'Scully's having the Homicide Squad bosses in at six for a briefing. He wants you there,' Battaglia said.

I was certain McKinney had been lobbying to take me off the case. His girlfriend had just been dumped from the head of the Gun Recovery Unit for general incompetence, and Pat kept looking to insert her into other high-profile work. The fact that he hadn't dragged her into this mess suggested he didn't have any ready solutions for these murders and feared things would get worse before we made headway.

'All right if Nan comes along?' I asked.

'I'd prefer it. At least I can find her when I need something.' Battaglia had good reason to respect Nan's professionalism. She had tried some of the most challenging cases — from murder to multimillion-dollar white-collar frauds — and was one of his most trusted soldiers.

Chapman obviously hadn't reached Scully yet. 'Just so you know, Mike didn't take me on a wild goose chase. We found what we were looking for.'

'Are you serious? He found the woman's tongue?' The DA put his hand on the black phone that connected him immediately to the police commissioner's desk. 'Tell me where it was. I can hold this one over the PC's head.'

I explained what had led Mike to the campus chapel. A smile crept onto Paul Battaglia's face. He liked the church trivia and the forensic finding almost as much as he relished being the first in a position of power to know something.

'I've got a slew of calls to make before I go over to headquarters,' I said, rising to leave. 'We left Crime Scene at the chapel going over every inch of the place. The killer must have gone straight from St. Pat's cemetery up to Fordham.'

'I can head out from here,' Nan said. 'I'll tell Mike you'll be over in? . . . '

'By the time the meeting starts.'

We left McKinney with Battaglia and Nan asked me if I needed help with anything before she took the short walk from our office, through the cutaway next to the federal courthouse, to One Police Plaza, tucked away behind the United States Attorney's Office.

'Thanks. Laura's going to hang out and triage my list of calls. See you there.'

I went back to my office. Laura had just brewed a fresh pot of coffee and set me up with a steaming-hot mug.

Six of the lawyers from the unit were on trial. Only two had courtroom crises, and my longtime deputy had put out those fires. I clipped the notes together to take home with me, so I could check in on each of them that night.

There were case inquiries from victims, detectives who wanted investigative guidance, and one bureau chief complaining about a judgment call we had made in a new case. My internist's office reminded me of the need for an annual checkup, my nephew wanted theater tickets when the family came to town for spring break, and a date had been set for the fall trunk show at Escada. It seemed that everyone but the man I loved was looking for me.

'This guy was beyond rude,' Laura said, handing me a slip with her red exclamation marks and underlining all over it. 'Let him cool down a day before you call.'

The message was from Vincenzo Borracelli. My meeting with his wife had only been Thursday but felt like a week ago. 'It's imperative that I hear from you today. *Do you know who I am?*' The italics were Laura's — it meant that Borracelli had been screaming at her. 'You can't treat my child the way you did. I'll have you taken off the case at once. I'll see that you pay for this.'

'Good luck to him if he can find someone else who wants the case,' I said, handing the slip of paper back to Laura. 'Let him stew until Monday. I'll return some of these others. Can you please remind me when it gets close to six?'

'Will do.'

I picked up my private line to deal with the more important matters and let Laura continue to fend off callers and passersby. I slipped a couple of Tylenol from my desk drawer and tried to make a list of details that might be useful for Scully's meeting.

When Laura told me it was time to go, I left all the papers in discrete piles on my desk. We both put on jackets and walked to the elevator. She went into the revolving door first, and we parted on the sidewalk in front of the Hogan Place entrance.

'Good night. Stop pushing yourself so hard, Alex,' Laura said, walking off to head north to the Canal Street subway station.

'Thanks for everything. See you tomorrow.'

I took the shortcut along Baxter Street, crossing to avoid the loading dock that was blocked by a large truck. The small park that separated Chinatown from the courthouse was on my left. School-children who played kickball and tag there were long gone, and it was too dark for the seniors who did their Tai Chi exercises at the beginning and end of the day.

The wind picked up and shadows from the trees in the park danced under the dim glow of the streetlights.

I held my cell in both hands, texting Mike that I was on my way. I had forgotten that the new security system at One Police Plaza would slow me down by an additional five or six minutes.

I heard the footsteps before the man spoke. He came rushing out of the park after I passed the gate in the southwest corner, running at me from behind.

I turned to look at him and stumbled on the cracked sidewalk, falling to my knees, my BlackBerry skipping off the curb between two parked cars.

He was coming at me so fast that his feet caught on my extended leg and he landed on the ground, half of him squarely on top of me.

'Ms. Alice,' the slight young black man said. 'I'm not going to hurt you, Ms. Alice.'

I didn't realize I had screamed until two uniformed cops pulled the kid off and cuffed him.

23

'It was Luther Audley,' I said to Mike. I was forty-five minutes late for Scully's meeting, but the commissioner himself had been called to City Hall to explain things to the mayor, so we were all on hold waiting for him.

'How'd you recognize Luther? By the crack in his rear end?'

Guido Lentini, the deputy commissioner for public information, had given us his office to use until Scully arrived. Nan was standing behind me, kneading my shoulders. She knew I was rattled and was just trying to calm me down.

'Where is he now?' Mercer asked.

'I asked the cops not to arrest him. I believe his story. I'm fine. If I hadn't tripped on that jagged piece of cement, he wouldn't have become entangled with me.'

'C'mon, Alex. Where's Luther?'

'I told them you'd call. It's two guys from the Ninth Precinct,' I said, unfolding a piece of paper with their numbers. 'They're holding him in Central Booking till after we sort this out.'

'What did Luther say to you, exactly?' Mike asked.

'He might have been calling my name to get my attention. I'm not sure, but I thought he said 'Alice' so it didn't concern me. Anyway, I thought it was street noise and I ignored it 'cause

I was texting you. I didn't hear him speak until after — '

'After he brought you down.'

'He didn't bring me down, Mike. I really don't think that's what he had in mind.'

'He was waiting for you, wasn't he?'

'How could he possibly have known I'd take Baxter Street?'

'Your office is the only place he'd think to find you,' Mercer said. 'Maybe he just skulked around till he figured you'd be getting out of work, saw you walk out and separate from Laura, and got lucky when you took the darker route.'

'But he didn't do anything to me.'

'Tell her, Nan. The kid cost her at least a manicure,' Mike said.

'Twelve dollars, Mike. Still only a misdemeanor.' Nan pinched my shoulders.

My knuckles were bloody from scraping the sidewalk, and several of my nails had broken.

'Here's what he said, when the cops let him open his mouth. It's all about his grandfather.'

'I like that old guy,' Mike said.

'The trustees have decided to fire Mr. Audley,' I said. 'It looks bad for them that Amos has been letting Luther hang out there. By hindsight, people in the office claim that stuff is missing — cash, some of the silver objects that would bring in a fraction of their worth being sold on the street, books and hymnals.'

'Then keep a leash on Luther,' Mercer said. 'Why punish Gramps?'

'He's the one person in the world that Luther cares about. The one human being who's always looked out for him. The kid knows that and feels bad about it. That's why he was trying to catch up with me. That's all he wanted.'

'He's not familiar with the concept of office hours?'

'Right, Mike. With his batting average, you think he's just going to show up for an appointment with an assistant district attorney? Not likely to be his comfort zone.'

'What does he expect you to do?'

'Talk to Wilbur Gaskin. The kid's not wrong. Luther says Mr. Gaskin's behind the whole idea. He feels personally embarrassed about what happened in front of us with him and his friends. Gaskin thinks he needs to send a signal to everyone at the church.'

'Ain't nothing sacred if Amos Audley's expendable,' Mercer said. 'That'll have everybody shaking in their boots.'

'So you called, didn't you? That's why you were so late getting over here.'

'I was late because I had to make the cops understand why I wasn't pressing charges.'

'But I'll bet you called Wilbur Gaskin. Fess up, Coop.'

'Sure, I tried to call him.'

'Without discussing the idea with your partners, huh?' Mike gestured at Nan and Mercer. 'Without letting us weigh in on whether it was a good plan.'

'Not a problem, Mr. Chapman. I didn't reach him.'

'Nobody home?'

'Remember, Wilbur Gaskin spends every other

weekend in Atlanta? Keeps a place there, where he grew up. Likes to go down to play golf.'

'I'm not surprised, Coop. You scared him out of church on us, just when we could have used his help. Now Amos Audley's job is on the line, and you've run Gaskin right out of town.'

24

Guido Lentini cracked the door open. 'Everything okay with you, Alexandra?'

'We're good. What's with Scully?' It was almost seven thirty.

'Everybody in the room is getting antsy. All I know is that the first dep called to say the mayor has info for Scully, for a change. He asked me to keep all you cats herded in the big office. You ready to join us?'

'Couple more calls, Guido,' Mike said. He had already convinced the pair of 9th Precinct cops to let Luther Audley go and void his arrest for third-degree assault.

'I want you to be in there when Scully shows, okay?'

The office of the DCPI was one of the most high-tech communications hubs in the department. Lentini's phone bank could auto-dial any bigwig in the city, and the flat screens that hung on three of the walls could call up everything from local breaking news to on-the-ground action in Afghanistan or Israel, Abu Dhabi or Singapore.

'Give me a heads-up when he's crossing the street, will you?' Mike asked, one hand on the television remote.

I stood up and walked into the restroom to splash water on my face. When I came out, Mike pressed the power button and five of the large screens lit up with Alex Trebek's face.

'Get ready, Nan. I expect you to ante up,' Mike said.

'What makes this okay, Mike?' she asked. 'That the body isn't actually in the room with us? Or do you just like being the poster boy for bad taste?'

'You know a body wouldn't stop him,' Mercer said. 'Never has done.'

'That's right,' Trebek said. 'Tonight's Final *Jeopardy!* category is CRIMINAL SONGBIRD. First time we've had this one. CRIMINAL SONGBIRD.'

All three studio contestants laughed and shook their heads.

'Fifty bucks, ladies and gent. We're bound to know this,' Mike said. 'All crime, all the time.'

'Twenty-five,' Nan said. 'I've got those little mouths to feed at home.'

Trebek stepped back to reveal the answer. '"Singer convicted of pinching buttocks of a woman in the Central Park Zoo."'

'I'm going inside. I have no idea.'

'Don't throw in the towel, blondie. You know every Chester Molester in history.'

'Who is Frank Sinatra?'

'Are you crazy? If you were a player on the show, ninety-nine percent of the viewing public would be throwing rocks at the telly. Ol' Blue Eyes never had to pinch.'

I was only a bit ahead of the accountant, who guessed Keith Richards. Nan and Mercer — like the other two contestants — threw up their hands without an answer.

'I'm in a cultural wasteland with you mooks. Who was Enrico Caruso?' Mike cheered for himself when Trebek confirmed the question. 'In 1906. The great tenor was arrested by the NYPD for ass-grabbing a society dame in the monkey house.'

'You learned that at the Academy?' Mercer asked. 'I must have been dozing.'

'Nah. My dad loved Caruso. But Aunt Eunice wouldn't let him listen to the records 'cause of what he did. She thought he was a perv. Convicted too. He testified at his trial that the monkey did it. How's that for a new low?'

Mike was gathering up his papers to shift to the conference room adjoining Scully's office.

'Fits with your orangutan theory,' Mercer said. 'Let's move out, okay?'

Nan and I left first. We had long ago ceased to be surprised by the black humor of homicide work. These were detectives who faced down the darkest corners of the human condition every day and found relief — like small air pockets for someone gasping for breath — in the most unlikely manner.

The group waiting for Scully had grown considerably in number. Lieutenant Peterson led the Manhattan North contingent, chatting with his South counterpart while the men — and one woman homicide cop — stood in clusters around the long table. Somehow, Manny Chirico was still wide-eyed and alert. I recognized guys from Anti-Crime and the Harbor Unit, Highway Patrol and Housing. The only people not invited seemed to be the Counter-Terrorism teams.

219

Lentini stepped out to make a call, clutching his ever-present clipboard. He was back in a minute. 'Take your seats, men. The commissioner's in the elevator.'

You could almost smell the testosterone in the room as the city's best murder investigators staked out places and readied their notepads.

Sadly for the victims, not all homicides are created equal. The choice of religious institutions as this killer's backdrop and tortured young women as his prey ratcheted up the level of interest and outrage of this select team. Gang members, junkies, and the great unwashed dead of the metropolitan area would be shuffled to back burners until this perp was caught.

'Thanks for your patience, men.' Keith Scully entered the room with his first dep and a second man carrying a laptop, and it was as though the spine of each of us around the table automatically stiffened as we mumbled some version of 'good evening' to the commissioner. His professionalism was unmistakable, as was the ramrod straightness of his Marine bearing, physically and metaphorically.

I had known Scully for six or seven years, from the time when he had been chief of detectives, on the steady climb up the ladder to the top cop post, which was a mayoral appointment. He was tall and sinewy, with close-cut hair now gone silver, and as many creases etched into his face as there were constant crises thrown onto his lap.

'How many guys you got on this, Ray?' Lieutenant Peterson was the senior man in the room, so Scully started with him.

'A dozen, Keith.' The two privileges the old-timer was allowed were still addressing the commissioner by his first name and smoking his cigarettes inside headquarters. No one else dared do either.

'Double it. By tomorrow's day shift. Same goes for all of you.'

'Manpower's an issue,' Peterson said. 'My men each got a full plate as it is, and then you sent that new directive about limiting overtime — which, I gotta say, pissed everybody off.'

'Tell them to eat their overtime. Shove it. You've got tonight to organize yourselves. Get a good meal and whatever rest you can in the next twelve hours. I don't expect you to sleep again till you bring this guy down,' Scully said. 'Your world turns upside down tomorrow when we let the media know we've got an ID on the victim.'

Manny Chirico pushed back from the table. The rest of us were riveted on Keith Scully.

'Her name is Ursula Hewitt.' Scully pointed to his tech aide, who flashed one of the crime-scene photos of her from his PowerPoint file onto the wall screen.

If you hadn't seen the body in the churchyard firsthand, there was nothing like a life-size color blowup to jump-start this crew for a full-on manhunt. I could hear the intake of breath and a few 'holy shits' from around the table.

'Female Caucasian,' Scully went on, like he was calling cadence. 'Thirty-nine years old. Born in Forest Hills. Flushing Boulevard. Attended church and parochial school there.'

Most of the men in the room were Catholic.

That fact was probably intended to juice them a bit more.

'Our Lady Queen of Martyrs,' Mike whispered. He often said that New York and New Orleans were the only two cities in the country in which the devout identified themselves by their parish affiliations, rather than neighborhoods.

The next slide was a photograph of the young Hewitt from her high school yearbook, offering all the freshness and promise of youth. She was slimmer then, and the contrast between her slender neck and the slashed throat of the morning's scene was horrifying.

'Ursula's uncle called the mayor's office at five twenty-three this evening. He lives in San Francisco, but he's got a high school buddy who works at City Hall. She'd been staying with friends in Manhattan but never made it home last night. It was his birthday, and she was certain to call. Then he heard about the body at St. Pat's on the radio, but he thought he didn't have enough reason to call the police. Just that it was one of her favorite churches, which snagged his radar. We went over to compare photographs from the scene with the one from her last visit that her uncle scanned in to his friend at City Hall.'

The next picture went up on the third screen. It was a more recent image of Ursula Hewitt, dressed in flowing clerical vestments. The floor-length alb of white linen was perfectly draped over her, with a scarlet stole on her shoulders that ran down the length of the garment, and a large cross around her neck.

222

'This is Ursula Hewitt,' Scully said, his lips clamped tightly together as he paused. 'Three years ago, when she was ordained as a Catholic priest.'

There was dead silence in the room as we all took in the photo, till a split second later when one of the guys from Manhattan South broke in with a nervous laugh. 'Hey, chief. We don't got lady priests. We got nuns.'

Keith Scully didn't brook interruptions.

'Ursula Hewitt was a Catholic priest. She was ordained in a neighborhood church in Back Bay, Boston. She even celebrated Mass a few times at Old St. Pat's.'

Most of the men looked perplexed, as surprised as I was to hear that fact.

'She was excommunicated by the Vatican a year later, because of that ordination. So we've got another outcast on our hands, gentlemen,' Scully said. 'Another pariah.'

25

'Form your pods, guys,' Scully said. 'Put your working groups together tonight, figure out a way to keep each other up to speed on anything you discover — one from each team who can be the contact person — and report to the first dep every couple of hours, even if to say you've got nothing new. Nobody talks to reporters except Guido. Nobody.'

'The vic's uncle, Keith. He got any ideas?' Peterson asked.

'The usual. She's had stalkers, hate mail from the faithful, and worse from the Vatican. He was keeping close tabs on her because she was getting overwhelmed by the way she'd been treated.' The commissioner was going in ten directions at once. 'You're not only looking for the perp himself — or maybe it's more than one person. Find me an abattoir — a slaughterhouse, a cage of some kind, a basement or rooftop, maybe a commercial van he's turned into his chop shop. Check for stolen vehicles. A place these killings happen without this bastard calling attention to himself.'

'One more thing, Keith, if you don't mind,' the lieutenant said. He had earlier told Scully and the group about Mike's coup on the Fordham campus. 'Do like Chapman today. Think outside the box for a change.'

The sergeant from Mounted slapped Mike's

back. 'He's lived an entire life outside the box. That's all this guy knows. Don't start giving him credit for it.'

'This wasn't my original plan for the six o'clock meeting,' Scully said. 'But the ID changed the whole point of having you here. Let's hit the ground running at daybreak.'

Mike, Mercer, Nan, and I huddled with Peterson. He wanted us to have someone familiar with the waterfront, at least two men from South, and anyone Chirico could spare from the Night Watch crew.

'Can you step out for a minute, Alex?' Scully asked.

'Of course,' I said more eagerly than I meant. I figured that he wanted to get some assurance from me that he — not Paul Battaglia — would be calling the shots in this investigation. 'Nan too?'

'No. Just you.'

I looked over at my friend for support. She could do no more than raise her eyebrows.

Scully took me into the hallway and around the corner so our voices wouldn't echo. 'I need you to step down from this case, Alex.'

'I can't believe you just said that. You're joking, aren't you?'

'You know me better than that. Step down. I don't want any further discussion.'

'You don't want to discuss this? Neither do I, Keith, because there's really nothing to talk about,' I said, flailing my arms around more than I wanted to be doing. 'I don't work for you, Commissioner. You can't give me an order like

I'm one of your troops and think I'm going to salute you and slink away.'

I could feel the color rise in my cheeks as the anger swelled up inside me. I struggled to keep my temper under control.

'Don't raise your voice to me, Alex.'

'What are you worried about? That Battaglia might hear you trying to take over his operation? Have you bothered to speak with him yet?'

'I don't need to do that. This directive comes from the mayor.'

'Is it some kind of grudge match held over from our case at Gracie Mansion?' The mayor had been embarrassed by a crime scene at his official residence, so maybe that had me in the crosshairs. I was furious.

'You're more insightful than that, Alex.'

'Maybe some days I am, Keith.' I was crossing a line, I knew, trying to remind him by the intimacy of first names of nights we spent sitting on bar stools at dives in the worst part of town, celebrating victories after breaking our asses together on the city's toughest cases. 'This isn't one of them. Give me a reason.'

'I'm the PC. I don't have to give you a reason.' He had lowered his voice. We were staring each other down, just inches apart.

'I'm on this case,' I turned my back to him and started to walk, but he grabbed my arm.

'Not if I tell my men not to work with you.'

'This is so not your style, Keith. I didn't know you had a bit of the bully in you.'

'You need me to spell it out?'

'That would help.'

'How's your relationship with the cardinal?'

'Not as good as the mayor's, if I had to guess. I've never met the man.'

'Slamming Bishop Deegan in the courtroom, were you?'

'Ah, the fog is lifting a bit.'

'I'm trying to take you out of the frying pan, Alex, before you burn up to a crisp. Back out gracefully. You got the transit rapist, you got the cold case with four victims that's still likely to grow, you've got an endless array of crimes to keep you busy.'

'Is it because I'm a Jew?' I hadn't raised my voice intentionally, but a door opened down the hall behind me. A detective looked out and Scully brushed him off with a wave.

'Don't be ridiculous. There's got to be a man as the lead prosecutor here. Don't you understand anything about the church?'

'I know you wanted a woman at the wheel when that sociopath killed an eighteen-year-old in Central Park. Compassion and sensitivity and bonding with all the teenage girls who were witnesses. 'The jury, the public, will identify with a strong woman speaking for the victim.' Remember that pitch? And I know you pleaded with Battaglia to keep Nan on top when you had the mother-son grifter team who left you to prove murder without a body.'

Keith Scully was really in my face now. 'You want to be the distraction in all this, is that what you want? I can't name five prosecutors in this country besides you who've gone after rogue priests. I'm as good a Catholic as they come, and

227

I'm not proud of those guys, but the cardinal would rather not see you as the point person in this case. The mayor is standing with him on this.'

'And Battaglia's already in bed with the bishop. How convenient. If it wasn't so twisted, I might laugh.'

'How much do you know about the Vatican's position on the ordination of women?' Scully asked.

'Absolutely nothing. If it's your superior wisdom on this issue — and the cardinal's inside track — I'm happy to say you've got me beat. But I'm a quick study, Keith. Asphyxia, the insanity defense, polymerase chain reaction in DNA testing. Ask the cardinal to tutor me for a few days and I promise to pass the tests.'

Scully gritted his teeth. 'He doesn't want to tutor you, Alex. I'll give you the talking points.'

'Shall I take notes?'

'You won't forget.' The commissioner's hands were on his hips, confronting me head-on. 'In the summer of 2010, the Vatican issued some new laws.'

That spring, the pedophilia scandals that had rocked America over the past few years had erupted as virulently in England and Ireland and across Europe. I assumed Scully was going back to finger-pointing at my role in that issue.

'You're right, of course. I had no idea.'

'They actually extended the period during which a clergyman could be tried by a church court, under canon law, from ten to twenty years, starting from the eighteenth birthday of the victim.'

'How enlightened,' I said.

'At the very same time — and I'm not apologizing for this — the Vatican took a tougher position on the ordination of women.'

'How tough?' And why was it any different from Orthodox Jews, who wouldn't allow female rabbis?

'They've bolted the door to women becoming priests. The Vatican declared the attempt at ordination to be a *delicta graviora*.'

'Where's Mike when I need him? My Latin's no good,' I said, making a half effort at a smile. 'Oh, that's right. You're going to slap his hand if he tries to help me.'

'It translates as 'grave crime,' Alex.'

'You're kidding me. It's a grave crime for a woman to try to be ordained in the twenty-first century?'

'The Vatican declared it one of the most serious offenses in church law — as serious as heresy, or as schism. They raised it in punishment to as grave a crime as the clerical sexual abuse of minors.'

This was all new to me. I had no idea of the storm this subject had created.

'Do you understand now, Alex? Do you see why you're the wrong man for this job?' Scully's impatience with me revealed itself in his facetious remark.

'I think it's called misogyny, Keith. Both you — and the church. The Vatican equates women priests with pedophiles?'

'Yes. At the moment, yes it does.'

'This is new?'

'Well, Rome had a different solution until recently. Between us, it actually makes me worried we've got a religious fanatic on our hands with this case. The next highest punishment, before excommunication, is called silencing. Any priests or nuns or theologians who took a stand against established doctrine have been forbidden to speak in the church — they can't teach, they can't preach, they can't participate.'

I closed my eyes and thought of the women in our case. 'Naomi Gersh, then Ursula Hewitt, and before them, the woman pastor in Wayland, Kentucky. One's throat slit so deep and wide it hung by a thread, the next decapitated, and this time a severed tongue.'

Keith Scully was convinced he'd made his point. 'Wouldn't you say they've been silenced?'

26

'Does Scully think you're taking yourself off the case?' Mike asked. We decided to use my apartment as a command center for our team's strategy session. It offered space, privacy, and a well-stocked bar.

'He didn't wait around for an answer. He's so damn used to getting his way.'

It was ten o'clock, and we had spread out the police reports and our notes on my dining-room table. Nan was on the phone ordering pizzas, Mike was fixing drinks, and I was opening a bottle of wine. Peterson had banded the four of us with another foursome assembled from different squads and, after a brief discussion with them about how to communicate in the morning, we left to regroup at my home.

'You see what he's done, Coop. He's silenced you, too,' Mike said. 'First Battaglia clips your wings. Then Scully gives you the boot. Sitting behind the cash register in a restaurant in the south of France keeping count of every escargot the chef sells is looking more and more like your future. The glory days may be behind you.'

'Jack her up, Mr. Chapman,' Nan said. 'Just what she needs.'

'I don't want to be a lightning rod for anything that will affect the case.'

'Running scared.'

'Hardly. How about if I just fade into the

231

background for the time being, let Nan take the lead, and we carry on as usual?'

I poured a glass of white wine for Nan and one for myself. 'And I thought you were my pal,' she said. 'I get to deal with Battaglia, the archdiocese, and the unhappy mobs. And you?'

'Whatever you need. I can do witness interviews — '

'Find me a frigging witness first, will you?' Mike said, clinking his glass full of vodka against my wine. 'I smell what you're up to. You'll do everything except having to interface with the bosses. You get the fun part. And then I'll get pounded when Scully finds out.'

'By Monday we'll have a better sense of where this is going. I'll poke my head out and test the waters.'

'Kind of like a groundhog, looking for his shadow,' Mike said. 'But you'll have to see Battaglia tomorrow morning. That won't be pretty.'

'It's Friday, and he's got meetings in Washington all day. Probably took the last shuttle tonight,' I said. 'To which I add a 'hallelujah' and let's get to work.'

Nan had opened her laptop and begun her research on Ursula Hewitt. 'What do you want to know?'

'I'm the wrong one to pass judgment on the idea of ordaining women. It seems smart to me.'

'Amen,' Mercer said. 'Overdue by a millennium or two.'

'But then it's not my church, so what I think doesn't count for much.' I looked to Mike and

232

then Nan, who were both practicing Catholics.

'Here's the latest *New York Times* poll,' Nan said, Googling faster than we were talking. 'For more than twenty years, a large majority of American Catholics favor allowing women to be ordained as priests, even though the church hierarchy is opposed. More than sixty-four percent think it's a good idea. Another eighty-one percent support women as deacons.'

'Let me speak for my aunt Eunice,' Mike said, raising his glass in the air. 'And my aunt Bridget and my sainted mother and the good ladies of St. Anselm's of Bay Ridge. Not happening. Hellfire and damnation before they'd approve ordaining women. You want a poll? Poll my relatives.'

'Women are so often more judgmental about each other's conduct than men,' I said.

'You can't let Nan take the heat on this,' Mike said. 'Don't we have a kick-ass atheist on board who won't care when crowds start picketing the courthouse?'

'I can deal,' Nan said.

'It's like an ancient fraternity,' Mercer said. 'Somebody needs to bring these guys in Rome into the modern world.'

'Men in dresses. That's who's in charge,' Mike said. 'Men in dresses with more gold rings than even Coop's got. Ought to be a signal right there. You want to make my mother crazy? Some days I tell her I think I was the only altar boy in town who wasn't abused. I must have been homely as sin. Just ask her about that.'

'This is interesting,' Nan said. 'There's

actually a formal organization with its own website. Roman Catholic Womenpriests. They claim that more than one hundred women have been given ordination ceremonies as priests or bishops or deacons.'

'There were women deacons till the ninth century, in case you girls didn't know. St. Lydia, St. Phoebe, St. Tabitha.'

'It's like celibacy, isn't it?' Mercer asked. 'I don't believe priests were always celibate, were they? There were sure a bunch of popes who didn't get that part right.'

'The first Lateran council required celibacy,' Mike said. 'In 1123. It's a discipline in the church, based on the way that Christ lived his life.'

'I've got quite a learning curve ahead,' I said. 'I can spend the weekend doing an immersion course in religion.'

'About time.'

'What else do we know about Ursula Hewitt?' I asked.

'While Scully was dressing you down in the hallway,' Mercer said, 'we were getting the rest of the facts, few as they are. Her uncle said she'd been staying with friends the last six months. All he had was her cell. He'll get us the names and addresses by tomorrow.'

'Involved with any particular parish?'

'Certainly not officially. But still connected to the church, still hoping she and her sisters could effect change.' Mercer was reading from notes. 'Deep and abiding faith. Believed that priests should look like the people they serve.'

'Can we talk to some of these other women?' I asked Nan.

'The site says that the movement started in Germany in 2002. The first women ordained were called the Danube Seven. The ceremony took place on a boat in the river. And it lists the names of all the women priests, including the seventy-five Americans.'

'So we split up those calls, starting tomorrow.'

'Hewitt was teaching too,' Mercer said. 'According to her uncle. But he doesn't know where.'

'Excommunication means she couldn't teach in any Roman Catholic church or school. Even silencing her would have done that much,' Mike said.

The house phone rang and the doorman announced the food delivery.

'I'm up,' Mercer said, opening his wallet and going to the door. 'Last thing I got was that she was working some other kind of job.'

'What?'

'He didn't know.'

Nan was searching again. 'There are an awful lot of Hewitts coming up.'

'Keep going. Ursula's certainly not a common name.'

'All the hits are articles connected to her ordination and excommunication. The *Boston Globe* and the *Irish Echo*. Then a lot of women's press outlets. I'm not getting much else.'

'Try this,' Mike said. 'Plug her in again and add Naomi Gersh. Maybe their lives intersected at some point.'

'Peterson's right, Mike,' Nan said as she typed. 'You are totally outside the box today.'

She paused to grab the plate that I passed her with a slice of pepperoni pizza. 'You're going to faint if you don't eat something.'

'A few things popping up on Gersh.' She had one hand on the keyboard and one held a slice of the pie. 'Some articles on the protests with Naomi's name. Then a Norman Gersh in real estate, a Norton Gersh hedge fund. Gersh and Hewitt — got it!'

'Pizza and cloth napkins? Too rich for my blood.' Mike was halfway through his first slice, circling the table to look over Nan's shoulder. 'What is it?'

'A short piece in a newsletter called *On-and-Off-Broadway*. January of this year. I'm skimming the article as quickly as I can.'

'Faster. And out loud.' ' . . . in a limited run of the controversial play entitled *Double-Crossed*, which was staged last month at the Chelsea Square Workshop, to coincide with the holiest time in the church calendar. The controversial piece about the Vatican's attempts to punish American nuns for their social activism was staged by the feminist theologian Ursula Hewitt.''

'There's her day job,' Mercer said. 'Directing an edgy play about the church.'

'What social activism?' I asked. 'They're after nuns now?'

'Talks about the playwright. 'She was inspired to create the piece when Rome launched its investigation into the feminist work

236

of communities of American nuns several years ago. In Washington State, for example, three groups were targeted. They include the Tacoma Dominicans, which consists of thirty women — average age, seventy — who have begun to shelter victims of human trafficking. Their untraditional ministries, such as social justice work, is viewed as inappropriate by the Vatican hierarchy. Even their refusal to wear robes is considered a form of rebellion.''

'A seventy-year-old nun who's willing to step out of her robe?' Mike said. 'Give her a medal. If I could get my mother out of her housecoat once in a while, I'd say a few novenas.'

'What does it mention about Naomi Gersh?' I asked.

'Nothing.'

'But that's her in the photograph,' Mike said. 'The image is grainy, but it sure looks like Naomi, doesn't it?'

'Here's the caption. 'Director Ursula Hewitt, greeting several members of the audience — including an ordained minister and a nun — and Jewish activist Naomi Gersh.''

'Nothing more in the article?'

'No.'

'Does the Chelsea Square Workshop mean anything to you?' I asked Mike as he flipped through his notepad.

'Yeah. That's where Naomi's brother was working this winter.'

'So Daniel Gersh,' Mercer said, 'is the common denominator between our two victims. I'd call that fact into the PC's office right now.

Somebody better ramp up the effort to find him.'

We had set midnight as a time to quit.

Nan and I would work from our offices in the morning, trying to contact some of Ursula Hewitt's colleagues and waiting for her uncle to give us the information needed to retrace her last steps. Nan would try to press Bellevue to speed up their record search. Mercer would tackle the Daniel Gersh piece of the case, going to the theater itself and expecting that the DCPI would have blasted the young man's photo and information to the media. Mike was heading back to the Jewish Theological Seminary to try to talk to other students about Naomi Gersh.

'What time should we talk?' Mercer asked.

'Why don't we check in with each other at nine? In case anything breaks overnight,' I said. 'Then again at noon.'

'I hate to leave you with all this mess,' Nan said, carrying some of the glasses to the sink.

'Nothing to it.' I lifted the lids of the pizza boxes. 'Mike was good for five slices. There's not much garbage to deal with.'

'How are you going to handle Pat McKinney?' she asked. 'What if Scully calls him?'

'Scully's one of those boss-to-boss-only guys. If Rose tells him Battaglia's out of town, and I sit there chained to my desk like an obedient dog, he'll think I've seen the light and wait till Monday to confirm with the district attorney. Is Mercer driving you home?'

'Yes.'

Nan lived in Brooklyn, and it wasn't far out of his way to drop her as he headed for Queens.

'Give my love to the prince,' I said, our nickname for Nan's adorable, smart, long-on-patience husband. 'And a kiss to the kids.'

'Will do. C'mon, guys,' Nan said. She had packed up her laptop and folders. 'See you tomorrow, Alex.'

I closed the door and went inside to shut off the lights. Nan had stacked the napkins in a pile for my housekeeper to launder.

The last thing I wanted to wake up to was the smell of pizza crust and tomato sauce. I took the garbage with me and shuffled down the hallway, through the swinging door at the end, to throw the empty wine bottle in the recycling bin and the flat cardboard boxes in the incinerator.

I came out of the service area to return to my apartment.

The only thing between me and my front door, twenty-five feet away, was a tall stranger with his hands in the pockets of his black overcoat and a vicious expression on his face.

27

'What do you want?' I hoped the feeling of panic that seized my chest didn't show as obviously on my face. 'Who are you?'

I thought of making a break for the stairwell, but I didn't know if the man had a weapon in his hand or not.

'Keep your voice down, Ms. Cooper,' he said calmly. 'My name is Vincenzo Borracelli.'

'You are so far off base, Mr. Borracelli.' I clasped my hands together to stop them from trembling. 'Get out of here right now or I'll call the police.'

'They've just left, Ms. Cooper, haven't they? I've had to wait way too long as it is to get answers from you.' His accent was heavier than his wife's. I kept telling myself that he had nothing to gain by becoming physically violent, but it was shocking to me that he had found a way to impose on my personal space in the middle of the night.

I raised my voice and shouted at him. 'Get out!'

If I couldn't rouse my good friend David Mitchell in the adjacent apartment, then perhaps I could get Prozac, his gentle Rottweiler, to start barking.

'Your voice, Ms. Cooper,' Borracelli said, holding a finger to his lips. 'You gave my daughter your cell phone number, in case she wanted to contact you. That was a lovely courtesy. Uncharacteristic of you, as it turned out, but lovely.'

He withdrew his hands from his pockets, and they were empty.

'May we step inside for a few minutes? That's all I need of you.'

'You must think I'm insane. Say what you want, right here. Then go.' It was no surprise that a well-dressed businessman had gotten through the concierge desk where our doormen stood. There was a steady flow of traffic in the large building, and I was certain Borracelli had used his charm to convince one of them he was attending a cocktail party or dinner.

'Do you know who I am?'

'Gina's father.'

He laughed, and I sensed the same arrogance that Laura had when he left his message earlier that afternoon. 'That, of course, Ms. Cooper. I mean, do you know — '

'How important you are? Is that what you're trying to tell me, by trapping me here in a hallway tonight? Do you think I give a damn about whatever it is that you think entitles you to threaten and harass me?'

'Have I threatened you, young lady? That's nonsense. You were rude not to return my phone call.'

'I had a bad day at the office, Mr. Borracelli. Two women are dead and — '

'And that's reason to abuse my child?'

I took two steps back toward the swinging door in the service area. There was an elevator inside that was for the maintenance crew, although it was the slowest-moving piece of machinery in the world. I didn't speak.

'I'm the CEO of a major international telecommunications company, Ms. Cooper. Once I had your phone number, it was easy for me to get the rest of your personal information.'

'Everybody seems to know how to find me. A house call really wasn't necessary, Mr. Borracelli. I'll be at my desk all day tomorrow. Now, press the down button by those two elevators or I'll scream.'

'I don't imagine you as a screamer. Just listen to me. Two minutes.'

I continued backing up, closer to the service area, and just a few steps away from David Mitchell's door.

'Gina is my baby. She's a very, very sensitive child. I know she has issues.'

'Issues' was one of those dreadful weasel words that didn't begin to articulate what Borracelli referred to. Binge drinking, substance abuse, sexual promiscuity, and the ability to look someone in a position of authority straight in the eye while lying. Gina had more issues than her box of bad things could begin to contain.

'She's trying to act like one of the big girls. You'd better rethink the whole 'baby' idea.' The law still protected Gina, but she had chosen to start playing with fire.

'There was an urgency to my phone call, Ms. Cooper. Anyone who works for me and didn't return a call by day's end wouldn't have a job.'

'I apologize.' Days like this, I'd be willing to

give up my job too.

'Gina has been talking to my wife about hurting herself. She's distraught about having to face this boy at school. She said she has pills. She has razor blades,' he said, his anxiety apparent for the first time in this confrontation. 'She says that she'd rather kill herself than face the embarrassment of seeing Javier at school.'

'That's quite serious, Mr. Borracelli. I can get her a counseling appointment first thing in the morning.'

'And until then, Ms. Cooper? If she hurts herself tonight, it will be all your fault.'

I closed my eyes and took a breath. It wasn't the kid's doing that her father was a horse's ass. 'What is it you expect of me right now?'

So far today I was responsible for everything from the next Holy Wars to a teen suicide.

'I promised my Gina I wouldn't come home until you telephoned. Until you apologized for your mishandling of the case, to keep her from hurting herself — with pills, or with something sharp. Gina has tried to cut herself before this. My wife is with her now, keeping watch. They're waiting up for your call.'

This wasn't the moment for me to stand on principle and defend my actions if a kid's life was hanging in the balance.

'And for your promise that in the morning, you'll speak with the headmaster and insist that Javier be expelled.'

Vincenzo Borracelli took a step in my direction and I recoiled.

'It's just the phone I'm handing you, since you

243

won't let me come inside. No need to back away. Just press on it and it will dial Gina's number.'

I took the handheld from him and waited while it connected. It went directly to voice mail. 'Gina? It's Alexandra Cooper, from the DA's Office. I'm here with your father. We're concerned about you, of course. I'd like to apologize for anything I said or did to make you unhappy. We can put this entire event behind you and get you on a safer path. I'd like you to meet one of the counselors we work with. Let's talk tomorrow.'

I flipped the phone shut and handed it back to Borracelli.

'You didn't say anything about the boy, Ms. Cooper. Something has to be done about the boy.'

Vincenzo Borracelli took another step forward and I reached for David Mitchell's doorbell, pushing against it repeatedly. I had awakened a large, sleeping dog that began to bark fiercely and scratch at the door with his front paws.

'David!' I screamed for my friend and Vincenzo Borracelli turned to the two elevators and pressed the button between them.

I could hear David shouting the command to his dog to get down, opening up just as the out-of-bounds Borracelli disappeared behind the sliding elevator door.

28

'Alex — my God, you look frantic. Come on in. Is everything all right?'

'I know that 'I'm sorry' is woefully inadequate at this hour of the night,' I said, explaining the bizarre situation to my neighbor and good friend, who had a thriving practice as a psychiatrist. 'Go back to sleep. I'd just love to borrow Prozac for the night.'

'You want to talk?' David asked, belting his bathrobe around his waist.

'Not right now, thanks. I'm fine. It's been a tough week and I need a good night's rest,' I said, bending down to stroke the smooth back of the gentle dog for whom I frequently babysat. 'A cold nose beside me and the security blanket of her loud bark, just in case that prick tries to come back, will lull me to sleep. I'll walk her in the morning before I return her.'

'No need. I'll pick her up at seven,' David said. He often took the dog with him to his office.

I was truly ready to crawl into bed and put my head on the pillow. Prozac curled herself into a ball beside me and I was sound asleep before I relived even half of the day's events.

I was showered and dressed by six forty-five, and brewed a pot of coffee. David came in and I gave him a summary of what was going on over slightly well-done English muffins and a strong

Colombian roast. His insights into the psychopathic personality were often useful to me.

'I'll stay in touch. Let me think about the pathology here, Alex. I'm sure I can find you some things to read over the weekend. Take care, will you?'

I checked myself out in the bedroom's full-length mirror. I felt better than I had in two days, and dressed for comfort in a navy-blue double-breasted jacket and jeans, for dress-down Friday. The cashmere turtleneck I wore beneath, for warmth, matched the pale lavender pinstripes in the dark fabric.

My BlackBerry was beginning to load up with the usual morning spam. I refilled my mug and answered the handful of personal messages.

I was almost ready to leave for the office when my landline rang at exactly eight a.m.

'Alex? It's Justin Feldman.'

'Do I have you to blame for last night?' The prominent litigator was one of the most distinguished lawyers and political advisers in the city. He headed a successful white-collar defense team in a large corporate firm, so rarely crossed professional paths with my sordid category of crimes. 'I should have figured Borracelli to be in your client bank.'

'Did you wake up on the wrong side of the bed this morning?' Justin asked, making light of the situation with his throaty laugh. 'What's a Borracelli?'

I took my tone down a notch. 'Vincenzo Borracelli. He's not yours?'

'Should he be? What am I missing?'

'Never mind, Justin. A family member of a witness got out of line last night. I'm not sure how he got the information to find me at home.'

'Not my usual approach Alex. I'm trying to give you a hand, actually. Don't bite it.'

'A hand with what?' Feldman had advised presidents, senators, and high-profile clients of every variety. He was well respected for his wisdom and legal acumen, and there were often cadres of young lawyers in the federal court-house studying his storied cross-examinations when he was on trial with a high-stakes case.

'The late Ursula Hewitt.'

My loud sigh must have been audible.

'I thought as much. I took the liberty of calling because I wanted to get you before you were on your way downtown.'

'Are you in this, Justin?'

'No. But I've got someone who wants to talk to you about her, Alex. Someone in a bit of a delicate situation.'

'Delicate situation' was often a euphemism for guilty. 'I'm not making any deals.'

'I wish I could walk your perp in the door, but that's not what I mean.'

'Who is it?'

'She's a minister. An ordained minister.'

Another country heard from, as my grandmother loved to say. We had Baptists, Jews, Catholics. Now a Protestant in the mix.

'I thought most Protestants were good with that,' I said. My mother had been raised as an Episcopalian until her conversion to Judaism when she married my father.

247

'I think many of them are. Do you have time to meet with her today? I'm sure it will be worth your while.'

'If she can afford your fees, I guess I'll have to meet with her.'

'Glad you still have your sense of humor. We've taken her on pro bono. I think you'll really like each other. She's one of the smartest people I know.'

I grabbed a pad to take down the information. 'Who is this woman?'

'Her name is Faith Grant.'

'You're kidding me. Faith?'

'Her father was a minister too. She came by it naturally.'

'Can she meet me at the office?'

'Would you mind very much going to see her?'

'Where?'

'The seminary. Union Theological Seminary.'

I didn't want to tell Feldman we had just been to its Jewish counterpart as part of this investigation. 'I don't know it.'

'Uptown on Broadway. The entrance is at 121st Street.'

Harlem again. Just north of the Columbia campus, and one block away from JTS, where Mike would be arriving just about now. I could ask him to meet me for this conversation.

'Mind telling me what's so delicate about Faith's situation?'

'She's a graduate of Yale Divinity School and taught there for fifteen years. Now she's in contention to be president of Union — you know it's more than 175 years old — which is an

248

enormously prestigious post.'

'And probably never held by a woman,' I said.

'Exactly. I'd just like to shelter her a bit from the controversy of the two homicides, so we don't spoil her chance of an appointment. She may have something to offer you in terms of a lead — she apparently knew this new victim — or she may just want to do what she thinks is the right thing. May I tell her to expect your call?'

'I'll grab a cab and be to her in half an hour, Justin. Will that do?' This way we could see what Faith had and I'd still be at my desk by midmorning.

'I'm forever in your debt, Alex. And still holding a partnership for you when you're ready.'

'To come over to the dark side with you? Do I at least get a corner office?'

'I'll think on that. I should have known you'd want prime real estate. Thanks very much for doing this.'

My files were neatly ordered in a large tote bag. I threw on an all-weather jacket and waited until I was out on the sidewalk, hailing a taxi, to call Mike.

'Good morning. How'd you sleep?' he asked.

'Pretty well. And you?'

'Loaded for bear.'

'Where are you?'

'About two blocks south of the seminary.'

'I'm taking you on a slight detour,' I said, explaining Feldman's call.

I caught up with Mike in front of Union

twenty minutes later. The entrance was in the middle of the block, a stone's throw from the Jewish seminary.

We entered and were met by security. We had already decided to show our driver's licenses instead of our law enforcement IDs in case Faith Grant hadn't told anyone in administration we were coming.

'Mr. and Mrs. Chapman,' Mike announced to the sleepy-eyed guard. 'She's expecting us.'

'My maiden name is Cooper,' I said. I didn't mind Mike's humor, but the minister was expecting me, not the Chapmans. 'Alexandra Cooper.'

As I announced myself, a petite young woman, a bit younger than me, walked briskly through the lobby. She was a striking strawberry blonde, with shoulder-length hair and a dazzling smile.

'Ms. Cooper?' she said, stopping next to me at the security desk when she heard me say my name.

'Yes. Are you Faith?'

'No, no. I'm her sister. I'm Chat. But I just left Faith's office and I know she's expecting you. She's on her way down.'

Chat beamed one of her smiles at Mike and held out her hand. 'Chat Grant. And you are? . . .'

'Mike Chapman. Good to meet you.'

'Likewise.' Then, speaking to the security guard, she said, 'I'll take them through, Henry. Faith's just a minute or two behind me.'

Mike wouldn't say 'homicide' to a pretty blonde if he didn't have to. He was ready to go

250

wherever Chat Grant led him.

'This place is like a medieval labyrinth,' she said. 'Chapels and libraries and cubbyholes of all kinds. You can really get lost without a guide.'

'I'm all for guides,' Mike said. 'You a minister too?'

Chat's head tipped back as she laughed. 'Faith and I look an awful lot alike, but that's where the resemblance ends.'

She led us through the double-glass doors into the middle of a quad. If JTS most resembled a European's idea of a New England college, then Union Theological Seminary looked like a prototypical cloistered campus lifted out of Oxford or Cambridge and deposited across the ocean on Broadway.

'What do you do?'

'I'm looking for work.'

'Well, what line?' Mike asked.

It was another gray March morning, but the one or two streaks of sun that broke through the dense clouds found their way to Chat Grant and highlighted her hair like a Botticelli Venus.

'Are you just nosy, or do you run a search firm?' Chat said, good-naturedly. 'Where I come from, folks don't ask all these questions to people they don't know. It's not polite.'

'Don't mind him, Chat. He's just nosy. It's meant to be a compliment that he's interested in what you do.'

Students were already crisscrossing the walkways, probably on their way to their first classes. She looked at Mike again. 'Well, I certainly don't mind compliments. They're hard to come by on this island.'

One of the quad doors opened and there was no doubt the woman walking through it was Faith Grant. She was older than Chat and a few inches taller, with the same features and coloring. The hair was a dead giveaway, too, though the minister kept hers shorter and held back, today, by wire-rimmed reading glasses.

'This is my sister,' Chat said as Faith approached and extended her hand.

'Hello. I'm Alex Cooper. I hope you don't mind that I've brought along a detective.'

'Not at all,' she said. 'I'm Faith Grant.'

'Mike Chapman.'

'So you're professionally nosy,' Chat said. 'You're a cop?'

'Yeah. But I'm still interested in what you do.'

'Why don't we find somewhere quiet to talk?' Faith asked. 'You're welcome to stay, Chat.'

'You know I don't want to,' Chat said. The smile disappeared, replaced by an intense expression, as if some unpleasant thought had reappeared to trouble her. 'You know I've got things to do.'

'Ms. Cooper's a good friend of that lawyer who's been so helpful to us here at Union. You might want to talk to her someday.'

Now Chat fixed her attention on me. If I wasn't part of a career search, that comment probably meant the younger sister had a problem in her past that had not been resolved. That was a typical introduction to so many of the women I met.

I tried to restore her more cheerful aspect. 'Happy to talk to you anytime.'

Chat smiled and thanked me. 'I've really got to go. Nice to meet you both. See you later, Faith.'

'Dinner?'

'Yes. I'll be home for dinner.'

Faith blew her a kiss and Chat laughed at her sister as they waved good-bye. The sun caught her again as she moved in the opposite direction, luminous and delicate, like a free spirit without any of the responsibility of the scholars who scurried to class around her.

'Sorry to delay you.'

'Not a problem,' I said. 'Do you have an office here?'

'Yes, but there are too many eyes and ears around it, not all of them well-wishers. Then I'd have to explain to everyone who you are.'

'Where to?'

'This is a good hour of the day to find a quiet spot. Come with me, please.'

Faith walked several paces ahead of us, and when she reached the far side of the quad, she asked us to give her a few minutes to poke around. 'There's a small prayer chapel off that entryway.' She pointed as she spoke. 'If it's empty, we might talk in there.'

She went inside and I took myself around the quad — another of the city's hidden sanctuaries — admiring the gardens that were, like the rest of us, waiting for spring, and the benches placed throughout the maze of pathways so perfect for contemplative reveries.

Faith emerged from the building and descended the steps, closer to Mike. 'Why don't you come with me? This will work fine.'

As Mike walked toward her, there was a sharp noise like a crack of thunder directly overhead. The three of us looked skyward as a large carved figure broke loose from its base on the chapel tower and toppled over, hurtling toward Faith Grant.

Mike yelled her name and tackled her by the knees, taking her down on a muddy patch of lawn.

The statue crashed against the concrete sidewalk next to the spot where Faith had been standing, its saintly head split from its long, thin body.

29

'Matthew, no doubt,' Faith said as Mike pulled her to her feet.

'What do you mean?'

'See those spires on top of the tower? Each represents the writers of one of the Gospels. Mark, John, Luke. This one must be Matthew,' she said, nervously trying to defuse the tension of the frightening near miss. 'He'd be the first to tumble at the idea of a woman running this place.'

I'm sure Mike made that connection to the stained-glass window of Matthew and the winged figure in the old Fordham church even faster than I did. 'Good to know.'

Staff and students spilled out of every doorway and came running to see if Faith was all right. Someone had summoned the janitor, who tried to push all the bystanders out of the way and see what the property damage was.

Mike was scanning the rooftop from where we stood to check whether anyone was there. 'If you're okay, I'm going to take a run up to see what happened.'

'No, no. Please don't. It's just one of the problems we're having with the infrastructure. We're old, Mike, and we're literally crumbling. That's part of the trouble with this place.'

Faith kept glancing over our shoulders, as though looking for someone in particular. 'Why don't the two of you go inside? Just use that entrance behind me before the crowd breaks up. I'll join you as soon as I explain things to the dean of faculty.'

I took Faith's direction and didn't look back until I pulled open the heavy door. A man with a severe mien and pinched expression had approached her, causing the remaining students to take their leave. Mike followed me through the doorway, then charged up the flight of stairs that appeared to lead to the tower that dominated the rest of the interior campus.

The small chapel was off to my right. I let myself into the dark, cool chamber, silent as a tomb. The faint smell of incense hung over the room, and I walked around, studying the painted icons that hung on the walls.

Faith arrived before Mike. 'Lovely, aren't they? The priest's wife made them. We use this for our Greek Orthodox services.'

'Greek Orthodox, at Union?'

'Yes, we've got a lot of diversity among our students and in our programs.'

She was shivering, and saw that I was watching her try to still the movement of her hands. 'Why don't we sit?'

'Are you sure you're all right, Faith?'

'I will be. It's not the falling statuary that scares me, Alex. There are faculty members — and trustees — who don't want me to take the next step here. I'm not usually high-strung, but the politics, the backstabbing that seems to be going on, has unnerved me. Where's Mike?'

'I don't know. He probably — '

256

'I hope he's not wasting his time on the roof,' she said, now wringing her hands. 'That will only make them more unhappy.'

'Who are 'they,' Faith? Tell me about all this.' I sat on a long wooden bench against the wall, and she sat opposite me, at the end of one of the pews. I wanted to get a sense of the dynamic we'd just witnessed and then move on to discuss the more urgent questions I had about Ursula Hewitt.

'Some of the people in administration — not all of them — but there are some who don't want to see me promoted. Did Justin tell you that I'm in line to be president?'

'Yes, he did. Is it fair to assume that the man who just came to assist you in the courtyard isn't one of your supporters?'

'Mrs. Danvers?' Faith laughed. 'That's what I call him. Do you know who that is?'

'Yes,' I said, smiling back at her. 'The brilliantly drawn housekeeper in Daphne du Maurier's *Rebecca*. I've got my own Mrs. Danvers at the job. I'll have to remember that image.'

I relished the thought of Patrick McKinney cross-dressing like the severe Danvers, a gray wig pulled back into a tight bun.

'I get a lot of 'You just stay in your office and think great thoughts, Faith. I'll take care of everything else.' Meanwhile, the physical plant is falling apart and my allies have to wonder if I'll be up to reestablishing control of the substantive issues here, not to mention raising the money we need for upkeep and programming. He's the bane of my existence.'

'What's his name?'

'I don't want to take you in that direction, Alex. He wasn't up in the tower, pushing poor Matthew over the edge. He's not going to hurt me, physically.'

I wouldn't pressure her on the man's name till she got comfortable with me.

'Justin said that you wanted to talk with me, Faith. To talk about Ursula Hewitt.'

'I was horrified, of course, to hear about her murder last night. It's so unspeakably sad — so tragic.'

'How did you learn about it?'

'Ursula had been staying with me from time to time.'

'Here, on campus?'

'No. I'm in faculty housing, around the corner. Her uncle phoned late in the evening, to see if she was still with us.'

'Are you married?'

'I'm divorced.'

'Who's the 'us'?'

'Oh, I've got two sisters. They both live in Kansas, where I grew up, but Chat has been here visiting, trying to decide about whether or not to move east,' Faith said as she shuffled her feet and re-crossed her legs. 'I had to ask Ursula to find another place so Chat could be with me.'

'She's living with you right now? Is she also part of a religious community?' I asked, even though Chat had suggested otherwise to Mike.

'No. My father had a plan for each of us, I

258

guess you'd say. It worked for two of us. My older sister is named Serenity, and the baby is Chastity. That's why we call her Chat.' Faith loosened up as she talked. 'It was pretty tough growing up as the minister's daughters in a small town with that label.'

'I'll bet.'

'We're not much alike in temperament. There's a strong physical resemblance — people mistake her for me all the time around school. But she's sort of the black sheep, not that my parents would label anyone like that. It's how the world sees her, I think. Still finding her way after experimenting with some unconventional choices. That's why I'm trying to look out for her.'

'How unconventional?' I asked.

'Nothing that would stand out here, but Manhattan, Kansas, is a different place than this island. Chat was a chronic runaway as a teen, did the tattoo thing, tested my mother's great good nature all the time. No one in the family even knows that she was abused by a neighbor, back when she was fifteen. We got her through the runaway phase. Now she's just a free spirit, and I'm trying to keep her under my wing.'

'Nice of you. If I can ever help talk her through that period, my door is always open,' I said. Now I understood why Faith had made that suggestion to Chat.

'We might take you up on that.'

'What can you tell me about Ursula?'

Faith Grant removed the glasses from her

head and placed them in the pocket of her shirt. 'In a way, I feel responsible for what happened to her, for her death.'

'Why? What do you know about it?'

'Not anything at all, except what's in this morning's newspapers. It's just that the fact that she was murdered likely has something to do with her role in the church. And I encouraged her to come teach at Union after the Vatican silenced her.' Faith was soft-spoken but direct. 'I'm one of the people who urged her to carry on with the work that she so loved.'

The door opened and Mike came in, giving me a quick shake of his head to indicate he had come up empty.

'Did you go to the top of the tower?' Faith asked. 'Did anyone see you?'

She was more interested in whether Mike had been noticed by her superiors than whether he had encountered a criminal.

'No.' He sat beside me on the bench while I continued to ask questions.

'Back to Ursula Hewitt,' I said. 'How long have you known her?'

'I met her about a year and a half ago, not long after she had been excommunicated. I had the idea that she might be in need of a place to teach.'

'Why not a Catholic institution?' I asked.

'That's the whole point of silencing, Coop,' Mike said, leaning forward to engage Faith Grant and me. 'No can do. That message is from the top, from the Magisterium.'

I looked at Faith for confirmation.

'He's right. A very formal letter comes from Rome. The Magisterium is the teaching office of the Vatican, and according to their rules, the task of interpreting the Word of God is entrusted solely to that body — the pope and his bishops. Ursula was forbidden to teach in her own church.'

'But allowed to do so here?'

Faith smiled. 'Well, according to our vision, she is. We've done this before, Alex. We've had a silenced Jesuit theologian here, taken him in and made him a scholar-in-residence.'

'Did you face any opposition to inviting Ursula?'

She stopped to think. 'Not really.'

'What did she teach?' I asked.

'Feminist theology, of course,' Faith answered without hesitation. 'The history of women in the church fascinated her.'

'Before those who became priests, had women been silenced?'

'Certainly. There are loads of examples. In modern times, they've had to do with obvious issues. In 1979, a nun — a Sister of Mercy on the Yale faculty — signed a document along with twelve others supporting abortion, supporting a woman's right to control her body. She was told by Rome that if she didn't recant, she'd be excommunicated.'

'Was she?'

'Sister Margaret agreed not to publish the document, but she wouldn't recant. So she was silenced. Many of the most progressive nuns have been punished by the church for speaking out on abortion or on homosexuality,' Faith said, shaking her head. 'And despite the wonderful work they do in the most underserved communities — and in these times when Rome is having a very hard go attracting young people to service, women or men — they're shunned.'

'And the formal position of the Vatican on silencing?' I asked. 'What's the reasoning?'

'The primary argument used to be — centuries ago — that it would prevent confusion among God's people caused by contentious issues. Roman and Spanish Inquisitions, the index of forbidden books, the outlawing of scientific thinking by geniuses like Galileo — you know all the historic examples. It might have been a means to quash dissension in those days, but now all the issues involved are commented on by the mainstream media on the nightly news.

'Let me ask you this,' Mike said. 'Ursula Hewitt knew that much of what she did was unpopular. Was she ever afraid?'

'She was fearless,' Faith said, biting her lip. 'Principled and smart and totally fearless. There was nothing about her I didn't admire and look up to.'

'Was she still teaching this week?'

'Only one course this semester. Sort of a new direction for her. She'd been involved in stage work with a community group. She'd been researching medieval dramatists.'

'Why's that?' Mike asked.

'Because they wove so many scenes of torture into their work.'

'Religious themes?'

'Indeed. Around the time of the Inquisition, stagecraft often depicted sadistic acts and intense suffering. Ursula had developed a fascination for what was called the Theater of Cruelty. It was common in the Middle Ages for dramatists to stage violent acts — like the Passion of Christ. They did it to make accounts in the scripture more believable, and by doing so, they hoped to inspire more religious faith in the audience.'

I was familiar with some of these works from my study of French literature. '*Il faut du sang*,' I whispered.

'You know it, Alex? That's exactly right. 'There must be blood.''

'Sounds pretty gruesome,' Mike said.

He was correct about that. And I knew that he realized, as I did, that for at least one evening in the theater, the lives — and perhaps the deaths — of Naomi Gersh and Ursula Hewitt were linked in that milieu.

'What interested her about it?' I asked.

'Everything. Ursula questioned everything. When the word came from Rome that barring women from the priesthood wasn't a human-rights issue, it was Ursula who stood up to the Magisterium. 'Is it because we don't have rights?' she asked. 'Or is it because we're not human?''

'That's pretty direct,' Mike said.

'Ursula referred to the church as a place of

hope — and a place of horror. 'What does it say about Christianity' — she used to challenge her students — 'what does it say that at the center of Christianity, of all its writings and beliefs, is torture? Torture, and the murder of a man?''

30

'What is it that you wanted to tell me?' I was leaning forward, trying to get Faith's eyes to meet mine.

'Mike just asked if Ursula expressed her fears,' Faith Grant said. Her voice dropped and her spirit seemed to flag. 'As I said, she didn't have any that I know of, but I do.'

'So do I, Faith. Want to tell us about yours?'

She took her glasses out of her pockets and played with them while she talked. 'I'm afraid that Ursula's murder had something to do with the fact that she was here, that I convinced her to come to Union.'

'Why would that put her in harm's way?'

'There are things I said to her, ways that I prodded her that probably put her a bit more 'out there' than she needed to be.'

'Doesn't seem like she needed any prodding,' Mike said. 'Are you worried for your own safety?'

Faith Grant had tears in her eyes. 'I hope that's not what has my gut in an uproar. It's much more self-centered than I like to think I am.'

'Why?'

'Has anyone threatened you?' I asked, pausing for an answer but getting none. 'Have you been harassed or stalked?'

'Threatened, yes. And harassed. Neither of those are new to me.'

'But this week? These last two days?'

'Matthew aside,' Mike said, trying to play to Faith's good humor.

She finally looked at me. 'I don't know. I had an unusual encounter last night.'

'What was that?' Mike asked.

'Maybe nothing, but I can't shake it. Could just be because it happened right before Ursula's uncle called.'

'That's all right,' I said. 'Mike thinks I see ghosts everywhere. Sometimes I actually have.'

'And I talk to spirits,' Faith said, her dimples reappearing as she braved a smile. 'No visions yet, but we'd be quite the pair. Anyway, I left here to go home to make dinner for Chat and me, so roughly around seven. It's not a very long walk. I sort of just square the campus and it puts me onto Claremont.'

'Was Chat with you?'

'Oh, no. I was alone. At least, I thought so, until I got to 122nd Street. A man started following me from the corner of Broadway.'

'What made you aware of him? Did you hear footsteps?'

'I didn't hear anything. That's part of what was so strange. I just had that sixth sense that someone was too close to me. Do you know what I mean?'

'I get that all the time,' I said before Mike could interrupt with his personal view. He preferred hard, cold facts to women's intuition. 'It's the kind of instinct that has saved a lot of potential victims.'

'I kept walking west but I glanced over my

shoulder,' Faith said, looking at the floor again. 'No one was there. So I sped up a bit, and I fished my cell phone out of my briefcase. This time I'm sure I heard him speak.'

'Actual words?'

'One word only. A name. I thought he said 'Ursula.' That made my head snap around — not because I thought anything was wrong with her, but because I thought maybe she was coming by to surprise me. She'd often drop in if she was around the school. I thought maybe this man saw her, called out to her.'

'And when you looked?' I asked.

'Unless my eyes were playing tricks with me, I saw a fleeting glimpse of a figure — a man, not Ursula — but then he darted into a recessed doorway on the side of one of our buildings.'

'Did you note anything about him?' Mike asked.

'You'll think I'm stupid, but he was so fast, and he moved so gracefully, I couldn't make out anything about him. It would have been like trying to catch a shadow and hold it still.'

'Nothing stupid about you. Not your fault,' I said. 'What next?'

'I actually stood my ground. I stopped and called Ursula's name myself. But there was no one else around. No one answered. So I kept on walking, under the scaffolding now.'

'What scaffolding?' Mike asked. 'What's with all these churches and their scaffolding?'

'Our spirit may be strong, Detective,' Faith said, smiling again. 'But our bones are weary. There's always something to be repaired here.

267

We're a very old institution. This piece of it runs along the northwest corner of the campus, ending right opposite the entrance to my building.'

Mike's wheels were turning. His right hand went to his hair and began to comb through it. He was wondering where and how the scaffolding connected to the roof from which the statue just fell, and I was remembering Lieutenant Peterson's remark that the structures around the never-finished St. John the Divine offered shelter to all the wrong people.

'What next, Faith?'

'I couldn't see any light in my apartment when I turned the corner onto Claremont. I speed-dialed the number, hoping that Chat would be there and open the window, make contact with me in some way. But no such luck. I broke into a run, and I swear I heard Ursula's name again. Closer this time, almost above me.'

'Okay. Go on.' I didn't want Mike belittling this experience, which had obviously shaken Faith deeply.

'I looked back again.'

'Did you hear anything, any noise from the scaffolding?' Mike said.

'That's what's so creepy. Nothing like that at all. And yet when I ran across the street with my keys in my hand, the man that I thought I had seen the first time was ahead of me. He'd somehow crossed the street and was coming at me. Directly at me.'

'How could that be?' I asked. 'How could he have gotten past you, if he ran into the street?'

'That's sort of why I worried about telling anyone. It sounds incredible.'

'Look, the figure you saw behind you the first time, you told us you hadn't even noticed anything about him then,' Mike said. He stood up now, pacing back and forth, trying to make Faith articulate facts from which he could work. 'What do you mean it was the same man?'

'Well — I — uh, I couldn't describe features or recognize him from a photograph, Detective,' she said, becoming more flustered as he pressed her. 'But it was his shape, his silhouette that was identical.'

I nodded my understanding and now Faith looked to me. 'Yes,' I said.

'You understand what I mean, Alex? There was something distinctive about his movement. It was almost — well, almost fluid.'

I was thinking of the man who had entered the courtroom to watch some of Bishop Deegan's testimony. When I enlisted Pat McKinney to look at him, he had disappeared, as if by magic. And when I saw him again — as I was certain that I had — he had glided down the aisle and out the door of St. John the Divine, as gracefully as Faith described.

'Did you see his face?' I asked, hoping that angry red blisters might have been visible under the streetlights, if he was the man I thought.

'Barely. I think he was white-skinned. And no eyebrows. There was something weird about his look. Almost — well, phantasmagorical.'

Mike rolled his eyes. He probably thought Faith was being a bit too dramatic.

'Hair?' I asked, hoping for the long ponytail that I had noticed.

'Dark. Just dark. Which is why it was so weird that I couldn't see eyebrows.'

'Long or short?'

'I only saw him from the front. I don't know.'

'Anything else about his skin?'

'No. I was just drawn to his eyes, because it was such a bizarre contrast with the dark hair.'

The man in the courtroom two days ago had been wearing sunglasses. I had no idea whether he had eyebrows or not.

'Do you know how he was dressed?'

'A winter coat, I guess.'

'I don't want you to guess, Faith,' I said. 'Just give us what you remember.'

'Outerwear of some sort. A long jacket or coat.'

The last thing I wanted to do was put words in her mouth. I knew Mike would kill me for suggesting it but I couldn't help myself. 'By any chance, was he wearing a clerical collar?'

Mike threw his hands up in the air in mock despair of my methodology. I was grateful to have such an honest witness who was not willing to be led.

'I'm not sure I would have noticed that, Alex. Riverside Church is my back door. Between that and the seminary, I see collars on everyone most of the day. Stay long enough and I'll think both of you have them too.'

'Of course,' I said, disappointed in her answer. Maybe I was trying to push pieces of the puzzle into shapes they didn't fit. How could someone so brutal and ferocious be at the same time so graceful and fluid?

'I was about to punch 911 into my cell phone, sort of panicked that the man was headed straight at me. I don't know whether he was put off because he caught me fidgeting with the cell or that he saw one of my neighbors coming out of the building, but he just brushed past me and kept going, as swiftly and quietly as he had come up from behind. By the time it occurred to me that I should have snapped a photo of him, he was gone.'

'Did he say anything to you?'

'I don't want you to think I'm crazy or anything, but he was right in front of me this time. It was so faint that I couldn't be sure he was saying 'Ursula' again, because that's what I had already heard earlier. Or maybe the noise he made was — was, um — just a hissing sound.'

Faith knew she sounded confused, so she took a few moments to clear her throat, and her mind. 'Of course, after I got inside and Mr. Hewitt called, everything began to sound like Ursula.'

Faith Grant dropped her head and clasped her hands, as though she was praying.

'And that's all you heard?' I was silently repeating Ursula's name, comparing the sound to a hiss.

'He picked his head up right as he passed me, for just a second. The only other word he said was 'sorry.''

31

'What would be involved in having you move in to a room here in the dormitory, in this quad?' I asked Faith.

'That's the last thing I'd want to do, Alex. I don't need the front office to know about this.'

'What if I gave you a choice of having Mike Chapman handcuffed to you for the weekend, or bunking in the dorms?' I said, reaching out to put my hand over hers.

'I'm partial to ministers with dimples,' Mike said. 'I might let you out of the cuffs, but I'd hang pretty close to you.'

'There must be some guest rooms, Faith.'

'Yes, we use them for visiting scholars. I really don't want to do this.'

'Give us the weekend,' Mike said. 'There's nothing I like better than a brave broad who wants to tough things out. But we need you to be safe till we sort through this.'

'Do you think the man I saw last night was the killer?'

Mike hesitated. I guessed that to be because he wasn't even sure that Faith knew who or what she remembered correctly. She seemed flightier to him than she did to me.

I spoke to assuage her fears. 'We're not sure what we're dealing with yet, Faith. There have been two vicious slayings in the city — maybe more somewhere else. And both victims here, just twenty-four hours apart, were strong women, outspoken about religious issues. We'd rather know you had some kind of security system in place.'

'Just tell them the heat in your place isn't working right.'

'That's not a stretch,' she said, flashing an impish grin at Mike. 'You sure I can't choose the handcuffed option?'

'I'm expensive to feed,' he said.

'And to water. You'll be replacing the red wine with Absolut or Ketel One. Not to mention how he'll try to rewrite your sermons,' I said. 'I'll tell you what would help a lot, Faith, is to understand this place, to see how you fit and what you do. If you think you're a target for this guy, we'd like to know who else might be in danger.'

'I'd be casting a wide net, Alex. We're such a liberal arm of the church — the most progressive, viewed as the most left-wing.'

'Has that always been true of Union?'

'For a pretty long time. Think of this country's earliest institutions of higher education — Harvard, Yale, Princeton,' Faith said. 'They were all founded as divinity schools. The only reason for a man to be educated at that time was to become a minister.'

'So this seminary was part of a bigger school?'

'We started as a mission school in the early 1800s. Part of Princeton University, which was the most powerful of the group for religious training. But the radical leaders grew to believe that you couldn't do God's work on a cloistered campus. The whole point of the ministry was to be in the cities, working with orphans and paupers, immigrants and prostitutes. Princeton was too isolated. So we split from the university, on the theory that cities are the best classrooms for knowing God, knowing Jesus.'

'And Union Seminary was that breakaway institution?'

'Yes, as a Protestant seminary, in the Reformed tradition. At first in Greenwich Village, moving up here in 1908, as the city spread north,' Faith said. 'We needed to be where the heathens are, Alex, as they were called in those days. Still, it's a primal impulse in our ministry to deal with social injustice in our work — to go to the margins.'

'Exactly what some of the Roman Catholics have been silenced for doing,' Mike said.

'Let's say we're more welcoming. We've got three hundred undergraduate students here, half of whom are women.'

'Is that a new thing?' I asked, trying to gauge the exposure of Faith and her colleagues.

'Not at all. It's been that way for a couple of decades. A quarter of the group is African American, a fifth is Latino. And we've got a large LGBT community.'

'I hadn't thought of the Lesbian Gay Bisexual Transgender presence as a big part of the professional church community.'

'Many institutions aren't quite as embracing as we are. So we train a lot of these students, even though many don't get placed in jobs.'

'What do they do then?'

'Some of our best graduates are running secular organizations, nonprofits, mostly. Just another way of working on the side of the angels.'

'And women in the Protestant Church?' I asked. 'How have they been received?'

'Pretty well, in America. They've even had an ordained woman bishop heading the Episcopal Church here. At one point I thought they were going to completely divide over the role of women. Then that moment passed, and all the turmoil has been about the acceptance of gays in the hierarchy. One thing you can count on is that any church that is anti-gay is also anti-feminist. Basic rule of thumb.'

'That doesn't surprise me in the least,' I said.

'One of my good friends is a Lutheran pastor from South Dakota. Openly gay. The Evangelical Lutheran Church in America — the ELCA — is the largest Protestant church in the country to let noncelibate gay ministers serve in the clergy, something that has caused wrenching dissension in many denominations. In her home church, her fellow Lutherans treated her sexuality as a demon that had to be exorcised. So we'll take our victories as they come.'

'And you, Faith? Would you tell us about your beliefs?' I asked.

'I'm a Calvinist.'

'How'd you come by that?' Mike asked.

'Three generations of dirt-poor Kansans. Some were Lutherans, Dutch originally, from Pennsylvania. There's a little bit of Cherokee in me that came on the Trail of Tears. The rest is a healthy mix of sharecroppers and horse thieves. The Grants were a rough bunch, but they were always religious. And how they hated the elitism of some of the Protestant sects.'

'It's hard for me to imagine the way religion took hold on the frontier.'

'It was the only thing that held poor folk together, Mike. It was the idea that God loved them. You could accept the love of God and become a new person — a Christian. You weren't just a product of your history and your culture — or should I say your lack of culture.'

'There were great divisions in the Protestant Church, too, weren't there?' I asked.

'Certainly so. Around the turn of the last century, the Protestants divided,' Faith said, animated now, talking with her hands. 'That split was between the head and the heart. The mainline church — the Eastern elite — that was all about the head. If you wanted to adore God, in their view, you built universities and you educated people.

'But it was the evangelicals that ran off with their hearts,' she said, tapping her chest with her hand. 'Calvin and Wesley, Edward and White-field. They created churches instead of schools. These were men devastated by witnessing slavery, and by walking among the impoverished and the ill. Heart and hope — people with little else to cling to could have that. And the great irony? Union broke free from Princeton because our founders were all about the heart. But we managed to keep the head too. We do both very well.'

'So who are your enemies, Faith?' Mike asked.

'I never thought I had any, really. This hasn't been a hard road for me, Detective. Many people don't understand my choices, but I've never been as 'out there,' say, as Ursula was.'

'The other woman who was killed, Naomi Gersh,' I said, 'did you ever meet her?'

'No. Where do you think I would have?'

'She took a class at Jewish Theological.'

'Good neighbors, they are. But I didn't know her.'

'The play that Ursula directed — *Double-Crossed* — did you go to see that?'

'I didn't. It was performed over the Christmas holidays. I'd gone home to see family for ten days,' Faith said. 'Chat went with some of my friends to see one of the performances and told me about it.'

'Chat knew Ursula too?' I asked.

'Not well, but they met a few times. Why?'

'When you told us that Ursula had to move out of your apartment because Chat moved in, I made the wrong assumption. I didn't figure they overlapped. My own mistake. In fact, I would have urged Chat to stay so we could have asked her about Ursula.'

'She obviously didn't want to be here — I think you saw that. She didn't know Ursula nearly as well as I did. I'll tell her you want to talk.'

'Thanks. It's just better if you don't discuss it with her,' Mike said. 'Better if we handle that.'

'I understand.'

'So Chat didn't travel with you for the holidays?'

'It's hard for her to go home. It's — well, that's neither here nor there. Even she told me the play was over-the-top.'

'What do you mean?'

'Very graphic. Like we talked about earlier.'

'What people — what groups — do you think would be most outraged about someone like Ursula Hewitt?' Mike asked.

'She got it from all sides,' Faith said, shaking her head from side to side and biting her lip again. 'The actions that made her beloved to so many feminists were offensive to scores of her coreligionists.'

'How about someone with no religious attachment at all?' Mike said. 'Maybe it's my own head, but as someone who goes to church — maybe not as often as I should — it's impossible to imagine a believer capable of this kind of violence.'

Faith Grant looked away from Mike. 'The second largest group of people in the world, if you want to look at it that way, are the religious unaffiliated. Say they're lapsed, or uncontained if you will, or even searching for an institutional form to hold them.'

'Okay. I get it.'

'I don't view them as dangerous at all. They're in twelve-step programs or yoga camps or ashrams. They don't worry me in the slightest,' she said with a laugh.

'So who does worry you?'

Faith hesitated, as though she didn't want to

278

speak ill of anyone else. 'The fastest-growing religious group in the world today is Pentecostal.'

'I didn't know that,' I said.

'Many, mind you, have been accepted by Rome and by Protestant sects as part of the flock. It's a serious movement, and encompasses a wide variety of believers. The poor and the disenfranchised really gravitate to it.'

'I imagine so, if it's that fast-growing.'

'But there's a whole sect of Pentecostal churches that are completely outside the constraints of the dominant culture,' Faith said. 'They've overtaken the evangelicals.'

'Aren't both about expressing the passions of the heart?' Mike asked.

'Well, yes. But evangelicals believe in regulating those passions. Not a lot of talking in tongues where I come from.'

'Can you point us to any specific organizations?' Mike was hoping to get direction from Faith Grant.

'I'd be looking at some of the extreme ministries that have sprung up.'

'Extreme?'

'Yes. You know that a lot of nondenominational churches — evangelicals in particular — have used popular culture to reach new followers. Rock music, skateboarding — including pop things like that has been going on for years.'

'So what do the extreme groups do?'

Faith paused before answering. 'There are a lot of ministers who think that the church has become too feminized. I don't mean just because of women in the clergy. They think, in this new movement, that we've gotten too far away from Christ, emphasizing compassion and kindness rather than strength and responsibility.'

'So what's their solution?' I asked.

'Fighting. Using mixed martial arts as part of the church service.'

'You got to be pulling my leg,' Mike said.

'I wish I were. They believe that using violence — or sport, I guess they'd call it — explains how Christ fought for what he believed in.'

'You know where these extreme ministries are? You'll give us names?'

'I can work on that today. They're pretty much springing up everywhere.'

'Have you had any personal experience with anyone in particular that you think marks you in one of these fringe groups?' I asked.

'Oh, no. Not that at all. But when I look for — I don't know — someone capable of this kind of violent behavior, I'm not thinking he comes out of any church that I know.'

Mike lowered his voice. 'Then you haven't seen what I've seen, Faith: every one of the deadly sins committed by the righteous and the religious, sometimes before the preacher even gets to say the last amen.'

32

Mike and I walked Faith back to her apartment and waited while she packed a small suitcase with clothes, toiletries, and books to get through the weekend in the dormitory. She had arranged through the secretary of the soon-to-be-retired president to stay in one of the guest suites for the weekend. No one questioned the problems with the aged heating system that she complained of in her apartment.

'Are you sure we aren't putting you into the reach of someone here who could be dangerous?' I asked as we entered the lobby and passed into the center courtyard.

'I'll be very safe,' Faith said.

The small quad looked like most other campuses at eleven a.m. A few students were throwing Frisbees around while others tossed a football. The music that came from classroom windows was the sound of a gospel choir at practice, and the kids who greeted Faith on the path were a mix of earnest and upbeat.

'How about your nemesis?' I asked. 'The guy you didn't look too happy to see when the statue nearly got you. Won't you tell me his name?'

She looked up at me and smiled. 'Would you mind if I turn the other proverbial cheek, Alex? He spends weekends in Connecticut, and the only serious backstabbing he does is with a very sharp tongue.'

We exchanged phone numbers and e-mails so that we could stay in communication. 'You'll call us if anything happens?' I asked. 'No matter how insignificant it seems to you.'

'Of course I will. I'll have Chat here with me too. That's why I told them I needed a suite. As soon as she comes back today, I'll have her join me. Might be a bit more church than she's used to on an average weekend, but she's fiercely loyal to me.'

'That's excellent. We'll talk later.'

We let ourselves out and walked across Broadway toward Mike's car. 'Wasn't that woman pastor in Kentucky murdered in a Pentecostal church?'

'Yeah, but can you imagine how many of them there are all over the country?' I said. 'I wouldn't go leaping to any conclusions from that. Are you still going to JTS to canvass?'

He checked his text messages. 'Peterson's got two guys on site now. Why don't we work out of your office, with Mercer and Nan.'

'I won't tell Scully if you don't,' I said, getting into the passenger seat. I held my forefinger against my mouth to ask Mike to be quiet. 'I've got a call to make.'

I dialed Information to get a listing for New Amsterdam Prep. 'Connect me,' I said to the operator, then asked to be passed along to the headmaster. 'Good morning. My name is Alexandra Cooper. I'm an assistant district attorney in Manhattan. I'm calling about two — '

'I was expecting your call, Ms. Cooper. Mr.

Borracelli said you'd be phoning.'

If Paul Battaglia and Keith Scully were cutting back my duties, it looked like Borracelli had my day's work lined up for me.

'Is Gina at school today?'

'Yes, she's in class now.'

'And Javier Valdiz?'

'No. No, we suspended him when he showed up this morning. He'll be expelled once you confirm that he violated the school's honor code.'

'Violated what?' I asked.

'The New Amsterdam Prep code.'

'Mr. Borracelli is gravely mistaken, sir. My jurisdiction is strictly the penal code. I'm not calling on behalf of Gina's father. I'm calling because I conducted a criminal investigation which involved two of your students and several others as witnesses.

'I want you to know that Mr. Valdiz, in fact, didn't commit any crime. He's not going to be prosecuted, and I would suggest — before I advise his lawyer to take legal action — that you reinstate him as quickly as possible.'

The man on the other end of the phone sucked in air. 'May I have your callback number, Ms. Cooper?'

'Because you want to talk to Mr. Borracelli before you hear me out? He'll be happy to give it to you.' And my home address, too, no doubt.

'He told me that Gina wanted to withdraw charges. That she's too fragile, emotionally, to go through with a prosecution.'

'I'll say it again. Javier Valdiz did not commit a

283

crime. There was no rape. Gina admitted that to me, after all the evidence was evaluated.'

'But . . . but surely statutory rape? She's underage, Ms. Cooper.'

'So is he. A man has to be over twenty-one to be prosecuted for having sex with a minor.'

'Tell him it's called Hooking Up in the First Degree when two consenting teens hit the mattresses,' Mike said. 'I'll have his whole upper school in lockdown by the end of the day.'

The headmaster was mulling over what I told him, clearly surprised by the news. When he spoke, it was about the school honor code. 'It's still a violation for Javier to be drinking alcoholic beverages.'

'Even though it was Gina who served them to him, and had a lot more than he did? I think my count was seven intoxicated New Amsterdam students at the party. You'll toss them all? Or does the code only apply to the scholarship students who don't have a pitbull parent fighting for them?'

'I'll have to discuss this with my staff. And with Mr. Borracelli, of course. We're not about to expel seven students, Ms. Cooper.'

Not at thirty thousand a year, I wouldn't think. 'My more important immediate concern is Gina's mental health. She has threatened to hurt herself if Javier isn't thrown out. I'd suggest you have her parents and maybe a counselor present when you complete your findings and inform her of them.'

'Aren't you going to do that?'

'I've done my job, sir. I have no role in the rest

of your internal decisions. I'm just making sure you're aware that Gina has expressed suicidal thoughts to her family, whether true or not, and I think you need to pay attention to that as you go forward.'

'Take a line out of Borracelli's book,' Mike said, poking me in the ribs with one hand as he guided the steering wheel with the other. 'Doesn't this joker know who you are? Tell him who you are and be done with it.'

I covered the phone. 'Who am I, Detective? This guy knows exactly who I am in Borracelli-speak. Nobody. I'm absolutely nobody and now I'm dropping a monster headache in his lap to boot.'

'Were you talking to me? It was muffled,' the headmaster said. 'I couldn't hear you.'

'No, sir. I'm driving into a dead cell zone. I think we're done.'

'You may be finished with me, Ms. Cooper. But I don't think you've heard the last from Vincenzo Borracelli.'

33

Nan Toth had set up our team in a conference room in her building, which was directly across the street from the main office on Hogan Place. At one point, the courthouse held the entire district attorney's staff, but thirty years ago we'd annexed an adjacent government building as we more than doubled in size to close to six hundred lawyers.

I was on the phone with my secretary while Mike searched for a parking space. 'Laura doesn't even want me to show my face on the eighth-floor corridor. She's given Pat McKinney the impression that I've taken the day off, like I'm taking the commissioner's advice seriously. She's sending Maxine over with all my papers on the case.'

'Excellent.' He backed into a no-parking zone and tossed his laminated police plate in the windshield. 'So Nan's your shill today.'

'She's the ideal cover to take the lead. Battaglia thinks she walks on water.'

'Perfect talent for this case.'

We made our way into the 80 Centre Street offices, which were so antiquated that the elevators still required operators to ferry the hundreds of lawyers and support staff up and down all day.

The tired machine groaned its way to the fourth floor, and I led Mike through the maze of

286

security checkpoints and cubicles the size of rabbit warrens — homes to the rookie prosecutors — to the small conference room that serviced the Cold Case Unit and the Child Abuse team.

Nan and Mercer had established themselves at corners of the long table. My supersmart and good-natured paralegal, Max, was just unloading stacks of my Redwelds, already overstuffed with police reports and paperwork related to the two murders.

'Anything else you need?' she asked.

Mike and I staked out territory opposite each other. 'Don't you dare leave,' I said to Max. 'We're going to suck that powerful brain of yours dry today. Grab a seat.'

She was obviously pleased to be part of the team, and I valued the fresh pair of non-law enforcement eyes to reexamine all the facts that we had.

'Make yourself useful, Max,' Mike said. 'You take dictation?'

'No, but — '

'I'll talk slow. Turkey and Swiss hero. Lettuce, tomato, and mayo. Plenty of onion. Two Cokes. Big bag of chips. Get everybody's order and have lunch here at one sharp.'

'I can handle that.'

She wrote down his order and passed the pad around so we could add our choices while he talked.

'Let's all get on the same page.' Mike spent the next ten minutes summarizing the minister's interview for the others. 'Faith's going to try to track down some of the women who knew Ursula best, who may have been with her last week. And get more info on these extreme ministries.'

'Faith sounds so interesting,' Nan said.

'Yeah,' Mike said. 'I think I'm in love.'

'That would be a full-time ministry for the good woman,' I said. 'You were making a good play for Chastity.'

'A bit more of a challenge there, I'd have to say. I like the idea of a sister act,' Mike stroked his chin and pretended to be giving the choice between the women a serious thought. 'Have you given Max copies of those scraps of paper that Daniel Gersh tried to flush down the toilet?'

'I got them from Laura last night.' Max reached for one of my folders and extracted a much thicker stack than I recalled assembling. 'I've put together a few hundred words and phrases, just pushing around the letters. I can refine the search once I hear more about what you know. Maybe certain words will make sense.'

'What else is new?' Mike asked, looking to Mercer. 'What have you got to say for yourself, my man?'

'I stopped at the Chelsea Square Workshop on my way in this morning,' Mercer said, flipping open his notepad. 'Lucky to find anyone there at all. Nothing running at the moment, so the house was dark, as they seem to say in the theater.'

'Who'd you talk to?'

'Guy says he's the stage manager. He doesn't have anything to do with the business end of the

288

shows, but he hires the crews to work them.'

'Daniel Gersh?'

'Yes.'

'Does he know where that weasel is?' Mike asked.

Mercer shook his head. 'Just like Gersh told you, he got to town in the late fall. He worked a couple of shows in November and December. *Double-Crossed* was one of them. He was still around in January, but they've only had two stagings since then, and Daniel Gersh wasn't involved in either of them.'

'He must have information on Gersh,' I said. 'Where he lives and how to reach him, no?'

'Unfortunately for us, it's not a union operation. The place is like a funky, oversized coffee shop. The stage is just a raised platform with a homemade curtain. Doesn't look ready for prime-time.'

'Latte and lowbrow drama,' Mike said. 'How'd Gersh get to him?'

'They advertise in all those supermarket giveaways. Don't pay scale and don't really care who signs up to work. When they haven't got a live play, they show classic cinema. This guy runs the projector and his wife makes the brew.'

'What does he remember about Daniel Gersh?' Nan asked.

'Precious little. He's the cranky sort. He didn't like anything to do with Ursula Hewitt's play — not the subject, not the script, not the shots at the church. So he kind of shut down to everyone around him.'

'How about the team who worked the show with Gersh?'

'Two regulars — he gave me names and numbers — and another drifter.'

'Did he describe the drifter?' I asked.

'Nothing distinctive. You know the type. You could ask him to describe his wife of thirty-two years and he'd probably say 'nothing distinctive.''

'He'd probably be right,' Mike said. 'Was there a Christmas party? I think maybe that's what Daniel was talking to us about. A party after the performance Naomi attended.'

Mercer held a printout of the story that Nan had pulled up on the computer the night before, about the play. 'I showed him this. He remembered that night because — you're right — there was a celebration of sorts after the show.'

'That's a start. Did he recognize anyone in the picture, besides Ursula Hewitt?'

'No. But it reminded him there was a man in the audience that night who got really angry during the performance.'

We all sat up at attention.

'How angry?' Nan asked.

'Angry enough to stay for the party so that he could have it out with Ursula Hewitt. A loud argument that Gersh and the other hands had to break up. He thinks Gersh took him outside to cool him down, maybe even left with him. My witness says the guy was about as angry as the thick red blisters on his cheeks.'

290

34

'Is there a credit on that photograph?' I asked.

'I printed out a copy for each of you,' Max said. 'No credit listed.'

'Whoever took this picture must have other snaps from that night. Call the newspaper, pronto.'

She nodded at me and walked to the corner of the room with her cell in hand.

'Was he wearing a clerical collar?' I asked Mercer.

'The stage manager couldn't recall another thing about him except sunglasses, even though it was indoors, at nighttime.'

'If he really has no eyebrows, then maybe the frames of the glasses conceal that. Maybe it's why he wears them.'

'I want Daniel Gersh,' Mike said. 'I'll call Peterson and tell him to send somebody over to the offices of Local One.'

'What's Local One?' Nan asked.

'IATSE. International Alliance of Theatrical Stage Employees. The stagehand's union,' Mike stood up to speed-dial the lieutenant and started pacing. 'Someone will know if that scab is still working in this town.'

I took notes while Mike talked.

'Loo? We need a guy over at Local One. Yeah. It's on West Forty-Sixth off Tenth. See if the Gersh kid has signed up there. See if anyone can help us hunt him down.'

'But if he didn't join the union — ' I started to say.

'But if he did, Coop, they'll have him. They do scenery, sound, and light for every show in town, from Radio City to the Met, Broadway to network television.'

Mike and Mercer were meticulous about the need to run down every lead.

'You, Coop, you need to call the kid's stepfather.'

'I'm the last one he'll want to hear from — a sex crimes prosecutor. I'm sure Daniel has confronted him by now about the pictures of him in bed with Naomi.'

'Then call the mother, okay? Worm some information out of her. Tell her that her boy is likely to get hurt if she doesn't help us find him. What else?'

I fished through my notes to find the name of the suburban Illinois town to get to work on reaching Daniel Gersh's mother.

'I'm tracking the guy from Highway Patrol,' Nan said. 'Every precinct in the city turned out on the day shift with orders this morning to look for abandoned trucks as possible crime scenes. They're doing stops at the bridges and tunnels too. He'll check in on the hour.'

'Good.'

I was in another corner of the room, dialing Information for Lanny Bellin, Daniel's stepfather. The robot that helped me get the number offered to connect me at no extra charge.

'Hello? Hello, Mrs. Bellin? I'm calling about

your son, Daniel. My name is Alexandra Cooper, and I'm a lawyer — '

The line went dead.

'You got a machine?'

'No, I got distinctly hung up on.'

'Get the local cops to her house,' Mike said.

I dialed the area code again, asking for the nonemergency police number and explained our situation to the detective on duty. 'He doesn't know the family,' I said. 'But he has my number and they'll get someone to do it as fast as possible.'

Mike knew how close Mercer was to his minister, who had helped counsel him through a horrendous period after he had been shot by a deranged killer. 'Can you call your preacher man and see what he knows about these far-out Pentecostals — these extreme ministries that Faith told Coop and me about this morning?'

'On it.'

Nan was glued to her laptop. 'I don't know if this is anything, but I'm following up on Sergeant Chirico's body count.'

'Murders in other jurisdictions?' I asked.

'Yes. Pastors, priests, ministers. There are more of these than you'd think.'

'What have you got in the last six months, maybe a year?'

'Tennessee. A minister shot to death by his wife in the parsonage.'

'Not ours.'

'A nun strangled and raped in Baltimore.'

'Solved?' Mike asked.

'No, but appears to be in the course of a burglary.'

'Well, say a prayer for her, everybody. Doesn't sound like our boy.'

'Here's a love triangle in Texas,' Nan said. 'A pastor hired his own son to kill his wife — the killer's stepmother. The son's still on the loose.'

'Cause of death?' Mike asked. He was restless and itching to break through to a solution.

'She was drugged. Then suffocated with a pillow, to look like an accidental overdose.'

'I'll take the drugging part of it. Our vics must have been drugged to be moved to the killing ground. But accidental isn't his style.'

'Okay. This next one had me at the headline, but wrong gender. Skip it.'

'Read,' Mike said.

' "Community Grieves Slain Pastor.' It goes on to say that he was found inside the large church building — a converted warehouse — his throat slit — '

All of us stopped at those three words and gave our complete attention to Nan. She was cherry-picking phrases from the story. 'No known motive. No suspects. Parishioners being questioned.'

'What kind of church?' Mike was running fingers through his hair and barking questions.

'Pentecostal. Happened last November.'

'Any 'scrip of the kind of Pentecostal? Anything about extreme?'

'I'm reading as fast as I can, Mike. I don't see anything like that.'

'Where'd this go down?'

'The town is called Alpharetta.'

'It's right outside of Atlanta,' I said.

'Details?'

Nan was pulling the follow-up story. 'Beloved pastor. Eleven years at the church,' she said, taking a breath. 'Whoops. Some think the killing may be connected to the fact that he just came out to his congregation a month ago. He's gay. Wanted them to accept it, to welcome his longtime partner. Wanted to continue to serve. Split the community, to put it mildly.'

'There's your outcast,' I said. 'There's your pariah.'

'Does it say anything about how he was dressed?' Mike asked.

'Fully clothed. Except for his collar.'

Maybe the killer wanted a trophy from his victim, a collar of his own. Maybe he wore it to the courthouse to watch Bishop Deegan testify. Maybe he used it to approach his trusting victims, knowing the simple clerical vestment would disarm them.

'One of the worshippers speculates the killer must have wanted the poor man defrocked.'

'Silenced,' Mike said. 'Defrocked and silenced. That's his signature, all right.'

35

I studied the photograph taken at the Chelsea Square Workshop after a performance of Ursula Hewitt's controversial play.

'The newspaper doesn't have a credit for that, Alex. One of Hewitt's friends e-mailed it to her, and she forwarded the downloaded image to the editor herself,' Max said.

'Thanks.' I covered my ears with my hands to think, while Mike tried to light a fire under a small sheriff's office in Georgia to get police and autopsy reports, and someone who knew the case to talk us through it.

I scribbled a note to Faith Grant on the bottom of the page with the photograph. I had put her e-mail address in my BlackBerry earlier, so I wrote a note above the picture, and asked her to call me as soon as she received it.

'Hey, Max. Would you please scan this for me and get it out?'

'Sure.'

She was back in three minutes and placed the paper in front of me. While I waited for my phone to ring, I kept staring at the four women. There was Ursula Hewitt, basking in the congratulations of her acquaintances. Opposite was Naomi Gersh, who appeared to be engaged in conversation with the others. The photo was so blurred — maybe even taken by a cell phone, from a distance, that it was hard to make out the faces clearly.

Four smart, vibrant women celebrating together in December at a controversial play that would obviously have been offensive to many devout worshippers — and now two of them were dead, victims of torture and mutilation.

'This is Alex Cooper,' I said, answering my cell.

'Hi, Alex. It's Faith.'

'Thanks for the call. Is everything calm on your end?'

'Just fine, thanks. How can I help?'

'This photograph I forwarded you was taken at the workshop after one of the performances of *Double-Crossed*. I'm thinking that whoever took it might have more shots from that evening.'

'That's probably true.'

'One of the detectives visited the theater this morning. It's quite small, and since there was a party of some sort, there's a chance some other audience members could have been captured in the images.'

Faith Grant took a moment to follow my thinking. 'Why, Alex? Do you think the killer was among the guests?'

'We don't know. I'm not hiding anything from you, Faith. We're just trying to run it all down. The newspaper editor tells us one of Ursula's friends supplied the photo. You said you knew women who were there. Maybe it was the night Chat went to see it. That would help us to start tracking back for information.'

I wanted information from these two other women in the photograph. I also wanted to make

297

sure they were not also in the sights of our killer, that they were not currently in danger of being silenced.

'I see.'

'Of course you recognize Ursula.'

'Yes.'

'And the dark-haired woman on the far left is Naomi Gersh.'

'Okay.'

'The caption says one of the others is an ordained minister. By any chance — '

'Yes. I know who that is shaking hands with Ursula. Jeanine Portland, a graduate of this seminary. She's wonderful, and I'm sure she'll be helpful to you. I believe she's at a church in New England.'

'Can you get that contact information for us?'

'Of course. The front office will have it.'

'So that leaves the young woman next to Naomi.'

'I can help you there, too, but she's no nun. I'll swear to that on a Bible.' Faith Grant was laughing. 'That's my sister, Chastity.'

I held the paper right in front of me and examined the picture again. 'It doesn't look anything like her.'

'That was her goth period, Alex. Dyed her hair black and straightened it. Lucky for me it was her New Year's resolution to lose that look.'

My heart raced. I didn't want her to hear any concern in my voice. 'I need to talk to her, Faith. I need to talk to her as soon as I can.'

'I'll tell her that when she returns my call. I've left her a message explaining that I'd like her to

298

spend the weekend here with me in the dorms.'

'And she hasn't called back?'

'Don't sound so alarmed about it, Alex. It's only been a couple of hours. I told you that Chat's a free spirit.'

'So you haven't talked to her since she left the seminary this morning?'

'No. It's just been a few hours, Alex. There's nothing worrisome about that.'

'Do you know where she is or what she's doing that was so important she couldn't stay to talk about Ursula?'

'I don't keep her on a leash, Alex. And she isn't responsible for what happened to Ursula, even if I am.'

'But under these circumstances, Faith — I mean with Ursula's murder, and the fact that Chat spent time with her too — '

Faith Grant was calm and measured, perhaps even a bit annoyed with me. 'Do you do this to your friends, too, Alex?'

'Do what?'

'Manage to put the fear of God in them whenever a child gets lost or a man looks at them the wrong way?'

'I didn't intend to upset you.'

'I guess my calling, my professional training, is all about trust and belief and — well, faith. You don't trust anyone very much, do you?'

I didn't even have to close my eyes to recall the sight and the smell of Naomi Gersh's body on the portico of Mount Neboh Church, or the treacherous slit in Ursula Hewitt's throat as she lay in the ancient graveyard at Old St. Pat's.

'I apologize for that. You know Chat's habits and, of course, I don't.'

Two of the women in that snapshot with her are dead, is what I wanted to say. Two of them were outcasts and pariahs, one in her church, the other to her family. It was Faith who had described her sister to us as the black sheep of the Grant clan, who told us it was so difficult for her to go home that she hadn't made it back for Christmas, who alluded to a troubled past that might benefit from my counsel.

'I understand you'd like to have her help you figure out who was at the play that night. Is there anything else, for now, besides that and locating Jeanine Portland's congregation?'

'Thank you. That's all I need.'

'Then I'll call you later.'

It was prosecutorial cynicism that had my wheels spinning. 'Chastity Grant is the fourth woman in this photograph. Different hair and stuff, but it's Chat, all right.'

'What's your point?' Mike was standing over Max's shoulder, playing with the words and partial phrases she had cobbled together from Gersh's scraps of paper.

'Faith isn't bothered by that at all.'

'Why should she be?'

'Think about what she told us. That they're often mistaken for each other because they look so much alike.'

'Brilliant, Coop. What next?'

'I'm wondering about the guy who was following Faith to the apartment last night.'

'What of it?'

'That when he finally came at her face-to-face, like he was going to do something to her, he looked at her instead and the only thing he said to her was 'sorry.''

'The word means nothing out of context.'

'That's why I'm trying to frame it. Maybe he was sorry because he had mistaken her for Chat. Maybe he was after Faith's sister because of the contact they had at the playhouse in December. Maybe what's driving him — '

'Maybe if your aunt had balls, Coop, she'd be your uncle. Stop with the spooks and speculation.'

'I don't want a third corpse.'

'Nobody does. So far, no churches, no synagogues, no mosques heard from today. Let's concentrate on solving what's been done.'

'Anybody want to go to a service?' Mercer said, towering over us as he got to his feet.

'A prayer service?' Mike asked. 'I'm ready to get me some inspiration, Rev. Nothing else seems to be working. Where to?'

'Avenue C.'

'Alphabet City,' Mike said. 'Same 'hood as Naomi's apartment.'

'My minister's been doing his own research on these characters. Said if we want to know more about it, the closest operation to this office is in the back of a converted garage. Just look for the orange neon sign and the big cross.'

I stood up, anxious to do something more proactive than brainstorm in the conference room. 'I'm in. What's it called?'

'X-Treme Redeemer,' Mercer said. 'The church where fists and faith collide.'

301

36

'Hard punches! To the head! Again, to the head!'

The man's voice was yelling commands to someone farther back, out of sight, in the cavernous, dark space. An old garage had been split into a series of large open areas, the one through which we entered decorated like a primitive church.

'Work the head! Finish him now!' The shouts were loud and delivered with fierce direction, incongruous as the words were within a house of worship.

As my eyes adjusted to the dim light, I could see the makeshift altar and the white cloths draped over it. Brass stands held tall candlesticks, not lit now, on the floor at the end of a few dozen rows of benches without backs.

We followed the voices past the pews, through an open, undecorated area, winding up in a brightly lit corner of the garage where a handful of men who appeared to be in their twenties and thirties were noisily cheering on the two figures punching at each other on a raised platform that resembled a boxing ring.

'Punch again! Finish him!' The screamer was older than the others, dressed in a sports jacket and slacks, while the onlookers, like the pair in the ring — were in black T-shirts and gym pants, all heavily tattooed and well-muscled, with shaved heads and carefully shaped goatees.

No one noticed us until Mercer stepped up to the side of the group. All the spectators stared at him, then at Mike and me. I didn't know whether the hostility of their expressions was because we so obviously looked like law enforcement or because Mercer's ebony skin was so different from the complexions of the all-white onlookers.

'Whoa! Hold it right there,' the man in charge called out, wanly smiling at us while he ordered his subjects to stop throwing punches.

The obvious winner of the round didn't want to be halted. He continued to pummel the guy who was on his back on the platform floor.

Two of the men vaulted up into the ring to grab their friend. Before they could calm him, he slammed one knee down and placed his opponent in a choke hold.

'Did Jesus tap?' he shouted.

'Break it up, you hear me?' Mercer said, stepping in to stop the fighting.

'You tapping?' the fighter asked, throwing more punches when his opponent didn't give him an immediate answer. 'Jesus never did, did he?'

Mercer wrapped one of his enormous hands around the wrist of the guy who was on top and wrenched him back. He fell over onto his side, screaming up at Mercer, who was palming his gold detective shield for the group to see.

'What's this fuss?' the man in the sports jacket said. His Southern drawl was as thick as the blood running from the mouth of the injured

303

fighter, who was trying to roll over and catch his breath.

'Exactly what I'd like to know,' Mercer said. 'What was Jesus tapping?'

'That means giving up in our sport. Christ never gave up, don't you know? Now who might y'all be?'

'NYPD. Homicide,' Mike said. 'I'm Chapman. That's Wallace and Ms. Cooper. Never tapping either, till we get our man. You mind telling us who you are and what your sport is?'

'And why you're beating the holy crap out of each other in a church?' Mercer added, shaking his head as the bloodied fighter refused his hand, struggling to his feet unaided.

'I'm the Reverend Harold Kelner. This here's my church.'

'And your flock?' Mike asked. 'Is this one of the lost tribes, or they really think they're doing the Lord's work in a boxing ring?'

'Timothy 6:12. 'Fight the good fight of faith,'' Kelner said, motioning to us to step away from the men gathered around the platform.

I couldn't stop looking at the guy who was trying to steady himself and rise to his feet, blood dripping from his chin and holding his neck at an angle, as though the choke hold had made a permanent impression.

'Would you mind telling us something about your ministry?' Mercer asked.

'Why, sir? Has one of my worshippers done something illegal?'

'No reason to think so, Reverend. We're just trying to help some detectives in another state.

304

Trying to get an understanding of these extreme ministries. Found you in the phone book and thought you could give us some general answers. May I ask where you're from?'

'Came here about a year and a half ago from Nashville, Detective.'

That city wasn't directly in our path of homicidal destruction.

'To establish this church?'

'Exactly so, Mr. Wallace. And this academy.'

'What academy would that be?' Mike asked.

'You must be here because you've been told that some of our brethren in the evangelical movement have taken on mixed martial arts as a way of reaching out to young men.'

'Only men?' I asked.

'That's correct, ma'am. Surely you're aware that in churches across the country, the attendance numbers for young males — well, young white males; you'll excuse me, Mr. Wallace — is regrettably low. Dropping all the time. Go to our services on a Sunday and you won't have but a handful of men between the ages of eighteen and thirty-six. That's a sad fact. Pretty much all pastel and girly-like, so our programs are developed to be an outreach tool to the community.'

'How so?'

'Many men are led to find Christ when they come to understand that Jesus was a fighter. Do you know what mixed martial arts are?'

Kelner's voice was syrupy but he sneered at my ignorance. 'No, I'm afraid I don't. What we walked in on,' I said, 'just looked to be brutal and violent. Anything but spiritual and uplifting.'

'What you saw was a sport called cage assault. Highly popular, ma'am. Always draws a crowd, especially when you put on a show before the prayer service.'

'A blood sport, obviously.'

Mike could see I was offending Reverend Kelner. He slid behind me and pinched my forearm to urge me to keep quiet.

'So, mixed martial arts,' Mike said. 'Kickboxing, wrestling, full-contact karate — ultimate fighting, is that it? A little more machismo in your ministry.'

'Yes, sir, Detective.'

'I get you,' Mike said, although I knew him well enough to know he was stroking the reverend. 'The church is becoming too feminized for your folk.'

'Gentle shepherding is just fine,' Kelner said, 'but not at the price of strength. There are so very many young men who've grown up without fathers, without direction. They've struggled to find hope, and today's religious institutions don't really have a place for them. Our group tries to make Christianity more appealing. Fighting as a metaphor — like Christ fought — is very attractive to many fellows.'

'Joining faith to fighting,' Mike said.

'That helps us promote true Christian values. We've got almost seven hundred churches across the country.'

I was sickened to think of this as a religious movement. It seemed so antithetical to the teachings of every mainstream culture. I turned away from Kelner and watched one of the fighters mop the stained floor of the platform.

The loser had limped off to sit on the sidelines, against the wall of the old garage, still marked with faded red paint in the shape of a road sign that warned drivers to stop.

'So what were we watching?' Mike asked.

'One of our new recruits. He's going to fight tonight, in fact. I call him the Fury. That was some Muay Thai he was angling to do.'

'Asian.'

'The Art of Eight Limbs, as they call it in Thailand. American boxing involves two points of contact — just the fists.'

'Yeah,' Mike said.

'This lets you go at the other guy with eight points,' Kelner said, pleased with the telling. 'It allows punching, kicking, kneeing, elbowing.'

'And some Brazilian jujitsu thrown in, wasn't there?'

'You know your stuff, Mr. Chapman. Tell your girlfriend over there — she's seeming a bit squeamish — that's the only one likely to do more than bloody a boy's nose. That was the choke hold you saw.'

'Full-contact combat sport.'

I whispered to Mercer, 'Just ask him about the case — and a possible perp — and let's get out of this place. It's disgusting.'

'Oh, and some sambo,' Kelner said. He was pushing the envelope with me now, sensing my displeasure. 'You know sambo? That's one to kill with. You maybe came in too late to see the takedown.'

'What's sambo?'

'How's your Russki?'

'*Nyet*. Nonexistent.'

'A Russian acronym, Detective. Stands for self-defense without weapons — sambo, in their language.'

'Now I know what you're talking about. It was a top-secret Red Army technique to create a deadly kind of hand-to-hand combat after the Revolution, right?'

'Entirely. Didn't even make it to the US until recently. Focuses on getting your opponents to the ground, Detective, no matter how you do it. It's all about submission,' Kelner said, almost gloating at the way he had suckered Mike into his pitch. 'Now, is one of these martial arts how your mysterious killer works, Mr. NYPD Homicide Detective, or can I go back about the business of building God's army?'

'No sambo, Reverend. Don't even think there was kickboxing involved.'

The truth was we had no idea how Naomi and Ursula had become hostage to the maniacal killer. Neither body bore the bruising of the mixed-martial-arts takedown, and the toxicological tests were still days away from yielding clues.

'Then why y'all coming around my church, stirring up my men, Chapman? We've been scapegoated for just about everything in town, one place or 'nother.'

'You think this idea of yours is gonna fly in the big city, Rev?' Mike asked. 'I can point you to more fighting fools than could fill up your benches.'

'Bring 'em on, Mr. Chapman. I'll lead them to the Lord.'

'You know if there's an extreme ministry anywhere near Atlanta?'

'Quite a few on the outskirts.'

'How about eastern Kentucky?'

'You bet. Kentucky and West Virginia. We're growing like hayseed down South.'

Mike had printed out the photograph from Daniel Gersh's driver's license. 'Ever seen this guy?'

Kelner pretended to give it his best shot. 'Not one of ours.'

'How about a tall man, maybe long dark hair, his face kind of scarred with blemishes of some sort?'

Kelner thought about it but gave a firm no.

'Many other of these churches in town?'

'Not yet, Mr. Chapman. But we'll take hold. We have a way of doing that where we're most needed,' Kelner said. 'Meanwhile, you might try across the river. We're becoming real popular in south Jersey. And you might give some mind to being a bit more prayerful yourselves — all three of you.'

'Thanks for your help,' Mike said. 'Peace to you.'

Reverend Kelner just grinned and stood his ground, making sure we were on our way.

I wondered how much blood had been mopped from the floor of the church in the short time it had been in existence. It would be a forensic nightmare for Crime Scene to try to sort out the samples if someone was actually killed in the deep recesses of the old garage.

We were halfway down the center aisle of the jury-rigged church when my cell phone vibrated in my pocket. I retrieved and opened it. The woman on the other end was trying hard not to sound hysterical.

'Alex? It's Faith Grant.'

'Yes, Faith. What — '

'Chat called. She's in trouble.' I could hear now that she was crying. 'I wasted time ignoring your concerns and now she's in desperate trouble.'

'What do you know? We've got an entire police department ready to mobilize. What did she say?'

'It was impossible to understand her. The words were all slurred. Nothing made sense. She sounded like she'd been doing drugs.'

That would have been the first step in the killer's routine — more likely to have been administered involuntarily.

'Did you make out anything at all?'

'It was so hard, Alex. I tried to get her to keep talking, but either the cell went dead, or someone grabbed it away from her. She kept telling me she was cold.'

'Cold?'

'Yes, freezing. That's the clearest thing I could make out.'

'Did Chat say where she was?'

'Believe me, Alex. I asked all the questions I should have. First she said something about a truck. But then she said it was a train. Everything was muddled and confused.'

I was playing with the letters of the words that

310

Max had strung together from the Gersh papers. Train had been one of them. Truck was a longer shot. What would there be to connect the two?

'It will take us about twenty minutes to get up to you, Faith. Are you safe? Are you still at the seminary?'

'Yes. I've got two faculty friends with me. They know everything.'

'What number did Chat call on? Your office phone?'

'No, no. My cell.'

'Did she say who was with her? Did you ask her a name?'

'No names. She wasn't listening to me. She was just trying to talk. A bridge. Chat said something about a bridge. Then a truck and a train.'

'What bridge, Faith? Think.'

We were out of the church now, and I was jogging behind Mike and Mercer as we ran to the car. The island of Manhattan was linked to the rest of America by bridges and tunnels. Picking the right one would be crucial.

'She didn't say,' Faith said, trying to regain her composure. 'There's something about Chat I didn't tell you, Alex.'

This was real life. There was almost always something the most well-meaning witness decided not to tell me. In this case, the omission was probably to protect a loved one.

'I know she's a free spirit, Faith. Don't worry. If it's about drugs, it's not a problem. We'll find her.'

'It's not drugs, Alex. That was never one of Chat's problems.'

'She strikes me as gutsy. Chat had a little attitude going with Mike this morning. If she's got some fight in her,' I said, hoping to bluff some confidence into our operation, 'she'll hang on till we get her.'

'She's got fight in her all right,' Faith said. 'My sister left Kansas because she killed a man.'

37

'Murder'll make you a black sheep in any town,' Mike said, after we excused Faith's friends from her suite and closed the door to talk.

We had raced uptown with the siren blaring, Mercer and I fortifying ourselves for the long night ahead eating the sandwiches Max had ordered to the office before we left, while Mike drove.

'It wasn't murder,' Faith said. 'It was self-defense.'

It was my turn to get Mike to push back and let me talk. 'Will you tell me what happened?'

'I should have done that this morning. There I was, worried about myself, and all the time it was Chat who was in danger.'

'You can't go in reverse, Faith. Just tell us everything that might help to find her.'

We couldn't know whether Chat's abduction, if that's what this was, was connected to her past. But if the killer was targeting pariahs, then he might have found another victim to suit his appetite.

'I've counseled a lot of women who'd been abused as teens. I should have seen the signals in Chat's life, but I was too close to the situation.' Faith had dried her eyes and was trying to regain her composure.

While we talked, Mike had put the tech guys to work triangulating the cell activity from

Chastity Grant's phone. We had given them the number as we drove north to Union, and it wouldn't be long before they could pinpoint the general location — from the signals sent to the closest surrounding cell tower — from which the call had been made.

'It was two years ago, right before Chat turned thirty. She'd been dating a guy she'd known all her life.'

Mike had called the lieutenant on our drive up to Union to ask him to pull Chat's record — and photograph — from the state system in Kansas and the FBI crime reporting office.

'Did you know him too?'

'Yes.'

'What's his name?'

'He's dead, Alex. That hardly matters.'

I grimaced at her. I didn't want resistance to my questions at this point and now she seemed to get it.

'I'm sorry, Alex. Kenny Trimble. My dad called him Trouble. Kenny Trouble. It suited him just fine.'

Mike was texting the name to Peterson. The more info we could pull up, the faster we could move.

'What happened between them?'

'They'd been dating on and off since they were kids. I think Kenny was the first guy Chat got involved with.'

I needed to fast-forward from the high-school romance, but Faith had things she wanted to say.

'He was always way too controlling, even then. Jealous and possessive. I remember a time Chat

314

got a ride home from another boy and Kenny was jumping all over her. Still, when she ran away from home, odds were you could find her with Kenny. Off to Oklahoma for two weeks with him, my mother scared to death that we'd never see her again. Texas the next time. Like that over and over again.'

'Tell me about recently, Faith. Tell me what Kenny did.'

Kenny Trouble had fathered kids with two other women. He'd been in and out of jail for stealing and for assaulting the mothers of his boys. The pattern was as familiar to me as Mike Chapman's blazer and jeans.

'Chat started dating a man — a really nice man named Jonas — while Ken was in jail. He was put away for almost two years, so she had a good chance for some stability. We were all so proud of her because we thought she'd broken the cycle. Never visited him once in the penitentiary, wouldn't accept mail from him. First time ever that she got an order of protection for herself. Turns out it wasn't worth the paper it was written on.'

If I had a dollar for each time I'd heard that expression, I could find a cure for every disease on earth.

'The day Kenny was released from prison — the very same day — he came back to town. Spent the night at his favorite bar, 'cause neither of the women he'd been roughing up wanted him back. Someone told him about Chat.'

'Told him what?'

'That she was happy, I guess. That she was in a

healthy relationship for the first time in her life. Had a job,' Faith said, and couldn't help but smile. 'She was even going to church.'

'And then?'

'Kenny drove straight from the bar to the little house where Chat's boyfriend lived. At daybreak, when Jonas left for work, Kenny let himself in. It's the kind of town where nobody locks doors, if you folks can relate to that. Chat got out of the shower and he was waiting for her right there in the bedroom.'

'They struggled?'

'No,' Faith said with a frown. 'There was no struggle.'

I had violated my own strict rules, suggesting an answer rather than waiting for my witness's words. But I was anxious to get on with the search for Chat.

'She thought she could reason with Kenny. She was in somebody else's home, and she was mortified that she had brought Trouble — with a capital *T* — into it.'

'I understand.'

'So Chat calmly started to put her clothes on, trying to talk Kenny down as she did, telling him how well his kids were doing, how he could get himself a fresh start. But I think he knew better than believing he could get anybody in that town to stand behind him. That's when the fighting began.'

'What did Kenny do to her?'

'He had taken a butcher knife from the kitchen on his way into the house. After letting Chat exhaust herself trying to make him go away, he picked up the knife from the bureau and held it against her neck. That's when he made her undress.'

Faith stopped and took a sip of water from the glass on her desk.

'She refused at first, but then he pressed the knife against her. Not hard enough to leave any marks. There wasn't a bruise anywhere on her body, which is one of the reasons the cops didn't like her story at first. It's one of the reasons they arrested her.'

'It's good she wasn't physically injured.'

'I'm not sure the jury agreed with that.'

'Jurors never do, Faith. Makes their job easier to see black-and-blue marks, to count the number of stitches and feel the scars.'

'The first time he raped her, he only put the knife down on his pillow long enough to lower his pants. He held it against her neck the whole time he — he, uh — penetrated. Then he stopped for a while. Used a necktie to bind Chat to the headboard. Kenny got up from the bed, found her cell phone, and readied it to dial her boyfriend. He told her what to say.'

'What?'

'Kenny told her to call and tell Jonas to come right back home. That she was scared because someone had broken into the house and she could hear him downstairs.'

'And she did it?'

'Yes, Alex. With the point of the knife held tight against her breast, she made the call. Then Kenny got on top of her again, untied her hand. Asked her how long before her boyfriend could

317

get there from the factory. She told him eight, maybe ten minutes.

'That's when Kenny told her his plan. That he'd be making love to Chat — 'making love' is what he called it — when her boyfriend returned to the house. And when the guy came after him — or her — he'd stab both of them to death. No point either of them being happy when he couldn't be. He tortured her for those eight minutes, telling her how he was going to make her die, slowly and painfully, after watching him slice Jonas into little pieces.'

'So Chat knew she was walking her boyfriend right into a death trap,' I said.

'Yes, she did. And she also knew that once again, people in town would accuse her of being the bad girl, the one who was always looking for trouble.'

'Understood.'

'Chat could hear the door open, then Jonas pounding up the steps three at a time, calling out her name. Kenny rolled onto his side and gripped the knife tight in his hand, telling my sister to smile her best smile. That's when Chat reached down, under the bed.'

I could see the murder charge steamrolling down Interstate 70, headed straight for Chastity Grant.

'I'm not supposed to like this part of the story. It's not very Christian of me, but I don't mind telling you that it's all just fine,' Faith said. 'Chat's been on the receiving end of bad business for way too long.'

'We understand that.'

'Jonas kept a gun on the floor, in a box beneath the bed. Locked and loaded, like they say back home. Chat picked it up — she'd been around guns all her life — and the minute Kenny pressed the knife back into her side and started to rape her again, my sister fired the gun.'

'Where?'

'No chance for a miss, Alex. One shot, right against Kenny Trimble's ear.'

I was silent, steadying Faith's trembling hand with my own.

'And she got cuffed for that?' Mike asked.

'Arrested, indicted, and tried for murder. Even Jonas turned on her. He couldn't fathom why she hadn't resisted, and why she was willing to drag him into her old feud with Kenny.'

'Willing? Resist a man who's beaten you up before and now has at you with a butcher knife in your ribs?'

'People don't really understand the crime of rape, do they?'

'No,' I said. 'Most people don't get it at all. Especially when it comes to an estranged lover. If the same story happened with a stranger as the assailant, the whole town would have thrown a party for Chat.'

'Thank God — and I do mean that — the jury listened to her, believed her, and finally acquitted her of all the charges.'

Mike checked his cell. 'That's why Peterson's not coming up with any mug shots of her.'

'No, you won't find those arrest photos. I hired a good lawyer for her. The entire record's

319

been expunged. It's her only chance to start clean.'

'I hope she's still packing heat right now, Faith,' Mike said, trying to add some good cheer to a dark situation. 'Make my day if she gets our perp for us.'

'Then I'm sorry I've been such a good influence on Chat. All she packs now is a pocket-size copy of the Bible. Can that stop a madman?' Faith said, her spirits clearly flagging.

'You know better than I do. I'm sure you've saved your share of wretches like me — or worse. Just takes amazing Faith.'

'Grace,' she said softly as he drew a reluctant smile from her.

'My money's on Faith. You stay strong for us today, you hear me?'

Her eyes locked on Mike's handsome face, falsely reading in it a promise of some sort of hope from his fortitude and energy.

'I'll do anything you tell me to do. You just find Chat.'

'Have you got a recent photo?' I asked. 'Something more current than that newspaper picture with Ursula and Naomi that we can get out to the public?'

'Yes, of course. Right here on my computer,' she said, turning to her files to open a series of shots of Chat in the courtyard of the seminary. 'I just sent them to my mother last week.'

'May I forward those to headquarters?' Mercer asked.

'Please,' Faith said, moving aside so he could get to her desktop. She picked up a slip of paper next to the computer. 'And if it's any help, Alex, the dean gave me the contact information for Jeanine.'

'Jeanine?'

'Yes, Reverend Portland — the ordained minister who's also in the photo with Chat the night they went to Ursula's play. You asked me about her this morning.'

I reached for the slip of paper and was startled to see the 508 area code, which was the same as the code for my home on Martha's Vineyard. But the prefix for the phone number began with a two, not the six of all the Vineyard accounts.

'Is she at a church on Cape Cod?' I asked.

'Nantucket.'

'You'd better call, Coop. Let's make sure she's okay and see what she knows,' Mike said, jerking his thumb as a signal to Mercer to get moving.

Jeanine Portland needed to be warned — and perhaps assigned police protection — since she was the only one of the four women in the Christmas photograph as yet unharmed.

'Would it help if I come with you?' Faith asked, standing up with us.

'I need you to stay right here, no matter what temptation comes your way,' Mike said. 'You can help your sister by doing what you do best. Give it every prayer you got, Faith.'

'But you don't know where Chat is. It might be useful if I — '

'No offense, but I've got technology as reliable as you to lead me out of the wilderness,' Mike said, answering his vibrating cell phone. He turned his attention to the caller. 'Loo? They pull up a hot spot?'

Peterson was telling Mike the general location of the cell tower that had transmitted Chastity Grant's aborted phone call.

'We got the bridge, Coop. It's the George Washington. Chat made her call from a rail yard in Secaucus, New Jersey.'

38

I was belted into the backseat of Mike's car as he rocketed out of the parking space, up Broadway toward the entrance to the GW Bridge at 178th Street and Ft. Washington Avenue.

'Peterson's got the local cops ready to shut down the town. Get us backup from the State Police if we can figure out whether she's still in the area. What does our time look like, Mercer?'

'Give it twenty minutes from the bridge,' he said, checking his watch. 'Say Chat called two hours ago. No telling where she is now.'

'Why Secaucus?' I asked.

'Remind me to ask Chat after we find her, Coop.'

Mercer was thinking it through. 'If somebody is on the move with her, Secaucus is the perfect transportation hub. You're directly across the river from Manhattan. You've got the north-south stretch of the Jersey Turnpike, which is intersected by local highways up and down the entire line. And acres of rail yards.'

'Amtrak?' I asked.

'Freight. Not passengers. It's a major transfer station for truckers too. Our killer could be scatting in or out of there any which way. I wouldn't hold out a lot of hope that Chat's sitting in a terminal waiting for us.'

'I got a worse thought than that,' Mike said. 'Secaucus used to be the hands-down winner of

323

the most odorific stinking town in the US of A. Back before it became a destination shopping-outlet strip mall.'

The town had long been infamous for its foul smell, a stench so powerful that even as kids riding down the turnpike in the family car, we literally had to hold our noses for miles and miles along the drive.

'What causes the odor?' I asked. 'My father used to tell us it was sewage.'

'The doc was sparing your sensitive nature, kid. Didn't want to disconnect your olfactory nerve from your big brain.'

'Pig farms, wasn't it?' Mercer asked.

'That would have been the part of town closest to the Chanel counter at Bergdorf's. The rest of the distinctive Secaucus fragrance came mostly from rendering plants.'

'Rendering. You don't mean — animals?'

'Oh, yeah, Coop. Yes, I do. The process that converts waste animal tissue into useful materials — everything from lard to tallow.'

My fingers reflexively pinched my nostrils. We were high above the Hudson River on the upper deck of the bridge as Mike weaved in and out of the heavy flow of traffic heading to New Jersey.

'Butcher-shop trimmings, expired grocery-store meats, deadstock,' he went on, listing things I didn't want to envision. 'Blood, feathers, hair. What? You think the Mob used the old Meadowlands as a dumping ground for dead bodies 'cause they were Giants fans? A murder victim could get good and ripe before anyone in town suspected a stray whiff of death.'

324

'The girl was alive two hours ago,' Mercer said. 'Fingers crossed.'

'Be careful what you wish for. Being alive in this guy's hands isn't likely to be time well spent.'

'Freezing,' I said. 'What about the freezing cold she described?'

'Take off your long johns, blondie. It's twenty-six degrees outside.'

'Her *silk* long johns, you meant to say.'

'Now how would you happen to know that, Brother Wallace?' Mike asked with a grin. He had cut off two cars at the exit as he careened onto the southbound highway.

''Cause Alex was kind enough to give some to Vickee for Christmas, for that ski trip we took in January. Now I'm expected to keep my wife in silk underwear.'

'Coop dresses so she don't know from freezing. The wind blows off the Hudson, that cold air can bite like a king cobra. That's freezing.'

'So Secaucus is remote, industrial, and a ghost town at night. But just a short hop into Manhattan,' I said. 'Trucks and trains and the smell of death in the air — maybe Chat wasn't all that confused when she called Faith.'

'I'm telling you, Coop. This town is a natural killing ground.'

39

I tried the number for the Reverend Jeanine Portland as Mike sped south. My message went to voice mail, and when I rang the landline at the Nantucket church office, I reached a secretary who told me that the minister was off-island until later in the evening. She was sorry, she told me, that she had no idea where Portland's trip had taken her.

'You'd better call the police department there, Mercer,' I said. 'Someone is bound to have a relationship with Portland. I'd like them to track her down and make sure they sit on her for the night.'

'What time's the last boat?'

I knew the Woods Hole to Martha's Vineyard ferry schedule cold, on- and off-season, for all of the years that I had been summering there with my family, before my late fiancé and I bought our home. Nantucket was even farther out to sea, and many fewer ferries ran there from the Steamship Authority dock in Hyannis.

'Probably eight tonight. If she's traveling by car, there should be a reservation in the computer that will give us a clue to her travel plans.'

Mercer was on the phone, patching through from Information to the small police department that watched over the winter population of ten thousand. He explained the situation to a duty detective, who knew Portland and promised to track her down. He would have her met on the Cape side, escorted onto the ferry, and not left alone until we contacted him about the status of our hunt for the killer.

We took the Secaucus exit and at the bottom of the ramp were joined by two patrol cars from the local department. Lieutenant Peterson had given their boss the coordinates of the only triangulated call and sent his men to guide us to the area that was most likely the cell source. Mercer got out of the car to introduce himself and listen to their suggestions.

'Follow these guys,' he said when he climbed back in. 'They're going to take us to the spot our tech team plotted from the cell-tower coordinates.'

Not far from the highway, the cops led us off the local streets and onto a dirt road. It was lined with amber reeds, tall and willowy, that waved in the strong wind and made it impossible to see far on either side of the trail.

Mike drove for more than a half mile before the landscape cleared. Strong odors rose in intensity the farther from the highway we went, unless it was my imagination that had taken hold of all my senses.

The Crown Vic rattled as we rode over a series of gravel-lined railroad-track beds. The tracks themselves trailed off in both directions, crisscrossing back and forth as far as I could see. Old freight cars, with rusted metal trim and weathered paint chipped off the sides, stood at dead-ended points along the way as though they'd been abandoned years earlier.

'Where the hell are these guys headed?' Mike asked, honking his horn at them to slow down. 'It's the ass end of nowhere out here. We're going to need an army to search.'

'Peterson says he'll give us one.' I leaned forward, peering over Mercer's broad shoulders as we rounded a curve, crossed the tracks again, and came upon a sea of white trucks, maybe thirty of them.

Mike pulled up even with the second patrol car. 'What have we got, guys?'

The caravan of commercial vehicles were all the same shape, double the size of vans but only half as large as eighteen-wheelers. They were painted a glossy white, with strips of metallic silver material outlining their sides and tops. Unlike the vintage freight cars we had just passed, this looked like an entirely new fleet of trucks.

The cop in the passenger seat pointed with his right hand, and I followed the tip of his leather glove. 'That's a warehouse parking lot.'

'Active?' Mike asked, opening the door and stepping out of the car. Mercer and I followed suit.

'Yeah. It services one of the food-delivery companies based in Newark.'

Close, but not so close that anyone in the main warehouse would be stationed in this lot at all hours.

Mercer and I walked up behind the last van and around its side. Like all commercial vehicles, its name and logo were stenciled on it in bright red lettering.

The words ALDEN'S ANGUS appeared above a picture of a cow grazing in a pasture, blissfully unaware of its fate.

'Are these trucks refrigerated?' I asked Mike, who was on his knees examining the underside of one of them.

Chat Grant had complained of the cold when she called her sister. I knew Mike had that on his mind.

'Beef delivery trucks? Count on it, Coop.' He stood up and turned to the Secaucus cops. 'Get your boss to call the main shop in Newark. Somebody needs to get over here yesterday and open every one of these up.'

The driver got back in his patrol car and radioed headquarters.

Mike kept shouting questions. 'Find out how many trucks like this there are in the company. How many are supposed to be here. Somebody has to tell us if any of them are missing.'

'I'm not waiting for that answer,' Mercer said, stepping away to make his call. 'I'm telling Peterson to get out an APB right now. Use it with the photo of Chastity Grant. I-95 runs from Maine to Florida and passes right through the 'hood. If she isn't in one of these trucks right here, then our boy is on the run with her.'

'Are you thinking what I'm thinking, Mike?'

'A mobile abattoir. A slaughterhouse on wheels.'

A chill went through me. We had lost the

329

afternoon sun and the March wind was showing off its strength.

'Help yourself to one of these trucks and you could travel all over the city — any city — and you'd just be one more frigging deliveryman, no matter what time of the day or night. The refrigeration would keep a body cool. No one would make much of the sight of a little more blood inside the rear, and it would be damn impossible to hear anything from within these walls,' Mike said, slamming his hand against the side of the heavy vehicle.

A train whistle blew nearby and I started. 'I thought these tracks were dead.'

The second uniformed cop laughed at me. 'They don't see too much action, but one of them's got a load pulling out now. You're fine where you are. Gettin' jumpy, ma'am?'

'High-strung type, she is,' Mike said, walking around from truck to truck, pulling at the handles on the rear of each one and banging on the doors to try to elicit a response, in case Chat Grant was locked inside. 'Coop'll jump if you keep staring at her the way you're doing. She takes everything way too personally.'

There was an engine coming into sight from around the bend in the tracks. The black locomotive seemed to be headed straight toward us, moving at a snail's pace.

'Just an optical illusion, ma'am,' the cop said. 'He'll be on that outer rail, nowhere near you.'

The whistle blew again and the train chugged along in our direction. I stepped back anyway and could see the long chain of railroad cars trailing behind, their brightly colored sides a sharp contrast with the ebony steel of the lead engine.

It didn't look like any train I had ever seen before, because of the reds and blues and yellows that decorated it so gaily. I counted as more than fifteen cars took up the lead in the procession out of the Secaucus swamps, with no end in sight.

Now I could begin to make out the writing that was highlighted by the bold paint. Chat Grant hadn't been confused when she mumbled something to her sister, Faith, about both trucks and trains.

And my paralegal, Max, hadn't been far off in her wordplay with the torn papers Naomi Gersh had left behind in her apartment. Max had figured the *U* and *S* to have formed the word 'bus,' making a trifecta of three forms of transportation — bus, truck, and train.

'Where's the lightning, Coop?' Mike asked. 'You look dumbstruck.'

The whistle was competing with me for Mike's attention. 'Make it stop, Mike. Stop the damn train, will you?'

'What am I supposed to do for you, kid? Throw myself down on the tracks?'

They were all laughing at me, but now I knew what words the letters on Naomi's note to herself had formed before she left her apartment for the last time. I was on the adjacent bed of railroad tracks, weeds tangled around my legs, waving at the engineer to stop the slow-moving train.

'Yes, if that's what it takes to keep it from leaving town. I thought you'd do anything for me,' I said, flashing him a smile.

'That was before I met Chat Grant.'

'Well, then, do it for her,' I said as Mike walked toward me. 'Remember the notes that Daniel Gersh was ripping to shreds in his sister's apartment, just hours after her murder?'

'Yeah.'

'They had something to do with a train.' The more frantically I waved, the more times the engineer sounded his whistle at me.

'So?'

'Look where we are. Refrigerated trucks, a whole caravan full of them in a desolate rail yard. And this train.'

'What of it?'

'From the first kids at Mount Neboh Church who said the killer flew over the gates, like he somehow got over the wall with Ursula Hewitt at Old St. Pat's.' The images were clear in my mind, forming faster than I could speak. 'The guy who somehow lowered himself down from the balcony at St. John the Divine — fluid, agile, graceful — like he was when he disappeared on the scaffolding following Faith last night. He's got to be some kind of acrobat, Mike.'

It was getting through to him that I might be right. 'Swinging from the rafters, maybe, to get to the chalice in the Fordham chapel. I could go with the idea of a high flier.'

'Then, think circus train, will you? That's where she was headed. Naomi Gersh was going to meet a guy on the circus train.'

The uniformed cops looked baffled as Mercer and Mike joined me, wildly waving in unison, both displaying their gold detective shields.

The bold yellow letters on the side of the cars were visible to all of us as the powerful engine ground to a halt just feet from where we were standing. Smoke poured out of the stack, swept into the sky by the wind, as the train idled impatiently on the tracks.

''Ringling Brothers and Barnum and Bailey,'' I said. 'It's the circus train.'

40

'What the hell is going on here?' A loud voice boomed from the platform of the second car behind the locomotive. It had the deep resonance of a ringmaster, but the man who stepped forward wore business attire that suggested a management role.

'NYPD. Homicide. We'd like to get on board for a few minutes to talk with you. I'm Detective Chapman. Mike Chapman.'

'This is absurd, Detective. I've got to keep this train moving.' The man tapped the dial of his wristwatch. 'We've got a matinee tomorrow. We've got to set up an entire show.'

'I said we'd like to come on and ask some questions. It won't take long. You are? . . . '

'Delahawk. Fontaine Delahawk. Murder where?'

I doubted P. T. Barnum himself could have better named the character in charge.

'Where have you been playing these last two weeks, Mr. Delahawk?'

Mike had one foot on a rung of the metal stepladder that was suspended from the platform.

'Manhattan. That's no secret, is it? We're still the greatest show on earth. Don't you read the newspaper ads, Detective, or the theatrical reviews?'

'Only the funny pages, sir,' Mike said, trying to swing himself another step up on the ladder. 'I got no time for Broadway and I hate how you guys push those elephants around. I really do.'

Delahawk called to someone behind him. A teenage boy appeared with a wooden footstool, scooted past the heavyset man, and jumped off the platform. He placed the stool underneath the stepladder, reached up a hand, and Mike had to move aside to let Delahawk onto the ground.

'Now, what's this about, Detective?'

Mercer was walking alongside the train, around the bend, and briefly out of sight. He seemed to be counting the cars and using his great height to peer into windows.

'I've got reason to believe that there might be evidence connected to the commission of a crime on board your train.'

Mike sounded so tentative that even Delahawk caught it. 'Rather vague, Detective. I'm betting the chief of police himself might have come out in full uniform to stop the circus, if you had legal grounds. No warrant?'

'There's an exception for an interstate vehicle traveling with land-roving mammals, sir. We've got joint jurisdiction with the ASPCA to board any moving conveyance en route out of the state. Ms. Cooper here is our legal expert. She'll explain.'

'This isn't even your state.' Delahawk's expression combined his annoyance with a touch of humor, recognizing Mike's effort at complete overreaching.

'Where are you off to this evening?' Mike asked.

'Providence, Detective. I can't imagine you'd

335

want to be the cause of such disappointment to all the children there.'

'Can't get to Rhode Island without going through the Empire State. You kindly let us board right here, or you'll be stopped by the police commissioner of the city when you cross over the Hell Gate Bridge.'

The old red span that arched above the deadliest current in the East River had been built as the New York Connecting Railroad Bridge, the only way to link trains from Manhattan to the mainland, and to the Northeast Corridor route that led to New England.

Fontaine Delahawk motioned to the teen who waited beside him and held out his hand as he put one foot back up on the wooden stool. He seemed to know the sound of brazen deceit when he heard one. 'Have the proper papers, Detective. Will you do that?'

'May we have a moment, Mr. Delahawk?' I asked as Mercer approached us.

He turned to look as I spoke. 'It's almost five o'clock, young lady. Don't play games with me.'

'I wouldn't dream of it, sir. Where did your trip start, and how long ago?'

'Sarasota, Florida. That's our home. We left last fall, if it helps you to know.'

'And did you travel through Georgia?'

'Yes. We played Atlanta, of course.'

'And you'd have dates? Exact locations the train parked?'

'Certainly. We have to make those arrangements far in advance.'

'And your performers, do they live on this train?' I asked, raising my arm to point at the length of this village on wheels.

'Our artists, our stage crew, our mechanics. Two hundred and fifty of us. This is home, my dear. We're not gypsies or carnies. We're serious working people and this is our home for the better part of a year.'

'I need to talk with the detectives, if you'll allow me that, Mr. Delahawk. Perhaps I can persuade you to change your mind, to just give me five or six minutes.'

'More likely for you than for your mates, miss,' Delahawk said as the teenager assisted him back onto the platform.

'Thirty-five cars is what I counted,' Mercer said as the three of us took a few steps away from the train to talk. 'Some with great big windows; looks like there are entire families living inside. Others are closed up, with scenery in them, maybe. Or animals.'

'What do you want me to do here, Coop? I'm fresh out of bullshit for Delahawk. He's got that takes-one-to-know-one style.'

The whole picture of the killer, the combination of traits that fit his modus operandi was coming into focus for me. I kept my eyes on the locomotive and talked fast.

'Get me on that train, Mike. That's all I'm asking you to do. This killer could fly, just like your winged man in that stained-glass window he led us to. Come with me and I'll show you how.'

'Well, try again to cozy up to chubby old

Fontaine, 'cause he ain't buying my cruelty-to-animals angle. You got probable cause or anything close to it besides your green-eyed intuition?'

'I'll sniff out probable cause. The smell of it on that cattle car is stronger than the stink of Secaucus,' I said. 'Think about how the toddler found Naomi's severed head in the church fountain. What drew her to it?'

Mercer was in my corner. 'A child's backpack. A bright yellow backpack with cartoon characters and smiley faces. Like you'd take to the circus.'

'Or buy at a concession stand. Or lose there in the crowd.'

Mike was still mulling the whole situation over.

'Delahawk's probably glued to the second hand on his cheap watch while I try to twist your arm,' I said. 'Go back to what Faith Grant described this morning. The man who stalked her went from walking behind her on the sidewalk of 122nd Street to coming directly at her — facing her — from across Claremont Avenue. He went up like a cat on that scaffolding, bypassing the streetlights below. I think he's got Chat confused with Faith. He probably hasn't seen her since the night in December at Ursula Hewitt's play. That's why he kept on walking past Faith with a simple 'sorry.''

'He disappeared from your courtroom 'like magic' that day the bishop testified,' Mercer said, adding to my fuel. 'Isn't that what you told us?'

'That's exactly how Pat McKinney described it.'

'I'll get Manny Chirico checking those murders in Alpharetta, Georgia, and Wayland, Kentucky,' Mercer said. 'See how the dates match up to when the circus came to a nearby town. I'm beginning to like the possibilities here.'

'I know you wanted the killer to be an orangutan, Mike, swinging over the church gates,' I said, 'but unless there's one of those on board for an animal act, you better give me some cred. It's totally logical. Think Poe, that's fine with me. Think ratiocination.'

He had both hands on his hips, working through my ideas as though they were starting to make sense.

'Come with me, Mike.' I meant it both literally and figuratively. 'Strong, fluid, graceful, agile. Gymnasts, trampoline artists, illusionists. What better candidate for our perp than a circus performer?'

'A suspect with his own private rail car to take him away from the scene of his last crime — no flight in a stolen vehicle with bum tags,' Mercer said. 'And the train puts him firmly in our territory when his spree begins. No lousy motel room to leave a record of your driver's license or your timetable.'

'But we don't know what set him off,' Mike said. 'We don't know what he was doing here over the holidays, if he was actually the guy in the audience at Ursula's play.'

'Well, don't you want to find out?' I was imitating Fontaine Delahawk, tapping the dial on my watch. 'They're going to ride on if we don't bite this bullet now.'

'What's your gut, Mercer?' Mike asked.

'Take Coop and go.'

'Call Peterson first. Make sure he's got a squad waiting in the Bronx, in case we catch a break and move this fast enough to offload there. He'd better have a couple of cars all along the route, if they can figure out what that might be.'

'Probably parallels the Northeast Corridor passenger trains, on freight tracks. New Rochelle, New Haven, New London, Providence,' Mercer said. 'I'll wait here until every one of these Angus trucks is opened. And yes, Alex, Nan and I will stay on top of the lady minister from Nantucket too.'

'You going to try to sell this one to Fontaine?' Mike asked me. His words were almost drowned out by the double-blow of the whistle.

I looked to the engineer and could see Fontaine Delahawk talking with him in the cab. Slowly, the great hulking locomotive belched its smoke into the air and like a sleeping beast, awakened and started to move.

Mike pointed to the empty area from which Delahawk had earlier descended. We looked at each other and began sprinting toward the train. I beat Mike there, then reached out for him and pulled him with me onto the stepladder, holding on tight as we climbed up to safety on the platform of the rolling rail car.

41

'Stand still. Don't move a hair,' Mike said. He had opened the door of a coat closet in the front car, which seemed to be Delahawk's office, directing me inside and pressing against me while the train lurched forward and picked up speed.

'How long?' I mouthed to Mike.

He held up five fingers and whispered, his lips against my ear. 'He obviously gave the engineer the signal to start running. He'll either ramble back and check on his charges, or he'll settle down in his office, in which case we'll already be out of the rail yard and on the live tracks.'

I closed my eyes as the train swayed around a curve and tried to keep my balance by holding Mike's shoulder.

'What is it with the eyes, Coop? The onions? I shouldn't have had that second sandwich.'

I shook my head, unable to get the vision of Faith's sister out of my mind. 'Chat. It's Chat. Not knowing where she is or what condition she's in. How did I ever let that fragile girl walk away this morning?

'You can't go there, kid. We didn't know then what we know now. We're pulling out all the stops to find her. Stay cool. Wrap your mind around P. T. Barnum.'

'There's a sucker born every minute, is that what you're telling me?'

'He never said that, Coop. Some guy said it about one of his exhibits. The Cardiff Giant. Remember him?'

Mike was trying to keep me calm. He could read me as well as anybody. He was so close to me he could probably hear how fast my heart was pounding.

'Yeah.'

'Let's hope our perp stays away from Grace Church.'

The elegant Episcopal landmark on Broadway at Tenth Street was, like St. Patrick's Cathedral and the old smallpox hospital on Roosevelt Island, another stunning design of the architect James Renwick.

'I give up,' I said.

'Built with stone cut by the inmates at Sing Sing and shipped down the Hudson. That's where Barnum held the wedding of Tom Thumb and Lavinia Warren, his two dwarfs, in 1863. Bet there's not a true Barnum scholar on this whole train.'

'Is there anything you don't know?' I asked. He had managed to draw a smile from me. 'That's right. Barnum called Tom Thumb a general, didn't he? A four-year-old general. Of course you'd know about him, even if it was only a stage name.'

The train had suddenly gone from a slow canter to a noticeable trot. We were on the straightaway now and moving at a good clip.

I could hear Fontaine Delahawk's voice as he reentered the car. He stopped close to where we were hiding, wheezing until he finished a violent

342

coughing spasm. The teenager who had helped him off the train must have been his assistant. The older man again barked orders, telling someone — presumably that same kid — that he was going back to his room to await dinner.

'I've always wanted to come out of the closet. Too bad there's nobody here to see me,' Mike said. 'How about you?'

He reached behind his back and twisted the handle on the door. The large office was empty, except for the sound of the steel wheels.

It was smartly outfitted in the finest of wood finishes. And like a fancy yacht, everything was built into the walls of the windowless car so that it would be difficult for objects or furniture to be dislodged by the motion of the rocking train. There were several desks and a row of filing cabinets. Brass fittings were mounted on every drawer, more likely to secure them in place than to protect from intruders — like the two of us.

'Snap some photos, will you, Coop?' Mike asked. 'We may need to come back to this later on.'

He waited until I aimed my phone for a few shots, then pulled back the heavy arm of the car's exit as we made our way carefully onto the next platform.

There was a single door on the right-hand side of the long car. On the wall adjacent to it, a small whiteboard was affixed, and someone had written eight names — many of them foreign-sounding — in alphabetical order. The men and women who occupied this suite were a mix of Italian and Spanish, Russian and Czech, French and Hungarian, with a couple of Americans thrown in.

Mike opened the door and we entered. Directly opposite was a small cubicle — like a tiny college dorm room with a bed, dresser, and desk — occupied by a striking, raven-haired woman dressed in a sweatsuit. I'd guess she wasn't much older than twenty-five.

'Hey, guys. What's up?' she asked. Her back was supported by three pillows, none of which disturbed the well-lacquered beehive updo atop her head. She was balancing a hardcover astrology book on her knees. 'Who are you?'

She seemed amused and curious about our presence, not concerned.

Mike showed her his shield and identified himself.

'Awesome!'

'We're with Missing Persons, Ms. Cooper and me. We're looking for a young woman who went missing.'

It was a long-standing police department tactic. People were always much more willing to cooperate to find someone who may have just run away than become ensnared in an ugly murder investigation.

'You think she's with us? No way.'

'Mind if we talk?'

'Sure. Mr. Delahawk says — '

'Yeah, we met him on the way in.'

She leaned over and patted the end of her bed, and Mike sat down, motioning me to the desk chair. 'I'm Kris. Kristin Sweeney.'

Not from the long line of European circus

families, I guessed, as so many of the performers with foreign names might be.

'You a Cowboys fan?' Mike asked. There was a poster over the bed of the Dallas football team, autographed by many of the players.

'Can't grow up in Spur, Texas, and root for anyone else. I was a cheerleader for them before I took this job.'

'Awesome,' Mike said, smiling back at Kristin, and I knew he meant it sincerely. 'Hard act to follow. What are you now? A lion tamer?'

She giggled, pushing the book aside and wrapping her arms around her knees. 'I'm a stunt rider. Bareback, acrobatics, leap through fiery hoops. All that kind of stuff.'

'I'll have to buy a ticket for tomorrow's show,' Mike said. 'I've spent most of my life trying to find a girl who can jump through fiery hoops. How long you been with the circus?'

'I joined up last fall, in Florida. Had to go to school all summer before that. Circus school.'

'Have any new girls been around lately?'

'New girls? Doing what? I mean we always bring on some locals — you know, as ushers or ticket takers. But I don't have anything to do with any of them.'

'I wouldn't think so, you being a pro and all.'

I might as well have been on another planet. Mike seemed totally taken with his Dallas cheerleader. Maybe it was the bareback thing.

'There must be lots of guys hanging out at the stage door for you, Kristin.'

'Yeah, if you're into twelve-year-olds,' she said with a laugh. 'Not so much as you'd think.'

345

'And girls, looking to hook up with guys?'

'Occasionally.'

'Anyone been coming around named Naomi since you've been at the Garden?'

'Nope.'

'Ursula? Or Chat — short for Chastity?'

'I'd remember that one for sure,' she said. 'Are all these girls missing? That's so weird. But then, my mother warned me that New York was like that.'

'Not usually. Not with me on the job.'

'People always joke about running away to join the circus, but that's not how this works, Mike. There's all kinds of training before anyone gets hired. We don't pick up any strays along the way. We're a family, is what we are.'

'Tell me about this family, Kris. We got a long ride ahead of us tonight.'

'You both coming to Providence?' she asked, shooting me a sidelong glance.

'Yeah. What should we know?'

Kristin Sweeney was practically gushing now. 'So, think of this as an apartment building. Like, thirty-five stories tall, except it's horizontal. The only thing we don't have is a zip code.'

And, I guessed, a police department.

'Doesn't look like you have any privacy,' I said. 'Eight of you to a suite? No bathroom?'

'There are just a few cars like this. Works fine if you're single, like I am.'

'Who gets to ride the train?' Mike asked.

'The artists, of course. Cooks and stagehands and prop guys. Mechanics and electricians. Elephants, horses, wild animals. The costume

346

lady and all our glitz. Cast and crew, Detective. We're all here.'

'Some of the rooms are larger?'

'Yeah. Some of the couples have their own little apartments. They bring their kids along, or their in-laws. Flat-screen TVs and toilets and all that. Kitchenettes, which is something I miss a lot, 'cause I enjoy cooking. The rest of us eat in the Pie Car. That's what it's called, but it's really a diner. Mr. Delahawk even has an electric fireplace in his suite.'

'You like this kind of life?' Mike asked.

'I like it fine, for now. Better than what was waiting for me home in Spur after my cheerleading days were over. Better than circus life used to be, moving from hotel to hotel, always packing and unpacking. I've made friends here. I said it's like family, right? Well, for me it's better than hanging with most of my family.'

'How about the guys, Kris? You know all of them?'

'I sure do. It's not like I date any of them, if that's where you're going. Most of us in the troupe are pretty young. Hardly anybody over thirty-five. We work together, we live together. Spend a lot of time with each other. Some of them have grown up in this business, Mike. They'll have kids who'll be Ringling babies.'

Kristin Sweeney stopped talking and pointed at me. 'She's looking at me like it's all strange, what we do. It's not. It's really not.'

'That's not what I was thinking,' I said. 'I apologize. Your life sounds really interesting to someone like me who sits at a desk a lot of the time.'

I was actually thinking how lucky we were to get such a cooperative talker in the first room at which we stopped. And trying to remember the last time I'd spent a full day at my desk.

'You ride this train from town to town?' Mike asked.

'All over the country.'

'Can you — do you — ever get off?' Mike asked. 'Have you been into Manhattan on your own?'

'Oh, sure. They run a shuttle bus for us, almost wherever we go, so we can get around. And there's a flatbed freight train that travels behind us. It's got some motorcycles and cars on it. Lots of guys use those for their socializing and such.'

Everything suddenly went dark and I clutched the edge of the desk. Two seconds later, the lights went back on and I realized we had gone underground, into the vast tunnel system that fed an endless flow of trains below the Hudson River, across to Manhattan to be routed around Penn Station for the trip northeast. For a little while, we might arguably have a claim to proper jurisdiction.

'So, let me ask you about a guy I'm looking to talk to, Kris,' Mike said.

'Okay.'

'He's a performer. Maybe worked with the troupe a few months back. Maybe still does.'

She sat up straighter and listened attentively.

'He's a tall guy, very thin. Has dark hair, keeps

348

it long — sometimes tied back like a ponytail. Don't know what kind of artist he is, but he moves real smooth and graceful.'

Kristin Sweeney wasn't smiling at Mike any longer. She had her right arm raised to the wall next to her before he finished his description, and was pounding on it with her fist as he spoke.

'He's got bad skin, some kind of blisters — '

'I don't know a guy like that, but why do you want to talk to him anyway?' She was quick to answer, and there was almost a snarl in her voice. 'About those girls? About?'

The door opened and a hulking six-foot-six-inch man put a foot forward in the room. He had the torso of a comic-book strongman.

'Nico,' Kris said. 'Thanks for coming in. These guys are cops.'

If someone had posted a Doric column in the doorway, it would have been easier to work my way around it and out of the room.

'Nico Radka. Pleased to meet you.'

So he was the Czech performer in the next room, whose surname had been on the whiteboard. To the rescue, as Kristin had hoped.

'Mike Chapman. Alex — '

'Nico, they're all into asking questions about some missing girls and stuff. That's why I was answering them at first. Now they want to know if we got a guy that looks such and such. Tall, ponytail, red face or something. Maybe you should find Mr. Delahawk. I don't know anyone like that.' She was talking to Mike but staring at Nico Radka, as tense as if Mike had struck a nerve underneath a bad tooth.

'Why don't you step out with me, Mr. Mike?' Nico asked the question politely, almost as though he was giving us a choice.

'We met Mr. Delahawk on the way in. He has no problem with helping us,' Mike said, foolishly assuming that we wouldn't encounter the manager in our passage through the cars.

'Very well then. We shall get him.' The young man's accent was thick. So were his lateral deltoids.

'What's your gig, Nico?'

'Tumbling. Acrobatic tumbling.' Nico turned sideways to wriggle his way down the narrow corridor of the train as it emerged from beneath the river and hurtled north on the tracks that ran parallel to the Jersey Palisades. 'Come, please. Lock your door, Kristin. Is best you do.'

We followed Nico down the length of the hallway, across a platform with protective railing on both sides that linked to the next car.

This one seemed to be divided into two suites, obviously larger than the cubicles in which Kristin and Nico lived.

'So you know this guy I was talking to Kristin about?' Mike asked.

'Which guy?' Nico's head went from side to side as he walked toward the rear of the car but continued to turn back to Mike, whether to answer questions or make certain we were staying in line behind him.

'One of your buddies. Tall and lean, ponytail — '

'Why you want to know who we know? Somebody does something wrong?' His muscled arms braced against the window as the train rocked along the tracks.

We hadn't been so lucky with our first contact after all. Kristin and Nico had joined forces to circle the wagons around their extended family the moment she figured our interest had shifted from finding missing women to fingering one of the men in their troupe.

'We're looking for people, that's all. We think one of your friends may have known them.'

The first whiteboard we passed bore the names RAMON AND RAMON under the hand-drawn images of two stars. I heard Mike ask Nico who they were.

'Illusionists, Mr. Mike. Best in the world.'

Good enough to occupy half a train car. The other label at the far end said THE FLYING ZUKOVS. Again, someone had added a sketch, this time of a stick figure hanging from a trapeze.

Nico opened the door to pass into the next wagon. On the platform, which was like a small open vestibule, a man sat in a folding beach chair, looking at the scenic vista as we raced along the Hudson River.

We entered another dormitory-style car, and I scanned the names of the eight occupants as we hurried past.

Another platform and there was the brass nameplate, a more permanent fixture than in the other cars: FONTAINE DELAHAWK.

Nico faced the door and rang the buzzer.

Mike saw a chance to get around him, grabbed my hand, and pulled me in the direction of the next twenty-odd cars in the long train as we heard the deep voice of Delahawk ask who was at the door.

I looked over my shoulder as I ran behind Mike. Nico appeared to be stunned as he waited for Delahawk to open up for him. We were already through the rear of the car — a solo apartment — and into the next one.

Here the names were also illustrated by an amateur artist. The four suites seemed to hold the all-important costume designer and three performers who worked with animals.

'Keep running, Coop,' Mike said as he led the charge forward. 'Let's get as deep into the company — as many cars back as we can — before Delahawk lumbers along. We just need to talk to somebody. Anybody who'll point us in the right direction, or tell us we're off base.'

I paused to catch my breath. 'We can't be too far wrong, Mike. Kristin only called for Nico, only knocked on the wall to summon him, when you described our suspect. She was eating out of your hand till that very moment.'

We were on the move again, working our way back through the train. Three cars later, Mike stopped to adjust to the darkness as we entered another subterranean tunnel. We were crossing under the narrow strip of water that would take us east and out of Manhattan, into the Bronx, for the trip to New England.

I was leaning against the window and skimming the eight names on the whiteboard that faced me. One of them was familiar, not just because it was more American than the foreign surnames. I repeated it to myself silently, then said it aloud. 'Bellin.'

'What?'

'That name. Bellin.'

'Yeah?'

'Daniel Gersh,' I said. 'You told me to call his mother this morning.'

'So?' Mike was ready to move ahead. He pushed off from the wall.

'That's her name now. Bellin. His stepfather is Lanny Bellin.'

Mike made an abrupt about-face and stepped in front of me to open the door to the suite of cubicles.

'It's the fourth name on the list,' I said to him.

He counted three doors and banged his knuckles once on the fourth one, twisting the handle at the same time. I was at his shoulder, peering in.

Reclining on the single bed, listening to his iPod and looking almost as surprised as I did, was Naomi's brother, Daniel Gersh.

42

'The elusive Daniel Gersh,' Mike said. 'Aka Bellin.'

Gersh backed himself up into the corner of the bed and removed the earphones. 'What do you want?'

'I know you told us you were going to take acting classes in the fall, but somehow I didn't figure you for clown school.'

'I'm not — '

'A real Pagliacci, huh? A homicidal clown. Great act to take on the road, Daniel.'

There was a crackling noise overhead and I could see a small speaker in the ceiling, next to a recessed light fixture.

'Ladies and gentlemen.' There was a cough as the person cleared his throat. 'Ladies and gentleman, good evening. This is Fontaine. I need your attention for a moment.'

'You're out of your mind, Detective. You got this all wrong,' Daniel said.

'It would appear that two officers of the New York Police Department have joined us for the next leg of our trip. This is no cause for alarm. None at all. I'd ask that you all stay in your rooms for the next hour or so. We will of course keep the Pie Car open later into the evening. Do not — I repeat — '

'Make it right for me,' Mike said. 'Tell me what you're doing here. Tell me about your friend and what cubicle he's holed up in, Daniel.'

'Do not have any conversation with these officers,' Delahawk continued. 'I suggest you keep your doors locked and do not have any conversation with them, nor answer any of their questions.'

'What are my rights?' Daniel asked, looking at me for an answer. 'I've got rights, don't I?'

'The closest you come to that on this friggin' train is having my right fist in your face,' Mike said, stepping toward the cowering man, ready to pull him off the bed onto his feet.

'It's my sister who's dead, Detective.'

'And there's another woman missing now, you dumb bastard. A woman who was with Naomi at Christmastime, when you worked that play. She was at the same performance that Naomi attended.'

'Nico and Giorgio will be passing through the train,' Delahawk droned on. 'Do not open your door to anyone except either of them. And use your intercom to call my room if you see these police officers. One is a man, the other a woman. They are not dangerous, of course. They are police officers. But there will be no conversation with them unless I am present. Thank you, ladies and gentlemen.'

'What are you doing here, Daniel?' Mike asked.

'You heard him. I work for Mr. Delahawk. I can't talk to you.'

Daniel kept looking over at the desk. I could see a switch and a mouthpiece. He had given

355

away the location of the intercom. I squeezed past Mike and seated myself.

'If anyone sings, Daniel, it's gonna be Ms. Cooper. And nobody'll like that. You talk to me instead. What do you know?'

The kid knew he had his back against the wall. 'Nothing. I only came on here yesterday.'

He had gotten off the bus from Philadelphia just hours before Ursula Hewitt was killed.

'Here?' Mike asked. 'On this train?'

'Yeah.'

'What's your talent? You had a pretty good vanishing act going when you skipped out on us.'

'I'm a stagehand. I told you that.'

'Tell me again and lose the attitude this time. Ringling Brothers isn't the Chelsea Square Workshop. They don't hire scabs. You got a union card?'

'I do. Temporary.'

'Funny about that. My boss was having someone check Local One today. I think I'd have had a phone call if they'd confirmed that was true. Lying to me is a bad way to start.'

'I'm not lying,' Daniel said, reaching toward the desk for his wallet.

Mike grabbed his hand. 'You scope it out, Coop. This kid's a natural paper shredder, remember?'

I opened Daniel's wallet and pulled out his credit cards and identification papers, which were wadded together in a side compartment. The driver's license with his photo were in the name Daniel Gersh, but the union card — like two of the credit cards that probably linked to

356

his stepfather's account — said Daniel Bellin.

I handed the Local One temporary ID card to Mike. 'You scammed me on that one, Daniel. Now tell me what brings you to the big top, okay? Don't waste any more of my time. If we'd had your help from the get-go, two other women might still be alive. I'm praying for one.'

'Don't try and guilt me, Detective.'

'What's the guilt factor? Did you introduce Naomi to her killer?'

Daniel Gersh didn't answer.

'I know you didn't do that on purpose,' I said. 'Talk to us about it. We can all save a life if you move on this now.'

'Does that make me an accessory or anything?'

'Just the fact that you may have introduced the two to each other? No, Daniel. This isn't about you. We're working against the clock,' I said.

And against the knock on the door by Nico.

'His name is Ted. At least, that's what I thought when I got here last night.'

'You came looking for him?' I asked.

'Yeah.'

'Because you knew he killed Naomi?'

Daniel looked at me with the earnest expression of youthful trust. 'I didn't believe it at first. I'm still not sure that I do.'

'Why not?'

'When I met him — it was in December — and he came to the show I was working on. The same night Naomi came.'

'*Double-Crossed*,' Mike said.

Daniel nodded. 'Ted — at least that's what he told me his name was — got totally freaked out during the show. One of the other guys and I had to take him outside to cool him down. Get him away from the lady who wrote the show.'

'The priest?' I said. 'Ursula Hewitt.'

'Exactly. I don't remember her name, but Ted was crazed that she — that any woman — claimed to be a priest.'

'How did he even know about the play?'

'Through his church,' Daniel said. 'What's your name again?'

'Alexandra Cooper. Did he tell you anything about his church? The name of it, or where it is?'

'Nah. I'm not into that. I didn't really care. But he was only in New York for a week or two. Some special thing he had to do here. I think he said he came from Atlanta.'

'When did he meet Naomi?'

'There at the theater, that same night. She heard the argument Ted had with the lady-priest. Just her kind of thing, you know? So when I walked him out onto the street, she came out after me. Or after him, I guess. I — uh, I didn't know she was going to do that.'

'Of course not. Did Naomi leave with Ted?'

Daniel Gersh pulled back his arms, his palms facing out. 'Whoa. I have no idea about that. I went back into the playhouse to close up, to do my job, and I left the two of them talking. Her usual feminist crap. That'd be just like Naomi, thinking she could change his point of view about something like his religion.'

'She never told you whether she went for a drink with him?'

'They may have gone for coffee or something,

358

but she . . . well, she was . . . I don't have to tell you guys, do I? She was already involved.'

'With your stepfather?' I asked.

'Yeah. I guess he's a bigger jerk than I ever thought he was.'

'But you must have figured, when we met you at Naomi's apartment on Wednesday, that Ted could have been her killer.'

Daniel looked taken aback by that idea. 'Hardly. That's not what I thought at all. I mean, the guy was so going on and on about how religious he was, I never figured him to be capable of hurting anyone.'

'Daniel,' I said, 'you've got to be straight with us. You were in Naomi's apartment the morning after she was killed, ripping up pieces of paper, tearing pages out of her diary so no one would see them.'

'So what?'

'One of them had the words 'circus train' on it. You must have known about Ted. You must have realized that Naomi had made a plan to see him.'

'She didn't make any plan with him back in December. He was only here for a few days then.'

'Forget it, Coop,' Mike said, his right hand propped against the door and the left one combing through his hair. 'He just can't be honest with us. He's in this up to his neck.'

'No, I'm not!' Daniel shouted.

'Keep your voice down, kid. Start talking sense. Talk fast.'

'Yeah, I was ripping pages out of her diary. You

359

think I wanted my mother to read about the affair Naomi had with my stepfather in the newspapers? The other notes were about me, not my sister.'

'What do you mean?'

'When I was talking to this guy Ted that night in December, out on the street after the play, he was telling me I was crazy to work at a dump like the playhouse. I already knew that.'

Daniel squirmed in his corner on the bed. 'He told me he could get me a better job, without any of the feminist bullshit — sorry, Ms. Cooper — when he came back to town in March. He said he'd call me if I gave him my number. Turned out to be two weeks ago, just like he said.'

'You believed him?' I asked.

'Why wouldn't I? I wasn't getting a hell of a lot of job offers where I was. Naomi's the one who wrote down his name, who wrote down the part about the circus train that night. But she did it for me, only she kept the paper and e-mailed the information to me. It wouldn't surprise me if she got in touch with him this time around. You never know. She was always trying to make people see things her way.'

'And this train — the circus — Ted told you this is where he worked?'

Daniel Gersh answered me, his voice soft and low. 'Yes.'

'He's a stagehand too?' Mike asked, ready to rip open the door and confront Fontaine Delahawk. 'A prop guy? What?'

'No, Detective. Ted's an aerialist. High-wire

360

stuff. His family's been in the circus business for generations. They're trapeze artists too.'

Graceful, fluid, agile — and fiercely strong as well. Our killer was a skilled aerialist — an acrobat used to performing in the air, without a safety net.

'Zukov is the family name,' Daniel Gersh said. 'Ted's one of the Flying Zukovs.'

43

'It's Chapman, Mr. Delahawk. Call off your dogs. We're coming back to your place,' Mike said, speaking into the mouthpiece of the intercom. 'Do me a favor and wait there.'

Mike nudged Daniel Gersh, and the lanky young man, now entirely crestfallen, made his way out of the room between the two of us, with me in the lead.

I could see out the window as we passed the well-lit Amtrak stations that we had breezed through Westchester County and just gone over the line into Connecticut.

The corridors were empty. We passed through the cars with no sign of Nico or Giorgio until we reached Delahawk's door. He opened it himself and admitted us, clearly seething with anger.

'Come in and sit down,' he said, used to giving directions that were obeyed. 'You're the new boy, aren't you?'

'Yes,' Daniel said.

'Is he the problem?' Delahawk asked, and continued on before either Mike or I could answer. 'I'd stop and let you off with him in New Haven, but that would compromise our arrival time in Providence and cost a bloody fortune on top of it to get the emergency parking and unloading fee. Starting up again and all that. Not possible.'

'We'll take the ride,' Mike said. There were

other people on board he wanted to interview.

'What has he done?'

'Nothing wrong,' Mike said. 'Daniel's sister was murdered earlier this week. I'm assuming you follow the news, Mr. Delahawk. The girl who was decapitated. Her body was found in Harlem.'

'Shocking,' he said, lowering himself into a well-worn leather armchair. 'Why didn't you tell me you were in distress, son? I'd have done anything to make you comfortable.'

Daniel Gersh stared out the window.

'Well, we'll see you all have some dinner and send you on your way,' Delahawk said.

'Now that you know how serious this is, we need a little more of your help.'

'Yes?'

'Tell me about the Zukov family, Mr. Delahawk. Tell me how many of them are in your troupe.'

'What does this have to do with Daniel's sister, sir? The Zukovs are an international legend. One branch of the family has been with us at Ringling for thirty years. Tony Steele, the American; Terry Cavaretta; and the Zukovs — that's your circus royalty, Mr. Chapman. You're not going to make an international incident out of us, are you?'

'Tell me about the Zukovs. I've got two hours to listen, with time to meet them before we disembark. I can have the train stopped anywhere along the way because I've got Daniel, and every agent from here to Florida will want to press him for details he might remember.'

Delahawk's head snapped in Daniel's direction. 'What does he know?'

'It's not like that, Mr. D. I'm asking the questions. How many Zukovs on board this buggy?'

Delahawk cleared his throat. 'There are four of the family members in the current act.'

'And they are? . . . '

'Yuri. He's about thirty-five years old. His wife works with him too. She's quite good. And they have a four-year-old who travels on the train, of course. I hope you'll leave the children alone.'

'What's their specialty?'

'Trapeze. They're trapeze artists. The Zukovs are trained to do everything that might be expected of an aerialist.'

'Who else?'

'Yuri's younger sister, Oksana. She works mainly with her husband. That's Giorgio, one of the men I sent to search for you two. His family is from Italy, so most of them work in Europe. We're lucky that Giorgio fell in love and came with Oksana. His people also have a long tradition of circus performance.'

'And their act?'

'Oksana and Giorgio are aerial contortionists, Detective.'

'What's that supposed to mean?'

'It's been a long time since you've come to the circus.'

'I live it, Mr. Delahawk. Twenty-four-seven,' Mike said. 'What's a contortionist?'

'The Zukovs perform aerial acrobatics while hanging from a special fabric. No safety lines, of course. They can suspend themselves from almost anywhere.'

I thought immediately of the tall gate that separated the steps of Mount Neboh from Adam Clayton Powell Jr. Boulevard, the tree that hung over the cemetery at Old St. Pat's, and the beams suspended above the silver chalice at the Fordham chapel.

Delahawk went on. 'The best aerialists, like the Zukovs, can spiral their bodies into just about any position. They sort of, shall I say, fly through the air — but without the trapeze.'

Had Zukov been the apparition who had disappeared from the balcony at St. John the Divine when I called after him, and terrified Faith by climbing on the scaffolding above her without making a sound?

The large man hoisted himself out of his chair and moved to his desk. He had a stack of photos — eight-by-ten color glossies — and flipped through them till he found some of Oksana Zukov to show to us.

'Look at this, Mike,' I said. The attractive woman was dressed in a lacy black bodysuit and sheer tights, her lithe body bent back to form a semicircle, hanging on to a red fabric suspended from the ceiling of a tent. Her left leg was hooked over a vertical piece of the ceiling support, and the top of her auburn hair almost touched her right foot, which pointed straight down, also wrapped in the lower length of fabric.

'How the hell can she do that?' Mike asked.

'It's in the DNA, Detective,' Mr. Delahawk said. 'These families have it in the blood, I tell

365

you. They're incredible artists.'

'What's the fabric?'

'It's called aerial silk, but it's really a very strong, flexible, stretch material, which gives the performers all the control they need.'

'Aerial silk,' Mike said. 'I'll bet that's the type of cloth that was found under Naomi Gersh's arm.'

The shiny blue fragment that had been shielded from flames by the flexion angle of her armpit might yet be a forensic link to the killer's train compartment.

'So why don't you tell me about Ted, Mr. Delahawk?'

The older man screwed up his face and answered Mike with a blank stare. 'Ted? Who do you mean by that?'

'There's a Zukov named Ted, isn't there? You leaving him out for a reason?'

'I don't know who you mean. The only one I haven't mentioned is Fyodor.'

'That's the Russian equivalent of Theodore, Mike,' I said. 'There's your Ted.'

'So where is he, this Fyodor? What suite?'

'You've missed him, Detective. He's on leave.'

'What do you mean?'

'Just what I said. He's taken a leave. Young Daniel here is his replacement.'

'I didn't know that. I swear I didn't,' Daniel said, jumping to his feet. 'I'm just a stagehand. I'm not like Ted.'

'Are we talking about the same person?' I asked. 'Can you describe him, Mr. Delahawk?'

'He's a Zukov, young lady. That's what he

looks like. Tall, like all of them are. Thin. Supple body, like you see in his sister's picture. A Zukov.'

'Any unusual features? What about his hair?'

Delahawk thought for a moment. 'Dark hair. Very long. That's all.'

'His skin?' I asked.

'It's marked or pitted or something. But around me — when he was appearing in the show — I am used to seeing all these kids with so much makeup on that I wouldn't really notice.'

'Makeup?' Mike asked.

'Yes. Theatrical makeup. Very thick, almost like a white paste for the aerialists, so you can see them highlighted against the dark background of the tent, or in contrast with their black costumes.'

Phantasmagorical, like Faith Grant said, when she encountered Ted on the street.

'So is Fyodor a stagehand or an artist, Mr. Delahawk? Russian or American?'

'His parents came to this country when they were in their twenties, sent by their families. The three siblings were all born here. In Florida, in fact, near our headquarters.'

'Accent or no?'

'Not a trace.'

Mike was ready to call in to Peterson with a description of 'Ted's' actual birth name and other information.

'Do you know if he's religious?' I asked.

'The whole lot of them are religious,' Delahawk said. 'In our business, I suppose it's either religion or superstition that gets you up on the high wire. I'd pray a lot more if I was seventy feet in the air and had nothing but the wooden flooring to break my fall.'

'What religion? Do you know where he worships?'

'Eastern Orthodox. For years now we've had to make sure there was a church for the Zukovs to attend near every stop we make.'

I didn't know the Orthodox position on feminist theology.

Fontaine Delahawk held his forefinger against his lips. 'With Fyodor, everything changed after the accident last year. He doesn't go to church with the others anymore. I'm not sure what he does about that.'

'What accident are you talking about?'

'Fortunately, we were in a backwater town in the Florida Panhandle,' Delahawk said. 'If it happened at Madison Square Garden, it would have been front-page news.'

'What was it?' I asked again.

'Fyodor Zukov dropped a girl.' Delahawk spoke each word distinctly. 'He was on the trapeze, during a performance, and his partner — the girl he was training to work with him — fell to the ground. She trusted him to catch her while he was on the trapeze — he's done it thousands of times. He's done it almost every day of his life, since childhood. But she plummeted like a rock.'

'Did she live?'

'She's alive, last I knew. But both of her legs were crushed. If she ever walks again it will be a miracle.'

'And this was an accident, you say?' I was skeptical, thinking of the violence that had seemingly engulfed Fyodor's life throughout this year.

'It proved to be a medical situation, Ms. Cooper. You can be certain the doctors — and the police — confirmed all that. So, yes, it was an accident. Fyodor can no longer do the wire acts or trapeze. He had a brilliant future, of course, but now that's gone. That's why he's been moving scenery and carting the props around. I've offered to keep him on payroll, but he's very angry. He's angry at the world.'

'What medical condition is it?'

'Something to do with his nerves. I simply don't know. Patient privacy and all that.'

'You mean he's lost his nerve?' Mike asked.

'Oh, no,' Delahawk said, almost chortling while he spoke. 'Fyodor's got ice water in his veins, Detective. Nothing scares him, I can promise you that. It's the nerves in his hands that are shot.'

'When did he leave the company?'

'He hasn't been back to the train all week. That's why we had to hire an extra young man for the next leg of the trip,' Delahawk said, gesturing to Daniel Gersh. 'I haven't seen Fyodor Zukov all week.'

44

'We need to talk to Fyodor's family,' Mike said. 'I'll ask them if they're willing to — '

'You'll ask them nothing, Mr. Delahawk. It's almost time for dinner. Pour yourself a nice stiff drink, stay off the airwaves there — no intercom warnings — and we'll pay them a visit. No illusionists or jugglers. Don't send in the clowns. Do I make myself clear?'

'But I've told them not to talk, Detective.'

'I can be very persuasive, sir,' Mike said. 'C'mon, Daniel. You're with us.'

As we retraced our steps through the narrow corridors toward the Zukov suite, we stopped in one of the vestibules between cars. Mike called Lieutenant Peterson and I turned away from him to speak with Faith Grant on my cell.

'Do you have any news for me?' she asked.

'Not yet, Faith. But I think that's a good thing. I'm going to ask you the impossible.'

'What's that?'

'To try to keep it together tonight. The photograph of Chat may already be on the news.'

'It is. It's on every station.'

'You'll make yourself crazy trying to watch it. Have some dinner. You're not alone?'

'No, no. I don't think that I could be.'

'Good. Mike and I will be working all night, so you may not hear from us till morning. But we're on this. There's going to be a suspect's name

370

released shortly, with photographs. Stay as calm as you can.'

'You are indeed demanding the impossible.'

'May I ask you something about the Russian Orthodox Church?' I had my back to the window, holding on to the handrail behind me as the train pitched around a bend in the tracks.

'Of course.'

'Do they have a formal position on women in the priesthood?'

'Most definitely. They're completely against the ordination of women.'

'For a particular reason?'

'Well, most of their teachings claim such an act would disregard the symbolic and the iconic value of male priests, who are a representation of Christ himself, and of course, of Christ's manhood.'

'That's all I need to know. Call my cell if you have anything to tell me. And thanks, Faith. We'll talk with you soon.'

I waited for Mike to finish his conversation. 'Is there anything else about your friend Ted that we ought to know? Anything at all you remember?' I asked Daniel.

He answered softly. 'No.'

Every trace of Mike's good humor had disappeared by the time he hung up the phone. I asked Daniel to step away for a few minutes.

'Is it all bad news?'

'Peterson will have state troopers waiting for us in Providence. May even bring in some feds because of the interstate abduction possibility.'

'And the Zukovs? What if they don't talk to us?'

'Fine with me. They'll be climbing the monkey bars in the local jail.'

'No sign of Fyodor?'

'Not him. Not Chat. There's one Angus truck missing from the lot. The commissioner's doing a stand-up with the mayor at nine p.m. to release all the photos and ask the public for help. The APB on the truck has gone out to every police department and highway patrol. AMBER Alerts and all that. Maybe the guy's going home to his roots, to Florida.'

'And the rest of whatever has you so bummed?'

'The Secaucus cops broke open the back of every one of the trucks still on the lot. There's dried blood in all of them.'

'No surprise. They're butcher shops,' I said.

'One of them had a sleeping bag in it. There's blood in that too. Don't tell me the filet mignons didn't like the cold. ME's testing to see if it's human. It'll take a while longer for DNA, but this may be where he finished off Naomi or Ursula.'

'Could be he was camping out in one of the trucks, getting handouts from his family. That would still have let him use the train as home base, without anyone else aware he was around.'

We started to walk single file, catching up with Daniel Gersh.

'I need you to go back to your room, Daniel,' Mike said. 'Ms. Cooper and I got work to do. Don't talk to anyone. Not about Naomi or your

372

job or knowing us. Stay put, and when the train gets to Providence, you come out on the platform and look for me. Understood?'

'Yeah. I get it.'

We continued back to the suite that had the Zukov name on the door. Mike opened it and entered without knocking.

In the living area, a man and a woman were sitting on opposite ends of a sofa. The woman cradled a sleeping child in her arms, while both were fixed on a flat-screen TV on the wall, watching a twenty-four-hour news broadcast.

The man rose immediately — I guessed him to be Giorgio, the Zukov brother-in-law — and called out for Yuri and Oksana. 'The police are here,' he shouted to them.

The child was awakened by the commotion and started wailing.

Mike rushed back to the closest bedroom, heard the lock click shut from within, and kicked open the flimsy door with his foot.

Yuri and Oksana Zukov, the brother and sister of our probable perp, were being briefed on our intrusion by Kristin Sweeney, the stunt rider from Texas.

45

'Where's Fyodor?' Mike asked.

Kristin Sweeney had cost us the element of surprise. Mike directed her back to her compartment, but there was no way for the two of us to secure people or possessions.

'We don't know where he is,' Yuri said, turning to face us with his arms folded across his chest. That kept his sister positioned behind him while she dried her eyes and tried to compose herself.

'Let me have your phones,' Mike said.

'I don't have one.'

'Bullshit. Both of you, give me your phones.'

Yuri held out his arms to the side. He was wearing the classic bodysuit of an acrobat or dancer — a leotard and tights, with a zippered sweater over them. 'No pockets, Detective. I use the satellite phone only,' he said, pointing to the nightstand next to his bed.

'Coop — take her into the other bedroom,' Mike said, pointing to Oksana. There was no hope of getting information unless we separated them. He was giving me a shot at the weaker link.

'Why don't you come with me?' I said, smiling at the terrified woman. 'Is your room next to this one?'

She didn't speak, but she nodded.

'You can just do this?' Yuri asked. 'You know we're Americans.'

'Oh, yeah, we can just do this. I don't give a damn if you're flying Martians. There are cops from here to Sarasota looking for your brother, and if you want to see him alive, you'd better put on your thinking caps.'

Oksana slipped between Mike and the door without protest and took me into the adjacent compartment she shared with her husband.

'You understand why we have to find your brother quickly?' I asked. I didn't want to talk about the women who'd been murdered. 'If we can save the woman who's missing, maybe Fyodor has a chance.'

'It's not his fault, Ms. Cooper,' she said. 'None of this is his fault.'

The most tired lines in the perpetrator phrase book. I didn't care to think about who Oksana would blame. 'When is the last time you heard from your brother?'

'I'm not sure. Yuri probably knows.'

'Did you see him this week?'

'This week? What day is today? Maybe Yuri remembers.'

'Here's the thing, Oksana. Yuri is talking to Detective Chapman, so whatever Yuri knows, he'll eventually tell. When the train stops in Providence, all your friends will get off and stretch their legs, go out for a drink, get a good night's sleep for tomorrow's matinee. If you haven't answered my questions — and Yuri plays the same game — you'll both go to the police station and sit there, handcuffed to chairs, until your memories improve.'

She had the turned-out foot position of a

ballet dancer, feet planted firmly on the floor. I held the back of the chair to keep myself balanced as we hurtled forward along the tracks. She dabbed at her eyes and bent her head toward the wall, trying to make out the conversation between Yuri and Mike.

'Did you see Fyodor this week?' I raised my voice a notch.

'I think so.'

'Yes — or no?'

Oksana pouted.

'Sit down.'

'I'm perfectly comfortable, Ms. Cooper.'

She was so much better balanced than I that she was probably counting on me lurching over at the next bump on the tracks.

'I asked you to sit.'

Her fear was morphing into defiance now, like it was the Zukovs against the world. Slowly and with the graceful movements of her art, she pivoted and sat on the edge of her bed.

'Did you know that in the state of Georgia there's still a death penalty, Oksana?'

I wasn't sure whether she flinched at that prospect or at the tone of Mike's voice coming through the wall.

'There are more than a hundred murderers on death row there, most of them likely to be burned to toast in the electric chair.'

There were moments I knew I had spent too much time in Mike Chapman's company.

She swallowed hard. 'Georgia? What does that have to do with anything?'

'Your brother killed a man in Georgia.'

Oksana crossed and then uncrossed her long, slender legs. 'That's absurd.'

'The mayor of New York City is going to hold a press conference any minute now. Your brother's name and picture will be broadcast all over the country. Armed police officers, trained bloodhounds, and gun-happy vigilantes hungry for reward money will be looking to track him down.'

'I don't even know what you want him for. I don't know what he did.'

Every time I thought we would be moving forward, Oksana took a step or two back.

'I guess you haven't had the TV on for very long, have you? If Fyodor's still in New York — New Jersey — he'll have a better chance. You can convince him to turn himself in. He'll be safer in the long run.'

She tilted her head and stared at me, trying to divine the truth. Meanwhile, Mike was getting nothing from Yuri, as I judged from the noise level next door.

'Did you see him this week?' I asked again.

'Yes. Yes, we saw him.'

'Where, Oksana? What day did you see him and where?'

'Tonight's Friday, right? It was yesterday. Thursday morning.'

'Where?'

'In Manhattan. Where we were rehearsing, at Madison Square Garden.'

'He called one of you?'

'Yuri told you the truth. We don't use cell phones.'

'How did Fyodor get into the Garden?'

'He still has his identification card. He knows our practice schedule. He showed up, that's all I know.'

'How long did you talk with him?'

'I didn't. Just to say hello. It was Yuri he wanted. For money, for Yuri to give him money.'

'Did Fyodor say what the money was for?'

She hung her head and answered. 'No. But it must have been for food. For everything. I don't know how he's been living. I've been so worried about him.'

'And Yuri gave him cash?'

'Yes. Almost three hundred dollars.'

'But Yuri doesn't have any pockets, I thought. Where did he get the cash?'

Oksana didn't like my sarcasm. 'His gym bag. Fyodor was in the back row of seats, sort of in the dark. I saw him first. It's where one of us usually sits to spot the others when we're on the wire. Yuri went up to talk to him and came back for the money. He only let me say hello for a minute. To ask how he was feeling.'

I tried to sound empathetic, as hard a stretch as that was. Maybe she'd be more forthcoming if I showed interest in her brother's health condition. 'What's wrong with Fyodor? Why did he have to give up the act?'

'He — he won't tell me. He's embarrassed, I think. He's the first one in the family in more than three generations to cause — well, to have a terrible injury happen to a partner. I thought he was going to kill himself that first night.'

'Is he being treated by doctors?'

378

Rabbi Levy told us that Naomi talked about meeting a friend — probably Fyodor — at Bellevue, shortly before she was killed. Maybe it was psychiatric treatment that he was undergoing, as we had speculated.

'I don't think he has any use for doctors. He said they can't help him.'

'Did he tell Yuri where he was staying?'

'No,' she said, getting weepy again. 'If they arrest Fyodor in Georgia, are you sure they could put him to death?'

'I'm sure. A hideously painful death.'

Oksana was biting the inside of her cheek. 'But not in New York?'

'Not in New York.'

She was struggling with whether to confide in me, maybe encouraged that the conversation in Yuri's room sounded like it had taken a more civil turn.

'I don't know where Fyodor has gone, Ms. Cooper. But he doesn't have friends in New York. He doesn't really know people here.'

'That's very helpful, Oksana. Are there people he trusts somewhere else? People in whom he confides?' Was she telling me that she believed her brother would be on the move to the South?

'It used to be that he told Yuri everything. It used to be they were very close. When you work together like this — when you do what all of us do — you practically have to read the other guy's mind. It's instinct and trust. What wasn't passed on to us by our parents, we learned by spending our whole lives in each other's hands, literally. But then — the accident changed things.'

'I'm sure it did,' I said, not wanting her to register my impatience. 'You know who his friends are? Can you tell me their names and numbers?'

We were deep into southeastern Connecticut. Long, wooded areas bordered the tracks as we steamed toward Rhode Island, engulfing the colorful train in total darkness, broken by an occasional set of lights at the crossings.

'I don't know their names.'

'You can't have it both ways, Oksana. I get the feeling you're wasting my time. I'm going to step out for a few minutes and then — '

'May I come too?'

'No, no. You stay right here.'

'But I'm being honest, Ms. Cooper.'

'Where are these friends, Oksana? Are they in Florida?' I asked, but got no response. 'Do something to help your brother. If you don't care about the missing girl, do something to help Fyodor.'

'I told you it's not his fault. It's these guys he got mixed up with after the accident.'

'At home?'

'No, no. In Georgia. At home, in Florida, he'd have had the church. Our priest would have helped him through anything. He was a deeply religious boy, Ms. Cooper. Our whole family is religious.'

'I have great respect for that.'

'It was only his faith,' she said, and I shivered at the thought of Chat's sister, waiting out this dreadful ordeal back at the seminary, 'that got Fyodor through his adolescence.'

'But now?'

'He rebelled when he was a teenager. Hated my parents' accent — he so wanted to be an American kid. Hated everything about the circus and our traditions. Rebelled at any chance he had. With no provocation. It was our priest who found a place for him.'

'What do you mean by 'a place'? Did Fyodor go to jail?' Maybe she was trying to tell me something about a criminal history after all, something that would be useful in our efforts to find Chat.

'Never jail. No. But my parents sent him away for two years. To a really tough school. Far away from home, and sort of like a reform school, I think it was. He was placed there instead of a juvenile jail. He was grateful to come home, to join the troupe, to have a family that cared to take him back and embrace him again. But I think always bubbling beneath the surface was this rage. These new friends must have seen that side of him. Encouraged it. I can't think what else it could be.'

'Who are these guys, Oksana? These new friends?'

'Fyodor met them at the gym, where he was working out.'

'You know where the gym is?'

She hung her head. 'Yuri does. It's near Atlanta. After the accident, my brother had to find a place to build up his strength again. That's what our trainer told him. That's why I think it's all their fault.'

'Who?'

'These guys. Really crazy guys. They got Fyodor into very dangerous stuff,' Oksana said. She held her hands up at me and twisted them back and forth. 'We really need to be strong in our work — our hands and wrists especially — but these guys were teaching him to fight. Like that was a way to build strength.'

'Martial arts?' I asked.

'Exactly. But crazy. Really extreme. Like for combat, he told Yuri.'

Like the Russian combat sport, sambo, and other deadly ways to bring an opponent down that had been demonstrated to us that morning, at the X-Treme Redeemer.

'And church? Did Fyodor give up the church?'

'The Orthodox church, yes,' Oksana said, fingering the cross she wore around her neck. 'He told Yuri these friends had a stronger church. That he could only get his life back if he fought for it. That fighting could make him a better person. Crazy, isn't it?'

'I agree with you.' Totally insane. 'Why don't you rest for a few minutes, Oksana? Let me ask Detective Chapman if there's anything else we need from you right now.'

I wanted to get the information about the Georgia Pentecostal connection off to Peterson. I wanted to see if there was a juvenile record in Florida that had been resolved with an alternative sentence at a reform school, and where that might have been.

Oksana sat back on her bed and I returned to Yuri's room. He and Mike still seemed to be facing off against each other, seated and at arm's length. The questioning was contentious and I guessed that Yuri had held his ground more firmly than his sister did.

'You want to step out for a minute?' I asked, sweeping the small room with my eyes.

'Sure, kid. This prick needs a good tune-up with a barbell to make him talk. Short of that, he doesn't care that his brother's headed for the end of the line.' Mike stood up from the desk and started after me, then turned back. He reached for the telephone and yanked out the wire that connected it to the wall.

Yuri Zukov just laid back on the bed and laughed.

I stood on my tiptoes and grabbed the gym bag that was stashed on the luggage rack over the small sink in the corner.

Yuri leaped to his feet and tried to grab it from me, but Mike pushed him onto the bed again.

'Take this, Detective,' I said, passing the gym bag to him. 'His sister says he keeps his valuables in it. Of course he doesn't care if you rip the phone out of the wall. I'm betting he's got his cell right in there.'

46

'Here's the cell phone information for the perp's brother, Loo. Get somebody to run with it,' Mike said, then hung up with Peterson. 'Nice grab on that gym bag, blondie.'

It was after ten thirty and we were working out of a small office in the headquarters of the Rhode Island State Police. Several patrol cars met the train when it reached the freight track at Providence Station an hour earlier. Local cops and troopers had orders to sweep it from end to end, talking to all the troupe members, searching for evidence of a crime or signs that Fyodor Zukov had brought any of the women on board.

Mike and I had trailed the officers through the compartments for a first look at every possible place to conceal anything from a weapon to a body, then left them to their work. Daniel Gersh rode with us to headquarters, in case there was any way he could assist in the ongoing search. Yuri and Oksana Zukov were separated for the ride, and a prosecutor had been called in to discuss whether they could be held overnight as material witnesses.

'No sightings of Fyodor or the truck on the highway?' I asked.

'Nothing yet. You trust that broad?'

'Not entirely. She swore to the lie Yuri told about not having phones. But when we started to talk about Georgia's death penalty, she really got nervous.'

'So you think he's headed south?'

'I guess we wait to see if there's any info on Yuri's cell,' I said, opening the door to a cop who had brewed a fresh pot of coffee for us and handed mugs in to me.

The television was on in the main squad room, and all the news channels — local and national — were interrupting broadcasts to show photographs of the man wanted for the abduction of Chastity Grant and the possible murders of five other people from Georgia to New York. MANHUNT FOR CLERGY KILLER was the continuous crawl running at the bottom of the screen.

'I'm ready to start mainlining caffeine,' Mike said. 'Another hour and it probably makes sense to accept the captain's offer to drive us back to New York.'

'Whatever you think,' I said, yawning as I settled into a high-backed chair and curled my legs up beneath me.

'Did you reach Mercer?' Mike asked.

'He's not picking up. I left him a message.'

'Where are you, Coop? You're thinking something you're not telling me.'

'The one piece that stumped me was why Zukov was at the trial this week, why he was there when Bishop Deegan testified. He certainly didn't have his eye on me — I was a surprise guest, the designated hitter stepping in for the young prosecutor.'

'And the bishop?'

'No. Deegan's his kind of guy. Old-fashioned, misogynist, trying to uphold the dignity of the church. No, no. He was scouting his outcast.'

'Who?'

'The defendant on trial. Denys Koslawski. Think of it, a disgraced priest who had molested children.'

'Yeah, but how would he know?'

'I'll take the hit on this. There was a story in all the papers about Koslawski — no mention of Deegan's court appearance at the time because he wasn't expected to testify — when the original trial was supposed to start.'

'December?'

'Yes, December. There was a feature about rogue priests. And then we had the idea to adjourn the case for three months because juries tend to be so generous to the bad guys around the holidays. I didn't want a Christmas verdict for Koslawski.'

'So Koslawski goes and waives a jury in the end — wouldn't have been a problem — '

'And Fyodor Zukov had another pariah to stalk,' I said. 'I'm going to put that assignment in your lap when we get home. You check with Bishop Deegan. I'll bet he doesn't know Zukov and just nodded to him because he spied the clerical collar and assumed he was a friendly spectator.'

'Sure, I can do that — if you shut yourself off for a few minutes. You'll be no good to either of us if you're all worn down.'

I rested my head against the hard wooden slats and closed my eyes. Just a fifteen-minute catnap might help refresh me.

I went out so fast and deep that I didn't even hear my phone vibrating on the tabletop ten minutes later.

'Just a minute, Faith,' Mike said. It was his voice that woke me up. 'I'll put her on.'

He handed me the cell. 'Are you all right?' I asked her, startled out of my short slumber.

'Yes. But I've just had a call from Jeanine Portland.'

I sat up. 'Is she back on Nantucket? Is she okay?'

'She's fine, Alex,' Faith Grant said. It sounded like she was choking up as she tried to talk to me. 'Chat called her.'

'When? Was that tonight?'

'No. I wish that were so. It was this morning. Late morning, maybe right after her call to me.'

'Why did she call?' The timing made it all the more likely that Chat had been abducted shortly after she left us with Faith at the seminary.

'Chat told Jeanine she needed to talk to her. You see — ' Faith's voice broke, and she took a few seconds to put herself together. 'I didn't know this. I feel like I failed my sister entirely.'

'You know that's not true. Stay strong for us. Tell me.'

'After they met at Ursula's play, in December, it seems Chat and Jeanine struck it off. She said she found it easier to talk to Jeanine than to me. That she was — well, less judgmental than I am.'

'That's not about you, Faith. It was probably easier to unload some of her troubles on a person who wasn't aware of the whole backstory.

You've been Chat's lifeline. You keep that going all through this night, you hear me? She'll need you more than ever right now.'

'I so very truly want to believe that. I know I can give her all the love, all the support that she could possibly want.'

'You're the only one who can,' I said. 'Did Chat see Jeanine between Christmas and this week?'

'No. That's why Jeanine said she thought the call was so strange. She went up to Boston yesterday, from Nantucket. She got the call today, saying Chat needed to see her. Urgently.'

'What about?'

'Chat didn't say. Just that she needed help, and she couldn't rely on anyone but Jeanine to give it to her,' Faith said. 'She asked Jeanine to meet with her tonight.'

My head was pounding. 'Where? Meet her where?'

'On the Cape. She told Jeanine she could get herself to the Cape. She asked her not to take the boat home to Nantucket, but to wait for Chat to arrive. There was a friend, Chat said to her — a man who needed help too.'

'And Jeanine? . . . ' It sounded as though Zukov was shooting for two victims, using Chat to draw Reverend Portland into the trap.

'Agreed to do it, of course. She told me — ' Faith had dissolved into tears. I could hear the voice of a woman in the background trying to comfort her.

'Are you there?' I waited a few seconds before asking her.

'I'm all right. Jeanine told me that Chat sounded like she was in pain. I can't bear to hear that, Alex. About the pain. You've got to find her.'

'We're going to do that. I promise. Is Jeanine with the police?'

'Yes. The officers have her at a hotel room in Hyannis,' Faith said, sounding as though she had found something lighter to say. 'She's not terribly serene about that, Alex. She understands, but she's not happy about it. We're a stubborn lot.'

'That's how you came to be ordained. I'm counting on stubborn to help us here. I'll call her now, Faith. Get some rest, if you can.'

'The Reverend Portland?' Mike asked when I hung up.

'Yeah. I'll call her to get more details. I say you ask the captain for a cruiser and we head to Hyannis right now. Scratch what I said about the perp heading south.'

'I'm on it, even though I gotta think the fishing is better in Florida this time of year.'

'You're right, Mike.' I thought of the photograph of the four women, the third victim already in the killer's weakened hands, and the fourth one being drawn into his web. 'But tonight there's live bait in Hyannis.'

47

'You don't need to waste time programming the GPS,' I said. 'I know this part of the world like the back of my hand.'

It was close to midnight on Friday when we pulled out of the trooper headquarters.

'The back of your hand has gotten me lost more times than I can count.'

'In Brooklyn, maybe. But not on Cape Cod.'

'How long you figure?'

'No more than an hour and forty-five minutes at this time of night.'

After my brief conversation with Jeanine Portland, she had agreed to let the Hyannis police take her in to their station. She knew she would get no sleep in any event, and we would oversee a plan once we reached the famous resort town.

'Did the rev give you any more information about Chat?'

'Nothing new. She sounded drugged, terrifically frightened, and complaining that she was cold — and now, hurt. And in the company of a man who needed help.'

'That's our best hope for believing he'll keep Chat alive throughout this road trip,' Mike said. 'What was she talking to Portland about that she wouldn't confide in her own sister?'

'More of the same. She's just very needy, is the way Portland described it. I don't know if that's the truth or she simply isn't ready to offend Faith Grant yet with some deeper unburdening,' I said. 'Did you bring Peterson up to speed?'

'I did. And he tells me that Yuri Zukov's phone shows no calls from his brother since yesterday. Same cell zone as Chat.'

'Secaucus?'

'Yeah. So he's backed off communicating, even with his family, for the time being.'

We had traded our hot caffeine for cold. I flipped open the tops of two soda cans and placed them in the cup holders between us.

'You're going to take I-95,' I said. 'Through Fall River and New Bedford. Then the Sagamore Bridge and on out to the Cape.'

'Keep talking, kid.'

'Sleepy? Want me to drive?'

'I just want you to concentrate on the territory, the geography. You were totally thinking outside the box when you hit on the idea of the circus train this afternoon. Now find me a perp.'

We were in a marked black-and-white car, so the fact that Mike was doing eighty on the highway wouldn't get us stopped. We batted facts and theories back and forth, none of them particularly inspired.

'Is it twelve yet?' Mike asked.

'Quarter after.'

'Do me a favor, will you? Dial my mother's number, okay?'

'It's late for that.'

'Friday-night bingo at the church. One of her favorite forms of worship. She doesn't leave there till after eleven.'

391

I found Mrs. Chapman's number in the address book, pressed it, and passed my cell to Mike.

'Did you get lucky or what, Ma?' Whatever her answer, it made him laugh. 'Next week I'm gonna get a Brinks guard to drive you home. You shouldn't be walking around with fifty-six bucks in your purse at this hour of the night. Do me a favor and pour yourself a double — I'm grounded tonight.'

Mrs. Chapman chatted on with her favorite — and only — son.

'On my way to Cape Cod, Ma. Yep, she's with me — my lucky charm, like you say.'

She had called me that since the first time we worked a case together. I smiled at the thought of their loving, good-humored relationship.

'Did you TiVo *Jeopardy!* for me?' Mike asked. 'Great. Well, just leave the answer on my cell after you play it back. I'm looking to score on Coop tonight. You sleep tight, Ma. You tell Father Bernard we're gonna catch this son of a bitch. You tell him that when you see him on Sunday, and no, I swear to you he won't mind the language at all.'

He handed me back the phone.

'I meant to congratulate you on the great restraint you showed while we were on the train,' I said. 'Not turning on the television, I mean.'

'I just lost track of time is all that was. Never meant to miss it. She'll fill me in.'

'There's practically no traffic. The only trucks I've seen are supermarket semis and gas tankers.'

'Tell me something I don't already know.'

'When we get out on the Cape, you're going to have to watch out for deer. They're everywhere at this hour of the night.'

'So what did Oksana say about Fyodor's juvenile record?'

'No specifics. Just enough to send him away to a school for troubled adolescents.'

'Peterson hasn't been able to track anything yet.'

'If it's juvie, it's likely to be sealed. Who knows? She was just trying to give me her 'Officer Krupke' pitch.'

'I've heard way too many of those,' Mike said, speeding past the WELCOME TO THE COMMONWEALTH OF MASSACHUSETTS signs that bordered the highway. 'He's disturbed, he's misunderstood, he's got a social disease. It's never the bad guy's own fault. I'm surprised she didn't throw in growing up in a leotard and tights. Maybe that's what twisted him.'

'She might have reached that point by now. I think I shut her down,' I said. 'Tell you what. I'll be Alex Trebek. Here's your substitute question: The Final *Jeopardy!* category is FAMOUS AERIALISTS.'

'One ride on a circus train and suddenly you're a freaking expert on the subject?'

'The answer is the daring young man on the flying trapeze, Detective Chapman. I'll give you twenty seconds.'

'Give me nothing.'

'Who was Jules Léotard?'

'You and your damn ballet lessons. That's how

393

come you know from leotards. And the guy was French, to boot? Another likely heartthrob for you.'

'A lawyer who left the bar for a career on the high wire. It was Léotard who developed the art of trapeze, and for whom the song was written, in 1867. And he started a trend — wearing the one-piece outfit that dancers use too.'

'Then maybe this case is all his fault, you think?'

'I'm expecting that will be part of the defense — blame the victims, and then throw in a little bit of what was a man in tights supposed to do?'

We made small talk and bantered trivia and tried to reassure ourselves that every cop and agent in the northeast was doing something to find Chastity Grant while we made our way to Hyannis. By the time we reached the Sagamore Bridge, one of the two spans that crosses the Cape Cod Canal, it was one fifteen in the morning and the only thing lower than my hopes for Chat's safety were my spirits.

The cell phone slid off my lap as it vibrated. 'You losing it?' Mike asked.

'Not entirely.' I leaned down and picked it up, recognizing the displayed number. 'Hey, Mercer. Thanks for calling back.'

'I wasn't avoiding you, Alex. I had no reception. I'm just outside the ER at Bellevue.'

'Listen. We've got news — '

'And I've got news for you. What brought me here tonight is Gina Borracelli.'

'What?' I assumed the teenager and her box of bad things was behind me.

'Hold tight and don't let this throw you off course,' Mercer said. 'She's doing fine, Alex. But she tried to kill herself tonight.'

'Oh, my God. Is she all right?' I slumped down in the passenger seat, my head against the car window.

'She's going to be just super. Acting out, is what the docs tell me. Not a serious effort in anyone's view, except her parents'.'

'What happened?'

'She was out clubbing with her friends. Got liquored up. Every one of them had fake IDs so they got served. She went into the restroom around midnight. Swallowed a handful of pills and passed out on the bathroom floor.'

'Where was she?'

'The Limelight.'

'I should have guessed that. Uncanny, isn't it?'

'Unholy,' Mercer said.

The Limelight, on Avenue of the Americas at 20th Street, had been a nightclub for longer than I was a prosecutor. Drugs were as readily available there as alcohol, and many of our date-rape cases started as casual encounters in the trendy club.

For more than a hundred years before that, the landmarked building was anything but notorious. It was the glorious Church of the Holy Communion, an Episcopal church whose parishioners once included the millionaires Cornelius Vanderbilt and John Jacob Astor.

'EMTs just shot across town to Bellevue. Pumped her stomach out and Gina will be up and about by morning. They'll keep her a couple of days for observation and make sure she starts some inpatient psych care.'

'But she's conscious and alert?' I was sorry to have played any role in the mounting distress that had caused the teen's well-being to be compromised.

'Nothing to fret about. She's fine and her ol' man has a new punching bag.'

'You?'

'Yeah, but I think I scare him a bit more than you do.'

'Good to hear. In the meantime, while you're there, can you check for Fyodor Zukov's med records? His sister says — '

'I guess I buried the lede, Alex. They're going to give me the records, subject to a subpoena that Nan can cut in the morning. It's not what we thought.'

'You mean it wasn't an emergency-room admission?' I said, thinking of the problems with the nerves in his hands that cut short his career on the wires. 'Or it isn't psychiatric?'

'Neither one of those,' Mercer said, discounting the two things most commonly associated with the old medical facility.

'What then?'

'Zukov's been examined here at a new clinic. It's for Hansen's disease. Do you know — ?'

'I know exactly what it is, Mercer. It's leprosy,' I said to him. Then to Mike, 'Our killer — who targets outcasts and pariahs and black sheep — is a leper.'

48

'Stop the car!'

'Stop the train, stop the car — what is it with you tonight?' Mike asked.

'Zukov's not on his way to Hyannis. Pull over and let me drive.'

'What are you talking about?'

'I know where he's going, Mike. I can get us to Woods Hole with a blindfold on, in half the time that you can,' I said. The tiny village on the southwestern tip of the Cape is the home of the terminal from which ferries run back and forth to Martha's Vineyard. I'd spent countless hours there walking the harbor as I waited to get over to my island on standby, with no reservation.

'Where's he going? And why do you think you know?'

'Because this country didn't ever have more than a handful of places that were leper colonies, and only one of those was turned into a 'last chance' school for delinquent boys.'

Mike pulled to the side of the road and braked the car.

'Twofers, Coop. I'll bite. Where are you taking me?'

Mike opened the door to change seats and I answered him as I moved behind the steering wheel. 'A desolate little place in Buzzards Bay where they used to banish lepers a century ago,' I said. 'It's called Penikese Island.'

49

'Get on the phone to the Coast Guard. We're going to need their help to get to the island,' I said, adjusting the rearview mirror as I made the U-turn to take us south to the tip of the Cape. 'And don't let them send a chopper up yet. We don't want to let him know we're coming.'

'Penikese is a smart guess, Coop. A bit of a wild card, but smart. I just don't want to jump the gun. I'm not ready to pull any cops off Reverend Portland's detail yet on the theory that our perp knows about this little island.'

'Here's what you do. Call Peterson and ask him to get the feds moving. They'll bring in the Coast Guard. Then you call the captain in Providence. I blew Oksana off when she was talking to me about Fyodor and his reform school. Have him ask her where it was. I bet she and Yuri were old enough at the time to remember.'

'How long till we get to Woods Hole?'

'With any luck and no roadkill, I'd say we're there in less than half an hour. And the local cops — '

'How many are there? Two?'

'Off-season like this, maybe four,' I was only half joking. I had no idea what their resources might be, but Mike and I would need backup. 'They've got to start scouring the town for an Angus truck.'

'Doesn't really give me a lot of time to rally the troops. There's a slew of places to dump a truck, aren't there?'

'Ferry parking lots, marinas, residential areas, and plenty of woods that surround the little town. Get on it.'

'You like giving me orders, Coop?' Mike asked as he got on the phone.

'I love being in the driver's seat. Get used to it.'

'I'm allergic to the idea. Brake going into these curves, will you?'

'You don't know how many times I've raced this road to catch the last boat over. Stop whining and tighten your seat belt.'

'Don't steal my lines, Coop. You're the whiner,' Mike said as he waited for Lieutenant Peterson to answer. 'You know this is going to get worse before it gets better, don't you?'

Every trace of my smile disappeared. 'I'm well aware of that.'

'I'm in charge once we get where we're going. There's one gun, and I've got it. When we get to town, you're no longer the dominatrix. Am I understood?'

I swerved to avoid a raccoon — his beady eyes reflecting in our headlights as he lumbered across the road.

'Loo? We got a change in plans. Coop's brain is on double-overtime. Don't ask me to explain, Boss, just go with it and put some pressure on the locals,' Mike said, and then answered the question Peterson asked him, winking at me as I looked up from the road.

'Yeah, I do trust her. Just go with it.'

'Thanks for that,' I said.

'Eyes on the road. Tell me first what Mercer said about Zukov's diagnosis. And then you've got about twelve minutes to make me an expert on every inch of this little island.'

'I'll start with the disease.'

'Shoot.'

'Zukov saw a doc in Atlanta after he dropped the girl during their trapeze act. Admitted to him — but not to his family — that he'd lost sensation in his hands from time to time. That fact, combined with the lesions on his face, caused the physician to send him to New York.'

'In December?'

'Exactly. The diagnosis was made at the Bellevue clinic, one of the few in the country that specializes in the disease. Mercer read me the notes.'

'How was it diagnosed? How advanced is it?'

'To begin with, the germ that causes leprosy attacks the skin and the nerves. The skin lesions developed first, a couple of years ago. They were small initially, then became larger and larger — festered and blistered. But because of the tendency for Fyodor to use makeup for performances, he was able to cover it up.'

'He must have been in complete denial. That — and the fact that nobody thinks about leprosy today, except in third-world countries.'

'Mercer says Bellevue's got five hundred people in their program, right in New York City.'

'And Fyodor Zukov is one of them?'

'No. They wanted him to be treated, but he

was so devastated by the diagnosis that he didn't come back. Not until the day that Naomi Gersh disappeared.'

'Why then?' Mike asked.

'For pain medication.'

'Shit. And they gave it to him?'

'Yes, he promised to enroll in the program, and they gave him a scrip for pain meds,' I said, thinking of the drugged and drowsy voice of Chat Grant. 'Oxycodone. A two-week supply.'

'It's a narcotic and a painkiller, right?'

'Oh, yeah. It would do the job on our vics.'

'But if they were offering to treat him, why would he skip out?'

'The nurse who talked to Mercer interpreted the doctor's notes. The disease has progressed pretty aggressively. Even though Fyodor couldn't face telling his siblings — and certainly not circus management — he'd never be able to work again. The sensory impairment of his nerves — nerve paralysis, in fact — has already caused permanent deformities.'

'Where?'

'In addition to the weakness in his wrists, his fingers have begun to claw.'

'That's what it's called?' Mike asked.

'Irreversible clawing, yes, of the fingers and toes. It's no wonder he dropped his partner,' I said. 'The infection eventually invades the bones and destroys them. Without treatment, he'll lose his extremities.'

'I'd be pretty devastated too.'

'The other thing was his eyebrows. Remember Faith telling us he had no eyebrows?'

'Yeah.'

'Classic symptom of leprosy.'

'But he's got a full head of hair,' Mike said.

'That's 'cause the head is warm. The bacteria invade the eyebrows because they're much cooler than head hair.'

The road had narrowed from four lanes to two. Fog was settling in over the treetops and I could smell the saltwater as we neared the shoreline.

'Let me tell you about Penikese.'

It was hard to see the pavement for the thickening fog, and I slowed my pace briefly. I centered the car on the yellow line in the middle of the road and pressed down on the pedal.

'It's one of the Elizabeth Islands, just north of Cuttyhunk. It's only seventy-five acres.'

'The whole thing? Central Park's more than eight hundred acres. You're right about tiny,' Mike said. 'You've been there?'

'Scores of times, mostly as a kid.' I could see Cuttyhunk and its three sister islands from the deck of my Vineyard bedroom. Penikese was out of sight, on the far north side of Cuttyhunk.

'There's a ferry?'

'No ferry. No regular service at all.'

'Great. You planning a swim?'

'No. There'll be something moving in the harbor,' I said. 'My father kept his sailboat on the Vineyard. A Herreshoff — a twentyeight-foot ketch. My brothers and I spent a lot of time exploring the islands. Then I fell in love with Adam, and he was a sailor too. Penikese held a fascination for him 'cause he was a medical student, so the diseased history of the place and its tragic sadness drew him there. But it somehow terrified me.'

'Why?'

'It's jinxed — it's always been that way. It's got a miserably sad past.'

'How so?'

'Leprosy is one of the most dreaded conditions of humankind,' I said. 'Until very recently, people believed it was contagious. Incurable and contagious.'

'It's not?'

'Very rarely. There's a genetic susceptibility.'

'So Zukov's siblings might be in line?'

'It's possible. Ninety-five percent of all people are immune to the bacillus. But in the old days, lepers were sent off to live in quarantine.'

'Leper colonies.'

'Isolated from their communities. And islands were the ideal solution. There was one in the East River, another off the coast of San Francisco, and the infamous colony on Molokai. People were shipped off forever, separated from their families, to live the rest of their lives — and to die — among strangers suffering with the same affliction. There was no coming back.'

'Penikese was one of them?'

'In 1905, Massachusetts created the Penikese Island Hospital on this lonely rock in the middle of the bay. Two doctors volunteered to staff it, and five patients — ripped from their homes and their children — were forced to be sent there.'

'How did they live?'

'The patients had to build their own shacks

— small, wooden ones. They don't exist anymore. Fishing boats would drop off fresh food from the mainland, once a week, depositing it at the end of the dock. Letters from home, that sort of thing. One-way service only.'

'And no one ever returned?'

'Not a single soul. The tombstones and crosses are proof of that. Most of the wooden markers have rotted away.'

'What scared you there, Coop?'

'As a kid it was the idea of plague pits. My older brothers would tie up the boat and we'd sneak ashore. I was afraid to go with them, and more afraid to wait alone. Everyone says the island has ghosts. Even a haunted mansion, way back in time.'

'Mansion? In a leper colony.'

'No, no. Before the state took it over. Long gone, but my brothers used to play in the old shafts and tunnels beneath it. That didn't worry me — I was just too claustrophobic to go down into them — but the sad stories of the lepers really got to me.'

'Sounds like it.'

'The boys used to taunt me — tell me that if I stepped on one of the graves, the ghost of the leper would rise up and, well — kill me. When I was ten, eleven — I believed that.'

'You've been to ghost islands before.'

'Not so full of death as Penikese. Not with such a painful past. It's one of the loneliest little outposts in the world.'

'How long did the hospital last?'

'Only about fifteen years. The government

404

built a leprosarium in Louisiana. This pitiful place went out of business pretty fast after that. Then, about thirty years ago, someone had the idea to use the desolate setting as a school for delinquent boys — really dangerous ones. Kids who needed complete isolation to attempt to resocialize them. The success rate has been less than enviable.'

I could make out fog lights on the road ahead and I braked again, getting over to the right to avoid a pickup truck coming the opposite way. When I reached the traffic light in Falmouth, I could see that no one was approaching the intersection and I ran through the red signal. There was only one more stop sign between where we were and the harbor, then a twelve-mile boat run to Penikese Island.

'It's biblical, you know,' Mike said. 'Leprosy, I mean. Maybe that's what's haunting our killer.'

'It was considered a mark of God, wasn't it? A sign to the priests that the leper was someone who had sinned.'

'Your boy Moses started the whole phobia, Coop.'

'I guess so. I remember in Leviticus, he directed the Israelites to exile lepers, to exile all those who had offended their God.'

Mike knew as much of the Old Testament as the New. ' "Whosoever shall be defiled with the leprosy and is separated by the judgment of the priest . . . shall dwell alone without the camp." '

'Father Bernard might smile on you after all.'

The fog swirled around the car as we crested

405

the hill that over-looked the Woods Hole ferry terminal. The sturdy old *Islander* was sheltered in its dock below us, dark and still, out of service until the first run of the morning.

Off to the right, in Quissett Harbor, the red bubble atop a police cruiser was spinning in the haze, setting off an eerie glow.

'There,' Mike said. 'Head for that patrol car.'

'I see it,' I said, nosing the car past the row of stores and restaurants, beyond the scattered buildings of the Oceanographic Institute.

A solo officer was pacing the sidewalk at the end of the dock, talking to someone on his radio, when he saw us get out of the Rhode Island trooper's car.

The device squawked as he waited for a reply. 'You the New Yorkers?'

'Yeah,' Mike answered.

I walked beyond them to the shiny white truck that had been backed into a parking space, blocked from the view of traffic by a large RV that stuck out into the street.

'I was just calling this in to my office,' the cop said. 'It's the stolen vehicle from New Jersey. Got the broadcast a couple of hours ago.'

'How long ago was it ditched?'

'It wasn't here at eleven, when I came on duty. I'm pretty sure of that.'

'Get Crime Scene on it,' Mike said. 'Bust it open. We got things to do.'

The cop gave a halfhearted laugh. 'I maybe can get you Crime Scene in a day or two.'

'Then make it a locksmith or a safecracker. Break it open. We're looking for a woman who's

406

probably been locked inside there for twenty-four hours.'

The cop seemed shell-shocked by the orders Mike was directing at him.

'We can't take the chance that Zukov has left Chat behind in there,' I said. 'He's always staged his bodies at a far more dramatic setting. I don't want to wait till they get this open. We can't afford to do that if she's still alive.'

Mike pounded his fist on the side of the truck repeatedly. If Chat was inside it, she wasn't capable of sending a signal back to him.

He walked to the other side of the truck and called Chat's name, then turned back to the cop. 'Seen anyone around the docks this evening? People you don't know?'

'Just the regulars. A few old guys fishing for squid off the end. Only thing unusual I saw was a big black duffel bag out on the walkway leading to the dock as I drove through. But by the time I cruised the street and turned around, it was gone. Figured someone was picking it up off his boat.'

Mike looked at me. 'Didn't Luther's friend — what's his name? . . . '

'Shaquille.'

'Didn't Shaquille tell us the killer at Mount Neboh had the body in a large sack, like a duffel bag?'

'Sure he did. I'm telling you, Zukov's on the move with Chat.'

'I think you're right.'

'How about boats?' I asked the cop. 'You know the harbor well enough to tell me if anything is missing?'

'There's a twenty-two-foot Grady-White sits right over there most of the time,' he said, pointing to an empty space on the dock between two other motor boats. 'She belongs to the guy who owns the liquor store, but he's not usually on the water at this hour. The *Phantom Flyer*, he calls it.'

'Put out an APB for that one,' Mike said. 'You got a gun I can borrow for an hour or two?'

The cop shook his head. 'We don't patrol with guns.'

'Then you'd better rouse all the help you can get. We're going over to Penikese.'

50

'Where's the Coast Guard?' I asked the cop. 'We were supposed to have lots of backup here, waiting for us.'

'I can't imagine anyone promised you that. A trawler overturned in Nantucket Sound around midnight. Most of the guys are out on search and rescue. Four crewmen still missing.'

I saw a light in the little shack at the far end of the harbor and started to jog toward it. 'C'mon, Mike. I'll get you there.'

'Let's just untie a boat. Jump-start it.'

'I'd never be able to find my way. Fog, rips, shallows, the current. Let's get a pro.'

'At this hour? I thought you said that nothing runs.'

'Nothing commercial. But we'll make one take a run.'

I reached the shack, barely larger than a phone booth. The startled attendant was awakened from his nap by the sound of my footsteps on the dock.

'We're from New York. He's a homicide detective. I'm a prosecutor. We need a ride on the *Patriot* now. *Now.*'

'Everybody's in a hurry tonight. Are you two with that tall guy who was jumping from boat to boat an hour or so ago? I chased him right out of here.'

'We're not with him,' Mike said. 'We're after him.'

The man placed his arthritic hands on his thighs and stood up. 'Let me see what I can do about that.'

'Is the *Patriot* here?'

'Right over there. Morning papers should be aboard shortly.'

The *Patriot* fleet consisted of half a dozen workhorse boats — fortyfive feet long — each more useful than decorative. They were available for private hire all night, often by Vineyarders who missed the last ferry over, or entertainers leaving after an evening gig on the island. The things we counted on to make our lives normal — from daily newspapers to fresh bagels — motored across on one of these boats.

Unlike the Steamship Authority ferries, which halted service in severe weather, there was almost nothing that could stop a *Patriot* from making a trip.

Mike beat me to the boat. There was a light on in the cabin, and I lowered myself over the side and knocked on the window.

The captain was bundled up in a down jacket, with a Red Sox ski cap pulled down over his ears. He was reading a copy of the *Boston Globe*, probably waiting for the *New York Times* delivery before the first three a.m. crossing to Oak Bluffs.

'Captain? I'm Alex Cooper. This is Mike Chapman. What'll it take to hire you for an emergency run?'

To my surprise, when the captain's head picked up, I could see she was a young woman.

'Emergency?' she said, dropping the paper and

getting to her feet. 'To the Vineyard?'

'No, no. To Penikese?'

'At two in the morning?'

Mike took over. His charm might work faster with the attractive boater. 'Look, Miss . . . '

'Lynch. Maggie Rubey Lynch.'

'Give me that newspaper, Maggie.'

She picked up her copy of the early edition of the *Globe* and handed it to Mike.

'See this bastard?' he said, pointing to the head shot of Zukov that was on top of the fold of the morning news. 'We're thinking he's over on Penikese, and he's likely to kill the girl who's with him unless you can get us there. Just a drop-off. You just put us on the rock and head back to port. That's all we're asking.'

She didn't flinch for a second. 'Let's go. It's kind of rough out there. I need you to sit down, okay?'

'Whatever you say.'

I guessed Maggie to be about thirty years old. She had platinum hair, from the wisps that had slipped out beneath her cap, bright blue eyes, and an easy smile. But she also had the complete confidence of someone who had probably spent her entire life on the water, as evidenced by each of the steps she took to release the lines, raise the bumpers, and ease the *Patriot* out of its slip.

Mike got on his cell and again called the lieutenant. The reception was patchy, but it would be his last chance to reach out to anyone. The up-island half of the Vineyard had no cell service, so I knew that Penikese would

411

be a dead zone too.

'Where's the frigging Coast Guard, Loo? I can't hear you,' Mike said, shouting over the noise of the engines. 'I know there was an accident. We're on our way to this leper colony, you got that? Call the Navy, call the Marines. I don't give a shit what you have to do, but we need — hello? Hello?'

'You're talking to the wind out here,' Maggie said.

'You got that right.'

'We're into the bay now. It's going to get bumpy.'

The water was practically black. The boat heaved in the waves and tossed us from side to side. Maggie held on to the wheel, keeping an eye on the radar and GPS to guide us toward our destination. I knew the moon was almost full, but fog had blanketed Buzzards Bay and it was impossible to see the heavens.

'What's your plan?' I asked Mike.

'I'm working on one.'

He was a nervous flier, and I worried that motion sickness might overcome him on this short ride.

'Are you queasy?'

'It's not like a plane that's going to fall out of the sky on me, Coop. These are just bumps in the road.' He was trying to convince himself that was true.

The waves came at us hard. 'I'm counting on you for a plan. It'll take your mind off your stomach.'

'Just watching the captain calms me.'

Maggie smiled at him. 'This is nothing. They're predicting six-foot swells later this week.'

'Where are you able to put us off?'

'You know Penikese?' she asked me.

'I haven't been in years.'

'It's pretty uninhabitable. A few primitive buildings the school maintains, but they're completely shut down 'cause next weekend is Easter. I picked a teacher up about two weeks ago. There's a jetty on the eastern end. If the rip doesn't smash me up on it, it's the best place to let you go.'

'Can you try for something a little more optimistic?' Mike asked.

Maggie flashed a big, pretty smile. 'Hey, I can be as upbeat as the next guy, but there's not much hope on Penikese. You sure you don't want me to wait for you?'

Mike was clutching the rim of the life preserver that was mounted on the wall behind his bench. 'What I'd really like you to do is play Paul Revere for us. Hightail it back to base and raise an armada for me. Come back with any able-bodied seamen you can find. You'll get extra credit if they bring weapons.'

'That's a deal, Detective,' she said. 'We're half a mile out. You get ready to offload.'

I stood up and steadied myself by holding on to the metal rails above my head. The color had drained from Mike's face. I thought he was going to be sick.

'Don't look at me that way,' he said. 'I'm good.'

'Do you have any flashlights we can use?' I asked Maggie.

'Sure. Lift up the top of that bench.'

I removed two from her supply stash. 'And this length of rope?'

'Go for it,' Maggie said. 'It's likely to be slippery on the rocks, so watch your step.'

She had killed the engine and was maneuvering the boat along the end of the jetty. She stepped to the side and tossed another rope around a rotting wooden upright that once must have been part of a pier to hold us in place long enough to disembark.

I stuffed one flashlight in my rear pocket and hoisted myself up on the gunwale of the sturdy boat. Mike slowly got to his feet, and while I wrapped the rope I had taken around my waist, he stepped off onto the large, moss-covered rocks of the jetty.

'Thanks a million, Maggie.'

'I'll be back,' she said softly. 'I promise. You watch yourselves, will you?'

'You keep your half of the deal and we'll keep ours. See you later.' I pushed against the stern of the boat with one leg and waved her off.

The wind howled across the barren landscape. Scrubby trees bent and blew, and the spray from the waves dashing against the jetty drenched the calves of my jeans.

Mike started to walk toward land, taking deep breaths and being careful to step on the flattest rocks.

If either of us thought that moonlight might break through the mist to guide us onto the island, we were greatly mistaken. Our flashlights stayed lodged in our pockets. We were both unwilling to attract Zukov's attention, hoping he hadn't seen the lights of the boat.

The breaking of the waves was the only sound I could hear as we made our way forward, single file, and stepped at last on the hard earth of the desolate outpost.

'You recognize anything, Coop?' Mike said in a whisper.

I shook my head in the negative.

'Anywhere to hide?'

'A few wooden school buildings. Really small. We're talking only ten or twelve kids here at any one time, living dorm-style, and a couple of teachers. I don't know what's left standing.'

A gull screeched as it flew overhead and I ducked at the sound, though it was nowhere near me.

'Stay close,' Mike said. 'I'm flying blind, but let's get going.'

I was on his heels as we started along the shoreline. We had only gone about twenty yards when the night sky was pierced by a bloodcurdling scream.

Mike reached back for my hand and squeezed it. 'He's made us, Coop. He's putting on a show for our benefit.'

'You really think he saw us land?'

'He wants an audience for his next silencing, kid. That wasn't one of your Penikese ghosts.'

'I know that, Mike.'

It was the voice of Chastity Grant, who'd been carried to this pitiful island to be tortured and killed.

415

51

'We have to show ourselves,' I said to Mike. 'He'll go on torturing her until we do.'

'Correction, Coop. I'll show myself. You'll be my fog-enshrouded second, okay? You'll hang back until we know the lay of the land.'

There was no point challenging his machismo until we knew what Fyodor Zukov was doing to his prey.

'Where did it sound like her scream was coming from?'

Chat's cry had resonated around us like a thunderclap, carrying its mournful wail high above the open space of the small island.

'Everywhere,' Mike said. 'What's the shoreline like?'

'At low tide like this, there's a spit of sand — well, sand and rocks — that rings the place.'

'That's how we'll start, on the perimeter.'

I was tempted to take off my driving moccasins, which were soaked through, and go barefoot in the sand. But I knew that the stony, unforgiving landscape of Penikese would make me regret doing that before too long.

We moved fast, going northwest along a crescent beach. Waves lapped the sand, and beyond that steady sound, there was none of the noise I hoped to hear — no boats circling nearby, nobody looking for a spot to land his craft and aid us.

'What's on top of that rise?' Mike asked, coming to the end of the short beach.

'There's a pond up there. I'd expect it to be all dried up this time of year. It's kind of like a mud hole, so let's avoid it.'

Another fifty yards and I could see that the low cliffs that once faced westward had eroded and were nothing more than sand dunes.

'There, Mike. We can probably climb over those.'

The terrain slowed us down. Our feet sunk into the wet beachfront as crabs scampered away from the dead fish that had washed up in our path.

Each leg felt heavier as I pulled up, step after step, to go forward. Then, as I mounted the rising dunes, the dry sand crumbled beneath my moccasins and filled them like an hourglass turned upside down.

Mike had reached the top before I did. He waited for me to pull up beside him. We were still sheathed in silence and could only see a few feet ahead.

'What's that?' he asked, and pointed.

A low picket fence — maybe two feet high, painted dark green, as it always had been — was just ahead of us.

'The graveyard,' I said. 'Or what's left of it.'

'There's your plague pit, then,' Mike whispered.

'Don't be ridiculous.'

Mike grabbed my arm and held a finger to his mouth to shush me. 'Hear it?'

I waited for the current to draw the waves

417

back into the bay. Then I was able to hear a noise wafting through the dense mist. A whimpering sound, muffled now, not clear and shrill like the scream that split the night sky a few minutes earlier.

Mike pointed again, toward the south end of the picket fence and started to walk in that direction. He had drawn his weapon — the Glock 19 that was the duty gun of choice for most of the NYPD.

Now he was moving at a snail's pace, as was I behind him. He was trying to bypass every twig, every bramble that might snap when stepped on. I walked in the damp imprint of his large steps.

We inched along and seemed to be drawing closer to the whimpering woman.

Another step and Mike stood still. I looked down and saw, at the very place his toes were, a cement block — a row of them side by side, actually — then a gaping black hole ahead. It looked like a deep foundation — the only remains of an old building.

He tapped the flashlight in his rear pocket, and I pulled it out. He braced himself and held both arms straight ahead, nodding at me to shine the light into the darkened space that had been dug into the ground so very long ago.

Fyodor Zukov was directly below us, standing over the body of Chastity Grant. She was gagged now — probably after her penetrating scream — and bound as well, hands and feet. I could see the red fabric — aerial silk — that her captor had used to restrain her.

Next to her head on the dirt floor — nestled

418

on top of a large duffel bag — was a long-handled ax, the kind of tool that had been used to sever the neck of Naomi Gersh.

Zukov was holding an implement of some kind. He had clearly been waiting for us, as Mike had expected. As soon as the light hit him, he prodded Chat in the neck with the sharp end of his stick and she emitted another ungodly sound.

'Drop it, Zukov,' Mike said. 'Drop the bullhook or I shoot.'

I hadn't recognized it as a bullhook, the vicious steel-tipped instrument used to goad elephants, the inhumane device some circus trainers favored to push and yank deep into the animal's sensitive flesh to control its movements.

Mike took aim to fire, but Zukov's hands — though weaker, perhaps — were still faster than Mike's. He swiveled and raised the curved handle of his bizarre weapon, hooking it around Mike's left ankle and dragging him over the cement block, down into the hole.

I heard Mike hit bottom with a thud. I shined the light on him and could see that the fall had dislodged the Glock from his hand.

Zukov stabbed at Mike's back as he tried to struggle to his feet.

'I prefer to call it a shepherd's crook,' the killer said, referring to the C-curve handle that indeed resembled the staff used by priests and bishops. How ironic that the cruel circus tool was also a symbol of Christ's ministry. 'The Gospel of John, chapter ten, verse eleven. 'I am the good shepherd. The good shepherd giveth his life for the sheep.''

Mike got to his knees and Zukov thrust the bullhook into his back again.

'I'm not afraid to lay down my life, Ms. Cooper, like Christ did for all of us,' Zukov said, looking up at me. He obviously knew who I was from his courtroom visit. 'How about you? Are you ready to die?'

52

'Get out of here, Coop!' Mike yelled to me. I assumed that he hadn't gotten to his feet immediately to take on Zukov because he'd hurt his leg — maybe the ankle that had been so badly injured a year ago. 'Get as far away as you can till the Coast Guard arrives.'

'They'll be too late,' Zukov said. 'Whenever it is they get here, they'll be late.'

I was way too tired to think clearly. Running wasn't an option. I didn't know whether to stay where I was until the crazed killer decided which of his victims to go for first, or to lower myself into the old foundation and try to find Mike's gun.

'You must be one of the detectives, aren't you?' he said to Mike. 'I have to hand it to you. I never thought you'd find us on Penikese. I figured I'd have some time to get to know Reverend Grant more intimately.'

Fyodor Zukov had indeed confused Faith Grant with her sister, whom she so closely resembled. Chastity may have been the black sheep of her hometown, but when she showed up at the Christmas performance of Ursula Hewitt's play — surrounded by the other ordained women — he made the mistake of targeting her. Her changed appearance from the December evening when she had gone goth — and now the striking resemblance between the

421

sisters with Chat's natural hair color and style restored — had caused Zukov to kidnap the wrong sibling.

'She's not a minister,' I said, trying to keep an eye on Zukov while using the light to look for Mike's gun.

'You know, Ms. Cooper, she's told me that over and over. But I've done my research well. I've been to the seminary and I've talked to her friends, and I don't think I've made a mistake. She has offended God and she must be silenced for that.'

Now Zukov was using the long, pointed end of the bullhook to poke around for the Glock too. I could see that Mike was spread out on his belly, inching himself forward like a reptile. He must have had some sense where the pistol had landed.

'Stay as calm as you can, Chat,' I said. 'Every police department in the northeast knows you're here. Faith sent us to find you, and we're going to get you out of here.'

'Don't play games with me!' Zukov shouted, waving the bullhook wildly overhead. 'I know who this woman is.'

I could hear her racked sobs from beneath the silk ties that covered Chat's mouth.

'The Reverend Grant — the minister — is at her seminary in New York. Don't make this any worse for yourself, Fyodor. You can let — '

'They're not ministers,' he said, watching Mike carefully but yelling in my direction, as though the wind carried his message across the seas. He looked every bit the madman as he preached to me. 'None of these foolish women are ministers. They should all be silenced by the church. Silenced by me, before I die.'

'The woman you're holding is not — '

'Priests and ministers are linked to the person of the incarnate Christ. The Father begets the Son.' Fyodor Zukov was raving now. 'The priest presides at the altar and says what Christ said, does what Christ did. In that moment and in that ministry, he *is* Christ. And Jesus Christ was a *man*.'

Mike was using the distraction of this maniacal sermon to edge himself forward.

'Tell her the truth, Ms. Cooper,' Zukov said, switching gears to a soft whisper of a voice. 'No one will find any of us here. Not in time.'

Somehow, while he'd been ranting, Zukov caught Mike's movement, and swung suddenly around, kicking his right leg up in a wide arc that took dead aim at Mike's head.

I screamed and Mike ducked, but the martial-arts training combined with the grace and balance of Zukov's circus artistry was in full display.

'How's your sambo?' Mike called out, taunting the devil himself.

It looked like Zukov was waiting for Mike to lead him to the gun before he struck a deadly blow with the sharp point of the bullhook.

'I fight for Christ, Detective. That's why you'll be so easy to kill.'

'If you thought the Reverend Portland would be your decoy, Fyodor,' I said, hoping to get his attention, 'you were wrong.'

He looked away from Mike and up at me, surprised that we knew as much as we did.

'It's Oksana who told us about you,' I said, starting to walk around the base of the foundation. I wanted to know how Fyodor thought he would get himself out of this deep hole. 'Oksana who told us about your time at Penikese.'

'Oksana would never give me up!' he shouted.

I had sidetracked him completely from his two captives. He was enraged by his sister's betrayal, baying at me as I continued to prowl above him.

Three-quarters of the way around the rectangular ditch I came upon his solution. Zukov had tied a strip of aerial silk — a bright blue length of fabric, the color of the piece that had been found on Naomi's body — to the base of a huge boulder a few feet away from the hole. He had secured the other end of it to a corner of one of the cement blocks. He would be able to lift himself out with very little effort, after he disposed of Chastity Grant.

'How else do you think we knew about Penikese?' I asked, stepping over the silk and continuing to stalk the perimeter. 'How else would we know you'd been banished here, sent away to school instead of jail?'

Zukov was following my movements, ready to take out his unhappiness about Oksana on me, or whoever was closest to him. It gave Mike the chance to continue his crawl. It allowed me time to think about what action to take.

'Doesn't matter that you can't call her from here. She's in jail. She was locked up as an accessory to murder tonight.'

'You're lying!' he screamed at me.

'I don't have any reason to lie, Fyodor. Oksana was arrested when the train stopped in Providence. Would you have silenced her too? Is that your plan? To silence anyone who has offended you?'

'I'd never hurt Oksana. Those who need to be silenced are the ones who offend God!' he yelled at the top of his lungs.

'Pariahs and outcasts, is that it?'

Mike was sitting up now, his back against the wall. I guessed he was close to his gun, ready to take on Zukov, although ten feet of darkness separated them and I knew he couldn't see a human target clearly in the blackness of the hole.

'And lepers, right?' Mike added.

Zukov spun on a dime. He was ready to charge at Mike.

'Don't you know doctors can treat your condition?' I called out to him. 'The doctors at Bellevue can help you. You don't have to die, Fyodor.'

He turned again to look at me, wondering, I thought, whether I was worth chasing down.

Now it was Mike speaking. 'The Gospel According to Mark. 'And there came a leper to him, beseeching him, and kneeling down to him, and saying unto him, If thou wilt, thou canst make me clean.''

Fyodor Zukov seemed transfixed as Mike recited text from the gospel.

''And Jesus, moved with compassion, put forth his hand, and touched him, and saith unto him, I will; be thou clean. And as soon as he had spoken, immediately the leprosy departed from him, and he was cleansed.''

'Don't mock me, Detective. It's too late for that too. Don't you dare mock me.'

Zukov extended his arm with the bullhook, aiming for Mike's head. But Mike dodged the sharp tip and came up with the gun in his right hand. He fired once and I heard the bullet ricochet off the wall.

Zukov laughed and readied his weapon, like a javelin, for another charge at Mike, who had braced himself against the foundation as he tried to get to his feet.

The killer lunged again. The tip of his weapon dug into the wall, catching the sleeve of Mike's jacket and pinning him in place, just as his foot caught Mike directly in the gut.

'Coop!' he called out from the darkened pit. 'Hang tough. Catch this and you're out of here.'

Mike pitched something out of the hole. In the few seconds the object was airborne, I realized it had to be the Glock. He couldn't loosen his arm sleeve from the bullhook to take aim, but he had flipped the light pistol up over his head in my direction. Mike knew he was no match for Zukov's killer instincts, and ridding himself of the deadly weapon would eliminate giving it up to the skilled fighter.

There was no way for me to grab the Glock as it sailed over my head like a small missile. It must have landed on nearby rocks, clattering against them as it dropped.

'Run, Coop!' he shouted at me again.

'No, Mike. No. I'm not going,' I said, trying to keep my voice strong. 'You're trapped.'

It sounded as though Zukov had kicked again. There was a loud thud and an ungodly sound from Mike's throat.

'Get the gun and shoot this bastard, will you?'

'Are you pinned to the wall?'

'No more,' he said, sounding weak and exhausted. He must have ripped his jacket loose from the point of the bullhook. 'Beat it.'

Then I heard the resurgence of Chat Grant's desperate sobs, and the beginnings of a fistfight between Mike and Zukov. I knew I had no choice but to find the loaded gun and use it.

53

I beamed the flashlight down the slope behind me.

There was a dense tangle of brush and shrubs, and about ten feet beyond that, something flat that looked like a granite step. It was the only visible surface that would have produced the noise made when the gun fell to the ground.

The grunts and pounding sounds of Mike and Zukov hitting each other propelled me toward the large stone even faster. When I reached it, stood on it, and looked down, I could see it was just the top piece in a staircase of at least fifteen steps. They were dug deep into the ground, most of the lower ones covered by rotting wooden beams that framed the sides.

Now all was silent again. There was no noise coming from the old foundation and I got no answer when I called Mike's name.

I took a few steps in, then hesitated, staring into the blackness beneath me and smelling the dank odor from within the belly of this obsolete seaside structure. Even a quick glance showed it to be more formally crafted than the old laundry building that was simply scooped out of the Penikese dirt. It must have been the remains of the mansion that my brothers had explored as kids.

I looked back over my shoulder. Of course the pit had gone quiet. Fyodor Zukov's body was outlined against the low-hanging clouds. He had grabbed on to the strip of blue aerial silk that he'd hung between the boulder and the concrete slab from down below with his long fingers, and he was climbing out of his lair, swinging himself up with all the grace and agility of his craft, in order to come in search of Mike's gun — and me.

'Are you there, Coop?' Mike's voice sounded a million miles away now that the killer was poised in midair between the two of us.

I didn't want to answer or give my position away, so I turned off the flashlight and stuffed it into my pants pocket. Maybe Zukov hadn't seen me yet. I had already committed myself to take the steps down — most reluctantly — padding farther along in my soft moccasins, hoping not to kick any loose rocks or debris in my path.

'That's how they punished us, Detective. Two or three nights in solitary — 'in the hole,' as they liked to call it. Bracing winter air. Builds character, is what they told us,' Zukov said. 'I played with the snakes, actually. I found them nicer to be with than most people.'

And as cold-blooded as the young delinquent too. I was halfway down the steps, feeling ahead of me with one foot for any sign of the gun.

'You tend to those wounds. I've got to find your friend, haven't I?'

I froze in place. What had he done to Mike? I could barely breathe as panic seized my chest and fogged my thinking.

Fyodor Zukov was one of the few people on earth who had walked every inch of this island. If there was a crevice in which to hide, I longed to find it. But I knew that if he got the Glock before I did, Mike Chapman and Chat Grant were doomed.

Above me I could hear him tread on the brambles and branches, first moving quickly over the ground to the side of the opening. Then suddenly, with his catlike moves, he was directly above me, his arms outspread and almost hanging there, like a silent apparition.

There was no hiding from him now. He had obviously seen that the slope to the water's edge was too covered in growth for me to maneuver through in the dark. I had to get my hands on the gun before he had me trapped in this clammy cellar.

I took the last four steps as fast as I could move, listening to Zukov's triumphant laugh when he spotted me below him.

I looked up in horror as he launched himself from the overhead wooden beam at the top of the staircase. Gripping it tightly, he pumped his legs back and forth, throwing himself down and forward, suspended from the crossbars, coming toward me as easily as if he were sliding along a length of rope.

I crouched as he approached, fearful that he would kick me in the head with one of his long legs. As I put out my hands to balance myself on the floor, I could feel the coldness of the gun. I reached for it and secured it in my waistband, pulling myself upright with some reserve of courage I didn't know was there.

I was running across the smooth surface of the

cement flooring. There had to be a closet to hide in or some object to stow myself behind while I got the gun in position. I knew it had a spring-loaded firing pin safety, and it would be a struggle for me to remember what I had learned about the weapon from my last trip to the NYPD's range.

Zukov had his feet on the ground and was giving chase. This subterranean space was vast and full of as many apparent dead ends as a maze at an English country manor. I passed a dozen small rooms but none had doors, so I didn't turn to go into any of them.

In the dim light I could see a massive wall looming straight in front of me. I looked to both sides, surprised to find a narrow opening to my right, and charged through it. Another huge room opened up before me, baffling me with what its uses had been and where it would lead me.

We were on equal footing on the flat surface. I was fast, too, with long strides that were a pretty decent match for the aerialist when he was earthbound.

I raced past scores of wooden planks that had once probably served as shelving for something in this damp basement. There was broken glass all over the floor and I needed to get through this space before Zukov tried to bring me down on it.

Another turn and the darkness lightened a bit. There were no windows in this next great room, but the thick granite walls narrowed at the far end.

It looked like there was an opening to the

outside — almost as wide as the room itself — that had been boarded over with plywood, and someone had punched an enormous hole through it ages ago. My eyes had adjusted to the dim interior when I'd descended the staircase minutes earlier, but now it seemed as though the foggy exterior light beyond the room was, by comparison, as bright as neon.

I beat Fyodor Zukov to the wall by a matter of seconds. We were both winded and the only noise I could hear above the sound of his heavy breathing as he tried to grab hold of me was the waves crashing against rocks very nearby.

I bent down and stuck my right leg through the hole in the plywood. Zukov tried to pull me down by the collar of my jacket, but I threw back my head and the top of his hand was impaled on the jagged edge of the splintered wood pieces that hung like stalactites. He recoiled in pain and I pressed ahead, crawling through the space to what I assumed would be freedom.

I straightened up and inhaled the briny sea air. I opened my eyes wide and closed them just as quickly. I hadn't expected to find myself standing on a stone ledge only ten inches wide, hung out over a rocky precipice that bordered the Vineyard Sound.

Fyodor Zukov was coming out behind me. I guessed the trapeze platforms he had flown from were smaller than this ledge and higher off the ground and, like it, had no safety net. This was his territory and I needed to escape it.

With my back to the building, I moved step-by-step to the left. Heights made me dizzy, so I turned my head in the same direction and focused on getting to land — maybe twenty feet away — as quickly as I could.

Something fluttered above my head and startled me. I looked up, expecting to see a diving gull flapping its wings. But it was a bolt of silk, rolled into a ball, that Zukov had thrown, trying to secure it to a shrub just beyond my position. It landed short and he pulled it back toward him — drawing it across my body — as I continued my baby steps to the side.

'It's hopeless, Ms. Cooper,' he called out to me. 'I'm going to get you. You'll die here alone, like one of the lepers.'

'I've got the gun, Zukov,' I shouted into the wind. 'Stay back or I'll shoot.'

I sucked in some air to combat the dizziness and kept walking as fast as I could. The small ball of silk sailed overhead again and almost snagged on the bare branches of a bush but fell just short.

I could practically feel his cold breath on my neck when he laughed and said, 'That's not likely to happen.'

With three feet to go, he tossed the blue fabric over my head. It caught and wrapped like a lasso around a dense thicket of *Rosa rugosa* shrubs just in front of me. I stopped in panic and watched as Zukov yanked on the strip to make sure it was secure before dropping off the ledge and flying to a clearing in the dirt just above the rocks and below the rosebushes. The gust of air, the draft created by his movement, had nearly carried me with it, practically knocking me off-balance and onto the pile of thick rocks below.

I was close enough now to shuffle to the end of the precarious ledge and jump down to the ground. Zukov had overshot that position by just a few yards to get ahead of me and was scrambling up the slope to take me on face-to-face.

I needed to circle around the bottom of the hill that held the old basement enclosure and retrace my steps to the pit in which Mike and Chat were confined. I started to climb, pushing brambles out of the way and trying to ignore thorns that nipped at me from the sturdy rosebushes.

Zukov's hand reached almost to my foot. I could see the blood dripping from it, where the splintered wood had cut him. He was gaining on me, seemingly oblivious to the pain when his hand brushed thorns or scraped rocks.

At a break in the rise to the crest of the small cliff, I stepped to a clearing at my side and straightened up. I had only seconds to think through my decision as Zukov tugged on his silken bolt to retrieve it from the bush, no doubt planning to use it again, perhaps to restrain me when he caught up with me.

I would be fortunate to outrun him to return to Mike, but far likelier to be overtaken by him and fall victim to the combat techniques of his extreme ministry. In either case, the gun was a liability in my hands, without the opportunity to examine and prepare it for firing.

I went to my waistband to retrieve it, and

while Zukov watched in disbelief and stretched out his bloody hand to try to stop me, I heaved the pistol as mightily as I could, beyond the rocky shore and into the icy waters of the Sound.

I didn't wait to see where it landed, as he did. I knew from the splash that it was beyond his deadly reach, and that my best chance for helping the captives was for me to get to them before Zukov.

'You'll die here,' he called out to me again. 'I promise you that.'

As frightened as I was, the thought that I might die, that I might be too late to help Mike, juiced me to go even faster. I twisted and turned among the thickets, knowing that he had to do the same. On this scrubby terrain, it was impossible for Zukov to fly.

At the summit of the small slope I called out to Mike. 'Are you alive?'

I needed to know that he was, and I wanted his voice to guide me in the right direction.

'Don't come back here, Coop. Get help.'

I had only halted for a fraction of a second and was on my way again. As agile as Zukov was, the rough landscape had slowed him too.

I reached the granite coping of the pit, sat on the side of it, and lowered myself to the ground. Chat Grant was struggling quietly against her restraints. I ran past her to Mike's side. He'd been punched and kicked, and the bullhook was stuck into the ground, pinning both hands behind his back to hold him in place. It was unbearable — unthinkable, really — to see him incapacitated by this murderous perp.

'You're mad to come back,' he whispered as I tried to lift the long instrument out of the ground.

'Not a word more,' I said.

I could see Zukov approaching the edge of the dark pit. I removed my flashlight from my pants pocket and knelt beside Mike.

'You got the gun?' he asked.

'Take this,' I said, placing the flashlight in his hands. I knew he'd be furious if I told him about the Glock. 'Count to five and turn it on.'

'What will that — '

'I'm still in the driver's seat. Just listen to me,' I said, my mouth against his ear.

Zukov had turned his back to us as he retied a length of aerial silk to the boulder where it had been earlier. He was preparing to float down into the pit while I slipped across to the corner beyond Chat Grant. He would be looking for me as soon as he alit.

He was halfway through his descent when Mike pushed the button to illuminate the flashlight. Zukov turned his head as the eerie torch suddenly backlighted one of his captives. Neither of us could see much against the blackness of the dirt wall, but Zukov stormed in that direction, assuming that I was holding the torch, trying to set Mike free.

'Where are you?' he shouted to the heavens, unable to see me crouching alongside Chat.

'Shoot, Coop,' Mike yelled as Zukov worked to pull the bullhook out of the ground. 'He's going to use this on one of us. He's going to kill one of us with it. Shoot, dammit, will you?'

Zukov kicked Mike again and laughed as he pulled his weapon loose and raised it with both arms, over Mike's chest. 'I have not come to bring peace on earth,' he said, 'but a sword, like Jesus Christ.'

I lifted the heavy ax from the ground beside Chat's head and quickly took three or four steps that brought me directly behind the killer. Mike was wide-eyed, shocked out of his poker-faced expression at the sight of my armed advance.

Zukov turned his head to see what had captured Mike's attention. I swung the ax with all my strength and struck at his outstretched arm.

He fell to his knees, cradling his wounded wrist. I picked up the flashlight and shined it on him as he doubled over in agony, covered in his own blood.

Fyodor Zukov's scream was louder than any human sound I'd ever heard.

54

I took the gag off Chat Grant's mouth and untied her hands and feet. She wrapped her arms so tightly around my neck that I thought she'd never let go.

'Don't try to talk,' I said, stroking her matted hair. 'There's no need to say anything.'

There would be hours and hours of debriefing after she was treated at a hospital.

Mike was limping around the hole, about twenty feet by forty. Zukov seemed to have passed out — maybe his body had gone into shock from the blood loss — and Mike had bound his legs together. He wasn't going anywhere, but neither were we.

'His arm? . . . ' I started to ask. I had meant to disable the madman, not to sever his hand.

'Don't go soft on me, blondie. You took a healthy bite out of him, but you didn't get the whole thing. I don't think he'll put the word 'flying' in front of his name anymore.'

'Let's have your jacket,' I said, reaching out for it as Mike removed it.

'How come you didn't warn me about this place?' he asked.

I wrapped his blazer, with its shredded sleeves, around Chat and we kept her huddled in a corner, trying to warm her up.

'It wasn't a hole last time I was here. I think it's the foundation of the old laundry building,' I said.

'But what's that big old ruin you were describing?'

'I had forgotten all about it. In the 1870s, long before the leper colony was built, a professor from Harvard started an institution here. Built a home and a laboratory and a boathouse. The Anderson School of Natural History. That must have been the ruins of the Anderson mansion — much grander than the leper colony ever was.'

'One of the haunted houses?'

'Exactly. I'm sure my brothers will delight in telling us about it,' I said. 'How's the leg?'

'I'm likely to do a trapeze act before Zukov is.'

Both of us were pacing back and forth — Mike nursing a mild limp — grateful that the fog was lifting and counting on help to get to us soon.

It was about four thirty in the morning when I heard voices. Mike answered first. 'Come this way! Can you hear me?'

'Loud and clear.' I didn't know who responded, but I was elated that a team was on their way.

Within minutes, four uniformed Coast Guardsmen were standing over us, and beside them was Maggie Rubey Lynch.

'That's Mike Chapman,' she said with a smile. 'And Alex Cooper.'

'You're a woman of your word, Captain Lynch,' Mike said.

'Well, I promised an armada, but all I came up with was a flotilla. Best I could do on short notice.'

'I'm still buying the drinks if you get us out of

here,' Mike said, blowing her a kiss. 'Can you get Ms. Grant up first, guys? She needs medical attention.'

'We've got four more men on the boat. Two are on their way with a stretcher. Looks like you solved this problem yourselves,' one of them said, pointing at Zukov.

'For the moment, we have. She gets the first stretcher. I've got a tourniquet around his arm, but it's a big bleed.'

'Helicopter's on the way. We just airlifted the four crewmen from the trawler.'

'So that situation has a happy ending too,' Mike said.

We waited with Chat until the guardsmen lowered a portable ladder into the space of the old foundation. 'You think you can climb up that?' one asked. 'We'll ride you the rest of the trip.'

The dazed young woman told them she could, and slowly made her way up the rungs to the top. She collapsed onto the stretcher and two burly guardsmen prepared to carry her off.

I was next up the ladder, with Mike behind me. I took one of Chat's hands, reminding her that she was going to be fine, and that she needed to concentrate on getting herself better in the next few days. I was sure that Faith would be flown up to her sister's bedside at Mass General, the Boston hospital that was a short hop from these islands.

She clung to me until we heard the welcome sound of the chopper blades hovering over the island. The sky was lightening, and I could see a grassy field that would make an easy landing pad for the helicopter.

Once Chat Grant was airborne, the crew worked on rigging another stretcher to lift the unconscious Zukov out of the hole in the ground. The second chopper was on its way for him.

'You two ready to head back to the Cape?' Captain Lynch asked.

'I've got a better idea,' I said to Mike. 'Come with me to the Vineyard. It's what — Saturday morning? Let's just chill for the weekend.'

'You look more worried about hacking at Zukov than saving Chat's life. Of course I'll go with you, just to order your priorities if nothing else. Make sure your head's on straight.'

'Maggie, will you take us there?'

'Sure. You can explain to all the impatient Vineyarders why the newspapers are coming over so late today.'

'I'm in,' Mike said. 'Commissioner Scully will be looking for my scalp.'

'Yours?' I said. 'I might as well just hand him mine.'

'I'll take it back with me. May be my only hope to keep my gold shield.'

The *Patriot* was roped to the uprights on the old pier alongside the jetty. Mike let himself onto the stern of the boat gingerly, favoring his bad leg. He moved forward and seated himself in the wheelhouse, close to Maggie.

I wanted the brisk, fresh morning air. I stayed outside, watching the sun begin to rise, and letting my hair blow wildly in the wind.

Somehow, no matter what turmoil awaited me at the office, the peace and beauty of my island home always managed to bring back an inner calm. A few days and nights here would give me the emotional energy to deal with repairing Gina Borracelli's delicate emotional health and getting her in the proper professional hands. Mike would follow up on my hunch that Bishop Deegan had no idea who Fyodor Zukov was when he nodded at the stranger in the clerical collar, and instead that Zukov had the defendant, child molester Denys Koslawski, on his pariahs-of-the-church hit list.

There was a strong chop in the water and the whitecaps gleamed in the morning sunlight. I had dozens of questions for Chat Grant, but they would have to wait until doctors treated her and determined that she was able to cooperate with us to give us every detail of her long encounter with the crazed murderer.

I looked inside the cabin. Mike had engaged Maggie with tales of his exploits, no doubt. He had a bruise developing on his right cheekbone and lacerations on his chin, but his legendary resilience was already on display in full force.

I turned back to the soothing vista of the sea and the chain of Elizabeth Islands. The district attorney and police commissioner would shortly share a podium to describe the capture of the clergy killer. They could do nothing else publicly but praise Mike and me for hunting him down and saving Chat's life, but I smiled when I thought how Paul Battaglia would get me in his office alone to take me apart for risking so much in that effort. I would spend part of my day composing an apology to him and to Scully for disobeying their orders, but they would know as well as I did that it wasn't going to be sincere.

I wanted this serene interlude for a few days. I needed it. I had no illusion about the stack of cases — serial attackers, date rapists, domestic violence, child abuse — that would pile up on my desk to review on my return. But for now, I was headed for my own safe haven.

The strong boat worked its way through Canapitsit Channel, between Nashawena and Cuttyhunk, on its way to Menemsha Harbor. I would never be so happy to step onto the gas dock and look across the pond at the home I loved more than any place in the world.

55

'I've got a surprise for you, Alex,' Mercer said, calling in from New York.

It was seven o'clock in the morning. I had showered and changed into a sweatshirt and leggings, and Mike was upstairs in the guest room, rummaging through my brothers' summer clothes to cobble together a pair of jeans and a sweater to wear.

'I'm off surprises for the day. Be gentle.'

'There's an NYPD helicopter on its way to Penikese to help the feds with a thorough crime-scene evaluation.'

'Excellent.'

'And I guess Keith Scully still has a soft spot for you. He's letting them drop Luc off on the Vineyard.'

'That's amazing, Mercer. Do I have you to thank for this?'

Luc had been due in from France on Friday evening for a quiet weekend with me. Now we could spend it in front of the fireplace, far away from the madman who had carved such a murderous path up the coastline.

'Nan and I were in cahoots on this.'

'Well, then. You and your spouses need to keep my reservation at Patroon tonight. You can have their perfect steak and mashed potatoes, and we'll have oysters and lobster and a bucket of champagne on this end. I might even have a date for Mike.'

'A blind date?'

'Nope. I think he's hooked on a sea captain,' I said. 'How is Faith taking all this?'

'She's on her way to Boston. We haven't told her yet that she was Zukov's intended target. I don't think she'll be able to cope with that until she sees that Chat's going to be fine.'

'And Zukov? Have they given you an update on him?'

'He'll live. He's in surgery right now. They're sure they can put his hand back together again. And the docs in Bellevue can start treatment while he's incarcerated,' Mercer said. 'I'm not so sure he deserves it, but I'll keep that thought to myself.'

'Remember that when you're in church tomorrow.'

'I don't think there's a disease that's still as wrapped in ignorance as leprosy.'

'You're right.'

'The nurse at Bellevue told me that they can't even put a sign outside the clinic that says Hansen's disease.'

'Why not?'

''Cause there are still people — most people — who won't even put their hands on the door handle if they think there are lepers inside.'

It was an appalling image, and a disease with such a stigma that had attached itself to almost every society and culture, every religious faith, since ancient times.

'Do you mind if I take a few days up here?' I asked.

'Don't you come back till you're good and ready. Let your man take care of you for a change. Can you do that?'

'Of course I can. Have you checked with Reverend Portland?' I asked. There were endless lists of things to be done in cases like this. 'Is she all right?'

'Safe and sound in Hyannis. Probably on her way home right now.'

'That's good news.'

'You better get yourself to the airport, Alex. That package I'm sending your way should be there within the hour.'

'Thanks, Mercer. Thanks for everything.'

Mike came down the stairs and flopped onto one of the living-room sofas.

'Want me to make some coffee?'

'Are you kidding, Coop? I don't want to smell any java for a month. I'm just going to stretch out right here and sleep for the next twenty-four. Will I be in your way?'

'No more than usual.'

'All copacetic with Mercer?'

'Oh, yeah. He's on top of everything,' I said. 'So I'm going to shut off the phone, if that's okay with you. Luc's flying up from the city. I thought I'd go down to Larsen's Fish Market and pick up some lobster for the three of us. Put my *Iron Chef* to the test.'

'Luc? Coming here?' Mike asked. 'I almost forgot about your romantic weekend plans. Sorry to let something like murder almost interfere.'

446

'How about if I put something on your cheek so it doesn't swell? Or get a doc up here to check your leg?'

'How about you just get on with it and let me sleep? Stop yammering.'

He rolled over on his side and closed his eyes.

'Want anything special with dinner?'

'Just shut-eye. Do what you gotta do, Coop.'

I took the SUV to the airport, and was waiting at the gate when Luc came down the steps of the blue-and-white helicopter, ducking beneath the rotors and waving to me.

We kissed and embraced and kissed again. I was safe on my own island sanctuary, where my personal peace and happiness were always so richly and easily restored.

On the way to Menemsha to pick up dinner that came fresh out of local waters, I started to tell Luc the awful story. By the time we got back to the house, I was still only halfway through the week's events.

We set the groceries down on the kitchen table and I went in to check on Mike.

The living room was empty. I ran upstairs but the guest rooms were deserted too. I came down to tell Luc, who had found Mike's handwritten note on my bed.

'Don't worry, Coop. Commissioner Scully called. Wants me back immediately to give the whole story to Public Info. Called a cab to take me to the ferry. Car rental to the city. You know how I hate those little planes,' I read aloud.

Beneath his signature was a PS: 'Have a good

time with Luc. Chow down some of that lobster for me too. You might be the best partner I've ever had. Ever. But don't push your luck. I'll probably forget I ever said that by Monday.'

Acknowledgements

As always, great friends led me to many of the more hidden treasures of my beloved city. A conversation with Alan Levine opened the door to the Jewish Theological Seminary and a private tutorial with Rabbi Marc Wolf. A delicious dinner at Rao's with the inimitable Frank Pellegrino enlightened me about the old St. Patrick's Cathedral. A book signing with a new acquaintance who writes a fine crime novel herself, Hilary Davidson, surprised me with information about a gift to the people of New York from the one-time king of France.

And then there is the unique moment when someone makes an introduction that is as memorable personally as it is useful professionally. A casual lunch with my good friend Susan Reed ended with her insistence that I meet the Rev. Dr. Serene Jones, a brilliant scholar and the first woman appointed to the presidency of the 174-year-old Union Theological Seminary. Let me first assure you that Serene Jones is *not* a character in this book. The thoughts and words and familial relationships described by my fictional Faith Grant come entirely from my imagination. But I had the pleasure and honor of spending hours with the Rev. Dr. Jones, exploring the treasures (what exquisite libraries both seminaries have!) of Union, and scratching the surface of some of the most fascinating issues in modern theology. I also commend to you her writings, including the books *Trauma + Grace: Theology in a Ruptured World* and *Feminist Theory and Christian Theology*. My admiration and respect for Serene Jones is beyond measure.

The *New York Times* is a constant source of information for me on an endless variety of subjects. I am especially grateful to David Dunlap, R. M. Schneiderman, Anne Barnard, and Anne Midgette for such intriguing articles, each of which contained fascinating facts that found their way into this crime caper. The *Vineyard Gazette* is a great newspaper. Holly Nadler's story, which appeared in the *Gazette*, is an excerpt from her book *Vineyard Supernatural*, and Mike Seccombe's piece 'On the Midnight Run to America' was equally riveting. Two books that provided rich background detail were John Tayman's heartbreaking true tale *The Colony* and I. Thomas Buckley's *Island of Hope*. The deposition transcript in the case of *Rosado vs. Bridgeport Roman Catholic Diocesan Corp.* was as helpful as it is shocking.

Whether for business or pleasure, you keenly want my friend Esther Newberg on your side and at your back. I've been fortunate to have her there for a very long time, and it has been more fun than one could imagine. With her come the great crew at ICM, including Kari Stuart and Lyle Morgan, and now that I'm totally bicoastal, in the talented hands of Mark Gordon.

My team at Dutton is the classiest act in publishing. The support and enthusiasm starts at the top with my publisher, Brian Tart. Ben

Sevier's skill as an editor makes it a joy to work with him. Christine Ball is always a few steps ahead of me, a master at PR and marketing, aided by Jamie McDonald. Carrie Swetonic, Jessica Horvath, Susan Schwartz, Dick Heffernan, and the rest of the Dutton family have given me a truly happy home. On the road, it's Tammy Richards who keeps the ink flowing. My thanks to all, and to David Shelley and the UK group at Little, Brown. They've been with me from the start.

My family and friends have done it again. I owe them all my love and gratitude. And to my husband, Justin Feldman, words are inadequate to express how very much it means to me that you battle so valiantly to savor the joy of our life together.

We do hope that you have enjoyed reading this large print book.

Did you know that all of our titles are available for purchase?

We publish a wide range of high quality large print books including:
Romances, Mysteries, Classics
General Fiction
Non Fiction and Westerns

Special interest titles available in large print are:
The Little Oxford Dictionary
Music Book
Song Book
Hymn Book
Service Book

Also available from us courtesy of Oxford University Press:
Young Readers' Dictionary
(large print edition)
Young Readers' Thesaurus
(large print edition)

For further information or a free brochure, please contact us at:
Ulverscroft Large Print Books Ltd.,
The Green, Bradgate Road, Anstey,
Leicester, LE7 7FU, England.
Tel: (00 44) 0116 236 4325
Fax: (00 44) 0116 234 0205

Other titles published by
The House of Ulverscroft:

HELL GATE

Linda Fairstein

In New York, the body of a congressman's mistress is found dumped in the mayor's well. Assistant DA Alex Cooper is distraught that she wasn't able to prevent the death in time. Investigating the circumstances she uncovers a secret affair and an illegitimate child, supposedly fathered by the politician. Then after news of a tragic shipwreck off the coast claiming the lives of the human cargo on board, Alex is called to the gruesome scene. She discovers a strange connection between the seemingly unrelated cases: a young woman drowned in the wreck and the congressman's murdered lover share the same tattoo . . . Alex finds more than she bargained for: dark links to New York's powerful elite that will call into question all she ever believed in . . .

THE KILLS

Linda Fairstein

Prosecuting Andrew Tripping for the assault of Paige Vallis is already hard enough for Assistant District Attorney Alexandra Cooper. Without evidence or forensics, Alex is pinning her hopes on two contrasting individuals: Kevin Bessemer, Tripping's cellmate at Riker's, who claims to have incriminating information; and Dulles, Tripping's ten-year-old son. But on the way from Riker's to meet Alex, Bessemer manages to escape. Then, as the trial begins, a murder overtakes the events inside the courtroom, and Alex is plunged into a race against time to discover the truth: a terrifying journey that ends up in the Kills, the eerie waterways along New York's harbour . . .